Also by J J Rusz (aka J J Ruszkiewicz)

The Window Trail: A Big Bend Country Mystery

How to Write Anything

A Reader's Guide to College Writing

Everything's An Argument (with Andrea Lunsford)

The South Rim Trail

JJ Rusz

A BIG BEND COUNTRY MYSTERY 2

In memory of Don Graham
Writer, Critic, Texan

Characters and events depicted in *The South Rim Trail* are fictitious. Any resemblance to actual events or real persons, living or dead, is coincidental. Brewster, Davis, and Pecos Counties, Texas, and the towns described in the book are actual geographical and political locations. However, for purposes of plot and storytelling, not all places named in this work are real, nor are real places always as described.

With windlasses and with assays of bias,
By indirections find directions out.

Hamlet, Act 2, Scene 1

Prologue

He first spotted her on an evening in August. The employee lounge was quiet, an ancient vacuum-tube TV glowing in a corner. An old guy slouched on a worn sofa reading while younger employees stared at their phones. They could get a signal here.

And there she was. He made sure no one caught him, glancing at her at first, then studying her with more care. It would seem out of character, creepy. He got that. He was a serious guy.

But he couldn't help himself. Nor could he talk to anyone about it.

For weeks thereafter, stretching into a month, he watched. It *couldn't* be her, yet there she was—a shimmering image stolen from his memory. And mostly as he remembered. Full lips, dark eyes, skin like milk, nose turned up just enough to make him tremble. A smile that won his heart and he wasn't a romantic. Far from it.

She *was* his girl. She had to be. He would make it so.

Again.

Chapter 1

"**M**ore coffee, Mr. Harp?" the flight attendant asked, too cheerful in the first-class cabin for a 5:30 AM flight from Los Angeles to Denver. She knew his name. Alex declined the refill and smiled at his companion.

"It's because I've got the aisle seat," he said, guessing what Piper Robinet was thinking.

His TV co-star forced a smile and toyed with a fruit cup on her tray. "And I guess that's why the flight engineer wanted your autograph for his daughter?"

Luckily, Piper hadn't caught the nod a middle-aged business woman across the aisle gave him, telegraphing *I know who you are but won't bother you.*

"Alex?" Piper wanted a response.

He shrugged. How could he make her feel better? People knew him by sight now, well beyond the thirteen-year-olds who watched their cable sitcom *Brainiacs*, a program few adults ever heard of. In recent months, Alex Harp had appeared in breakout roles in several movies, graced magazine covers, and, hell, *People* recently named him Hollywood's new *It* boy. Which so appalled his mother she wanted him to return to Ohio. Until his father reminded her how much money he was making.

Their Monday morning flight was smooth and the dull roar of the engines soothing. Alex leaned back, pretended to snooze, but kept an eye open to admire Piper. He was glad the tray table was down.

His career *was* ahead of the curve, even measured against former Disney kid stars like Gosling and Timberlake. But it wasn't just luck. Alex's most recent film part as a drug addict's son melted hearts and electrified critics. Talk of an Oscar nomination next spring was serious. Fifteen minutes of screen time and he was a made man. Heady stuff. And he was not quite eighteen.

And neither was Piper Robinet—though Alex could never nail down when she was born. Girls were weird about dates. He knew she fell under the same restrictive WetBTE Network rules for underage performers he did. But his were even tighter since he lived with a watchful aunt in Santa Monica. Staying with her was the only way his mother would let him leave home in Ohio while still in high school.

And one reason Alex Harp remained—*how was it even possible?*—a virgin. But if this trip worked out . . .

⋇ ⋇ ⋇

PIPER HADN'T LIKED Alex at first. She'd kept her distance, suspicious of the Ohio jock who'd gained national attention for stepping in to sing the national anthem at his high school football championship game. A local diva hired for the night turned up drunk and the charming quarterback walked over and just nailed the tune. The video went viral and Hollywood came knocking. He won the game too.

Piper, on the other hand, labored through several auditions to get her *Brainiacs* part, and producers still had doubts until they noticed how well she paired with their new heartthrob. *You kids have chemistry*, they realized. Yet fanzines, mostly written by women, weren't kind—*Piper Robinet sparkles only because Alex Harp glows* one of them wrote. Worse, she feared the snotty appraisals were true.

But she came up to speed quick enough, once she grasped that he was more than a jock who could sing. *A lot more.* It didn't take much for gifted kids like them to play students at a school for gifted kids. But her new co-star wasn't content with *good enough*. He insisted they turn their stock sitcom characters into edgy originals and the producers went along. Fortunately, Piper shared Alex's gift for dialects, the two of them broadening the humor of *Brainiacs* by mimicking snooty Brits, dour Germans, and even the occasional Texan. Other cast members struggled to keep up with their cheeky performances. But their best episodes won media attention and Piper saw firsthand what a charismatic co-star might do for her stalled career.

Alex made his feelings for Piper clear right from the start, but she kept him at a distance. Which, Piper realized, likely made her even more alluring to the infatuated quarterback. This at a time when the network was already posting guards around his trailer to keep crazed fans from sneaking in.

In their cable series though, their roles were reversed. She played rich girl Mackenzie obsessed with Charlie, Alex's screen character. Piper was as all-over him as kiddie networks allowed while he spurned her, episode after episode. Which proved, Piper realized, what a gifted actor Alex was. But, slowly, they came to terms, not as girlfriend and boyfriend exactly, but as sincere, if oddly diffident, friends.

Diffident was Alex's word.

⋇ ⋇ ⋇

"WHATCHA DOING FOR the hiatus?" Piper had asked Alex one afternoon late in September just several weeks earlier, shortly after they'd wrapped the third-to-last episode of their sitcom's season. Alex knew what was on her mind: *Would Brainiacs be around for another?*

Rumor was Throng!Media, the parent company of their WetBTE Network show, now wanted Alex for its own A-list film, *Romeo and Juliet*. And for other blockbuster projects. And, for once, rumor had it right. He'd already signed the contract. Could *Brainiacs* survive without him? *Think* Hannah Montana *without Miley*, he'd overheard one cast member complain.

"Might go to see my sister Claire in Texas," was all Alex admitted to Piper.

"The professor mixed up with that murder last spring?" she said. "In that tiny town?"

Alex was surprised she remembered. He'd casually mentioned the case months before when it was, briefly, a national story. He knew much more about it now—all its complicated, even grisly, details. *Make a good movie*, he thought, smiling to himself.

"Claire wants me to visit Texas," he explained.

"Ever been there?"

"Nope."

"Dry and flat. I couldn't wait to get across it."

Alex knew that Piper, emancipated before she was sixteen, had driven an old Silverado from Arkansas to Los Angeles to find a better life. At least, that was the story she told. She'd covered eight hundred miles of Texas on her way to California.

"There are mountains where Claire lives," he said. "Place called Alpine. Not far from Big Bend National Park."

"Hey, you know what?"

Alex recalled now how Piper's dark violet eyes had flashed. He could usually guess what people were going to say, but not this time. Or maybe he didn't want to jinx it.

"We might maybe go to that park ourselves on break? Get out of Los Angeles and see what the real West looks like."

"Big Bend?"

"Yeah."

"Don't think we can fly there directly." In fact, he knew they couldn't because he'd already mapped a route to his sister's place.

"Better still! We'll rent a Jeep and have an adventure. Do you camp?"

"Eagle Scout with a merit badge." She rolled her eyes.

"I spent lots of time outdoors in Arkansas. We'll get a backpacking tent and do some trails after we see your sister. Won't that be cool? Maybe sneak into Mexico? October would be perfect. Past the heat. We'll go on holiday." She delivered the last line just like Judi Dench. Spot on.

Alex laughed. She had him at singular *tent*.

"Okay," he said calmly.

But he wasn't calm. Alone under the stars. In a remote campsite. Was she really proposing that? Well, there was already more to his trip to Texas than just visiting a sister almost twice his age. But he'd work anything around Piper Robinet if it meant getting laid. *Finally.* And they could do it all without publicity or studio supervision. Hell, if West Texas were as remote as Claire claimed, they'd barely be noticed.

⋅⋆⋅ ⋅⋆⋅ ⋅⋆⋅

ALEX WAS RIGHT about not being able to fly direct to Big Bend or Alpine or just about any town south of I-10 and the Pecos River. *The Trans-Pecos* they called it. It was a long haul and their 5:15 AM flight from LAX to Denver was just its first leg.

But he'd enjoyed the run-up to the trip. Even those final episodes of *Brainiacs*—likely the last TV he'd do—were fun. Piper was into the trip too, studying travel sites and proposing different hikes at Big Bend National Park almost every day. They discussed them during breaks in taping. One day she was all *Lost Mine Trail* for the romance of its name. Then she thought they might try the Marufo Vega Trail, a fourteen-mile hike in the Dead Horse Mountains, but she was concerned by warnings in a travel guide. *They could get lost or die.*

She mentioned the Window Trail, but Alex vetoed that without much explanation. Piper finally decided they *must* do the park's signature adventure—the South Rim Trail, camping overnight at a canyon overlook. Photographs of the view from the rim sealed the deal. They weren't bothered by an initial 1500-foot climb or the full hike's 12.5 miles. They were young. They'd barely notice.

No water on the trail, of course. And just pit toilets. Perhaps not the ideal locale for a rookie sexual encounter. But Piper knew what she was getting into and Alex kinda guessed it wouldn't be *her* first dance.

For a guy? Way simpler.

They browsed online for gear and clothing, hoping to look like native Texans but unsure what that meant. They spent an afternoon at REI selecting lightweight backpacks, hydration gear, and the all-important tent. Presently, that stuff was in the baggage hold and entrusted for the next several hours to United Airlines.

Alex's sister Claire had seemed chill when he'd explained he'd be bringing a girl with him to Texas. But their more-than-a-decade difference in age made Claire more parent than sibling to him. He'd always gotten along better with his two other sisters. But as the baby of the family and only boy . . . well, he'd have liked a brother or two.

Which oddly made him think about Piper and how independent and untethered she was—no immediate family to speak of. No home base in Arkansas. And now an uncertain future because of him. If *Brainiacs* folded, even a teen actor as capable as Piper might fade away. The track records of performers from kiddie networks just weren't good, and WetBTE TV was hardly cream of the crop.

Alex did know that Piper auditioned for the Juliet part in the Shakespeare film he already thought of as his own. No question, they worked well together. Looked good too. But Piper lacked his big-screen credentials. And media coverage they'd enjoyed on TV fansites meant nothing to filmmakers. Piper was a nonentity. Beautiful, for sure, but up against more experienced and famous people.

Especially pop star Tabreetha Bree-Jones, who was campaigning for the role on websites and TV talk shows. Alex disliked the Brit's style, music, and even her name. Worse, at twenty-six, Bree-Jones would be almost ten years senior to him. He'd be making love to an old lady.

That observation didn't make Piper feel much better when he'd mentioned it to her.

Chapter 2

"Looks good on you, Sheriff," a dark-haired man in jeans and purple western shirt said, admiring the leather belt Clayton Alton Shoot was sizing. They were at Big Bend Saddlery just east of Sul Ross State in Alpine, Texas.

Clayton smiled. "Buying it for the dang party you're throwing. Claire wants me to be presentable." The two shook hands, the sheriff several decades younger than William Ogden Lamb, titleholder of the 300,000-acre McCann Ranch in southern Brewster County. One of the storied properties in Texas.

"How *you* doin', Bill?" Clayton asked delicately.

"Okay for a guy about to be several million bucks poorer by the end of the week."

Clayton checked his belt in a mirror. "I remember when my daddy first took me here. All them saddles lined up in a row . . . the smell of leather. Cowboy heaven." The merchandise at the Saddlery was serious gear, much of it made on site. Not tourist trifles.

"Speaking of your dad, how's the family holdin' up?" Bill asked, eyes almost shut. Clayton realized he hadn't seen the rancher since the funeral. Clayton's long-ailing father Finis Shoot died late in May, just five months earlier. The man had been a rancher and, in his early days, a preacher.

"It's been rough," Clayton admitted, "but life's easier now for my mom and sisters. He kept a cabin near the main house, but couldn't manage much by himself at the end."

"Finis was a good man in his heyday," Bill recalled. "Fine kids, too."

Clayton nodded. "Thanks. But Beatrice especially has not been herself." Clayton's much older and only unmarried sister had pretty much run their property for years. But she seemed subdued and disengaged now.

"And you?" Bill inquired.

"Hasn't hit me entirely. Happened just when I became sheriff. So—no time for grief, especially with my mama needing support and Beatrice off her game. And Claire Harp turning me down."

"That belt should get her attention." Bill raised an eyebrow to lighten the mood.

"At the price, it better," Clayton smiled.

"Billy Jr.'s dropped a few bucks here over the years. Right now, I'm picking up a birthday present to mark his change in status." Clayton read that as a signal the rancher didn't mind talking about what was coming.

"The party's Nikki's idea," Bill continued. "To show the community we're one big happy family. Billy's invitin' the ranch crew and his younger friends and we'll have ours there too. You sort of fall in between, Clayton—and so does Claire. She was his teacher last spring."

Claire Harp, an assistant professor at Sul Ross State in Alpine, was also Clayton's girlfriend and might be more someday, though she'd rebuffed a marriage proposal in May—when they'd known each other less than three months. Sensible thing to do, he guessed.

"Believe me, I remember," Clayton said.

"You know she's welcome?"

"The invitation said Clayton Shoot and guest and I'm not about to bring my sister."

"Nikki wants Claire at the party, but couldn't bring herself to invite her separately."

"I kinda figured that." Claire had inadvertently entangled Nikki—William Lamb's second wife and Billy's stepmother—in a sensational murder investigation and, well, women don't forget.

"I'll send a separate invite if need be."

"Nah. I wouldn't be here if we weren't gonna show."

"By the way, Beatrice *is* comin'. She RSVP'd."

"Maybe a big event will make her feel better."

Lamb's expression darkened again, and Clayton guessed why.

"Things gonna be okay with y'all and Billy?" he asked.

William Ogden Lamb leaned against a rack of saddles and gave the young sheriff a once over. The two men had a good history.

Most Brewster County residents were saddened when the previous sheriff Arnie Paulsen decided to retire before he died with his badge on. Heart trouble. And three years left in his term.

Clayton applied for the opening as a long shot. He was hard-working and personable, with deep roots in West Texas and a solid service record. But he was very young—especially compared to Fiona Tusk, Alpine's police chief, who also wanted the job and had a much longer résumé. A specialist in self-promotion, Fiona lobbied county commissioners hard for the appointment.

William Lamb likely made a difference. The rancher appreciated the tactful way Clayton handled that thorny criminal inquiry involving not only the rancher himself, but his wife and son—and mistress. Fiona Tusk, on the other hand, had rashly accused Billy Jr. of the murder. No doubt, commissioners paid serious attention when the richest man in Brewster County weighed in on Clayton's side.

"I'll be honest with you," Lamb said finally, drawing the sheriff toward a counter displaying leather bags and briefcases and away from a cluster of shoppers who didn't look local. "The thought of Billy taking over the ranch terrifies me. If Nikki had her way, we'd of hired lawyers years ago to find loopholes in my ex-wife Delia's pre-nup and will.

"But the ranch was hers—lock, stock, and barrel—and Delia intended the property to fall to someone with her McCann blood. I had no problem with that. Billy's my boy too and, though I wish we'd had more kids, we didn't. Even then, Billy would have been sole heir of the land—that's how McCanns always settle things. One heir. Never let the ranch be divvied up.

"Delia loved me sure enough, but doubled down when she got sick. She knew about Nikki those final months too. Understood my needs. But made certain then that when Billy turned twenty-one the McCann Ranch went to him and him only. And here we are now. Billy reaches manhood Thursday. And when you come over Friday for the party just about everything you'll see, all those acres and all that prime beef, will belong to a kid with one more semester in college."

Clayton shrugged. "Billy's a rascal, but . . ."

"I know, I know. Can't blame him. I spoiled the boy and misread him too. I thought maybe I could talk him into an Ivy League school. You know, get him a degree in finance or law to handle what was coming? Hell, the way the world's changing, maybe computers woulda been best. But Billy weren't no scholar."

Clayton laughed. "Right priorities though. Loves horses and ranching. And women too."

"Got that last part from me," William admitted. "What I never appreciated all these years is how close the boy is to the land. Maybe he'll need to hire an accountant or two and put another lawyer on retainer. But Billy will never need anyone to advise him about the ranch. And he'll never let it go. Shit, I intend to be around to help too."

"You're his dad. That don't change."

Lamb's forehead tightened as if a headache were coming on.

The owner of the Saddlery walked up at that moment with a sizeable box and placed it on a glass counter. "Your cattleman's briefcase, Mr. Lamb. Do you want to open it?"

"Thanks, Gary. I will in a moment."

"Sure hope Billy likes it," Gary said, heading toward another customer with a question.

"You feel okay?" Clayton asked. William looked like he was hurting.

The rancher fiddled with the end of the box, peeling at the flap more than tearing it. Then he stopped to stare at Clayton. "Now more than ever, you must appreciate how much your daddy wanted you. Three daughters and Finis kept tryin'."

It was a strange observation. "Yes, sir," Clayton said. "Same in Claire's family. Three girls before a boy came along. Alex. He's visiting here this week."

Lamb showed the hint of a smile. "I was tickled with Billy. Couldn't know we wouldn't have more."

"But you got him."

"Yeah." He turned away for a moment, breathing hard.

"William?"

"We'd always been careful to give Billy his due as heir to the ranch. When Nikki and I redid the main house, we added a section for him with its own entrance and garage, even a small kitchen. He could have girls there without sneakin' 'em in. He's got a hunting cabin down in the south of the ranch too. His private place for playing cards and drinking with the hands. Nice rockwork and views almost to the border."

"Yes, sir."

"Nikki's worried now that Billy may want the main house with all its art and stuff—you know the theater and pool and such. I told her we could build a smaller place for ourselves if he did. We got the revenue. Hell, most houses in cities fit on an eighth of an acre these days and there's 300,000 in the McCann. Billy would have all the space he wanted."

"Yes, sir."

"Well, that's not what he wanted. He sat down with me about a month ago to say he'd been talking with our lawyer about a change he intended. 'Clarify things for the future,' he said. 'For the good of the ranch.' Never seen him so serious.

"'Daddy,' he says to me, 'I wanna change my name. The ranch and its owner should have the same one. I wanna be Billy McCann. Legally. I asked our lawyer to draw up papers.'"

Clayton shook his head.

Lamb gazed at the ceiling.

"Billy said he wouldn't sign and file the documents unless I said *okay*. Said he didn't intend to hurt me, but he wanted any first son of his to be a McCann—clear and direct. Not a McCann Lamb, like he was. Just plain Billy McCann II."

"That's hard."

"I told him I'd need time to think about it. Haven't mentioned this to anyone else. Not even Nikki. Well, except Gary."

"Gary?"

With a deliberate hand now, Mr. Lamb undid the flaps on one side of the box on the counter and pulled a medium-brown cattleman's briefcase, carefully wrapped in tissue, out of the box.

A leather circle above the latch identified its intended owner—Billy McCann.

Chapter 3

Piper and Alex had a brief layover in Denver, just a break to change planes with no time to explore the terminal. Piper hadn't travelled much compared to most people her age and still found airports a novelty. But she suspected they were all pretty much alike at ground level. At least Denver's concourse had a cool ceiling—like a tent.

The jet they boarded there at 9:30 AM for a two-hour flight to Midland–Odessa was small and lacked a first-class cabin. They now shared a row with an elderly woman who had the window seat, but claimed the aisle instead because she expected to use the restroom. She didn't recognize either of them, but a tiny African-American girl strolling down the aisle spotted Piper and waved excitedly, covering her mouth in delight. When she noticed Alex, she squealed. So did her mother.

Piper had never heard of Midland–Odessa before this trip and Alex explained that it was two mid-sized cities in Texas oil country, side by side. *Like Minneapolis–St. Paul*, he said. That didn't help because St. Paul was not on Piper's radar either. She felt no embarrassment. All most Californians knew about her home state of Arkansas was that Bill Clinton was its governor or something before moving to Washington with Hillary when he became president. Piper grew up not far from Hope, where Clinton was born.

Alex dozed off even before their second flight took off. She didn't blame him. She'd slept through half the trip from Los Angeles herself.

Piper enjoyed watching her co-star sleep. Envious. He had a profile that cameras loved. And why did men get such beautiful lashes? Piper was wearing little makeup on the trip but Alex, of course, had none and he still looked better close-up. And far more relaxed.

Maybe that was because he had nothing to worry about compared to her. Alex was just visiting a sister on this trip and, maybe, getting laid. For the first time—if he was telling her the truth! And what guy would lie about that? Piper had hinted to Alex that she too might be . . . well, she really hadn't said so, just implied it, and his eyes crinkled up the way they did when he was skeptical.

It didn't matter. First time, he'd be lucky to last five minutes. And she'd have a good story to tell in the future if she wrote a book.

Did it bother her that she wasn't being completely honest with him? Maybe. But she was rarely honest with herself these days. Story of her life, in fact. Things moving so fast now she hardly knew what she wanted. Or how to get it. Or *him*.

But when Alex said he was going to Texas, so much fell into place. Not in an easy way, but that was okay. Life was complicated. Always had been for her. She'd learned to roll with it. But maybe, this time, it would be different—as effortless as it always seemed for Alex.

⋆ ⋆ ⋆

ALEX NOTICED RIGHT away that Piper seemed uncomfortable. They'd landed at the Midland International Air & Space Port on time and grabbed their gear off the baggage carousel with no problems when a middle-aged couple dressed for safari approached them, waving large printed cards. The woman's read *Alex* and the man's *Piper*. Alex looked over to Piper.

"I may have mentioned to my agent that we'd be heading to Texas," she said. Alex did not have time to react.

"Hey, you kids! I'm Nancy Legeson," the tall woman shouted, looking directly at the actor. "And this is my husband Ethan and we are the advance team for your visit to Texas."

"Advance team?" Alex frowned. *A triathlete in her youth?* he wondered. Nancy was tanned and taut as a bow.

"We'll handle all the details so you and Ms. Robinet can have a wonderful experience."

As if to underscore the point, Ethan—more muscled than his wife but just as leathery—commandeered a baggage cart for what Alex assumed would be a short walk to the rental car counter.

"No need," Ethan smiled. "We've got vehicles already waiting outside the concourse."

"Vehicles?"

"I really didn't know," Piper insisted, though Alex could tell she was fibbing.

"Ethan wanted to find you a Bentayga," Nancy snorted. "But *I* thought that would be too stuffy for kids like you."

"What's a Bentayga?" Piper asked.

"A Bentley," Alex said.

"And they could get one! Midland's a wealthy town," Ethan added as they departed the concourse and headed to a parking garage. In the valet area, they spotted a shiny Tahoe and a glossier Range Rover.

"We'll take the Tahoe," said Alex.

"Ah . . . no," Nancy replied, as politely as she could while contradicting clients. "We've already packed the Range Rover with personalized items for your expedition—extra clothes, food, drinks, emergency gear, cameras, even liquor for any adult guests you may host. But please don't drive with open bottles in the car. You'll get arrested down here."

"We do have attorneys on standby," Ethan piped in. "We provide them for celebrities, especially younger ones."

Alex stared at the Range Rover. "We're just hiking."

"I understand, Mr. Harp," Nancy said, "but we want you to be prepared for all situations. We know how special you are." Both the Legesons were again looking at Alex. Mr. Legeson handed him the key fob.

The tang of leather—and maybe chocolate—assaulted him when he opened the hatch to stow their gear.

"As for accommodations at the national park, we've got that covered too," Nancy said, speaking to Piper now as if domestic matters fell to the girl. "Ethan and I will go there this afternoon to finalize them."

"You *do* know we're staying with my sister in Alpine tonight?"

"Of course, Mr. Harp. The distinguished assistant professor at Sul Ross State University and now the editor of *Madrone*. How proud you must be. You'll find a hostess gift for her in the car, Piper."

Did they bring condoms? Alex wondered.

"And we'll pick up the campground permits you'll need for Tuesday night at the South Rim," Ethan added. "Now, I know you were hoping to stay on the South Rim itself, but we've selected a more comfortable campsite. Closer to water and a toilet and better for you all the way around. Trust me."

"Of course," Alex said. "And you knew this—where we wanted to camp—how?"

"Just a reasonable assumption. Most first-time hikers want to stay right at the rim."

Alex looked over to Piper. She shrugged, "I may have mentioned some details to my agent."

"Don't worry about anything," Nancy laughed. She handed them cards with contact information. "For the whole trip we've reserved Roosevelt Stone Cottages near the main lodge for your group. They're very special. If you run into problems, just head back there. Ethan and I have excellent relationships with national parks staff." She paused, then suddenly looked conspiratorial. "So many young ladies at Big Bend are just tickled you're visiting, Mr. Harp."

"Call me Alex," he said.

"And I'm Piper."

"Yes, of course, Ms. Robinet."

❄ ❄ ❄

ALEX STARTED THE engine and watched as black screens lit up across the Range Rover's instrument panel and console. Before Alex rolled his window up, Mrs. Legeson mentioned that the navigation system was already programmed for his sister's house.

"Naturally," he said.

The Legesons waved and then headed toward their Tahoe for their longer ride that day to the national park.

"Are you pissed?" Piper asked while Alex flicked through options on one of the video panels, tapping icons that offered a half-dozen massage functions. He pushed more buttons and suddenly Piper felt air bladders inflating beneath her.

"They packed us lunches too," she giggled, reaching into sacks on the back seats. "Roast beef sandwiches," she sniffed. "And chocolate cookies."

The navigation screen displayed their route to Alpine. One hundred fifty-seven miles to Claire's house. Two hours, thirty-seven minutes, assuming no stops. Gas gauge, *full*.

Piper felt a twinge of guilt. "Don't be angry, Alex. My agent thought I needed publicity right now. He said being seen with you would help my chances to get Juliet. I figured maybe some pictures at the rim. The two of us and a photographer? I didn't imagine all this—or any kind of group thing." She was bending the truth a little.

He remained mute. The Range Rover's supercharged V6 murmured softly. Piper ventured a change of subject. "I hear Tabreetha Bree-Jones is a bitch."

Alex looked her square in the face, squinting. With anger? Disappointment? Piper couldn't tell.

He turned away again and rotated the shift knob to Drive, then floored the throttle.

"Yee-haw," the young actor squealed. "We're in Texas!"

Chapter 4

Claire Harp wasn't sure why she felt embarrassed to have Clayton Alton Shoot catch her vacuuming carpets in the house she rented just west of Sul Ross State University.

"Don't think many seventeen-year-olds care if a carpet's clean," Clayton said, slipping into the living room after a light knock on the door, kissing Claire casually on the cheek.

"Alex is bringing a girl."

"That makes a difference?"

"He said he might bring a friend when he first mentioned visiting Alpine. But I figured a guy, somebody from Los Angeles he hung out with."

"Think she'll be pretty as you?"

Claire rolled her eyes. "You tell me, Sheriff. You've seen her."

"What?"

"On the TV show. His co-star."

"Shit!" Clayton rarely swore. "Piper . . . what's her name?"

"Robinet." Clayton's reaction didn't thrill Claire. It got worse.

"The one that looks like Liz Taylor? Back when she made *Giant*? Same hair, eyes, figure."

"If you think so."

"Better if I didn't?"

Claire managed to smile, stepping out of the living room to stow the vacuum in a hall closet. She'd straightened up the bungalow, but it still looked like what it was, an academic's home cluttered with worn books and unreadable journals. Her tiny office upstairs was even worse. But it was a safe space for her cat, who disliked both vacuum cleaners and the sheriff.

"This will be strange for me."

"What?" Clayton had claimed a Dr. Pepper from the icebox, knowing she stocked them for him.

"Hosting my little brother. We're not what you'd call close—not like I was with my sisters."

"Issues?"

"Nothing specific. I was almost fifteen when he was born and away at college when he started kindergarten. Then I went off to grad school in Texas. I've been more *aunt* than *sister*. A very cool aunt, but still an adult dealing with a child. I barely knew what to get him for Christmas."

"Beatrice is older than me, but I didn't escape her 'til *I* went to college. Different relationship."

Claire laughed. Over the last several months, she'd gotten to know Clayton's eccentric sibling very well—she reminded Claire of her own domineering mother. "I just wish we'd been closer," she said. "I've no idea now how to deal with Alex and a girl. I mean, they're high school kids. I can't let them share the guest bedroom. But they're camping in the park the next night."

"If he's anything like the kid he plays in *Brainiacs* . . ."

"He's even sharper. I'm the PhD and I can barely keep up. But he's still my baby brother."

"Almost eighteen."

"And he makes ten times the money we do. More, probably. I'm glad you're having dinner here tonight. You guys might have things in common."

"Two good lookin' dudes with crazy sisters?"

"Wait 'til you see him in person."

"Seriously?"

"Oh, yeah," Claire laughed. "I'm roasting a chicken."

"Not BBQ?"

"He likes roast chicken and mashed potatoes and pistachio ice cream. I had to call my Aunt Clara in California to find out."

"A man after my own heart."

"I hope so. I really do." Claire softened her tone.

Clayton blushed a little. It didn't take much, but maybe the sheriff was thinking about their own relationship. A quick spring romance had drifted into a strange second act during the summer. Clayton unexpectedly found himself

Sheriff of Brewster County and then, when his dad passed after a long decline, he faced challenges at home too.

On her side, Claire had been asked to edit one of the most important works of fiction in decades—an amazing opportunity. But they both paid a price for the changes. Family pressures, deadlines, schedules, endless meetings. Clayton and Claire rarely saw each other now. And their typical date night? Catching Alex's TV show on Friday nights over takeout and wine. Ironic, Claire supposed.

They did think of themselves as boyfriend and girlfriend, even if the terms struck Claire as juvenile. Clayton, after all, was sheriff of the biggest county in the state and she was a professor and writer. But nothing else fit. They weren't *partners* because he was disinclined to sex before marriage and she'd nixed his hasty marriage proposal. So they weren't *fiancées* either. A faculty colleague habitually described Clayton as Claire's *special friend*, and Alpine's chief of police Fiona Tusk once introduced Claire as Clayton's escort, apparently unaware of the connotations. Or maybe she was?

"When's he arrive?" Clayton asked.

"Around five, I'd guess. I had a text. They're on their way from Midland. In a Range Rover."

Clayton whistled.

"Yeah," Claire said.

※ ※ ※

"MAYBE WE SHOULD turn back?" Piper mumbled to herself. But Alex understood her because he was thinking the same thing.

They were on Texas State Highway 18, an hour out of Odessa and somewhere past Monahans, sharing flat and dusty pavement with banged-up tow trucks and glistening tankers that ignored lane markers. Heavy-duty pickups too, more than Alex had ever seen in Ohio or California, many of them dualies. Passing them raised Alex's heart rate while Piper closed her eyes.

The featureless land was as rugged as the vehicles rolling over it, low-lying brush and scrub doing little to conceal battered sheds, rusting towers, and phalanxes of pumpjacks and storage tanks. No hills, neighborhoods, trees, shops, cyclists. Just miles and miles of industrial hardware that made the state rich. Oil country.

They sampled local radio stations and quickly reverted to Sirius. "Texas can't all be like this," Alex said.

"Maybe we should open a bottle of wine?"

"Right. Drinking under age and open-container to boot. Probably a life sentence here." They'd seen lots of state troopers.

"Your sister's boyfriend is sheriff."

"We're not in Brewster County yet."

"It's got to get better."

And it did, as soon as they crossed I-10 heading south where Highway 18 became Highway 67. Traffic ebbed noticeably as most trucks diverted onto Interstate 10, east and west. Almost immediately, a horizon of low hills and looming mountains gave perspective to fields fenced for cattle. Windmills pumped water for livestock.

"Another 60 miles," Alex said. Piper could read the navigation screen as easily as he. The sun was already in its late afternoon decline.

"What's your sister look like?" she asked.

"You've seen pictures. She gets lots of attention."

"You two close?"

"Not much in common. We talk. Haven't been face-to-face in more than a year."

"Text?"

"Barely."

"So why are we visiting?"

"She invited me. And like I said, haven't seen her in a year."

"Bad vibes?"

The question unsettled him.

"Why would you think that?"

"Don't know. Wouldn't you be jealous? Kid brother getting famous and making tons of money and she's out here in Nowhereland."

"She's done okay in Texas. Big book deal. Cool boyfriend."

"The sheriff."

"Yeah."

"Serious?"

"Don't know."

"Not sure I'd date a cop."

"Probably better than dating an actor."

"Don't get ahead of yourself, Mr. Harp."

"Just saying." Piper steered clear of defining their relationship. But Alex figured girls were like that. And they call the shots. "You had an older sister," he ventured.

"You know I don't talk about her."

He knew the girl died in a car crash. Somewhere in Arkansas. Piper and her sister were already living on their own then and moving to California after their mother—or *maybe* their dad?—died of cancer. Piper eventually got to Los Angeles. She was barely sixteen then. Alex didn't press for details.

They drove in silence until he called out a sign for Brewster County. The pavement changed in hue and texture. Hills were even closer to the road now and afternoon shadows made surrounding mountains and mesas mysterious.

Piper wasn't impressed. "Mind if I zone out?"

"Go ahead, but pass me a Coke."

"I'll stay up if you want."

"I'm fine," he said and was, despite the 2:00 AM wakeup. Switching to Real Jazz on XM, he thought about his reunion with Claire—likely in less than an hour. He admired her, for sure. Handsome and wicked smart, she was as professionally driven as he was. Good genes not shared with their two married sisters.

And they'd both learned how to deal with an intrusive and dogmatic mother. Endless stories to share there. He'd ask Claire about Texas and Texans too. And for sure about the murder case she was part of last spring.

She'd want to know about Hollywood and his show. And the movies he'd been in and people he'd met. Jon Voight. Clint Eastwood. Lady Gaga. Explaining Piper would be strange. One look should be enough. But what else? Was Claire on the job market? Was she happy? Would she talk about her handsome cop? Most of her previous boyfriends had been nerds.

About then suddenly Highway 67 veered sharply right as it headed into Alpine. The town was just big enough to have outskirts where the speed limit dipped quickly from 70 to 45. He tapped a steering wheel button to cut his momentum. Moments later, a black-and-white was flashing lights in his rearview mirror. No siren though.

The shoulder was plenty wide for him to pull over. The cop kept him waiting a few minutes, diddling with his computer. Alex thought about waking Piper, but she was fast asleep—even snoring. (Good to know. He'd rag her about it.)

Alex rolled down his window as the officer approached. Afternoon heat rolled in.

"License and registration," the officer said. Big guy, young and pale. Brown uniform. Cowboy hat. Name tag over the right pocket.

"What's the problem?" Alex asked.

"Just wanted to check you out."

Alex removed his sunglasses. "I'm used to it."

"You've got your sister's eyes."

"Hers are green. Mine are blue."

"I can see that. Welcome to Texas."

"What?" Piper roused. "Are we getting a ticket?"

"No, ma'am. Just sayin' hello."

"Haven't been 'ma'amed' since Arkansas. You must be . . ."

"The sheriff."

Chapter 5

A year had changed Alex a lot. It wasn't just the razor cut, Arc'teryx boots, Navajo cuff. It was how he held himself and gazed at her, like he was the elder of the pair. Not arrogant or cocky, eyes still flashing and lustrous. But they suggested something other than the good humor she remembered. Claire was almost intimidated.

The girl he'd brought along begged off for a nap almost immediately after handing Claire a gift of Wellness Oil from Neiman Marcus. *Thoughtful!* Claire escorted her to the bedroom upstairs. And, yes, this Piper with an Arkansas drawl (never heard on the TV show) *did* resemble Liz Taylor, especially around the eyes. And waist. And breasts.

Claire was relieved Alex hadn't followed them upstairs because she intended that he sleep alone on the living room sofa. She found him there sorting through a backpack. She'd taken only a few minutes to show Piper the guest room and a full bath they'd share. Alex would have the half bath downstairs to himself.

He looked up when she returned. "Come on in the kitchen. I have a chicken roasting," she said.

They embraced a second time, more affectionately than when he stepped across the threshold with Piper. Alex was taller than she was now and muscling up like a man.

"I met your cute boyfriend," he said. "Stopped us on the highway. Gonna marry the guy?"

"What a question," she laughed. "Let me look at you—Mr. Movie Star. I'm so glad you're here." Clayton would have blushed, but Alex just rolled with it. Claire didn't know what to say next.

Alex was no more eloquent. "Good to see you too, sis."

A line from a bad script.

"I'm sorry . . . you must be tired. Sack out on the sofa if you want while I finish dinner. We won't eat 'til seven."

"I'm okay." He sat at the kitchen table.

They mulled over family matters—their mother's social activities in Ohio, dad's impending retirement, sisters' reluctance to produce grandkids. Nothing consequential. She studied him as they talked—thick bronze hair scavenged from their father's side, blue eyes bigger and darker than her green ones, cheekbones and brows that created dramatic shadows.

Where did this kid come from?

Alex muttered polite words about how she'd decorated her rental house and Claire responded by observing that he and Piper picked a good time to hike. That Piper was very attractive.

He said nothing. Claire was orbiting a planet rather than landing on it.

"What have you two planned for this week?" Alex had been vague in his emails. "Will I see you after tonight?"

"Tomorrow, we'll be on the South Rim at Big Bend. Then if the park looks cool, we'll stay a couple nights at a lodge. Our travel people got us something called a Roosevelt Cottage."

"For you and Piper."

"Yeah."

Claire smiled. "And you have *travel people?*"

"They picked the Range Rover. I'd been happy with a Chevy."

"So I *won't* be seeing you again?"

"No, you will—if that's okay. I'll likely be driving Piper to Midland–Odessa midweek so she can fly back to California. Needs to be there about a movie part she wants."

"And?"

"I'm finished with the TV show. So I'm not going back right away. If you have time, maybe you could spend a day or two showing me Texas? Give me a feel for the place. Meet some cowboys."

Claire felt better. She'd make the time—maybe on the weekend. She wasn't teaching because of her book project, but it was on a demanding schedule. She wanted to tell him more about it.

Pounding on the foyer door off the kitchen interrupted them. An odd arrangement, but it made her living room more private. Claire got up to answer, doubting it was Clayton arriving early.

Four girls, maybe still in junior high, stood on the stoop in t-shirts, hoodies, and spandex pants, dancing nervously as if they had to pee.

A dark girl with thick hair sure to be a head-turner in senior high spoke for the group.

"Is Alex Harp here?"

Claire was not prepared for that.

"Could we see him?" It sounded like an order.

"Well, I don't know . . ."

Alex overheard and appeared like a shadow behind her. The girls gasped and giggled and waved books the size of diaries for him to sign. When he stepped forward, a tiny blonde girl touched his shoulder and screamed. The others pulled out pens for Alex to use, and one happy fan sniffed hers after he returned it. Alex thanked them for coming, then withdrew quickly into the house. As the girls skipped away, Claire called after. "How did you know he was here?"

❧ ❧ ❧

"ANSWERING THE DOOR may not have been a good idea," Alex said, explaining the role Piper's agent played in the trip. "I'm guessing he contacted local media. It's what PR people do."

Claire figured he was right. While there was no daily newspaper in the region, Marfa just thirty miles away had a public radio station, and the whole area was served by the *Big Bend Mercury*, a clamorous news site covering everything from murders to *quinceañeras*. Likely its editors Barney and Ella Nixon got hold of Alex and Piper's itinerary in West Texas and published it.

"Well, damage done," Claire said. Alex looked disappointed.

"I wanted private time. But like I said, Piper needs publicity. You heard about my next movie?"

Claire nodded. *His next movie.* They fell silent.

"We're not handling this well, are we?" he muttered. "Lots of things to say and I'm blank."

"And I'm just blown away," Claire admitted. "I want my baby brother back." She managed not to cry.

"And you the big-time writer and editor. Will *you* stay in Texas much longer?"

Nice deflection on his part, she thought. "For now," she said. She'd had queries from liberal arts programs all over the country and even an offer from her publisher in Boston. Moving up was on her mind.

"The cop complicates things," he said.

When'd he become a grownup? Her turn for a dodge. "Like Piper complicates your life? Are you two . . . ?"

"Maybe." He'd looked away. It was odd.

"I see."

"You won't tell Eugenia?" She wasn't surprised he called their mother by her first name.

"No. Of course not. But she'll phone."

"Yeah. She expects me to report on you too."

Claire laughed. "And does she know about Piper?"

"Piper and I aren't exactly a thing."

"But you just said . . ."

At that moment, the stairs above them creaked. "What smells so good?" Claire didn't know how long Piper had been on the upper landing.

"Roast chicken," Alex replied as the young actress slipped down the remaining stairs into the kitchen. "Didn't sleep long," he said.

"I couldn't leave all the work to Claire."

"Don't be silly. I've been looking forward to this. The food won't be fancy, but it's stuff my brother likes. Or used to. You've both probably been spoiled out there in California."

"They eat like rabbits. I'm looking forward to ribs and BBQ," Piper said.

"Well, it's Cleveland cuisine tonight."

⊰⊱ ⊰⊱ ⊰⊱

IT WAS WELL past seven before Clayton Shoot phoned. Claire took the call away from the tiny dining room, guessing business once again was about to interrupt pleasure.

"Big house fire in Fort Davis," he said.

"But that's in Davis County," Claire protested. "You don't have jurisdiction."

"Expected you'd say that. The sheriff there asked me to help. Seems the

35

distressed homeowners mentioned me. Their house is three-quarters standing, but smokin' like a kiln. Neighbors pulled a lot of furniture out and stuff. Belongs to the Nixons—Ella and Barney. You remember?"

"The couple that runs the *Big Bend Mercury*? I've never met them."

"Yep. They salvaged laptops and lots of files on disk," Clayton explained. "They intend to keep their site up. They even been covering their own fire."

He waited while Claire checked her laptop. "Sure are. And there you are in a photo, Clayton."

"Ella's almost excited about it," he said. "She's the one asked for me. Thinks it was arson and her husband—he's blind—*kinda* agrees. A mess. Their cats got out."

"Ella Nixon wanted *you* specifically? What's that about?"

"She has a crush on the Sheriff of Brewster County," Clayton laughed.

"Oh?"

"Ella would of been a looker—way back in the sixties."

"Oh."

"Too early to know how it started. Her husband mentioned his political enemies from Vietnam War days. But the fire marshal says a blaze a few weeks ago got traced to faulty AC repair. The Nixons just had theirs fixed by the same company."

"Dinner is off?"

"Looks like it. Hey, and this is *real* odd. Her house is smokin' and Ella Nixon asks me if your brother Alex showed up yet. How'd she even know that? You don't talk to her, do you?"

"Never, Clayton. But maybe she had a tip from Piper Robinet's agent."

"Story about them in the *Mercury* too?"

"Seems so, I'm looking at it right now. Some little girls already showed up at my door wanting Alex's autograph."

"Not Piper's?"

"They've discovered boys."

"Ella said she expects to interview your brother. Imagine her house burning down and she's thinking about the next story."

"Maybe that's how the Nixons get on in the news business? Grace under pressure."

"You want I should come by when things clear up? Might be a few hours."

"These kids had a long day and a bigger one on tap tomorrow. Bet they sack out after strawberry shortcake."

"Save some for me?"

"Dudn't keep well, Claytie."

"Did you just say *dudn't?*"

Claire smiled, hung up, and returned to the dining room.

"We overheard most of that," her brother admitted.

"So we won't get to see the sheriff again." Piper seemed disappointed. Or maybe she was thinking about whose autograph those teens at the door wanted.

⅏ ⅏ ⅏

CLAIRE STUDIED PIPER carefully throughout the meal, wondering what she was missing. The actress made all the right moves, smiled at Alex whenever he said something clever, parried Claire's questions about her life with queries of her own.

She admired Piper's hair and makeup too, both toned down for a trip into a rugged corner of the country. Artful, yet simple. She spoke quietly, her very slight drawl adding character to observations about her work or ambitions or even the upcoming hiking expedition. She'd mastered the feminine skill of asserting opinions while sounding deferential.

"How about a glass of wine to celebrate this evening?" Claire said as she gathered up dessert plates. "Or maybe a cordial—I have a nice Port or maybe a Drambuie or something sparkling?"

"Whatever you're having," Piper said, too predictably.

"Damn, sister. Texas has changed you," Alex laughed. "You know we're both underage?"

"One of the finer points of Texas law is that parents or guardians can serve alcohol to their minor children. I think I might pass as guardian tonight."

"Sparkling for me," her brother said.

"I've a decent Prosecco in the fridge. Piper?"

"Sure. I'd like that."

The three finished the bottle easily, just enough alcohol to make them mellow. Alex eventually stood up, stretched, and said he'd better shower before Piper and Claire retired. Claire told him which towels were his and he bounded upstairs, first recovering a travel kit and clean underwear from his backpack.

"I won't take long."

Both women watched him climb the stairs.

37

"Still a kid, isn't he?" Claire said, settling into an armchair and indicating a place on the sofa for Piper.

"Can't I help you clean up?" the girl said.

Claire shook her head. "Won't take long. You're on vacation."

"That's kind."

Claire poured Port for each of them. Piper took it gracefully. "Now tell me, Piper. How much older are you than my brother?"

Piper stared at the glass and then lifted it slowly to her lips.

"This is very good. Expensive."

"I figured you could tell."

"I'm a few years older than Alex."

"Enough to make a difference?"

"In California, yes. Here in Texas, I don't think so."

"So you aren't lovers yet?" Claire couldn't hide her curiosity.

Piper leaned back into the sofa and crossed her legs. Took another sip of the wine.

"I'm not making an issue of it," Claire added. "My brother can take care of himself. But I don't want him . . ."

"I've worked with Alex for a year now," Piper interrupted. "To be honest, I didn't like him much at first—just a lucky jock with a viral video. But I was wrong. He's incredibly talented."

Claire nodded. She'd seen her brother on screen.

"Neither of us is in love. But if Alex wants to give it a go, I'm fine. Happy, in fact. Might help him clarify things."

That sounded odd. Claire wondered what Piper was hinting at. "Didn't expect you'd be so frank," she said.

"Didn't expect you'd ask the question."

"So, you two came all the way to Texas . . ."

Piper smiled. "Some would say it's romantic."

"And what would you say?"

"That it's complicated. My whole life's complicated. In ways his isn't yet. I don't resent that and I don't burden him with my issues. We both want something from each other."

The stairs squeaked again.

"What's complicated?" It was Alex standing on the landing in just boxer

38

briefs, holding trousers in one hand and trying to pull on an undershirt with the other. Both women stared. Claire's cat was nuzzling his ankles.

"Not you, brother," Claire said, beginning to suspect she might be wrong. "Not you."

Chapter 6

"We look like skiers," Piper sighed.

In beanies and sunglasses, Alex didn't disagree. In fact, the weather *was* chilly enough for headgear, yet bright enough for Oakleys. They'd donned the accessories just before taking on the Pinnacles, the first stage of the South Rim Trail, hoping others on the climb wouldn't recognize them.

⊰⊱ ⊰⊱ ⊰⊱

IT WAS AN unexpected text that prompted the disguises. The message interrupted their drive to Big Bend National Park earlier that Tuesday, nearly spoiling it. They'd slept later than they should have and then gorged on Claire's blueberry pancakes before departing Alpine around 9:30. Piper got the text maybe thirty minutes later, just moments before both their phones lost service and she couldn't respond.

They'd already breezed through a Border Patrol checkpoint on Highway 118—they didn't stop because they were heading south toward the Rio Grande. The message pinged moments later, near Elephant Mountain, a sprawling hump of rock surrounded by a wilderness preserve area that harbored big horn sheep. Alex was enjoying the cruise through ranch country edged by mountains and broad-shouldered mesas stretching beyond sight. No traffic to speak of.

He was also imagining the upcoming night with Piper. They'd worked together for months now and he flirted as much as network overseers allowed. The two of them made out in limousines a few times, kissed during photo shoots, enjoyed playing starry-eyed teens in their series.

But Piper kept him at a distance too. Depending on her moods, she'd raise or dash his hopes. And she had lots of moods. Said *she* wasn't ready. Said *he* wasn't ready. Said *it* might spoil their onscreen rapport. Or make working together awkward. *Sure.* They were teenagers—by definition, emotional wrecks.

So he guessed her sudden itch to go camping with him in Texas was a career move. Good publicity just when she needed it. But he was okay with that. He wasn't looking for romance. Just a night alone with a girl in the mountains.

Then a terse and allusive text complicated their plans. It came from Annette, a name Alex didn't recognize, possibly someone working for Piper's agent. Or maybe the WetBTE Network? Or perhaps from Throng!Media itself, though Alex guessed the corporate overlords would text *him*, not Piper. She read the message aloud twice, slowly the first time as she wrestled with the syntax, more glumly the second as its implications settled in.

> Hey kids. Team in place for BBNP show. Legesons onsite: rooms and camp permits OK. Crews hndlg gear, shade, video, water, food, etc. No lighting permitd. Media event noonish: meet/greet with NPS people. Photogrs. Some press? At south rim afternoon. BC 2 campsite dinner. Entrtmnt cancld. See ya on rim. Head to Rosvlt cabins, if prblms. Txt if pssble.

"Shit," Alex mumbled. But with the endgame in sight, he saw no point in upsetting Piper or blaming her for whatever had been set in motion. A media event on a national park trail? Could her agent have pulled this off alone? He suspected bigger forces at play.

"What's *NPS* mean?" she asked.

"National Park Service."

They both knew what *meet/greet* entailed. An invited audience. But who'd climb fifteen hundred feet to see them on a Tuesday in October? *Brainiacs* fans would be in school. Could the event be aimed at tourists already in the park or locals needing exercise? Or park staff and employees? Alex knew they trended young in Death Valley and Yosemite. Likely here too.

"Photos!" he suddenly realized. "They want publicity shots."

"Of us . . . or you?"

Alex ignored that question. He figured the studio would focus on him because of the movie. But Piper's agent would want her in those photos—the perfect Capulet to his Montague.

Fortunately, the Texas scenery intervened and distracted them for a good many miles—sweeping panoramas of distant mountains and flat fields of skeletal bushes aligned in rows, as if planted. Freaky, brutal, yet oddly beautiful. True West. Alex turned the conversation to hiking.

Asked Piper where she'd camped before. *State parks in Arkansas,* she said. Who'd she hike with? That query went unanswered. He tuned in Sirius and they sampled country stations. They at least made Piper smile. She talked about singers she remembered as a child.

Maybe an hour down the road, Alex pointed to a turn-off for Terlingua Ranch Lodge. He said it had ties to racing legend Carroll Shelby. "Never heard of her," Piper said.

Yeah.

But signs of human presence steadily increased, much of it tied to long-abandoned digs in the desert. None of it pretty. Then just over a hill not far from the park entrance, the tiny town of Study Butte suddenly appeared like something built around a strip mine. Not a national hotel chain or restaurant in sight or a gas station franchise they recognized. Not even a Dairy Queen.

The western entrance station to Big Bend National Park felt derelict too, an empty booth with a sign directing visitors to pay entrance fees at park headquarters miles away. *Who'd bother?* But at least the surrounding hills were thick now with cactus and scrub, ocotillo waving thin green stalks against a blue horizon. No heavy equipment had mauled these federal acres in half a century.

They still had the western half of the park to cross before reaching the Chisos Mountains, where they'd be hiking. Twenty miles or more east of the entrance gate, their navigation system ordered a right turn at the next junction, sending them directly toward that ring of rocky peaks. The late-morning light set palisades and hoodoos along the road in harsh relief, softened by thriving oaks and pinion pines. Somewhere up there was the South Rim Trail.

Piper insisted they stop at a scenic pull-off and then again for photos at a warning about mountain lions and bears.

"Don't see that in Ohio," Alex admitted.

The road continued to climb. Cliffs edged its narrow shoulders, eliminating them entirely where turns tightened into switchbacks. They slowed near the top of the climb when they approached a row of parked SUVs and pickups. Tourists with backpacks and water bottles were prepping for a hike. A sign said *Lost Mine Trail.*

"Maybe tomorrow?"

Piper shrugged and they drove on, descending slightly now into a bowl-shaped valley. They passed signs for a campground and then turned into a parking area bordered by a restaurant, store, visitor center, and two-story lodges with porches. Still no cell service, Piper noted. They orbited the lot looking for the Roosevelt Cottages, finally pulling in at a visitor center for help.

"Oh, you mean the CCC cabins," a middle-aged ranger behind a counter laughed. "They're all booked by Hollywood people."

"We're the Hollywood people," Piper said. But the female officer was staring at Alex.

"What's CCC stand for?" he asked.

"Civilian Conservation Corps. A federal program to help young men during the Depression. They'd join the CCC and then be shipped to work at camps across the country. They built lots of the facilities here—trails, shelters, and even the stone lodges you're looking for."

The ranger suddenly smiled. "You're Alex Harp, aren't you? We heard you might show up. My daughter at Sul Ross State just loves you. Me too. You were so good in that movie." Other tourists in the visitor center overheard and stared. Alex did a perfect Texas *aw shucks*. Everyone laughed but Piper.

The ranger pulled out a map of the Basin area and marked where their accommodations were. They could have walked there, but needed to park the Range Rover. It didn't surprise them when a local outfitter was waiting to open their separate cabins. He then pointed them in the right direction. They stretched a few minutes, checked gear, tightened shoes, hoisted backpacks. Fortunately, the trail to the Pinnacles ran right past their accommodations.

They hadn't gone ten yards when Alex stopped.

"You know, it's a loop," he said. "We could screw them all by heading the other way. We'd still get to the rim but miss all the hoopla."

Piper just ignored him and kept walking.

"I need the hoopla."

⸭⸭ ⸭⸭ ⸭⸭

THAT'S WHEN THEY donned the sock caps and sunglasses, hoping to avoid attention from other hikers headed to the meet-and-greet. Running late, they caught up with and passed some older climbers unable to match their pace.

43

They were overtaken themselves by several even more energetic couples. And they didn't fool anybody looking for them. How could they? These fans mostly just smiled, nodded, and kept a respectful distance. Texans, they decided were, for the most part, cool.

There was, of course, the trail to deal with, initially a graveled path through desert scrub and cedar, then an easy climb through pleasant meadows but, soon enough, one switchback after another lined by rocks that might have dropped from the moon. Carved steps made some sections even tougher to climb. Aspen and pine somehow thrived at this elevation, competing for space with agaves, some with stalks twenty feet tall. One hiker paused on the trail to make sure Piper and Alex took note of a short tree with gnarled branches shedding orange bark.

"It's a madrone," she explained worshipfully. "Very rare and can't be cultivated. Even Texas A&M couldn't do it."

Alex and Piper nodded, unsure why that mattered. But they used the interruption to gaze back over the two miles they'd hiked. The elevation was impressive and the terrain eye-popping, if not quite Grand Canyon awesome. Good work for a late morning.

It took another hour to reach the edge of the rim they'd been scaling. Here hikers had gathered around a crude toilet, taking a breather on some logs, or standing in line to use the one-at-a-time facility. They'd climbed 1600 feet.

At a distance, they spotted two pairs of hands, belonging to a tall couple, waving them ahead. Nancy and Ethan Legeson again. And, past them, a troop of trail guides, photographers, a reporter or two, and even gofers, likely hired in Terlingua and Study Butte to assist the media folks. Mostly men, but women too. Alex thought he recognized at least one minor bigshot from Throng!Media itself—Sherman Farr. A slim executive with a dark mustache and an oversized phone, Farr took a moment to greet Alex.

"Come, come over here," Nancy Legeson quickly interrupted, gesturing them farther down the trail and away from the pit toilet. "People want to say hello."

It wasn't new territory for Alex and Piper. They'd handled press and fans before, only never on a chilly Texas mesa at 7000 feet. Their fellow hikers were mostly in-shape middle-aged folks able to take vacations in October and, as anticipated, a healthy assortment of young people in park gear, including rangers, guides, and possibly staff from the lodges, stores, and restaurants.

Cheery fans and tourists and some media types gathered around Alex and Piper—gradually pulling them apart, guys predictably attentive to Piper (who looked too sexy in her stretch pants, Alex thought) and women surrounding Alex. These at least didn't scream like the pre-teens outside Claire's door. Instead, they asked friendly questions about his movies and career, in part to show how much they knew about him. Native Texans asked for his impressions of their state. Several older women, just as eager as younger ones to rub shoulders with a celebrity, asked for kisses on the cheek. Alex obliged.

He couldn't help notice how attentive Piper was to her mostly male fans. She rested a hand on the shoulder of a muscular Hispanic ranger while she flirted with his buddy, a tall African American. She soon had a whole group of dudes laughing and, at one point, even casting eyes back on Alex. Was he the butt of some joke?

Some of the park people, Alex understood, would accompany then all the way to the South Rim, which was still miles off according to a dark-haired girl—a park intern she explained—who introduced herself as Gracie and touched his Navajo cuff. The name made Alex smile.

"My favorite old-time actress was a comedienne named Gracie," he explained.

"No way," the girl laughed. "Gracie Allen?"

"You've heard of her?"

"My grandfather named me after her! He loved her movies and a TV show she did with George Burns, her husband. Hard to catch either on the Navajo reservation, but he'd find VHS tapes. I'm Gracie Allen Yazzie from Kayenta, Arizona."

Alex was smitten. He quickly discovered that Gracie was poised, ironic, and sweetly gorgeous. The kind of fan he rarely encountered too—someone more interested in his work than him. Within minutes, she was explaining why his upcoming *Romeo and Juliet* should stick to the script Shakespeare wrote and not try to make the play *relevant*. She was so relieved when he concurred she almost hugged him. He wouldn't have minded. Attentive to others gathered around, Alex and Gracie still managed to keep their conversation going until the Legesons summoned the two actors to the campground, while encouraging the rest of the group to head on to the South Rim overlooks, maybe two hours away.

"I won't ask you for your email," Gracie said, "because you'd be crazy to give it to a fan. But let me give you my card, just in case, you know . . ." Her dark eyes sparkled. Alex saw Piper staring at him as he slipped the card into his wallet.

"Happy to meet you, Gracie Yazzie," he said. And he was.

Chapter 7

"So you don't think it's arson?" Deputy Alonso Rangel asked his boss, sitting with him late Tuesday morning at a table in Judy's Bread and Breakfast, their go-to place for quick coffee and breakfast in Alpine. "The Nixons have lots of enemies I can think of—oil companies, pipeline fitters, Republicans. My relatives."

Clayton Shoot munched a sweet roll. "Agree about the enemies. But not arson."

"That makes things simpler."

Clayton nodded. "The sheriff there in Davis County said the fire was electrical. Maybe an arc from a faulty contact in the heat pump. The insurance inspector agrees."

"Already?"

"Knew what to look for. They had an incident in Fort Stockton a few weeks ago traced to a similar component. Both units just recently repaired."

"And the Nixons still managed to report on their own fire?"

"Yep. To their credit, their story's not overblown either."

"Gonna rebuild?"

"Nope. Turns out they been leasing all these years. Ella Nixon said she'd look for a house here in Brewster County."

The dark-haired deputy laughed.

"What?"

"Fiona told me Ella Nixon is sweet on you. Maybe the old lady wants to get closer?"

Clayton grunted. The deputy was teasing. Rangel himself had just left the Alpine Police Department because he'd moved in with a woman nearly twice his age—Chief of Police Fiona Tusk. *His former boss.*

Poster children for opposites attract. She outweighed him by more than a few pounds too. The affair should have caused a scandal in Alpine, but most people simply felt good for the unlikely couple. Still, Alonso needed to find another job and Clayton got caught in the middle.

Alonso came by first, even before the affair went public. *Just between us, okay? Man to man?* At the time, Clayton didn't know what was up. He'd worked with the junior officer the previous spring when the city and county jointly investigated a difficult case. Liked the good-natured kid. Naturally, Clayton was intrigued when Alonso mentioned an older woman in his life. No big deal. Clayton's own girlfriend Claire had five years on him. Then Alonso mentioned Fiona Tusk.

Happened in Galveston, Alonso explained, at the Texas Police Chief's Annual Meeting in April. He was her co-driver *'cause Fiona said she don't like to fly*. At ease with each other after a 600-mile ride across the state. Dinner on the police chief's dime the next evening following a full day of boring sessions. Then, watching Fiona across the table. Sweet perfume. Perfect skin. All those curves. Breasts like . . . Alonso used a gesture. *Man, I never woulda thought,* he said. A little wine. More wine. Racy night. (Clayton more embarrassed than Alonso.) By the next day chief and deputy are holding hands under the table at the closing luncheon. *Whata I do now?*

Talking with Fiona the next morning was even worse for Clayton. She began the same way. *Just between us, okay?* Then, Alonso's sensitive eyes. Alonso's piquant smile. (She used words like that.) Alonso in her room, Alonso without his shirt, Alonso like Clayton would rather not imagine. Fiona seemed both horrified and giddy. *What's a woman to do?*

Didn't she have girlfriends for gossip like this? Clayton wondered. But Fiona wasn't after empathy or advice.

You need a deputy, no?

Yep. To fill a line that opened when he became sheriff. Hmmm. Alonso had computer smarts and good work habits and common sense. People skills too. Almost as important, the kid gave the twenty-eight-year-old sheriff some seniority. Rangel was only twenty-three.

So, what worked for Alonso and Fiona also worked for Clayton. And hiring him might lessen the bad blood between Clayton and Chief Tusk since he'd won the sheriff's star Fiona also sought.

What surprised Clayton, however, was not the May-September romance itself but was how much he found himself envying Alonso and Fiona. He and his own girlfriend Claire Harp were gridlocked. He'd wanted marriage and even proposed. She wasn't sure. But he wouldn't fool around until she was. Yep, that's how serious he was about the assistant professor.

But what if Alonso and Fiona had it right? *Smokin' love.*

Better than smolderin'—which was all Clayton and Claire were managing. Between her high-profile editing assignment and his figuring out how to be sheriff, they'd found less and less time for getting to know each other. His father dying was sobering too.

Stuck in second gear, Clayton was feeling anxious. Never expected he'd envy Fiona Tusk when it came to love.

⊰·⊱ ⊰·⊱ ⊰·⊱

"SHOULDN'T YOU GUYS be working?"

The question, only half in jest, came from Gus Stumpf, a stocky middle-aged woman joining Clayton and Alonso at their table in Judy's. Clayton had recently named this by-the-book veteran of the sheriff's office as his captain, stepping into the slot he'd formerly held.

"Just talkin' about the fire last night in Fort Davis," Alonso explained.

Gus nodded knowingly. "Better off with a swamp cooler than a heat pump, I always say." The men knew better than to argue. She'd have fifteen reasons why she was right about swamp coolers.

Clayton had surprised just about everyone, including Augusta Ryan Stumpf, when he'd asked her to serve as his captain. Gus was a low-profile officer who preferred fifties-style permanents because they fit neatly under her hat and wore tortoise shell glasses because her mother did. Married to a propane dealer exactly her own age, she was the mother of four rowdy boys. No doubt police work seemed like a cakewalk in comparison. For as long as Clayton knew her (and he remembered Gus policing football games when he was in high school), she'd looked exactly as she did now.

When the young sheriff first discussed the open captain's position with other officers and staff, they'd suggested a range of first choices—with Gus almost everyone's second pick. Reliable, knowledgeable, dependable, and fifteen years in the sheriff's office. Clayton decided to raise the issue with his retired mentor, Sheriff Artie Paulsen.

"She was my second choice, too, when I named you captain," Artie admitted,

48

a trifle grumpy. Clayton suspected he now regretted retiring, following his bypass surgery.

"But why not Gus? She had more experience than me."

Mrs. Paulsen had wandered onto the patio where the two men were talking, taking a seat beside her husband. The ex-sheriff looked uneasy.

"Well, you know what a community person Gus is. Drive through a neighborhood with her and she's naming people who live here and there and telling stories about 'em. Knows where everything is, how everything works, what state regulations apply, all that stuff."

"All reasons to pick her, not me," Clayton countered.

"Well, that's true. But you were just, well . . ." Artie Paulsen appealed to his wife. "Darlin'?"

Mrs. Paulsen did not mince words. "I told him to pick you, Clayton. I like Gus Stumpf. Gossiped with her all the time. Still do. But I thought about photos."

"Photos?"

"Yes, Clayton. Artie's been getting up there for some time and not as in-shape as he could be."

The retired sheriff didn't like that, but said nothing. His wife dug in.

"Put my old guy in the same picture with Gus Stumpf and the sheriff's office would look like Mayberry."

"And she's Aunt Bee," Artie Paulsen added, nodding to his better half.

"I don't have a clue what you're talking about," Clayton said.

Mrs. Paulsen patted him on the shoulder. "Handsome buck like you. I thought you'd give the place more energy, standing side-by-side with my husband." She said it to make Clayton blush and he did.

"But right now, you and Gus Stumpf would make a good pair. She's a mature, level-headed woman," Mrs. Paulsen explained, "and you're . . . Captain America. You won't go wrong picking Gus."

Clayton did and he had no regrets, so far.

❧ ❧ ❧

"THE NIXONS OKAY?" Gus asked, looking around the café and nodding at half the diners.

"I expect they've had better mornings," Clayton replied.

"You know what the talk is?"

49

Clayton knew she'd tell them. Gus took a slow sip of coffee—in a paper cup because she usually stayed just minutes.

"Word is they been rakin' it in lately. More ads on their site every week now that they're getting popular in Midland–Odessa. And Ella's been crowing about something big in her life."

"Her life or theirs?" Clayton asked. He thought of Ella and husband Barney Nixon as joined at the hip.

Gus took a deep breath while studying her cup. "They're about the same age, but people I talk with say Ella has all the energy. My impression too. Barney's still stuck in the sixties while Ella . . . isn't. She's political, but knows what ordinary people like. She keeps their news site afloat. More'n that, now."

"So she'd be aware of Hollywood kids visiting Alpine and Big Bend?" Clayton said.

A smiling Alonso guessed where this was going. Clayton had already mentioned he'd stopped Claire's brother and Piper Robinet on their ride into Alpine the previous afternoon.

"Whaddya you think of the girl, Sheriff?" Alonso asked.

After a long pause, Clayton said, "She's a woman a guy would notice."

Gus choked on her coffee. "My fourteen-year-old said the exact same thing. I gave him what for."

Chapter 8

Somehow Throng!Media Corporation had commandeered an entire primitive campsite near Boot Canyon, more than a mile from their initial stop at the top of the Pinnacles Trail. It wasn't much to look at, only a graveled scraping amid tall trees but big enough for four or five tents (three already erected) clustered around a bear-proof storage locker. Farther off was smaller clearing adequate for yet another pair of campers. An energetic trail guide, tanned and handsomely scruffy, asked Piper whether she had the tent she and Alex would be sharing. He identified himself as Donnie.

Her mind was elsewhere and she didn't respond until Donnie asked a second time. "Alex has the tent," she mumbled. "Can I leave my backpack here? I know I'll need water."

"Leave it. We have a CamelBak for you. Guides are bringin' refreshments too. I'll get the tent from Mr. Harp and set it up."

They'd thought of everything. Good, cause I'm not thinking straight right now.

The campsite already sported a camp stove, stacks of gear, lots of coolers, and a ridiculous sunshade. She watched at some distance as Alex surrendered his backpack to Donnie. The two pulled out the tent and headed toward the smaller clearing to set it up, just far enough away to guarantee privacy.

Great.

Piper wandered around the campground, wondering who exactly would be staying overnight. Fewer than a dozen? Everyone smiled like they knew her, but the only official person she vaguely recognized, the Legesons aside, was a red-headed woman in never-before-worn hiking clothes approaching her.

They shook hands and Piper heard the name Annette and recalled that she was a friend of her agent, who'd remained in California. Piper was now also certain Annette worked in some capacity for Throng!Media since she'd been the one who, hours earlier, sent the text announcing the meet-and-greet.

"Who are all these other people?" Piper asked.

Annette laughed and explained that many were locals hired to pump up the size of the crowd or to handle gear. "They'll be heading back down the trail soon as we're set up. Then come back tomorrow—some of them—to carry all this out. Park people are upset, but we'll make a nice contribution."

Annette seemed chatty. "Such attractive people on the park staff," she continued. "Did you meet the cute African American guy? Cultural resources manager. He'd be great in PR back in California."

Piper nodded. She'd noticed him.

"And that Mexican ranger, Sebastián? He's from . . ."

Piper interrupted. "That guy's cell phone works," she said, pointing to a tall man with a moustache very awkward in hiking shorts and standing with Nancy and Ethan Legeson. She was certain *he* was with Throng!Media. Big Kahuna. Why hadn't he introduced himself?

"Satellite phone," Annette sighed. "Wish I brought one. No cell service up here at all. That's Sherman Farr."

Piper didn't reply. When this Farr guy with the phone started moving away from the campground, everyone else did too and Annette quickly followed, abandoning Piper. She decided to keep her distance. Two more hours at least to the rim, the hike almost inconsequential now. *So much to think about.*

Alex, still accompanied by Donnie the trail guide, briefly noticed Piper falling behind, but a blonde ranger grabbed his arm and started chatting, drawing yet another woman into the conversation. Then, also up ahead on the main trail, Piper spotted the dark-haired girl Alex spoke with earlier—the one who handed him her card. And of course, Annette and Sherman Farr and others. Handshakes all around, laughter, comradery. Alex turned briefly again, saw Piper, waved and shrugged.

Some folks did hang with her, mostly tourists too old to know who she was. Odd how this trek to the rim was playing out, Piper thought. People shifting into and out of focus, randomly. Like in old foreign movies she'd watched with Alex. Piper wished she still smoked. It would calm her nerves.

But something was up with the Throng!Media people. She was certain of it. They'd peek back at her and then glance at Alex and resume intense conversations. Sherman Farr was the point man. The guy with the satellite connection.

Almost no one noticed when the trail entered a shallow ravine shaded by pines. The air suddenly cooled. There was evidence of water now too, depressions in the white rock creating algae-tinged pools. After miles of austere desert and the climb up the Pinnacles, Piper felt like she was in Arkansas again, the path atop the rim intricate, but less arduous than the steep climb to get there.

Boot Canyon someone said, pointing to a rock formation that gave this part of trail its name. Piper could imagine bears or mountain lions stalking them from behind the oak and maple trees, except this group, buzzing about jobs in the park, or road trips through Texas, or box office duds, would scare off most predators. The crowd had thinned noticeably, many park guests going their way once they'd met Alex Harp.

Eventually the Hispanic ranger Annette identified as Sebastián sidled up to Piper on the way to the rim. She didn't mind at all. He chatted about El Paso where he grew up and showed actual interest when she mentioned her Arkansas hometown. He even admitted to seeing *Brainiacs*.

"You know who you look like?" he said. Piper could guess, but then he surprised her. "Lindsay Lohan," he nodded. Well, Lohan *had* played Liz Taylor in a TV movie.

Even before she could reply, ever-busy Nancy Legeson appeared out of nowhere. She was in her element.

"I just want you to know that Ethan and I will be staying back at the campsite with you and Alex tonight. Most of the PR people and crew will be down in the lodges by then, but my husband and I will make certain you have what you need here." Piper didn't care. Her thoughts were on someone else in the crowd. But she was polite.

Mrs. Legeson spent the next quarter mile reviewing the dinner menu in the campground. They'd hardly be roughing it. "No alcohol, of course," she concluded, then winked to hint there might be. "But not for you and Alex."

"No, I wouldn't think so," Piper said, smiling at Sebastián, the ranger still shadowing her. But she was screaming inside, unable now to ignore the Throng!Media crowd orbiting Alex. Especially the photographer. Then she saw Sherman Farr pulling even farther ahead to be alone while Annette drifted back to Piper's lonely band.

Piper was angry by now. She pulled the redhead aside. "You do remember it was *my* agent and me who arranged this event?" she said. "Throng agreed it would be good publicity."

"Sure . . . and it is!"

"I need all the goodwill I can get," Piper said, trying not to sound needy. "Things are happening, aren't they?"

Annette was silent. Piper noticed that Sherman Farr had stopped on a rock ledge with the satellite phone glued to his ear. Nodding intently, staring at the ground. Had Farr even noticed the vista ahead of him, jagged peaks as far as the eye could see?

"I hope he has spare batteries." Piper couldn't conceal her sarcasm.

"Don't worry," Annette said, looking earnest. "You're a first-tier prospect for us and you have Alex Harp on your side."

Except that, at that moment, Alex Harp was side-by-side with that dark-haired girl again and she had him in stitches.

❧ ❧ ❧

ALEX FOUND THE rim view awesome. Like standing at the edge of the world. Or Mordor. Row after row of low rugged mountains, thick and deep, stretching far into Mexico. Way cooler than he expected and it made up for a lot. Everyone went silent. Even the folks from California. They'd nitpicked the hike until the view suddenly went IMAX.

"The South Rim," Alex said, sidling up to Piper for the first time in way more than an hour—maybe two. He'd finally ditched the photographer and his dwindling entourage to walk the hundred yards to where she sat on a cliff, studying the gnarled skeleton of an oak hanging over the rim's edge. Throng!Media people loitered at a wary distance. A red-headed woman shared their ledge, as did a youngish Hispanic ranger he'd met earlier. Piper's focus seemed elsewhere.

"Hey," he said.

She shrugged. Her ivory cheeks were sunburned.

"Not the way we imagined, huh?"

"See the guy with the satellite phone?" she said.

"Where?"

Piper pointed a few ledges over. Alex spotted Sherman Farr, staring into the clouds, talking feverishly into what looked like a walkie-talkie. He glanced in their direction, acknowledged Alex when he saw him, then turned away.

"Something's up," Piper said.

"Probably arranging flights out of here. There's an airstrip in Lajitas where you can get a jet to Dallas. Just forty miles outside the park."

Piper said nothing.

"A golf resort there too. An intern told me about it."

"The dark-haired girl?"

She'd noticed. "Gracie's from Arizona. Native American. Hopes to join the Navajo Rangers." Alex needed to redirect this conversation fast. "Have you seen our tent"?

Piper still didn't look at him. "The campsite's like Disneyland," she said.

"Hardly roughing it."

Farr looked in their direction now, pointing at the red-headed girl Piper seemed to know. Alex suspected she worked for Farr. Farr waved her over and then turned away again. Annette excused herself. The Hispanic ranger, suddenly alone, took the opportunity to edge over and re-introduce himself to Alex.

"Yeah, I remember," Alex said, "Sebastián Escobedo. We talked earlier with that other guy, the resource manager? What was his name?"

Piper interrupted their handshake.

"Sebastián is from El Paso," she said, in a snit, to judge from her tone. "But he's up for a transfer to Yosemite. That's just four or five hours from Los Angeles. He could visit our set. And isn't Sebastián a delicious name?"

The ranger looked embarrassed and Alex felt the same. Piper told Alex about Sebastián's job, his family, his ambitions. It sounded like a rant.

"You okay, Piper?" Alex said. But her eyes were locked on Annette, walking slowly back already, a troubled look on her face.

"I think if I had a son, I'd name him Sebastián," she said.

"Piper?"

Annette reached their rim overlook. "Can I talk to Ms. Robinet alone, Mr. Harp?" she said, including the ranger in her request. "And Mr. Farr wants to speak with you, Alex, if that's okay?"

Alex looked to Piper, signaled he was willing to stay with her. She motioned him off to the meeting with Farr.

"This doesn't feel good," Sebastián said as he and Alex left Piper with Annette.

Chapter 9

"Shouldn't *you* have spoken to Piper about this first? Let her know yourself?" Sherman Farr figured Alex might ask. The boy had manners as well as talent, a rarity in the business. The sort of guy you built franchises around. Sherman Farr couldn't afford a screw up. A middle-tier executive at Throng—*who else would you send into the wilds of Texas to keep tabs on horny actors?*—Farr nonetheless wanted Alex as an ally, someone whose goodwill might count for something long term.

"Annette's talking with Piper instead of me since she's our contact with Piper's agent. Besides, this decision is about *your* movie. Throng!Media wanted to pair you with a performer of more stature. We looked at dozens of girls for Juliet, not just Piper and Tabreetha Bree-Jones."

Performer was the right word. Farr didn't think much of Bree-Jones's film credentials. She was a singer mainly, song writer (allegedly), and media personality who'd played herself in a short-lived Netflix series. Hardly a stretch.

A creased brow suggested Alex's doubts.

"Okay, she's not a Shakespearean, but at least she's a Brit with a huge following in the right demographics—just like you—and that opens up the market." Farr knew Alex never had done Shakespeare either. But the kid displayed real chops in three movie roles loved by both audiences *and* critics.

"So, Piper didn't get this part. There'll be other opportunities for her." *That was a lie.* Throng!Media had no plans for Robinet and *Brainiacs* was caput. Annette would tell Piper about the series cancellation too, but Farr decided not to mention it to Alex. He'd left the show already. Smart enough to read the tea leaves.

"Look. For what it's worth, Piper was my first choice. You guys woulda been sensational. Both so great with foreign accents. I made that point in meetings.

I knew *you'd* handle the medieval stuff fine. I even mentioned Bree-Jones was getting long in the tooth." And he had. Farr also pointed out that Piper would cost a tenth of what they'd pay the Brit—who'd initially demanded double Alex's salary, but settled for parity.

Alex twisted his shoulders and looked down at his feet. Classic James Dean move, Farr noted.

"This decision won't affect you and Piper. You can make other movies together." Farr assumed the two were screwing like bunnies anyway. All WetBTE kids did, despite network policies for underage actors. Farr stopped short of hinting it might be time for Alex to move on from Piper. Say what you will, Bree-Jones was an eyeful.

Farr spent another quarter hour, maybe more, talking locations and schedules and the publicity tour Throng already had in mind for Alex and Tabreetha. "Stratford, Berlin, Cannes, Moscow, Singapore. And you'll really like her," he said almost certain the boy wouldn't. She was a bitch and dumb as a stump.

Which led to another five minutes about people cast for other parts. "Tebow's a fencer from Ohio State and the guy playing Mercury's been on a couple of BBC shows. Artsy shit." Alex smiled grimly, figuring the guy meant Tybalt and Mercutio. But Farr took it as a positive sign.

"Thanks, Mr. Farr," Alex said. "I expect I need to talk with Piper. Appreciate all you've done." The young man shook hands with the executive and headed to where he'd left Piper on the rim, a little John Wayne wobble in his gate, Farr noted.

Well that went well, he thought, immediately reporting the good news to his boss Ayala Topfer just as his satellite phone went dead. He should have brought spare batteries.

⁍⁘ ⁍⁘ ⁍⁘

ANNETTE WAS WAITING for Alex, clinging to her worthless cell phone like a totem, dancing nervously. Piper was gone.

"We didn't expect a casting decision this soon. We thought this trip would be good publicity—you two together."

Alex didn't buy the story. He'd noticed the videographer focusing on him all day. Piper was in shots early on, but got little attention on the walk to the rim.

"Where'd she go?"

"Piper? Back to the campground, I assume."

"With the ranger? That Sebastián guy?"

"No." Annette pointed. "He's over there." Sebastián had joined a group of park people, but he was gazing right at them. Alex waved him over.

"Piper wanted to be alone," Annette said. "She was upset, but not crying or anything. She acted like she expected this."

"She wouldn't let us go with her," Sebastián confirmed, sidling up to Annette. "You've seen the trail back. It's not rough."

"I'm going after her," Alex decided. She had maybe a twenty-minute head start? He'd catch her.

"We're coming too then," Annette insisted, surprising Alex. He hoped to reach Piper alone and talk.

"If you can keep up."

But Annette and Sebastián quickly fell behind the former quarterback, Annette lacking decent shoes. Or maybe those two wanted privacy?

Alex wasn't sure what he'd say to Piper. Gallantry was pointless. He'd nailed his part many weeks earlier and she'd always been a longshot for Juliet. She knew that. Still, Alex had some hope for the upcoming evening. Was that insensitive? *Sure.* But Piper knew what this trip was about. She'd even reminded him to bring condoms. He'd make her feel better. *Maybe.*

And then he thought how much easier it was to talk with Gracie Yazzie, how quick they'd connected, how sweetly she smiled. No games either. He didn't feel disloyal. That business with *Sebastián*—wasn't Piper trying to make him jealous? And now the same guy was flirting with the redhead.

There was stuff happening here he didn't understand. *Rank amateur when it came to women*, he thought.

Almost an hour down the trail, much of it easygoing, Alex still hadn't caught up with Piper, though he'd passed other members of the Throng!Media crew. They hadn't seen her either—even though they'd headed back to camp before she did. Strange.

Alex finally decided to wait for Annette and Sebastián to catch up, which took awhile. But it was just 3:30 and wouldn't be dark until 7:00 or later.

"You're sure Piper headed toward the camp?" Alex asked Annette. She nodded and Sebastián agreed.

"If she went in the other direction, she'd miss the campground and end up at the Basin," Sebastian pointed out. "It's a loop—a long one. But she definitely went this way."

"We've got a room at a CCC lodge down there."

"Sweet, I guess." Sebastián shrugged. "But wasn't she spending the night up here with you?"

"I told him," Annette chimed in before Alex could ask how Sebastián knew.

Another hour later, their Boot Canyon 2 campsite came into view. The turnoff was clearly marked. Piper couldn't have missed it. Members of the support crew were already serving food, especially to colleagues who'd be returning to the Basin soon. But they'd have no problem even if they stayed on too long. Plenty of moonlight in the offing, though clear skies meant the evening would cool down quick.

All the better for snuggling Alex thought.

Piper hadn't been in the camp when Alex, Annette, and Sebastián checked in, but neither was Sherman Farr and some others still at the rim when they left. Alex hadn't panicked yet, but he was getting there.

Word of Piper's failure to win the Juliet part circulated among the Throng people, who seemed unsure how to take the news. Officially, they had to seem delighted with Tabreetha Bree-Jones. But Alex overheard nasty comments. So maybe Piper had some supporters?

Alex's mood picked up when Gracie Yazzie dropped by the campsite to wish him well. Said she had to return to park headquarters because she worked the next day. "But let's keep in touch," she insisted.

Alex agreed but invited her to stay for dinner. "That might be awkward," she smiled and departed with a sandwich.

"I'll email you soon," Alex promised.

"This week?"

"Sure!"

When Piper finally showed up fifteen minutes later, the bustling campsite went quiet.

"Hey, I'm not dead," she said gamely. Alex started applauding and everyone joined in. Right thing to do. Piper teared up and Alex hugged her close, figuring the gesture guaranteed him a happy evening.

He was wrong.

⇥⇤ ⇥⇤ ⇥⇤

BY THE TIME the stars came out, just nine people remained at the campsite, chatting around a propane grille. Piper noticed the pairings. Sherman Farr and

59

Annette, for example. She expected the Throng executive to be in the Basin by now or maybe in a RV rolling on to Midland. Piper wondered how long Farr had been with Annette. The girl said nothing to her about any such connection.

The Legesons of course would share a tent. A happy couple after so many years. Nice to think they still existed. The video/camera guy stayed on too and he was friends with an equally middle-aged and non-descript WetBTE official who hadn't even bothered to introduce himself. And there was the essential muscle: three sturdy trail guides to keep things safe and organized. Two were business partners who would share a tent while sweet Donnie was on his own. Poor guy. But she noticed he had a one-person tent.

Poor Alex too. All caring and low-key at first, treating her like china. She evaded his questions, beginning with how they'd missed her on the trail. She made it clear she wasn't in a talkative mood. Let Alex figure things out for himself. He was clever enough to manage his career—beginning with spiking that singer's Cokes before his football game so he'd be the one to croon the national anthem. *He told her about that.*

But he was naïve in so many ways too, soft and privileged.

Well, she wasn't. Had never been. She'd get by without the movie or TV show. And land on her feet. There'd be a time to explain things to Alex. But not tonight. Not tonight.

Alex kept up a good front despite the brush off. Or maybe it wasn't a front at all. Though the youngest of the group, he was still its connector. Alex told stories around the camp stove better than anyone that night. Listened better too. Got others talking, joining in, even the trail guides. She felt his appeal. And was jealous.

Darkness and falling temperatures didn't faze the campers. If anything, the gossip and confessions grew more spirited. Especially after flasks came out. Piper passed, but Alex didn't. She noticed the trail guide Donnie eyeing Alex, falling for him no doubt. She'd do the guy a favor.

Annette brought the South Rim pow wow to a close by wondering why the stars were *so* much bigger in Texas. The guides muttered about dark skies. Everyone got up to gaze at them, walking the outskirts of the campsite and then heading for their tents. The Legesons were hand in hand. Alex took time (naturally) to point out constellations to Annette and Sherman Farr, who pretended to care. Piper used the moment to pull Donnie aside by a belt loop and make a request, rubbing his back gently, knowing the gesture was pointless.

"He's sure gonna be disappointed," Donnie said when she'd finished. "But it's fine by me." She knew it would be.

Alex, on the other hand, looked miserable. But how could he object, given the circumstances? She'd lost her TV show *and* a part in a movie just hours ago. Did he think she'd be in the mood for sex tonight? *With a virgin no less?* And, no, cuddling beside him wouldn't make her feel better. She wanted to be alone.

Then Alex brought up logistics. Did she expect him to sleep out in the open?

"I'll be using Donnie's tent. It's for one person. He's fine joining you."

"I'll bet he is," Alex said. *So he'd noticed.* She felt a twinge of guilt. But not enough to change things.

"I'm gut punched," she said, feigning tears. "I've lost so much." He had no answer to that. Alex *was* a good guy, always would be. And Piper wanted his goodwill long-term—though not tonight.

❖❖ ❖❖ ❖❖

DONNIE MAJEWSKI WAS a decent guy too. Even if he *had* cell service, he wouldn't text about who he was sharing a tent with tonight. His friends wouldn't believe him anyway. As he approached with sleeping bag and gear in hand, Alex Harp said, "Sorry about this, dude."

Donnie shrugged. *Oscar buzz, TV series, and soon-to-be friggin' Romeo, and he's apologizing to me for moving into* his *tent?*

Poor guy—he knew Alex was just seventeen and jilted by a girl. One who even Donnie found hot. *Sorta.* He could understand, too, why someone like Piper who'd just lost a movie deal might feel awful.

But, if you're normal, what makes everything better?

So Donnie assumed the actress was some weird Hollywood type. But all he said to Alex was *I'm cool with this.* And reintroduced himself in case the guy didn't remember him from earlier. But he did.

"Donnie with a Polish name. With an outfitter in Terlingua."

"Yeah. Majewski."

"Long crazy day."

"Yeah."

They fumbled with their sleeping bags and gear. But the tent was roomy enough. An expensive model, no surprise, with vestibules for backpacks.

They undressed by lantern, Alex down to his shorts, Donnie further.

Alex laughed. "I expected to be naked tonight too."

"Don't let me stop you." Donnie hoped the suggestion wasn't crude. But Alex slipped into his bag with boxer briefs and socks.

"I get cold feet," he explained, hint of a smile.

"For what it's worth, I think your girlfriend's nuts," Donnie said, settling in. He turned and they were face-to-face. Close quarters.

"Tell me about it!" Alex muttered.

And they talked. Far enough away from the other tents not to disturb fellow campers. About the hike, the park, and how crazy girls are.

"You're lucky," Alex said.

"What?"

"With guys. Must be easier."

Donnie rolled with it. Explained why it wasn't. Alex shrugged and went quiet.

"How'dya know?"

"Straight guys have gaydar too. Need it in Hollywood."

Donnie smiled. "I got rum. I know you're not legal. But what the fuck . . ."

"Sure."

And they sipped slow for maybe an hour, Donnie explaining his job in Terlinqua. Mostly on the river, but lots of trail-guiding too. Alex opened up about Piper. About making movies. About why he'd come to Texas.

"Hey, don't say nothing about this, Donnie. Or about the rum." Words a little slurred now.

"I won't," Donnie nodded. "I swear. First time drunk?"

"Maybe."

"First time for everything."

"I wish," Alex frowned, drifting off to sleep.

Chapter 10

Just shy of eighteen, Alex Harp rarely blundered. Parents, teachers, even directors explained his good sense differently. But the boy knew it was chiefly because he was *really* smart and in ways even he didn't always understand.

Smart enough now, for instance, to know he might be about to screw up royally on a cold canyon rim in Texas.

Blame *eros*.

That he knew the word and understood the concept only made it worse. Eros made men dumb and reckless, especially young ones. Eros *plus* rum? Yikes. Which explained why he was stalking a rocky campsite an hour or two past midnight in just Tommy Johns and hiking boots to persuade his maybe-also-underage girlfriend (in California at least; but Texas was different) to put aside her troubles and, well, you know . . . get happy.

They'd planned a month for the trip, he reminded himself, Piper as enthusiastic as he. Maybe more. She didn't object when he bought the two-person tent. And primitive camping had been her idea. Said she did it all the time back in Arkansas where she grew up.

She had disappointments today for sure. Big ones. But Donnie was right. The best way to fix a problem was to spend the night with a friend in bed. Or a sleeping bag. Well, he was a friend of Piper's just drunk enough to do something dumb. He'd heard alcohol diminished sexual performance, but the equipment was working great. *Eros* beckoned.

He barely felt the chill, despite a light breeze that stirred a hoot owl. Noisy bugger. The sky above was unbelievable. Moon bright enough to cast shadows—which you'd never notice in Ohio or Los Angeles. *By the light of a silvery moon.* Like Donnie said, *First time for everything.*

They could maybe do it under the sky.

No movement in the other tents, though Donnie was awake. Alex had kicked him slipping a boot on in the dark. Donnie lit a flashlight and wished Alex well. Just a few years older than he was, but way more practical.

Her tent was dark and motionless, its flap undone. Odd.

"Piper," he whispered about as loud as when people at a movie shushed you to be quiet. Tried it again and then pushed the flap aside. Enough light to see the tent was bare. No sleeping bag, no backpack, no gear. No Piper.

He was drunk enough to hope she'd gone to pee. But, dah! No one takes a sleeping bag to pee. Alex felt suddenly colder, aware of the breeze and night sounds. Of standing in just boots and shorts in a primitive campground. Alone.

He hustled back to his tent.

"Donnie?"

"Yeah?" Voice from inside.

"Piper's gone."

"Peeing."

"Nah. Everything's gone. Tent is empty."

Canvas rustling and flap unzipping. Donnie backing out and struggling into shorts. Moon shot. Maybe drunker than Alex?

"Shoes, Donnie. Hurry."

"Oh yeah."

At Piper's campsite. Donnie looked in. Pondered. "Maybe in another tent?"

Alex hadn't thought of that. A threesome? Possibly with Sherman Farr and the redhead. "We better get everybody up," he said. "Even if we embarrass Piper."

Serves her right though.

But the Legesons were stirring already, their tent just yards away. The flap opened.

"Oh, my," Nancy said, eyeing the two young men. Almost smiled. She was in a flannel nightgown, of all things.

"What're you guys doing?" Mr. Legeson said, looking stern and suspecting horseplay. He'd taken the time to put on pants.

"Piper's gone."

"Probably peeing in the bushes."

That script repeated three more times until everyone was up, accounted for, and decent. The propane stove was relit and lanterns too. Like a coven of witches, Alex thought. The trail guides huddled and then Donnie took charge. Alex guessed he was maybe the soberest member of the group, Legesons aside.

"Anybody know what's up?" Donnie asked. All eyes turned on Alex.

"She didn't want me in her tent tonight so I slept with Donnie." It was possible that not everyone had known his original intentions. Then Alex explained what he'd discovered just minutes earlier at Piper's tent.

"In his underwear," Mrs. Legeson added. Alex realized she'd maybe absolved him of suspicion, if there was any.

"She might be nearby right now just thinking about things," Annette said quietly. "You know, losing that part?"

"But why clear out of the tent?" Ethan Legeson asked. "It's empty, right?" Donnie nodded.

"And she'd be back by now if she was close, seeing our lights," Sherman Farr added.

Agreement all around. Alex noticed Donnie counting.

"Everyone's here who was here when we sacked out," Donnie said. "If Piper left, she went alone."

"Unless someone forced her to go." Sherman Farr again. Nancy Legeson shuddered. Silence for a beat or two.

"That'd be ballsy," one of the trail guides said. "We mighta been sleepin', but we'd of heard a struggle if there was one." The tents were near each other, all except the one with Alex and Donnie.

"And Ms. Robinet was supposed to be with Alex," Donnie pointed out. "If someone came looking for her they went to the wrong tent."

"Unless it was one of us who did it?" Annette said quietly. "Did something to Piper."

Mrs. Legeson huffed. "Did what? Drag her and her gear away, push her over a cliff, and then come back here. That's nuts."

Annette stuck to her guns. "We don't know when it happened."

"Donnie and I were awake for a long time talking," Alex said. "Way past midnight. What time is it now?"

"Quarter to two," Sherman Farr said.

"Ethan and I were up late too," Mrs. Legeson said. "We weren't talking however. We heard coming and going. People using the bushes we figured. But nothing like a struggle. No voices at all till we heard you and Alex." She directed the last sentence to Donnie.

Donnie folded his arms. "Here's what I'm thinking. We got a missing camper and need to let park people know asap. Cell phones don't work. Hey, what about your satellite phone?" He pointed to Sherman Farr.

"Batteries dead."

"Replacements?"

"No."

"Didn't think so. So we need folks to hike down the Pinnacles Trail to the Basin." Donnie was taking charge.

Farr perhaps feeling he should show authority, objected. "We have crews coming back in the morning to clear out this gear. Couldn't we just wait?"

Donnie frowned. "If those crews leave at 6:00 AM, they won't be up here till 8:00 at the earliest. But they might not leave early. And if we've got a girl out there somewhere on the trail, she might be lost or injured or having other issues. We can't wait. Someone leaving now could be talking to park police by 4:00 AM. Maybe earlier if they pick up a cell signal on the trail."

"Suicide?" Mrs. Legeson suddenly spoke the word, but it occurred to Alex at the same moment.

Donnie bit his lip and nodded. "Don't know her at all, but possible, I guess."

Alex felt all eyes on him again. But he saw the flaw. "If you're thinking suicide, why take your stuff? Maybe enough water to get you to the rim and then . . . I don't know. But I agree with Donnie. Cops need to know, even if she left on her own."

"She have car keys?" Farr interrupted.

"I got 'em," Alex said. "But we both have room keys for a CCC cabin tonight. Just in case."

"So she might have hiked down the Pinnacles on her own," the photographer suggested, quiet until then. "Get away from this group reminding her of bad things . . . Or maybe it's a publicity stunt?"

The trail guide who'd also been quiet to this point spoke up. "Moon's bright. Path's just one switchback after another. Tricky. But doable, so long as it don't cloud up."

Annette bristled. "What about animals? Bears and mountain lions here. I read that."

The guides nodded. "They mostly don't bother adults," Donnie said. "More likely she'd run into skunks. Javelina closer in to the Basin."

"So?" Farr wanted action.

"Okay, let's do this." Donnie pointed to his fellow guides. "You two pack up and hike to the Basin now. Contact park police and tell 'em what's happened. The rest of us will wait here until no later than daybreak tomorrow. Then we're all headin' out. "Mr. Farr and the girl with you . . ."

"Stephanie."

"Stephanie. You can wait here or hike down now. Your choice."

They answered simultaneously, Farr electing to go to the Basin with the guides, Stephanie to stay in camp. Farr probably thought he needed to manage this story.

"And Alex," Mr. Farr said, "you come with me. You're too valuable to remain here under the circumstances."

Alex felt bad for Stephanie. Farr was sleeping with her, but Alex was the more prized commodity.

"I'm gonna look for Piper," Alex said. And Farr didn't argue. Probably realizing it made better press if the actor stayed.

Donnie weighed in. "Alex and me can reconnoiter nearby campsites in case Piper showed up there. If skies stay clear, we might check out the rim again. That okay, kid?" Donnie figured the actor wouldn't stay put in the campsite with his girlfriend missing. "And the rest of you keep the fort in case Piper comes back. Wander around if you want, but don't neglect the gear."

For a moment, Ethan Legeson moved to join Alex and Donnie, but his wife stopped that.

"Make coffee, dear," she ordered. "The stove's fired up and the hikers need some before they head out."

But the hikers didn't wait.

Chapter 11

The call came at 7:00 AM Wednesday morning. From Velma Furcron. Clayton Shoot was finishing a second cup of joe in his cabin and about to head for work. Fifteen easy minutes from the Shoot compound to the sheriff's office.

He'd spoken to Furcron for the first time just weeks earlier when she'd taken over as Chief Ranger for Visitor and Resource Protection at Big Bend National Park. Promoted after ranger stints at Waputki, Mesa Verde, and most recently, Rocky Mountain National Park. He'd yet to meet the woman, a Harry Yount Award winner (big deal in ranger world), nor did he envy her job. It was one thing to deal with crime and justice in the county as he did. Caring for park welfare too, as she had to, was a whole different ballgame. It was like making a sheriff responsible for roads and fences and tourists.

Her concern this morning was Piper Robinet who, Furcron reported, had disappeared from a campsite at the South Rim the previous night. It was a courtesy call. But given the vastness of Big Bend National Park and the chunk of Brewster County that surrounded it, law enforcement in the area (including local police departments, Border Patrol, Texas Rangers, and his own sheriff's department) had learned to cooperate. Mostly.

Furcron about fell through the floor when Clayton admitted he'd met the young actress briefly Monday afternoon.

"So you know these people, Sheriff Shoot?"

"I do. And the boy Piper went hiking with . . ."

"Alex Harp? The TV star?"

"Yep. He's my girlfriend's brother."

"Girlfriend's brother? You weren't on this expedition yourself by any chance?"

"No ma'am." Furcron was being ironic, he hoped, but didn't know her well enough to be sure.

"I take it she's still missing?" Clayton knew from experience how rugged the South Rim and Chisos Basin were.

"She is, but we don't know what we're dealing with—a crime or just an upset actress wandering off on her own."

"Upset because . . . ?"

"Apparently she didn't get a movie part she wanted. Ain't life tough?"

So Furcron did sarcasm.

"People she was with think maybe her disappearance is no big deal. You know a Hollywood guy named Sherman Farr?"

"Don't."

"Lucky. He's been on the phone since 5:00 AM trying to get orders from something called Throng!Media in California. Didn't want us too involved. But your sister's brother . . ."

"Alex," the sheriff said.

"Yeah. He just arrived here at park headquarters with a local guide named Donnie Majewski and filed a missing person's report."

"Robinet's a minor."

"Actually, she's not. Farr swore up and down she's an adult, but couldn't give her actual age. Or wouldn't."

"Alex is seventeen, for what it's worth."

"That kid's sure blunt. Told us right out he expected to sleep with Ms. Robinet, but then discovered she'd left her tent. We'll talk with everyone at that campsite whenever they all get down here. But what I'm seeing is, maybe, a girl injured hiking somewhere on the rim. The trail branches off in places, so possibly she's just lost. We're searching on foot and have a helicopter coming shortly. But I don't suspect a crime, not yet. Seems everyone on the rim can account for everyone else—except Ms. Robinet. But then there was a whole bunch of strangers too up there yesterday meeting the actors. Big to-do for that Throng!Media company, not exactly cleared by us."

Clayton didn't know about any such event. But they talked for another ten minutes, Chief Furcron piecing together everything she'd learned so far about the rim hike and its aftermath.

Clayton figured a healthy young woman could hike down the Pinnacles

Trail and back to the Basin without a problem on a clear moonlit night. But like Chief Furcron, he could only guess Piper Robinet's intentions. She hadn't checked into any rooms reserved by Throng!Media, and the Ranger Rover she and Alex used was still parked where they left it.

"I told the out-of-towners to stick around for a few days," Chief Furcron added, "your girlfriend's brother included."

"That was his intention anyway. He and Piper were on vacation. Hiatus from their show."

"Which was cancelled, by the way," Velma added. "Double whammy for Robinet. Have to say *suicide* was mentioned once or twice."

"Hope not."

"Amen. Don't want our South Rim becoming the Grand Canyon. Three or four suicides a year now there."

For some reason, Clayton knew that.

"Tell me if my office can help," Clayton said, realizing he needed to call Claire —no, maybe better to go see her. She lived just a few blocks from his office. Since he'd be stopping for breakfast at Judy's, he'd invite her to join him.

Velma was psychic. "One more thing, Sheriff. If your girlfriend is pretty as her brother, you're one lucky guy."

"Yes, ma'am."

"By the way, I have two daughters who'd kill to meet Alex Harp."

Not the best choice of words. But Clayton got her point. He'd see what he could do.

◈◈ ◈◈ ◈◈

CLAIRE WASN'T SURPRISED when Clayton invited her to breakfast at their favorite spot. She'd seen his text after she'd gotten off the phone with her brother, who located one of the few spots in the Chisos Basin with cell service. He sounded worse than when the family dog died.

Alex quickly explained what happened on the rim. It worried him now that neither the local police nor Throng!Media's people were taking his co-star's disappearance seriously enough. Claire assured him rangers dealt with missing hikers all the time. But she recalled a book entitled *Death in Big Bend*.

Alex wanted to stay at the park until Piper turned up, one way or another. But much to her surprise, Claire laid down the law. *You pack up that Range Rover right now, brother, and drive to Alpine—or I'll come get you.* She'd sounded just like Eugenia Harp, their imperious mother. Alex surrendered.

Soon as the Head Ranger says I can go, he promised.

At least Alex wasn't a suspect in Piper's disappearance. He was sharing a tent with a trail guide when they discovered she was gone. So, off the hook. Except he didn't explain what he was doing with that trail guide. Had something gone wrong between Alex and the actress? Claire remembered Piper saying the situation between them was complicated, but she hadn't explained why.

What a muddle. And, of course, the *Big Bend Mercury* was already on the story and was updating it regularly online. Did the Nixons have a mole within the park police? Even CNN briefly mentioned Piper's disappearance on a morning show—describing her as an unnamed WetBTE Network actress at a national park with Alex Harp. Maybe the film company just wanted publicity for her brother's movie?

Claire's head was still in a whirl when she sat down in a familiar café on Alpine's main street. Clayton's quiet demeanor calmed her.

"What's on your mind, big guy?" she'd said.

He looked up from his coffee, startled. "Fiona Tusk and Alonso Rangel."

"Oh." She'd expected him to mention her brother and Piper. But she knew both the Alpine police chief and Clayton's newest deputy.

"It's nothin'. They're just very happy. Heard from Alex?"

"Just talked with him. You know all what's happened?"

Clayton nodded. "Afraid so. How's he doin'?"

Claire recapped her conversation, and Clayton filled her in on what Ranger Furcron told him. A waitress slid scrambled eggs, bacon, grits, and a muffin in front of the sheriff and took Claire's order for a cinnamon roll.

"I can see the girl upset and doing something dumb," Clayton said. "But where is she? Why leave your brother on the rim like that? She didn't use a room reserved for her in the Basin either, and no one fitting her description checked into other motels in Study Butte or Terlingua. She didn't have car keys either and there's no ground transportation."

"She's still on that rim?"

"Possibly. Or someone else is involved."

"Not Alex?"

"Can't be. But right now, the case is with park police. The rest of us in the county have Piper's description and we'll keep an eye out. I just hope they don't find her injured on that trail or worse. It's a long loop with connecting hikes, even one up to Emory Peak. Not the best place to be yonderin' at night."

"It's daylight now."

"If she's there, they'll spot her. The rim's a busy trail. And people will be looking now, given the publicity."

"CNN mentioned it."

"*Big Bend Mercury* too."

⊰⊱ ⊰⊱ ⊰⊱

IN AN ALPINE hotel room later that Wednesday, Ella Nixon was cursing the slow internet connection as she loaded yet another photograph of Piper Robinet to her *Big Bend Mercury* news site. Her husband Barney was taking calls from major networks, adding Fox, MSNBC, and even *Entertainment Tonight* to the Rolodex. (He still used one.)

To be honest, neither of them had heard of Piper Robinet twenty-four hours earlier. But Alex Harp was a known commodity because he was a budding star with a local connection—his sister Professor Claire Harp. Even Barney thought the boy newsworthy, though he usually dismissed pop culture stuff. Ella knew so much better.

She decided to call Claire. As expected, the professor hesitated to say much about the situation at Big Bend, so Ella mentioned Claire's book project—*How's that coming? The definitive edition of Mote McCrary's* Madrone! *Do you have a publication date yet?* Flattery got the woman talking.

Ella then returned to Claire's sibling. *So much younger than you. Almost a different generation. What's he like?* Still cautious and equivocal. *Well.* A profile of Alex Harp could wait until Ella met the boy herself—as she knew she would.

Claire did complain (politely) about a short item the *Mercury* ran Monday about her brother stopping in Alpine—which also mentioned that his sister taught at Sul Ross. Ella brushed it off with a laugh, admitting that they'd floated a *rumor* that the *Brainiacs* star *might* be in town, based on a tip from a colleague of Claire's at Sul Ross State. Ella knew some teenaged girls showed up later at Claire's door because of the piece. Apparently, kids these days still knew local phone books included home addresses.

Given her own contacts at Big Bend, Ella eventually realized she knew more about Piper Robinet's disappearance than the professor did—or Alex, for that matter. So she turned friendly and personal. *Must be nice to have the boy with you in Texas. Will you see him again soon?* And the news just slipped out from Claire. *He's returning to Alpine–right now in fact.*

Exactly what Ella expected; she just didn't know when.

After the call ended, Ella's husband Barney wandered up to see what his wife was posting to their site, squinting at the screen. *Alex Harp Back in Town!* "Harrumph," he said.

Ella quickly made sure the motel room curtains were shut. Didn't want anyone noticing (after all these years) that Barney wasn't blind—at least no worse so than other geezers his age with ripening cataracts. But did it matter anyway? Most of the sixties radicals Barney could identify from his underground days were six feet under by now. He posed no threat to them.

Still, the ruse *had* served them well. Oodles of sympathy over the years for a blind reporter. Sources opened right up to Barney—*God knows why*. Yet a quick trip to Mexico for cataract surgery would make sense now. And suit her own ambitions.

She was tired of squiring around a blind guy who, in fact, wasn't. Especially one who still acted like he was the brains of their operation. Hadn't Barney been spectacularly wrong about her special project? Yet he refused to admit it—even though the proof was in Brewster County right now, all five-feet-eleven-inches of him and growing. And he was apparently even more handsome than his sister.

Damn it—Ella was even *happy* now that the old house in Fort Davis had burned down. Like a good cleansing. Decades of moldy books and papers gone in minutes. And an insurance check on the way to supplement a hefty advance she'd just received for her special project. So what if she'd let the fire smolder a little before calling 911, carrying out cats and essentials? Even Barney thought that old place stank.

Irony of ironies—they'd found the perfect replacement too. Breathtaking view, comfortably furnished, and rock-bottom rent just because no one wanted to live in a murderer's house. Ella and Barney Nixon, movin' on up immediately to Alpenglow Ranch Estates in Brewster County just south of Alpine.

Chapter 12

Just because you have a PhD doesn't mean you're smart. A line Claire's mother deployed more than a few times the past few years to chastise her daughter, most recently over the matter of a cowboy sheriff boyfriend. But Claire now aimed the barb at herself. *How could she have been so stupid?*

Her poor exhausted brother. Unshowered and likely unshaven (couldn't tell yet), he'd arrived at her place in Alpine just past noon on Wednesday, trudged straight upstairs, and fallen dead asleep on the bedspread in the same room Piper Robinet used Monday. Alex hadn't slept since then.

He'd spent the previous night in a futile moonlight search for Piper, disturbing sleeping campers up and down the South Rim. And then, rather than wait until daybreak, Alex and an adventure guide hiked miles from their own campsite down to the Basin where rangers questioned them for hours. Then Alex drove a hundred miles to Alpine with, he admitted, a thermos of coffee in hand and the AC cranked to max to keep awake.

Claire's doorbell rang for the first time about 3:45 PM, shortly after public school let out for the day. Might have been the same four girls who stopped by on Monday.

"Alex is asleep and I'm not going to wake him," Claire insisted after going back and forth patiently for several minutes as the teens tried to negotiate a meeting with their *favoritist* celebrity. Claire may have raised her voice. Another group was running up to the porch as she slammed the front door. And ran to lock the back one.

In mere minutes, yearning faces pressed against every window a middle-schooler could reach. (They seemed taller these days.) The doorbell rang non-stop and a chant went up. *We love you, Alex! We love you, Alex!*

Claire called 311. No such thing in Alpine. She tried 911. Was told police might not be able to get to her quickly because there was a disruption in her neighborhood. "I'm the disruption," she explained. She could see cars full of young women pulling up on both sides of her corner lot. She hoped the drivers were sixteen.

"Just what seems to be the problem, ma'am?"

By that point Alex was plodding down the stairs. He must have partially undressed because he was shoeless and shirtless. Which made matters worse. The girls outside howled like puppies when those nearest the house spotted him. Thank goodness for agaves under her windows. Alex ran back upstairs to grab a T.

We want Alex. We want Alex.

Of course. Claire should have realized fangirls might return. With all the media coverage of Piper's disappearance, they knew Alex was in the area. And who told Ella Nixon he'd be in Alpine? *She did.*

Claire swore she'd never speak to the woman again.

Claire heard sirens wailing as Alex tripped down the stairs more modestly attired. "You want I should talk with them?" he said, expecting she'd say *no.*

She did.

There was solid thumping on her kitchen door now and a deep voice. "Alpine police." She told Alex to get in the stairwell out of sight as she let in a middle-aged officer with a paunch and a visibly excited rookie, a young woman.

"Ma'am, we have a traffic situation outside."

"Traffic?"

"Cars full of kids coming from all directions. We're gonna close the intersection to your place asap and bring some officers in."

The young woman interrupted. "It's gone viral," she said. "All these girls driving to Alpine because they heard an Alex Harp might be here. Is that correct?"

Claire looked to the male officer. He sniffed like someone farted. "Can you confirm that this Alex Harp is in your house?"

Alex stepped from around the corner.

"Oh my," the younger cop said.

Alex seemed confused.

"They're coming all the way from Fort Stockton and Van Horn," the woman said, shaking her head but keeping her dark eyes on the actor.

Claire weighed the implications.

"How long can this go on? My brother was up all last night and needs sleep."

"We can close the road, but crowds will probably linger till it gets dark. I think we'd best get Alex out of here."

"Would they follow him to a hotel?"

"Probably," the veteran cop admitted.

"I would," the rookie said, ". . . if I were their age."

Claire's phone rang. Clayton.

"Heard about the situation," he said before Claire said *hello*.

"It's a mess and my fault. I stupidly told . . ."

"Alonso showed me the story in the *Mercury* and I thought this might happen again."

"*Much* worse than Monday."

"Look, I drove the Wagoneer to work this morning. You get Alex to pack his things and I'll arrange with Alpine police to swing by your house and hustle him and you out of there."

"To a hotel?"

"Nah. Someone would go online when he checked in and the kids would just drive over there. This is too much fun for 'em to give up so easy."

"Where then? Out of town?"

"My place. They won't know where it is or how to get there. And they won't mess with the sheriff." Claire couldn't tell how serious he was about the last claim. But she did know that the Shoot family compound—acres of pasture and farmland off Highway 118 north of town—was hard to find and miles away.

"Let me talk with the officer at your place and we'll arrange it," Clayton said. He probably could hear the *We want Alex* chants in the background.

"Okay, but I'm staying in my house till things settle down," Claire decided, somewhat reluctantly. "My cat doesn't like strange places."

"You sure?" Clayton sounded disappointed, but only slightly. Maybe he wanted to talk with Alex alone—to explore the Piper thing?

"Yeah. I'll stay here till it's quiet." Claire looked at the cops in her living room who nodded in agreement.

"Best not leave your place empty," the senior officer said.

Claire was a tad heartbroken.

❧ ❧ ❧

A CITY OFFICER waved Clayton's aging Wagoneer through their roadblock and the kids thought nothing of it. But girls near the back of Claire's house squealed when the young actor leaped out a window and raced to the vehicle,

Clayton pushing its heavy passenger door open. Alex flipped his backpack and suitcase over the front seat and they were off. Some teens (and a few mothers, Clayton noted) sprinted behind them half a block. But the sheriff and Claire's brother were soon cruising north on Highway 118 unaccompanied. Clayton radioed their successful escape to city police and told them to thank Fiona Tusk for her department's assistance.

"The Alpine police chief?" Alex said.

"And how do you know that?" Clayton replied, glancing at a young man who'd obviously had a rough forty-eight hours since he last saw him.

The boy ducked the question. "Thanks for getting me out of there, Sheriff," he said.

"Call me Clayton."

"Really?"

"Yeah."

"I shoulda pulled out with my rental."

"The Range Rover? Where would you go with that?"

They slowed down passing a busy True Value Hardware store and Clayton turned to give the boy a once-over. Found him staring right back. "You doin' okay? Worried about that girlfriend?"

"Don't know how I feel. Not sure she was my girlfriend."

That surprised the sheriff. "I thought you were . . ."

"Thought so too. One of the reasons for the trip was to get away, you know?" Clayton nodded.

"It turned into a circus. Piper needed publicity and then the movie company got involved. And then that actress in London signed on for Juliet, leaving Piper out of the picture. Maybe the company was just using Piper for leverage. I don't know. But she spaced out, I guess. I feel stupid—more was up than I knew."

Clayton nodded again, impressed by the kid's frankness. Clayton heard all about *Romeo and Juliet* from Claire.

"I barely paid attention at the South Rim. Need to go back sometime to see it better. Amazing moon and stars though. I was out all last night with another guy hassling people in their tents, hoping to find Piper. Nothing went like it should. And I don't know where she is now . . . or who she might be with."

"Didn't see it coming?"

"Hell, no. But I know squat about women. And I came here to see my sister too and for other reasons. Now I can't even be at her house."

"You'll be staying with me tonight," Clayton said.

"Sure don't mean to cause you and your family trouble."

Clayton smiled. The only person who might fuss was his sister Beatrice. "I got a cabin away from the main house. Just me and two old dogs," he explained.

They didn't say anything for a quarter mile, the road curving gently on the fringes of the small town before it skirted the Big Bend Regional Health Center to the right and, farther on, Alpine's tiny airport on the left.

"You really proposed to my sister?" Alex asked out of the blue.

Clayton swallowed, pausing before he responded. "I did. . . And I'm sorry she said *no*."

"So we might have been brothers-in-law."

"Still could be, I guess," Clayton said after another pause.

"I don't have a brother."

"I know. Got only sisters myself."

They looked at each other.

"I could use a brother right now," Alex admitted.

And, being guys, that's all they said for several miles.

⋈ ⋈ ⋈

CLAYTON LIVED IN what he called a dog-run house on the Shoot compound, separated from a sizeable stone lodge and a smaller wooden cottage by a pasture and a thicket of trees. *Texas oaks*, Clayton said, but it seemed Texans did that with everything. Texas toast, Texas BBQ, Texas pride.

"People call it a dogtrot too. It's just two log cabins separated by a breezeway, but under the same roof. In the summer, that opening between the cabins pulls cool air through. Except I got air-conditioning now and other upgrades. And both my rooms are oversized."

Still it was weird, Alex thought. A covered wood-plank porch fronted the house and in the breezeway two old German shepherds lay half asleep, lifting their heads to greet Clayton and dismiss Alex. *Pearl and Daisy*, Clayton explained.

They entered the cabin to the right, centered around a stone fireplace, with a full kitchenette and shelves and cabinets across a side wall. Bookcases and a sizeable sofa against the opposite one. A table filled some of the space between. Native American rugs on the wood floor, paintings and photographs on the

78

paneled walls. Gun cabinet in one corner, sports paraphernalia in another. Leather recliner. The room smelled of the surrounding pines.

Perfect guy space. Alex threw his gear on the sofa.

"No," Clayton said. "You'll sleep in the other room."

It was, of course, the cabin across the breezeway—a big bedroom with a sitting area, desk, laptop, closet, and more space for gear. Bookshelves too with titles Alex admired. No TV, but an ancient record player and lots of vinyl LPs. Bathroom with shower, no tub. Manly, like the other cabin, with natural wood and more Navajo rugs on the floor. It looked great, but Alex didn't set his backpack down.

"Hey, Clayton. I'm not pushing you out from here. I slept on Claire's couch and yours looks way more comfortable."

"Guests get the bathroom."

Alex hadn't considered that—most of the sheriff's sleepovers, he expected, would be women sharing his bed.

"I can piss off the dog run," Alex said.

"You wouldn't be the first."

"I'm serious. But I do need a shower. Fell asleep before I could use the one at my sister's and you know the rest."

"Didn't want to say, but you do smell gamey."

"Could use something to eat too."

"*Jeezus.* Some host I am," Clayton said slapping his head. "We'll go to the main house soon as you clean up. But don't tell my sister Beatrice I neglected you. She's real into Texas hospitality."

Another of those phrases.

There was a solid thump on the door across the breezeway. A female voice with its own echo. Alex knew enough about old Hollywood to think *Marjorie Main.*

"Clayton, are you home?"

Clayton turned red. "Jeezus," he said a second time. "I shoulda warned you about Beatrice."

Alex thought, maybe, his sister had mentioned the woman once or twice.

Chapter 13

Alex's first view of Beatrice was of her formidable butt. In boots, work jeans, and a sturdy denim shirt, she'd come right out of the fields and was pounding on the door across the open passage.

"Beatrice!" Clayton said, as he pushed the unlatched bedroom door open. She turned slowly. Clayton's dogs wandered out to lick her hands, already cupped to fondle them. Clayton sensed Alex right behind him when he stepped into the breezeway.

"Beatrice?" he said again and paused, bewildered by the expression on her face. His middle-aged sister, who faced longhorns and tax assessors with equal ferocity, was suddenly wide-eyed, pale, and, maybe, quivering. Her mouth hung slightly open and, unbelievably, a hand went up to fix her auburn hair. She pulled a bang away from her right eye.

Clayton feared she might be having a stroke. "Beatrice?" he said a third time.

"Mr. Harp," she said reverentially, almost curtseying.

Alex was baffled.

"This is my sister," Clayton said pointlessly.

"Just Alex," the boy said, offering his hand.

"Oh, no," Beatrice said, some color returning. "It would not be right. Look at you . . . look at him, Clayton!" Clayton watched her eyes dart between them. "He already has the bearing of men like Gable, Tracy, Cooper, Poitier."

Clayton thought he heard Alex mumble *Jeesuz*. But this was as animated as Beatrice had been since their father had died. It was like she'd awakened from a stupor.

She stepped nearer to Alex. "I intended to ask your sister Claire to introduce us while you were in Alpine, Mr. Harp. I have seen your movies. One of them in Midland. And now here you are. Clayton, what is Mr. Harp doing here? Have the park police found that woman yet?"

"No, Beatrice. Let's go sit in my living room and talk. Alex here wants to take a shower and then we need to get him somethin' to eat."

Beatrice looked abashed. "He is staying *here*?"

"Tonight at least. There are teenagers hanging about his sister's house wanting autographs and . . ."

"Detestable! Do not waste time explaining. I am *so* sorry, Mr. Harp. I will go to the main house and prepare something for you to eat—beef fajitas with maybe chipotle queso and fresh biscochitos. I will get right to that, Mr. Harp. And then we will talk about *Romeo and Juliet*. Over sherry."

"I would like that, very much," Alex said. "But please ma'am, won't you call me Alex? And then I won't have to call you Ms. Shoot."

Clayton laughed. The kid was sure pickin' up the lingo. And what fun seeing Beatrice making a fool of herself over a seventeen-year-old. He'd never let her forget it.

Beatrice charged down the breezeway to prepare the meal but stopped at the porch steps.

"*Alex* it will be," she said, "and now tell me, what is the most telling line Romeo delivers early in the play?"

"No time for a quiz, Beatrice," Clayton said, not wanting his eccentric but brilliant sister to embarrass their guest.

"He says it when he first sees Juliet. *She doth teach the torches to burn bright.*"

Even Clayton was moved. It was as if someone else had suddenly spoken.

"Correct answer," Beatrice said, clapping her hands. "Correct answer, Alex! Clayton, he must stay for a week!"

Might be good for Beatrice, Clayton thought. *Maybe for us all.*

⊰⊱ ⊰⊱ ⊰⊱

IT WAS ALMOST 11:00 PM on Wednesday and Claire's neighborhood had finally settled down. An hour earlier, she broke down and called the *Big Bend Mercury*, Ella Nixon picking up the phone.

"So will you run a story?" Claire said after explaining what had been happening in her neighborhood for the past several hours. "Let all these girls know that Alex is not at my home?"

"Oh, my golly," Ella said.

Pretending to be apologetic, Claire thought.

"Of course, yes. Where is your brother now?"

The woman never gave up.

"In an undisclosed location," Claire said, the jargon irresistible. And she wouldn't be budged, despite Ella's best efforts, all very polite, to learn where Alex was harboring. Claire simply said the police removed her brother, maybe taking him to a motel? She didn't consider that a lie, since Clayton might change his mind about sharing a cabin with a seventeen-year-old.

Weird that her brother would be spending a night where she never had.

The city police had been kind to Claire. Fiona Tusk, their chief, even called. She helped Claire find humor in the situation. But when Fiona hung up and the police cars departed the suddenly placid neighborhood, Claire felt glum. She considered driving to the Shoot compound and bringing her brother home, but the boy was probably sacked out already, given the day he'd had. Or more likely he was concerned about Piper—and who better to talk to about that situation than Clayton?

Clayton. She decided to call him.

Somewhat to her dismay, the sheriff sounded cheery.

"No. Alex is still up, on the patio with Beatrice talking 'bout *Romeo and Juliet.*"

Claire wasn't sure she heard that right.

"With Beatrice?"

"They hit it off. She got his mind off Piper quick and he's helped her too, I think. She made him fajitas and Mexican cookies and they're jabberin' like sparrows. My poor mother thinks something's wrong with Beatrice she's so happy."

"Oh," Claire sighed, hoping Clayton would sense her disappointment.

"I talked to him about Piper too," he added, "and about what law enforcement was doing to find her. He thought he should maybe be out there . . ."

Claire interrupted. "That would be crazy."

"Yep. But he seems a sensible boy. And just between us, he's saying all the right things. Pissed at Piper, even. But obliged to some trail guide who helped him search for her?"

"Doesn't surprise me," Claire said, not sure why.

"Wonder how much there was between 'em to begin with?" Clayton said. "He thinks she ran away from him, not that someone took her. I'm inclined to agree."

"So what happens now?"

"Park rangers keep searchin'. We've got an APB out in the county. We'll find Piper."

"One way or another?"

"Yeah. You need to talk with Alex?"

Claire thought maybe Alex should be the one calling her. But Clayton caught the hesitation.

"He's no problem at all. Why don't you come over? You can stay in the main house."

Claire was embarrassed, but glad Alex was comfortable with Clayton and his family. And, my God, forty-year-old Beatrice!

"Give him my love and I'll see him tomorrow."

"He says he's goin' to stay at least till Piper's found, for what it's worth. Says he has other stuff to do here too. You know what that's about?"

"I don't, Clayton. But I'm happy he's okay. Give him my love and don't you boys start drinking."

"Too late. Beatrice already offered him Sherry."

⊰⊱ ⊰⊱ ⊰⊱

"YOUR SISTER OKAY?"

Alex nodded to Clayton's question.

The boy had just spoken with her—at Clayton's insistence. Then they'd retired to the kitchen side of the dog-run cabin, walking back from the main house under a moon a tick brighter than the one lighting his search of the South Rim only twenty hours earlier. Alex sensed regret in Claire's voice when he mentioned how much he liked the Shoots.

Okay if I stay tonight? he'd asked Claire, explaining how he and Beatrice want to go over scenes from *Romeo and Juliet* in the morning. "We see eye-to-eye about my character," he explained.

"She knows about that?"

"She's seen all my movies. For the few scenes I was in."

"You know I miss you?" Claire said. "And you left a Range Rover here."

"Damn," he said, fingering the fob in his pocket. He mollified her by promising to stay in Texas until they did proper brother–sister stuff. "At least till Piper turns up, whatever that means."

83

Pretending he'd not listened in on the phone call, Clayton offered to make hot chocolate when Alex hung up.

"Sounds good," Alex said. And while Clayton fixed it using a double boiler, Alex studied the room. The sheriff repeated the offer to surrender his side of the cabin, but there were already pillows and a blanket for Alex on the sofa. He preferred that and Clayton said he'd leave his door open so Alex could use the bathroom.

"Never lock it anyway. But look out for skunks."

Alex assumed he wasn't kidding.

While Clayton stirred the concoction—real hot chocolate, not packaged stuff—Alex noticed a framed drawing on the wall above the sofa, a small work pushed toward the corner by larger oils and some photographs of a younger Clayton competing in rodeos.

The pen and ink sketch, meticulously detailed, was of a young man preparing to mount a stallion—spur on the visible boot, lasso down his chaps, left hand on the reins. Seen from behind, only the rider's ear and very light hair were visible under a black cowboy hat.

"That you?" Alex pointed to the item as Clayton settled on the sofa.

"Sure is. Done when I was exactly your age. Seventeen and a junior in high school."

"Awesome," Alex said, moving nearer the sofa for a closer look. "Very erotic."

"Damn!" Clayton said, looking mortified. "Damn."

"What?"

"That's what my mother thought. *Obscene*, she said. Wouldn't have it in the main house. My sisters agreed."

"Your butt kinda stands out," Alex said.

Clayton flushed. "It was done by a very famous artist."

Alex moved closer and squinted. "Iris . . . ?"

"Cobb. Iris Cobb Summerlin. She's a big deal now. Has her own gallery in Taos. Thing like that might go for five grand today. Maybe more."

"I bet." Touchy subject, Alex realized.

"My family know nothin' about art. That's just me and my horse. My favorite horse."

"I bet Beatrice liked it."

Clayton stared at Alex, surprised. "You'd be right."

Chapter 14

Beatrice awoke them at 7:00 AM on Thursday, pounding on Clayton's bedroom door with a large cooler in hand.

"Alex," she said, "I have brought you breakfast. You will find it outside on the breezeway and I will have Clayton make coffee so we can get an early start. I hope you slept well."

Clayton knew Beatrice was surprised when he opened the door, buttoning his shirt. She peered over his shoulder to find a bed already made bed. Her dark eyes—the deepest blue of any in the family—flashed.

"Surely you did not make our guest sleep on the divan!"

"He slept on my sofa. Wanted to."

She sighed and headed toward the door across the breezeway.

"I'll arrest you if you wake him up. Didn't get much sleep yesterday."

She turned again and frowned, the aroma of syrup and pancakes wafting from the cooler. Blueberries too, Clayton hoped. "I told Alex we would be up early to do morning rounds. He has not stayed on a ranch before."

The kitchen door swung open behind her, Alex up and dressed. "Mornin' Beatrice . . . mornin' Clayton." Clayton noted the dropped g's.

"You must forgive Clayton," Beatrice began. "He sometimes has the manners of a . . ."

"I'm fine, ma'am," he smiled, "and that divan was real comfortable."

She almost giggled. Clayton couldn't recall another man charming Beatrice this way—well, except maybe their late daddy.

"There is enough food for both of you," she said, stink-eyeing Clayton.

"I'll leave plenty for the boy, Beatrice."

"PERHAPS YOUR SISTER would prefer that you be with her in town?" Beatrice asked after breakfast, as she and Alex walked toward a corral, passing the cabin where Finis Shoot spent the last years of his life. Beatrice said that Clayton seemed different since the funeral some months earlier. Alex nodded, though he had no way of judging.

Alex told her that teenagers were still cruising Claire's neighborhood in Alpine, so Claire was okay with him staying with Clayton. "And she's got meetings this morning on campus at the university. So, since she's okay with it, I'm here for now."

"Do you ride?" Beatrice asked as two horses greeted them at the fence, nickering.

"Had to learn for a small part I had in a western. Film's not been released yet."

"The animals are biddable," Beatrice said. "The black one Sleipner is for you, the white one Grane is mine." Alex could guess who'd named them.

For the next hour, they quietly inspected the ranch, checking on both stock and crops, Beatrice making her regular rounds. Alex understood that she managed the large property.

"Your sister is an interesting scholar," she observed near the end of their circuit. "And this editing project is a challenge because she was not trained for textual work *per se*. But I am sure she will do a good job. It is not like she is collating editions of Renaissance plays."

Alex felt flattered Beatrice assumed he'd know what she was talking about.

"And how are you feeling about this woman who disappeared in the park—Piper Robinet? Did you make love to her?"

Alex pulled back abruptly on the reins and they stopped by a fenced pasture. A pair of longhorns stared at them. Alex studied Beatrice. Was she joshing? *Nope.* Her question was serious.

"I expected to," he said after a pause. "At the park Tuesday night."

"Had you two made love before, in California?"

"No."

Beatrice nodded. "It seems she disappeared rather than stay with you?"

Alex studied his pommel, said nothing.

Beatrice turned Grane neatly so she could face the boy.

"I do not know this Piper, nor have I ever watched your television program. But I will just say you must not let yourself be manipulated by women. Women are cleverer than men. They can destroy a man's career."

Alex smiled at the advice. Sure, Piper had used him. But he wanted something from her too. His eyes had been wide open in the relationship—until she disappeared. And now Piper might even be dead. Except he felt, down deep, she wasn't.

Beatrice had said her piece. They rode on farther, surveying fields of late crops—kale and pumpkins mostly—ready for harvest. Alex knew Beatrice was unmarried and wasn't sure how interested she was in men. But it would take a special guy to manage her.

⸙ ⸙ ⸙

"CLAYTON, YOU'LL WANNA see this." Alonso stared at his monitor and turned up the volume as the sheriff crossed the room, heading for his own office. The sheriff heard a female voice—a young woman. "It's on Facebook now," Alonso said.

Clayton pulled up a chair and sat behind the deputy. "I know what you're lookin' at. Just got a heads-up from Chief Furcron at the park."

"Piper's a looker," the deputy whistled. Clayton grunted. "No doubt about where she is either."

A hand-held video showed Piper Robinet standing in front of Paisano Pete—a twenty-foot-tall roadside effigy of a roadrunner that welcomed tourists to Fort Stockton, a town on Interstate 10 seventy miles from Alpine and double that from Big Bend. Maybe ten thousand people lived there.

"I want everyone to know I'm fine and just want to be alone for a while. I'm sorry I caused so much trouble. It was dumb." Still wearing her hiking gear, Piper spoke with the hint of a smile. Then the camera shook wildly as she bent over to pick up something—a newspaper, the *Odessa American*. Clayton assumed it was from this morning. They'd check. But he wondered. Did she think to show the paper herself or was that someone else's idea?

After a few seconds, she tossed it away, steadied the camera again, and stared directly into it, the big bird almost out of sight. Piper looked healthy. No makeup, but her face was clean and hair combed. Maybe sunburned?

"I also want Alex Harp to know I'm *so* sorry. But I had to do this, kid. I hope to see you soon and explain. I don't know when or where. Maybe California?

But don't worry about me. I'm fine. I'm happy." And there the video abruptly ended. Forty seconds? Too brief to stop traffic along the highway.

"I need to tell Alex," Clayton said, slapping Alonso on the shoulder.

"It's viral already. Bet he's seen it."

But he hadn't. Clayton's call interrupted a work session between the boy and Beatrice on Act II of *Romeo and Juliet*. Lines from Scene 2. And it was just mid-morning.

"Take a look."

"I'm on my phone with you."

"Beatrice has a computer in the office. Tell her you need to see this. Search Piper road runner. It'll come up."

"Road runner?"

"Just do it."

Beatrice led Alex to an office upstairs in the main house, as logical and organized as she was, and they found the video in seconds. Thousands of hits already.

"Lump in my throat," Alex mumbled to Clayton. "Where is she?"

Clayton explained.

"Going to pick her up?"

"She'd be long gone. Besides, there's no crime. She maybe cost the park and police overtime. But we don't bill folks for that yet."

"How'd she get there? Any busses between the park and . . . where is she?"

"Fort Stockton. Right on the interstate. But no public transportation."

"Did we pass through it driving to Alpine?"

"Remember a town when you crossed I-10?"

"Not even a gas station."

"Then you came down FM 1776. So Piper probably wasn't in Fort Stockton before."

"But she—or somebody else—knew where to take a picture."

"Right." Clayton had made the same assumption. "I'll let you know if we learn more. You and Beatrice doing okay?"

"Your sister's awesome."

"Not the word I'd use," Clayton said, smiling to himself and hanging up.

Clayton followed with another call to Chief Furcron at the park. Velma was now convinced the whole business was a publicity stunt. "She may not be Juliet, but a whole bunch of people now know the name Piper Robinet. I figured her to turn up at that fancy hotel in Marfa. The California people with her checked in there after they saw the motel rooms in our park."

"So you think Piper pulled a stunt on the rim after she lost the movie part?" Clayton said it like it was his theory too.

"I talked to her agent in Los Angeles and he told me Piper knew her series might be cancelled even before she arrived in Texas. Your boy Alex wasn't in the loop because he'd already quit the series. Seems Ms. Robinet lost her whole career in a matter of days—movie *and* TV show. People do crazy things."

"Yeah."

"But after this video, I think we're finished with her."

"No search and rescue fees?"

"We didn't need a medivac."

"Right."

"So best case, the girl decided to hike away from a group without telling anybody," Furcron said. "Stupid, but not criminal."

"I get it," Clayton agreed. "But I'd like to know who else was involved. How she got to Fort Stockton for one thing."

"And where she is now."

"I-10 heads right into Los Angeles."

"Does she have access to a car?" Furcron asked. "I know she came in a Range Rover. Where's that vehicle? *Damn*, we should have checked."

"It's in Alpine. Saw it last night."

There was a pause. "I understand the boy's at your place? I read about that riot at his sister's."

"I can't reveal that information, ma'am." Clayton could imagine Furcron smiling.

"I have two daughters . . ."

"So you told me. Hey, it's been great working with you, Chief. Hope we meet face-to-face soon. And I will see what I can do for those girls."

Chapter 15

Professor Harp was feeling sorry for herself this Thursday, maybe for no good reason. Both morning committee meetings were scheduled long ago and afternoon office hours on Tuesdays and Thursdays were all the university asked from her this term. The administration wanted her edition of Mote McCrary's *Madrone* in print almost as much as the publisher did. A prestigious launch party was planned for late winter along with a weekend conference honoring the legacy of the author who'd been a student at Sul Ross when he wrote his semi-autobiographical narrative. And when he died too, for that matter. Now, everyone in America knew about what happened to the manuscript after Mote's murder.

Just six months earlier, Mote's mother asked Claire to oversee publication of a revised version of the original book based upon a newly discovered and more authentic text. It was a labor of love for Claire. But labor nonetheless.

The project absorbed her office hours, though Claire spent much of day thinking about her brother too, still at the Shoot Ranch. What was Alex up to there? How had he won over Beatrice so fast? Was he avoiding *her*?

Probably not. After all, Alex *had* come to her place first, expecting a quiet night. Who could foresee what followed? Girls still lurked around her house this morning when she slipped out. City police were patrolling the neighborhood too. But that didn't make Claire feel better. Her only brother was in Texas, yet he was bunking with Clayton Shoot—a total stranger.

She was cheered, however, that Sam Vogt would be dropping by in minutes. He'd emailed saying he had an idea—no hint what it might be. But Claire always made time for Sam, her former student. And Mote McCrary's closest friend. She and Sam had bonded in the spring when, together, they'd figured out the real story behind Mote's manuscript. A poor kid then barely able to hold things together at school, Sam had prospered since, as she did, by those discoveries. He was even working for her this term as a research assistant.

More consultant than assistant. Sam wasn't a good writer—in fact he'd been taking a writing class from her in the spring when life changed for both of them. But he proved indispensable. A twenty-four-year-old who couldn't reliably get subjects and verbs to agree, Sam somehow managed to spot copyediting blunders invisible to her. Far more important, as Claire drafted an introductory essay to what she hoped would become the authoritative text of *Madrone*—it had been a best-selling novel in its counterfeit version—Sam supplied insights into McCrary's life no one else knew. Sam and Mote had been as close as young men could be.

He knocked on her door at precisely 2:00 PM, as promised. He was a plain-featured young man, but his hair was yellow as straw and his eyes blue as cornflowers. Invisible in the community once, Sam now sometimes needed sunglasses and a ballcap to preserve the anonymity he preferred. He removed an Astros hat as he entered.

"Hey, Professor Harp," he said pushing into her open office. She'd never get him to call her Claire.

"Come on in," Claire said, clearing books off a chair in the cluttered room. "You got pages for me?"

"Yes, ma'am," Sam said, handing over a thin folder. "This bunch was better."

Claire laughed and gave him a new set of proofs to examine. "So you see improvement in my work?"

"Yes, ma'am," he said, not catching the irony. "But I come here about somethin' else. An idea."

Claire leaned away. "What's that?"

"I hear'd your brother was in town and all?"

"I guess everyone knows."

"A movie star." Sam seemed wound-up.

"Not there yet," Claire said. "Someday maybe."

"Yes, ma'am. And he's in town, but no one knows where?"

So even Sam read the *Mercury*. Claire smiled. "I know where he is."

"Figured that. So, I was thinkin'. You recall that off-roading trip we talked about in spring when you first got your Jeep?" Claire had bought a new Wrangler to replace an ancient Cherokee and let Sam be the first to drive it. "We said we'd do the River Road in Big Bend someday with Clayton?"

"Yep," Claire said. The rugged two-track cut from one end of Big Bend National Park to the other, roughly parallel with the Rio Grande.

"But with Clayton so busy as the new sheriff, we couldn't do it all summer? And summer's not the best time anyway, given the heat?"

The questions were stacking up. "Whatya got in mind, Sam?" Claire fell into Texan more often with Sam than anyone.

"Well, if your brother's gonna stick here in Texas for a coupla days, maybe we could take him? Show him that part of Big Bend. Might be fun. Especially now that he dudn't have to worry about the girlfriend."

Claire sat up. "What?" As much as possible, Claire steered clear of distracting media when in her office.

Sam read her confusion and told her the news.

"They're sure she was in Fort Stockton this morning?"

"Yes, ma'am."

"My brother might head back to California then."

"I get that, but if he don't and wants to spend time with his sister?"

"Some off-roading might be fun."

"That's what I thought. This weekend. Sunday would be good for me."

Couldn't blame Sam for wanting to meet her handsome brother. And she guessed Alex would jump at the offer—if he was sticking around. Or he might want to pack up and leave, given all that happened.

"I'll ask him, Sam. I'd love to have him meet you."

Sam gave one of his quick nods, stood up, and flipped his hat back on.

"You don't have to go Sam," Claire laughed.

"I do. There's a fancy lady down the hall waitin' to talk. I told her I needed just a minute."

And that's just about all he took.

⹊ ⹊ ⹊

THE *FANCY LADY* was someone Claire had met briefly just once before. But she wasn't the sort you forget. Unfortunately, Claire had later uncovered compromising information about the woman in the same criminal case that involved Sam Vogt. Her visit was, to say the least, unexpected.

"I'm sure you remember me, Professor Harp," the very handsome middle-aged socialite said, ambling through the open door in cuffed boyfriend jeans,

92

tiered-sleeve snap shirt, beaded linen vest, and white cowboy hat. "I'm Nikki Lamb and we met back in March at a fundraiser at my home. At the McCann Ranch?"

"Of course," Claire said, sniffing Chanel and returning an embrace Mrs. Lamb initiated. The fundraiser had been a glittering affair with BBQ, an auction, and line dancing. The wife of rancher William Lamb was putting on almost as much of a show now in Claire's office.

"Was that Sam Vogt who just left?" Nikki asked. "Mote McCrary's boyfriend? What a striking young man."

"I wouldn't say *boyfriend*," Claire said. Or *striking* either, she thought. But flattery comes with fame.

"I do want to say how delighted William and I are that Clayton and you are coming to Billy's birthday party tomorrow night. He turned twenty-one today."

"Clayton showed me an invitation."

"And we got his RSVP for two."

Claire waited for the other shoe to drop, unsure what it could be. Or was Nikki just driving home the slight of not inviting Claire separately? Could Nikki be that petty?

Claire would be bigger. "We're so looking forward to it. Both Clayton and I know Billy."

"That's right. Billy was in your class last spring."

Claire nodded.

Nikki crossed elegantly long legs. She was William Lamb's second wife, Claire knew, and very much a stepmother to the randy and now very wealthy Billy McCann Lamb. Billy had hit on Claire and, truth be told, on Nikki as well.

Both women smiled sweetly.

"Well," Nikki said at last, fingering her gorgeous silk scarf. "Billy kind of asked me this morning whether you might bring your brother along to the party tomorrow night—you know, now that his girlfriend has been seen in Fort Stockton and is apparently okay. Billy thinks Alex needs a better introduction to Texas than he got there on the South Rim."

She said it with a straight face. Now, Claire *might* have believed it if Billy thought to invite the luscious Piper Robinet to his party. But seventeen-year-old Alex would just steal his limelight. Then Claire got it. She could see Alex on Nikki's arm at their lavish home, a handsome guest with Oscar buzz.

"Alex is so young," Claire said. "I'm sure he'd feel awkward at a party full of strange adults."

"Oh, Claire, no! He's used to parties in Hollywood. Why, everyone would be honored to meet your brother. And he'd have such a good time at the ranch. He could come for the music alone." Nikki dropped the name of a band even Claire recognized.

"Well, I can ask him," Claire said. No sense alienating a family as powerful as the Lambs. And Claire *kind of* liked Billy. She knew Clayton did.

"Why Claire," Nikki smiled, figuring she'd won, "maybe we can even find Alex a Texas girl who won't run away from him?"

Claire called Clayton the moment Nikki left her office. She noticed two messages from him earlier in the day. She'd silenced her phone during a morning meeting and forgotten to turn it back on.

Claire apologized to the sheriff and let him fill her in on Piper's video in Fort Stockton. She wondered whether to tell Clayton about Piper's admission to her Monday night that she was older than Alex—in Claire's opinion by at least five or six years. Irrelevant now? Maybe he knew already?

"I wish Alex were with me now," was all she said. "He must think I'm the worst sister ever."

"You including Beatrice in that?" Clayton asked.

Claire laughed and then told him about Nikki's invitation. "Should I even mention it to Alex?"

"Hell, yes," Clayton said. "After what he's been through? Nothin' better than a party. Good band, good crowd. And you should ask him yourself. Anyway, that's sorta why I was calling. I heard from Fiona Tusk that kids still are hanging around your place, hopin' to get a glimpse of the boy?"

"You're saying he should stay at your place another night?"

"Well, yeah. He's having the time of his life here. Not that he wouldn't be happy with you."

Claire said nothing, knowing what her work schedule was today and would be again tomorrow.

"We're having ribs and brisket outdoors tonight since the weather's so nice. Why don't y'all join us?" Clayton continued. "You could tell Alex about Billy's party then. I don't think he's all that eager to get back to California. He's still confused about Piper and got other things on his mind."

"Like *Romeo and Juliet*?"

"Yep. Beatrice is playing speech coach. They both got theories about that play and spend hours going over lines. It's good for her—best I've seen her since our dad died. She even took him for lunch today at that soda fountain in Fort Davis. Ladies at the counter recognized him."

"What time should I be there?"

"We'll eat about 6:30, but come anytime. You know, Claire, you kin sleep in the main house if you want. Don't have to go home alone."

"I'm used to it," she said. And then wish she hadn't.

Chapter 16

Clayton Shoot was able to leave the office early that day because he'd gotten in early and for once cleared his desk. The Piper Robinet matter wasn't quite closed. He expected Velma Furcron and the rangers at Big Bend still itched to talk with the actress. And Clayton guessed the girl might not be so eager to get back to California as the Throng!Media folks—after their PR stunt went south.

Thank God, Thursday had been quiet. Some drug buzz in the state park along the Rio Grande. And Alonso Rangel mentioned Fiona Tusk was feeling low. Clayton would check on that—even ask Claire if flowers were appropriate. He knew they were, but Claire liked it when men seemed clueless.

But Clayton wasn't. Hell, one of the reasons he was going home early was to rescue Alex from Beatrice and gear him up for the barbeque tonight and, more than likely, Billy's party tomorrow. He was sure the boy would go. To see how the other half partied—meaning Texans.

And he was right.

They started at Johnson Feed & Western Wear just east of the university. Alex found it weird that a store sold both ranch supplies and duds, but the combination made sense to locals. Ranchers dress up too. And right now, Alex needed a coupla pair of jeans, some western shirts, and a serviceable pair of boots. They'd maybe get a decent belt, buckle, and hat at Big Bend Saddlery across the road.

As expected, the boy was recognized. A girl at the front counter just about did a jig when he walked in. She and an older lady chattered like magpies while he tried on the jeans. Looked spectacular in them, they said. Tight as the ones Clayton wore in that drawing over the couch. He'd give Alex grief about that.

Boots were a pricier matter. Clayton knew the kid could afford any pair he wanted. But those at Johnson Feed topped out at what most locals could handle.

No ostrich or caiman skin here. Clayton recommended a pair soft enough for dancing without lots of break-in. He expected the boy might be on the floor at the McCann Ranch Friday night and maybe they'd be two-steppin' tonight if friends joining them remembered their fiddles.

Like his sister, Alex had clothes sense—which in his case meant he knew how to dress like a guy. Clayton suggested some shirts with pearl buttons and a bolo tie, and they were on their way. Alex signed autographs while the staff rang up his credit card. Slowly.

They dropped a lot more money across the road. Alex admired a silver buckle set Clayton liked and didn't flinch at the price. They had only a single Spradley hat in stock—most were custom ordered. But, yep, the item fit Alex perfectly. What were the odds? Clayton was beginning to believe the golden boy stuff. Must be nice. Not that he had cause to complain.

"Y'all be belle of the ball tonight," Clayton joked as they walked to his Wagoneer. "And you got another invite for tomorrow."

"What?"

"I'll let Claire explain."

⇥⋵ ⇥⋵ ⇥⋵

CLAIRE APPRECIATED THE roaring fire in a pit behind the main house on the Shoot compound. She could smell meat roasting and knew the guys tuning their fiddles were real cowboys. Her brother—*was he really that tall?*—fit right in, except his clothes looked too fresh and the bolo was a trifle much. Claire found herself saying *hello* to Clayton's two married sisters Mabel and Helen, trying to remember which was which. They brought kids too and their husbands Hector and Joe, who never quite looked her in the eye when they spoke. Maybe afraid what their wives might think?

Alex walked over and rescued her. "Gotta get these boots a little scuffed and didn't have time to wash the jeans," he admitted when Claire poked fun. But they approached the fire and sat on a log and Claire got right down to business.

"I'm glad Piper turned up," she said, watching his expression. "I was afraid this might go on for weeks." Alex looked relieved but wary.

"Sure'd like to know what she was up to," he said. Claire noticed the elision. Was it Texan or Elizabethan? Beatrice was watching them from across the circle. The woman nodded formally and Claire waved.

"You like Beatrice?" Alex asked.

"I do."

"She has opinions, but we're mostly on the same page with the part I'm playing. We've been working through the lines. I'm learnin' a lot."

"Clayton told me."

"I want to be a thought-provoking Romeo and she thinks that's right."

"You two have bonded."

Alex sensed resentment.

"I know how it seems."

Claire waved a hand. "Not your fault, Alex. Just I hoped to see you more."

"Same here," he said. But she wasn't sure he meant it.

"I've been busy," she conceded. "We couldn't have done anything today. And even tomorrow, I've got a conference call all morning with my editors."

"I did just drop in out of the blue."

"Did you ask him?" Clayton said dropping in himself, claiming the empty space on the log next to Alex, plate of ribs in hand.

"What?"

"The party at the McCann Ranch? . . . Guess I just spoiled it."

Claire sighed and then explained Alex's invitation to Billy Lamb Jr.'s birthday party. "He's turning twenty-one," she said when it looked like Alex thought Billy might be a child.

"And he gets the whole damn ranch. 300,000 acres and a house like maybe one you'd see in Beverly Hills," Clayton added. "From his late mother's will."

It took more explanation, but Alex eventually got it. "Sounds like *Giant*. But why'd they invite me?"

"Just being neighborly," Claire lied, impressed her brother knew the movie she so loved.

Alex sneered at Clayton. "So that's why you got me all tarted up."

"Just wanted to see you in tight jeans."

The men laughed. Claire didn't ask why. Clayton tipped his hat and left when the guys with the fiddles waived him over—their instruments glinting under a moon so bright it would cast shadows soon. Claire was used to the phenomenon now, almost invisible in the cities where she'd lived before moving to West Texas.

"You don't have to go to the party," Claire said to her brother. "You might be the youngest one there."

"Wouldn't miss it. Sounds like an episode of *Dallas*."

"You know that too?" Claire said.

"Hell, I might maybe find myself a Lucy Ewing. Let's get something to eat."

They filled their plates at a table overseen by Clayton's mother Anna, busy at that moment straightening a checkered table cloth. Three girls, one blonde and two dark-haired and ranging in age from maybe four to twelve, ran up and stared at Alex.

"*Abuela, abuela*," the youngest demanded. "Is this Charlie, Is this Charlie?"

Anna Shoot, Clayton's mother, smiled but Claire could tell she was confused. Claire leaned in and explained. "That's the name of my brother's character on a TV show."

Alex already had the little girl in his arms, assuring her he was, indeed, Charlie. "And where's Mackenzie? Did you bring Mackenzie?" she asked.

"Mackenzie's not here. She didn't come."

"Is she mad at you?" She frequently was on *Brainiacs*.

"She might be, I think." Alex winked at his sister, put the little girl down and then took selfies with the older ones. Claire could tell he did this all the time.

Standing next to Clayton's mother, Claire explained that Mackenzie was a character played by Piper Robinet in the same TV show Alex was in. Claire was cheered when the gray-haired woman just shook her head, clueless. "Such names," was all she said.

Alex stuck with his sister when they returned to the fire pit, stopping first to pick up Dr. Peppers from a tub. Claire liked that and then remembered the off-roading trip Sam suggested. Might be a way to make his time with her memorable. He'd not even noticed her Jeep.

"When are you heading back to California?" she began.

Alex shrugged his shoulders. "I'm on hiatus. Nothing on my plate for two weeks. Might have been longer if Throng!Media hadn't signed Tabreetha Bree-Jones."

Claire laughed. "A truly awful name."

"Brits." They bumped shoulders as the cowboys sawed at their *strangs*. Alex went quiet.

"You're so grown up," Claire said to break the pause.

"I'm not," he countered, giving her a pout she remembered from way back.

"Well, if you're still here Sunday, we could maybe go off-roading in Big Bend? My research assistant Sam Vogt . . ."

"Sam Vogt. Yeah—from the book. It's dedicated to him."

Claire was startled. Maybe he paid more attention to her work than she gave him credit? Mote McCrary had, indeed, dedicated *Madrone* to Sam—her first and maybe most important textual discovery.

"I sure wanna meet him," Alex continued. "He's quite a guy."

Claire nodded, trying to process her brother's enthusiasm. "Doing the River Road was his idea from back in May when I got my Wrangler. He suggested we go now so you could come along. He's been all over this county, Sam and Mote McCrary. Together."

"That would be *so* cool—meeting Sam. I need to . . . I've heard so much about him."

"Heard so much about what?" Once again, Clayton had stolen up, tipping a Shiner this time.

"Sam Vogt," Alex said. "We're gonna do the River Road in Big Bend on Sunday—Claire and Sam and me. How 'bout you come along, Clayton?" Genuine warmth in her brother's voice.

"Will, if I can, sure," Clayton said immediately. "Rugged country. We'd need an early start."

"Perfect!" Claire said. But she felt run over.

Her thought was interrupted by a full-throated howl from the surrounding hills.

"Coyote?" Alex asked, pronouncing it just like a Texan, with two syllables. *How'd he know?*

"Baying at that *purtee* moon," Clayton smiled. Claire opened her mouth, but he shushed her. "Listen now," he said. The single canine voice was joined by a vibrant chorus of high-pitched yips.

"Her pups," Clayton explained. "We bin hearing them 'bout every night since June. Some getting ready to leave her—the boys don't stick around once they're grown."

"That's for sure."

"Hey, young lady," Clayton said, grabbing Claire's hand, "let's take a spin."

The musicians were playing a slow tune and Claire noticed Clayton's sisters already dancing with their husbands.

And Beatrice was heading for Alex.

Chapter 17

"Claire?" A single syllable drawn out like a balloon about to pop.

How could she have forgotten to call her mother in Ohio? Well, it was easy. Eugenia Harp would blame Claire for all that happened to her brother since Monday in Texas. Surely Eugenia knew her eldest daughter had no control over where Alex went or what happened there to his girlfriend—if that's even what Piper was. And Claire was not the one who'd sanctioned his California adventures to begin with. He should still be in Ohio finishing high school.

"Yes, mother?" Claire said.

"Is your brother well?"

"Yes, he's doing fine. I saw him tonight."

"Oh, did you find time for that?" *Zinger.*

"Yes, mother."

"Is he with you now at your place?"

"No, he's with Clayton. On the ranch." Claire guessed Eugenia had already called Alex and knew precisely where he was.

"Why is that, Claire?"

She wanted her daughter to squirm through an explanation. Claire refused. "Mother, I know you know what's happened. I read your comments on the *Big Bend Mercury*." (Eugenia had signed in, using the handle *Concerned in Gates Mills.* It was an upscale Cleveland suburb, where her parents lived and Claire grew up.) "You must have talked to Alex already."

"The cell service is very bad down there, so close to Mexico." Eugenia wasn't entirely wrong. "Tell me at least about this Beatrice woman. Is she Alex's age? Are they a thing?"

Claire toyed with saying they were, but didn't want her mother on a plane to Alpine tomorrow.

"Beatrice is very middle-aged, mother, just helping Alex with his next movie role. I think you might even like Beatrice." *Birds of a feather.*

"So, she'd be playing Juliet?"

"They're going over lines, mother. And she's shown him the ranch. She manages it. There's no hanky-panky."

"I never implied such a thing."

"Of course, you did." Claire was often blunt with Eugenia. Long pause.

"What's really going on, Claire?"

Claire was wondering the same thing.

"Can we be serious for a change?"

"I'm always serious."

That was a lie. But Claire needed this conversation.

"Mother, it bothers me how tight Alex has become with Clayton and his family. In the few moments Alex and I have had together, we struggle like we've got nothing to say. We don't connect. I have so little in common with him."

"You are *much* older than he is . . . dear." A note of tenderness in the last word.

"Clayton's got a decade on Alex, yet they behave like brothers."

"There's that too."

"What?"

"They're men. Your brother's a man—in case you haven't noticed. I'm sure he's taller than you."

"He is."

"And you want to think of him as the child you chased around the backyard."

"I know he's growing up."

"He brought a girlfriend with him."

"And she was older than Alex too."

"What's that got to do with it?"

"Honestly, mother, I don't know. I just didn't get their relationship. The girl was evasive with me. Hiding something. Using Alex in some way."

"And you want to protect him."

"Well."

"Men don't like being protected."

"He's still in high school."

"Claire, you realize your father handles Alex's finances?"

"Father *is* an accountant."

"Does he handle your money?"

"I'm an adult."

"If you made as much money as Alex, you'd hire an accountant."

"That doesn't make Alex a man."

"We know that, dear, and I give him plenty of grief, the same as I give you. Did you talk with Alex about the girl?"

"No. It wasn't my business. But I wish now I had."

"I wonder if he's talked to Clayton about her?"

"He will in time, I guess."

"That's exactly right, dear. They won't say much either—but it will be enough."

"You think so?" Claire paused. "Clayton took Alex shopping this afternoon. So he'd have jeans and boots for a party we're going to tomorrow."

"Claire, do you want my opinion?"

"Of course."

"You won't get mad?"

"What's this about, mother?"

"Have you thought to ask why Clayton Shoot might be paying so much attention to your brother?"

Claire hesitated. "You're not thinking Clayton's gay?"

Eugenia's sigh resonated in Claire's ear. "No wonder you're still single, dear. Don't you see that Clayton is already treating your brother as a relative, a future brother-in-law? Sizing him up. Getting to know him. Getting to like him. Thinking in terms of *family*. You're the one who's out of synch. And I hate to say it, but maybe less serious in your relationship than Mr. Shoot."

Claire wanted to hang up on her mother not because she was angry but because, for once, Eugenia could be right. Yet Eugenia didn't have the whole picture either. She might be spot-on about Clayton. But about Alex?

"I'll think about what you've said, mother. Clayton is a good guy."

"You could do worse, dear."

Claire waited for a zinger, but none came this time.

Chapter 18

Very late the next afternoon, Deputy Alonso Rangel sat, with permission, in Sheriff Shoot's office, feet on the desk, thinking *someday all this might be mine*. Maybe after Clayton got elected to Congress? Or married Claire Harp and she dragged him off to Ohio.

In the meantime, he'd settle for captain or chief deputy, or, hell, any promotion that paired him up better with Fiona Tusk—his girlfriend and Alpine's chief of police. But Deputy Rangel was in no hurry either.

And he was okay, too, with the guff he took for pairin' up with a lady near twice his age. She was worth it. Too bad, though, they'd not been invited to Billy Lamb's birthday party—Alonso because the Lambs had no clue who he was and Fiona because she had history with the family. William Lamb probably paid a lawyer just to keep her off their acres.

Alonso had never seen the McCann Ranch up close. Heard the house was like an airport terminal inside, with walls of glass and stairways floatin' over galleries of fancy art. Probably fancy people too, in expensive clothes drinking cocktails he never heard of. But the Sheriff of Brewster County got invited everywhere. (The last one even met President Bush.) So that's why Alonso was sitting in this Friday for Clayton, who'd likely be dancin' up a storm soon with his pretty lady.

The dispatcher buzzed and, after Alonso pushed the right button, told him that a Ms. Regina Summerlin was wanting to report a missing person. Preferred *Gina*. Alonso didn't quite recognize the name. The call transferred with a click.

"Deputy Rangel here," he said. "How can I help, Ms. Summerlin?" The woman panting on the line sounded asthmatic.

"I need to speak to the sheriff," she said.

"He can't take a call now. I'm told y'all want to report a missing person?"

"She should've been home hours ago and is not answering her phone. It's not like her. It's my mother Iris Cobb. Iris Cobb Summerlin."

A name Alonso *did* know. He sat up.

"Ma'am, does your mother have health or mental issues or might her life be in danger?"

"She's an artist. Five or six pieces are missing from her studio too. Her work is very valuable. Something's wrong, I know it. Iris is in her early sixties and healthy. But she's been painting in out-of-the-way places lately. I think she was going to the desert today or maybe Big Bend or the state park."

"Where are you calling from?"

"The Cobb Institute. I live on the property."

Alonso got it. On Highway 118. Painters came from around the country to spend time there. An uppity place like Cibolo Creek Ranch where people like Alonso (and even Clayton) didn't go—except when guests got in trouble. Alonso calmed Gina Summerlin down by having her describe her mother and, maybe more important at this stage, the vehicle she was using.

"An almost new Escalade. Silver. That's a Cadillac truck."

"Yes, ma'am. Registered in her name?"

"Of course."

"When did you last see her?

There was silence for the first time since Rangel picked up. "I didn't see her this morning. I was awake by seven but she'd already left. Probably hoped to catch morning light in the desert. I guess it was yesterday before dinner? We live in different lodges at the Cobb."

Alonso ran through a missing person's checklist with Gina, getting down important physical details and contact information. Gina didn't know exactly what Iris was wearing this morning or where she was heading. In a county as big as Connecticut, going to the desert or federal or state parks wasn't much help. On the other hand, there were only so many roads to be searched, assuming she wasn't off road. And most folks didn't do that with Escalades. He asked Gina to text a recent photo of Iris, expecting there'd be plenty online too.

"Send us something that might show her in clothes she'd wear when working outdoors."

Things got more complicated when they returned to the business of missing artworks.

"Is it likely she'd have them with her?"

"No. They're were finished pieces ready to go to our gallery in Taos. That's where she sells her major work."

"Could you estimate their value?"

"Between 50 and 80 thousand dollars."

"That much?"

"Apiece. Together they'd be worth more than a quarter million. But that's not the point, officer. My mother is missing and I don't know where she is or where Mateo is either."

"Mateo?"

"Mateo Bottaio, a photographer who works with us here at Cobb. Jack of all trades. Iris and I depend on him."

Alonso wasn't sure what that meant. "It's gettin' on to Friday evening. Would he still be working?"

There was a pause. "He lives here at the Institute."

"Oh."

"It's just that with Iris so late, her paintings gone, Mateo not around . . . Something's wrong."

"Ms. Summerlin, I'm gonna contact the sheriff about this and get back to you. We don't have enough here for a formal missing person's search, 'specially since your mother is just a little overdue and a healthy adult. But you're right to report it, and we'll notify park police to be on the lookout for that Caddy for sure."

⋈ ⋈ ⋈

CLAYTON AND ALEX showed up on time at Claire's house, reeking of cologne or aftershave—though she wasn't sure either faced a razor, Clayton was so fair and her brother still a kid. Except he wasn't and sure enough she spied a tiny cut on his chin.

"Where's Beatrice?" she asked.

"Comin' later. Stuff to take care of first," Clayton said. "You look good."

Claire was happy he noticed. The guys were in jeans and western shirts, while she wore a burgundy pink tunic dress with a denim jacket, cowboy boots, and plenty of turquoise. She'd seen the outfit in *Cowboys & Indians* and ordered the items online. Clayton whistled when she turned to show it off, the effect she wanted.

"Never dressed like that in Ohio," her brother said.

"Could say the same about you."

His grinned, conceding the point.

They took Clayton's venerable Wagoneer. Claire remembered her own first ride in it to the McCann Ranch back in March, a dozen miles or more down Highway 118. The sun was setting then too, the sky glowing in ribbons of pink and orange just as tonight. Once again, Clayton's SUV stirred up a trail of dust on the mesa approaching the Lamb homestead and it wasn't long before they spied a ranch house glowing like a jeweled necklace on the horizon, most of it now owned by young Billy McCann Lamb.

"Little grander than our place," Clayton said, glancing toward Alex in the back seat. "Don't be bowled over."

"By the house?"

"By the welcome you'll get. Might be Billy's party, but Nikki Lamb's gonna make you guest of honor."

Claire assumed Clayton filled her brother in on the Lamb family, except maybe some scandals uncovered in the spring during a murder investigation. McCann hospitality would be an eye-opener for Alex, as it had been for Claire the first time she experienced it—at a fundraiser for the arts with Texan land barons. He'd likely handle it better than she did.

They were a trifle late. Clayton had paused to take a message from Alonso Rangel just before they left, nodding as he listened. Claire could tell it concerned him. But the delay only made their entrance grander. Claire adjusted Alex's bolo and let him follow her and Clayton through weighty antique doors into an elegant foyer above a sunken living area. A band was playing a country tune somewhere in the background, but all eyes were suddenly on them.

"Now h'ain't that a handsome young man!" a smoky voice declared from a posh settee in the entranceway. It was Miss Lucy Cavendar, a wealthy silver-haired *grande dame* who'd embarrassed Claire and Clayton similarly back in the spring. Lucy had been courted by Clayton's father decades ago, but she'd married more wealthily—several times in fact. And still regretted it.

"Thankee ma'am," Alex said in such gracious Texan that Clayton chuckled. Still seated, Miss Lucy stretched out the hand not clutching her glass of bourbon to embrace the boy. Then she kissed him so hard she almost pulled him over. A gathering crowd, sparkling in silver, laughed and applauded. A taut middle-aged woman in red boots, a black knit dress, and enough turquoise to open a boutique ran up the steps and embraced her guests, an arm winding tightly around Alex's waist.

"Won't y'all give our special guest Alex Harp a big Texas welcome!" Nikki Lamb said, smiling so broad Claire spotted wrinkles through her makeup. Alex hung his head just the right way and the moneyed Texans gave him a *yee-haw*, glasses raised all around. He was the only one there too young to drink.

"Holy shit," Alex whispered to Claire and kissed her on the cheek. He was enjoying this.

More women came up and a few husbands and Alex soon disappeared into a living area decorated by Russell and Terpning paintings, sculptures by Borglum, and a row of pots by Maria Martinez. Clayton and Claire followed at a distance but they were intercepted by William Lamb, who introduced himself graciously to Claire. They'd never met before, though she'd seen the handsome dark-haired man at the spring fundraiser.

"You guys sure know how to make an entrance," he smiled. "And thank you for bringing the boy. It's all Nikki's been yappin' about." He nodded toward a videographer who caught the moment.

"Where's Billy?" Clayton asked, looking around the room and noticing a mostly silver-haired crowd.

"The kids are down by the pool and patio—Billy and his friends and the ranch hands. Different band there too. Hard core country."

A group of women inched up to Claire and pulled her aside, eager for gossip about her celebrity brother and that *horrible girl on the South Rim*. Clayton waived as she was drawn away, happy to see her becoming part of his Texas crowd. Claire guessed she might not see Clayton for a while and she was right.

⋇   ⋇   ⋇

JUST MINUTES LATER, Clayton was in his Wagoneer driving south on Highway 118 toward the sprawling Iris Cobb Institute for the Arts to meet Alonso Rangel, also heading there at the sheriff's request. The handsome adobe structures at the Cobb compound were easy to spot just south of a Border Patrol checkpoint. Clayton knew, too, that miles of the acreage north of the Institute and spreading eastward toward some low hills were owned by a certain ICS Group—it didn't take a genius to figure out what the initials stood for. Iris's lush and ungrazed pastures might even skirt the sprawling McCann Ranch in places.

Clayton guessed Claire wouldn't appreciate his abrupt departure from the party there—he'd been disappointing her this way a lot since becoming sheriff. He texted her that an emergency had come up and then messaged Beatrice to be sure she got Claire and Alex home. Clayton's one-word explanation to both: *Murder?* And he instructed the women to say nothing.

Clayton soon had Velma Furcron on the radio. He'd installed the unit in his venerable Jeep just for situations like this. Velma was in maybe her third week as chief ranger at Big Bend National Park. And a homicide already. Pretty rare event there, but then he remembered another just a few years earlier.

"A body was discovered about 6:00 PM on the Old Maverick Road," Furcron explained. "You know Luna's Jacal?" Velma pronounced the *J* like a *J*, not giving it a proper Spanish *H*. But it was not the time to correct her.

"Sure. Halfway between the entry station and the river. Rugged area."

"In places," Velma acknowledged. Clayton wondered if she'd even been on the dirt road before tonight. "Ranger on routine patrol called it in. Suspicious to see an Escalade out there and an easel blown over on the ground but no artist."

"Where was the body?"

"A little way into Luna's Jacal—it's a low stone shed with a mixed sort of roof—mud and branches and a lot of what looks like heavy black canvas. She was painting it, I assume."

"Been there. Know it." Late in the nineteenth century, a Mexican farmer named Gilberto Luna had built the crude dwelling and then raised a huge family on the arid site. People were tougher then.

"Small caliber bullet to the back of the head."

"Iris Cobb?"

"Yeah. Just about confirmed. Face down. The lady probably never knew what happened. We got your deputy's missing person's report just minutes earlier. Pure luck the ranger was patrolling the Maverick Road. The body could've been out all night."

"Where's it now?"

"On the way to the Alpine medical center for identification—Big Bend Regional. The plates check out and the description we have matches Iris Cobb. No wallet or driver's license or purse. So maybe a robbery. We're bringing lights to the site and will start forensics. Waiting now on the FBI, of course. But one of your people is here. She'd been in Terlingua."

"Gus Stumpf."

"No, it's a woman."

"Gus is a woman. Augusta."

"Oh."

"I'm on my way to see the victim's daughter. Regina Summerlin," Clayton explained. "At the Cobb Institute on 118."

"Don't know anything about that."

Clayton suddenly remembered the sketch in his living room. "You know she's a *famous* artist? Iris Cobb."

"Guess I do now. This will be a big deal?"

"Yep. Very big."

"Ever heard of the ISB?" Furcron asked.

"Couldn't even guess."

"It's the National Park Service's version of the FBI. *Investigative Services Branch*. Just a handful of agents that specialize in high-profile park crimes. Not afraid to get their hands dirty. I might call in a guy I know who works out of Grand Canyon National Park. Head screwed on straight."

"As opposed to tight, like the FBI?"

"You got it. I'll see what I can do. Name's Perciak."

Chapter 19

Just a few weeks ago, it would have irritated Billy Lamb no end—his step-mother Nikki finaglin' some fancy Hollywood dude into *his* birthday party. Billy had never heard of Alex Harp, even though the kid's super-hot sister Claire had been his English professor in spring. She gave him a B, which he hadn't really earned.

Maybe she liked him?

But when his stepmom asked yesterday morning about inviting the actor, Billy realized he didn't care. It didn't matter.

She'd approached him in their Thermador-everything kitchen with stainless steel this and that—ovens on top of ovens, built-in refrigerators, racks of pots and rows of spices, and it hit him, just at that moment, that he owned it all. Everything. Right down to the artwork on the walls, according to his mama's will. And some of that art cost more than the kitchen.

Okay with me, invite the kid, he'd told Nikki.

Let the actor see all I got. My land. My acres. My friends. *Billy McCann*. Just startin' to sink in.

His daddy gave him that present yesterday—October 21—his actual date of birth. Billy wasn't sure Nikki even knew about it. He was standing out on a deck upstairs early in the evening. The highest one in the house where you could almost make out mountains people thought were in Mexico, but weren't. They were on McCann land. Chilly already because of a cloudless sky, but the walls on that part of the house were still warm.

The sliding door opened behind him and there was his dad, William Lamb, holding a box Billy recognized from Big Bend Saddlery. Not sized for a hat and way too big for a quirt, bosal, or fancy stirrups. Besides, he had all the gear he needed. He'd mentioned a hitched horsehair bridle—prisoners made them in Montana. But they wouldn't come in a Saddlery box.

Daddy looked choked up. Could barely speak. Billy hated when that happened and he glanced down, not wanting to see it.

"You're the man now, Billy. Happy birthday." That's all he said and turned back into the house. Billy sat on the porch sofa with the gift on his lap, tearing at the flaps, wondering if his father was watching from behind the glass doors. Slid the item out. Disappointed. A briefcase. Finest quality, for sure. But, a briefcase.

Then he saw noticed the embossed nameplate. *Billy McCann.*

Just like his dad—to accept his name change without a word. No more Billy Jr.—because he'd never been one. Middle name was always McCann. His mother saw to that. And now, well. The final papers for the name change were in his cabin on the south end of the ranch, just waiting for him to file. And put all these acres back in the hands of an actual McCann.

He'd do it next week, when the birthday thing settled down and he was done jawing and jugging.

Right now, though, he'd promised a *really* cute girl he'd met at the pool to invite Alex Harp down to the pavilion so his friends and ranch crew partying there might meet the actor. Herself included, no doubt. He didn't care.

Before this week, the Harp kid and the actress who'd dumped him on the South Rim were unknown to Billy and his crowd. Who watches kiddie TV or runs to movies about drug rehab? But Billy didn't see any downsides to knowing someone from Hollywood. He expected the boy might even appreciate being rescued from the wrinkled ranch wives upstairs wanting selfies.

And the girl was luscious. She'd arrived with his best bud Tyler Tribble, possibly a new girlfriend, though Tyler was *real* picky. He'd not talked about this one before. So, naturally, Billy was curious.

Come to think of it, hadn't Tyler also mentioned inviting Alex Harp to the party yesterday—same day Nikki had the idea? He bet the cute girl had something to do with that.

❄ ❄ ❄

ALEX HARP SPOTTED Billy approaching him from yards away. The older crowd in the main house—cattlemen, oilmen, and selected local artists invited by Nikki Lamb—parted ahead of the birthday boy, slapping him on the back like a football hero. "The eyes of Texas are upon him," whispered an elegantly tailored woman standing behind Alex and squeezing his elbow.

"Alex Harp?" the ranch heir said, extending a hand that felt hard and calloused. "I'm Billy McCann."

Alex noted slightly bowed legs, but the dark-haired guy was presentable enough. Nikki Lamb, standing with her husband William beneath the image of a colossal longhorn, watched the encounter. Alex thought she looked happier than the rancher.

"Good to know ya," Alex said, hunching his shoulders. Phones flashed around them. "This is embarrassing."

"Yeah. I figured that. Sorry. Come meet my real crew in the pool house. Less glitter, but we're havin' a better time."

"Cool."

Shuffling across the living area, shaking any hands offered under the crystal chandeliers, Alex spotted his sister. She was with Beatrice Shoot on a walkway above and both women looked uneasy. Clayton wasn't with them.

"You know, your sister—she was my teacher last spring at Sul Ross?" Billy said, following Alex's eyes, and directing him through a door and then down some stairs. Alex noticed an elevator.

"Claire told me."

"Never mentioned a famous brother then."

"No cause to. The buzz didn't start till late spring."

"Haven't seen your TV show . . . or movies," Billy admitted.

"I sure saw your ranch driving here."

"You know about that?"

Alex nodded and smiled. "Cool as shit."

"We'll get along."

Billy flashed a smile that Alex guessed won him plenty of girls. He might learn something from this young cattleman.

⋇ ⋇ ⋇

IN THE DIM light, she didn't think Alex would notice her right away. It's what Piper wanted. With just underwater LEDs on in the pool house, reflections bounced between glass walls and the water's surface. Two couples were skinny dipping in the deep end. Nobody paid them any attention, pretty as they were.

Piper's heart skipped when she finally spotted Alex, smiling at partiers dancing to country tunes. Most were deep into the bottle, or whatever. She was staying sober. Alex was in western duds, no doubt picked up recently. She was sure he hadn't packed any.

Others were taking notice now, gathering around, shaking his hand as he stood there with Billy—who Tyler introduced her to just an hour earlier. She guessed these party guests knew very little about Alex and much less, if anything, about her. She'd changed her hair and darkened her makeup before coming to the event so she didn't stand out.

Needn't have bothered. If she wore a sign around her neck that read "Piper Robinet," these cowboys would still say *who?* Which suited her fine. Tonight, she didn't want to be recognized, especially if the sheriff was nosing about.

Not that she went unnoticed. Billy Lamb sure paid attention. He played it humble when they first met, said he was Tyler's best friend. But she already knew the whole place belonged to him.

And, as it turned out Billy was only too happy to deliver Alex to her. She'd merely hinted the kid might have a better time down by the pool. *Younger people and a hipper band.* But Billy got it. Said he'd find and escort the boy down to the pavilion himself.

Now the challenge for Piper was getting Alex alone. And that took care of itself too—because cowboys and college kids care more about drinking and dancing than chatting up a high school dude. Naturally, the women couldn't keep their eyes off Alex. But hunky boyfriends weren't much into dates staring at other guys. And so, while Alex was not neglected, it wasn't difficult to catch his eye near a glass door and have him follow her outside. If Billy noticed, he didn't interfere. And Tyler understood what she was up to.

"Hello, Alex," Piper said. Almost added *I'm so sorry.* But she saw no reason to surrender right up front.

"I don't like your hair that way," he replied, almost catty. "You all right?"

She pulled him deeper into the shadows.

"I am—really. Better than in a long time."

"Okay."

She sighed, only partially an act. "I was confused about so many things. Stuff you don't know about. I thought this trip would help me sort them out, so I used you to get here. But I guess you figured that out."

Too much all at once.

But she couldn't stop. "I knew *Brainiacs* would be dead once you left. Girls only watch it because of you and boys aren't WetBTE's audience. So my agent suggested a romantic thing between us might help me get the movie part. *Like Liz and Dick*, he said. So when you mentioned going to Texas . . ."

"I figured as much," Alex said. "I didn't mind."

But she bet he did. Piper reached for his hand and he let her take it. She fingered his palm and stared down a dimly lit gravel pathway.

"Do you remember what you said about Tabreetha Bree-Jones, if she got the part?"

"I said a lot about her."

"You griped about making love to an old lady . . . Bree-Jones and I are almost the same age."

Alex looked embarrassed. That wasn't her intention.

"I'm twenty-four, Alex. I'll be twenty-five even before you turn eighteen and you really know nothing about my past. It caught up with me on the rim. All the baggage, bad and good. I *was* attracted to you. How could I not be? And it wasn't just physical."

"I'd been okay with that," he said. No smile though.

"Things are much better for me now," she went on. "That afternoon on the rim—you couldn't know . . . Everything fell apart for me and then came together almost at the same time."

"I'm not following," Alex said.

"What do you want to know? There's so much . . ."

They were moving toward a dimly lit rose garden still in bloom when Alex stopped and turned back toward the pavilion.

"Don't say more than what I can tell the sheriff. I'm staying with him and his family. I'm obliged now to let him know you're really okay."

"You're *staying* with Clayton Shoot?"

"In his dogtrot house."

"What's that? And how . . . ?"

"It's a long story. I just want what's good for you Piper," he said. "I was really worried . . . and angry."

"I know."

"And it wasn't because we didn't . . ."

She tried a smile. "I made you spend the night with Donnie."

"He's a good guy. We searched like hell for you on the rim that night." Alex's eyes softened. "You're so beautiful. I really wanted you."

She didn't doubt that. She pulled him close and kissed him lightly on the cheek. "A woman I talked to this morning said we make the world beautiful by seeing it that way."

"Maybe. But it helps to have something to work with."

"I think the woman recognized me."

"So?"

"She didn't care."

He shrugged. They'd reached the pool.

"I ought to go now," Piper said. "Don't tell the sheriff I was here until I have time to head off. And don't ask me how I got here . . . You'll find the right girl soon, Alex. Maybe you already have."

"Maybe," he said.

"Maybe what?" A smiling Billy Lamb crept up beside Piper and punched Alex lightly on the shoulder. "This guy's a fast mover."

"Billy, I'm leaving now," she said and kissed him on the cheek too. "Thank you for everything and happy birthday."

Billy hugged her. "Tyler's waiting," he whispered in her ear. "He's taking you to my cabin."

⊰⊱ ⊰⊱ ⊰⊱

WHEN PIPER VANISHED into the darkness, Billy tapped Alex on the stomach.

"Let's get you something to drink," he said. "Beer, bourbon, gin—full bar tonight and a decent bartender."

"Maybe one drink."

"You need it, kid—passing up on that."

"Like I had a choice."

Billy looked sympathetic. Pulled a card from his wallet. "Call me if you need anything else while you're here."

Tyler Tribble had just told Billy all about Alex Harp and Piper Robinet.

116

Chapter 20

Regina Summerlin was more composed than the sheriff expected Friday evening. She'd still have to drive to Alpine to identify her mother's body in the presence of the Brewster County Justice of the Peace. Then with the murder case formally in the hands of the FBI, Iris Cobb's remains would be taken to Lubbock for forensic examination. It might be weeks before the artist could be interred.

It fell to Clayton Shoot to handle this preliminary interview with the daughter of the deceased woman. Chief Ranger Furcron was tied up with securing evidence on the Old Maverick Road and the FBI agent assigned to the case— someone out of El Paso named Grimmel—was still in transit. So was the guy Furcron requested from the Park Service's Investigative Services Branch. He was flying in from Arizona.

Clayton had been to the Cobb Institute a time or two before as a deputy on petty matters. The compound lay ten miles south of Alpine on Highway 118 and well more than an hour north of where Iris Cobb was shot. Whatever the legal protocols this Friday evening, Clayton figured the victim's daughter needed support from law enforcement more than anything.

He wasn't feeling too good himself. It was just two nights ago when he and Alex Harp talked about Iris Cobb's pen and ink drawing in his cabin. Clayton realized he had an emotional stake in solving this crime.

Ms. Summerlin agreed to meet the sheriff in her mother's studio on the compound, the only building brightly illuminated when he and Deputy Rangel pulled up separately. If the FBI and park service were responsible for whatever happened in the park, the theft of any paintings in Brewster County itself would be their business. So, while Clayton talked with Regina, Deputy Rangel could examine the site of the alleged robbery—presumably wherever Iris Cobb stored her paintings or prepared them for shipment. The kid at least was in uniform. The sheriff felt conspicuous in party clothes.

They were greeted at the studio door by Aurora Mendez, a local painter who'd driven in from Marathon, nearly forty miles away to support her friend and fellow artist. Clayton remembered Aurora well from high school—she'd been sweet on him then. They hugged briefly.

"So good of you to come, Clayton. Gina's making coffee. She's hanging in there."

Clayton introduced Deputy Rangel and then Aurora ushered them into the studio and briefly explained the Cobb Institute's programs, seminars, and artist-in-residence fellowships. No one held one currently.

"Gina's a painter too, like her mother," Aurora added, "but her primary job is managing all this. The Cobb's become one of the most respected centers for traditional western art in the country."

"Like Marfa, huh?" Alonso said.

Aurora almost smiled. "The Cobb is for artists and clients who don't *get* Marfa." But that was already obvious from the realistic images of wild and domestic animals, rural landscapes, and even portraits of a few people Clayton recognized on its walls. The studio was spacious and well lit, cluttered with canvases, brushes, rags, scrapers—exactly what the sheriff expected. A beamed ceiling made the place feel airy, and during the day, tall windows would flood it with natural light. Several paintings and sketches in various stages of completion were on easels.

"Awesome," Rangel said and Aurora seemed proud.

Clayton assumed the dark-haired woman entering the studio from a small kitchenette near the back was Regina Summerlin. Clayton had never met her, or didn't remember her if he had. She carried a tray with a carafe, four cups, and the necessary milk, cream, sugar, and spoons.

"I've left this area and Iris's private gallery untouched since I noticed the missing paintings," Gina said quietly. "But that seems irrelevant now with her dead." She placed the tray on an expensive wooden table surrounded by comfortable chairs and offered her hand to Clayton. "I guess we haven't formally met before, Sheriff." She just nodded to Rangel.

Her hand felt firm but cold. Gina sure didn't resemble her tall, silver-haired mother—at least the woman Clayton remembered back from the time she'd drawn his portrait. Or more recently when he'd see her at civic events or even the occasional rodeo. Iris stole your attention the minute she strode in, steely gray eyes taking everyone else's measure.

But Gina's brown eyes were alert too, cheek bones taut, lips thin and expressive. More formidable that pretty, he decided, but handsome enough. She was in scuffed jeans and a paint-spattered shirt. Colors on her well-worn boots too. Clayton wouldn't keep her long, though she seemed composed and willing to talk.

"I spent all day on that trail above Fort Davis working," she said when she saw Alonso eyeing her clothes. "Haven't bothered to change."

The sheriff knew the hike well, a short but taxing ascent into and across cliffs and pinnacles high above a nineteenth-century military outpost once manned by Buffalo Soldiers. You could see almost to Marfa and Alpine from its best viewpoints, and, farther along, the trail crossed into the Davis Mountains State Park. Nothing but fond memories for Clayton out there, a few involving girls.

"Both you and your mother were painting today then?" he asked.

"In different directions. We'd just closed a seminar on Wednesday and were eager to be out on our own. I figured she'd head south to do plein air pieces in the park or maybe Terlingua. She'd just taken up that style the last several years. But I didn't know exactly where she'd be. We both preferred to paint alone of course—like most artists."

"*Plein air?*"

"It means painting outdoors, away from a studio and usually in one session. That's the only work I've ever done. Iris was a studio artist most of her life, using models or photographs or a combination of both, and then working and reworking those pieces."

Clayton recalled two days of standing in a barn with his horse. Iris asking him about ranching and riding and girlfriends.

"So when you returned from Fort Davis—what time was that?"

"A little before five."

"That's somewhat before you called my office. What made you concerned?"

"Because she'd been gone so long. Iris was off the property before I was today and still out there maybe ten hours later. She never did that. She had her routines. Be home in time for tea in the afternoon. Feed the dogs. Always. I told your officer that on the phone."

"That's me," Alonso chimed in.

"I'd probably have waited longer, but then I walked here to the studio just to be sure she hadn't returned. I looked into the storage vault."

"Where's that?"

"Let me show you." Gina led them across the cluttered studio and unlocked a tightly sealed door neither man had noticed on a side wall, revealing a very large and windowless room lined with rows of wooden boxes large enough to store paintings without them touching. A light came on when the door opened.

"The vault is climate controlled and fireproofed to protect the art." Gina pointed to a large empty box just inside the door. "I noticed immediately that five or six of her recent works were gone. I'd inventoried them only a day, maybe two, before. Iris wasn't very good about such details, so numbering and identifying paintings fell to me. They were some of the most brilliant pieces she'd ever done. And they are gone and so is Mateo Bottaio, our associate and my assistant manager."

Gina spoke with the rhythm of an old typewriter. Clayton recalled them from movies. She put strong pauses between her sentences. Expected you to pay attention.

"Has this room been locked since you noticed the theft?" Alonso asked, pulling on gloves for a preliminary look inside. More serious forensic work would follow in the morning, possibly by the FBI.

Gina nodded, looking nervous.

"We'll need to fingerprint you."

"An officer in Alpine said they'd do that when I identify Iris's body. This room was unlocked when I first checked. I locked it only afterward. But Iris almost always kept it open. She never worried about theft."

"But she has the combination and you do too? Anyone else?"

Clayton noted Summerlin's hesitation. "Mateo knows it. He moves items to and from storage and handles some of our shipping. Keeps his own work here too. He's a photographer."

"You mentioned an inventory?"

"I can give you a printout. All of Iris's art is named and photographed—something Mateo handles now—and then I assign a unique number. Iris usually just penciled a title on the back of the frame or canvas and I took care of logging it all in. With paintings as valuable as hers, we must be able to authenticate them for galleries."

Alonso smiled. "Makes our job easier." He pulled out a camera from a case he brought along and stepped into the vault. "I'll make this quick."

Clayton, Aurora, and Gina returned to the studio, the sheriff checking his watch to signal respect for Ms. Summerlin's long day (and his own).

"An FBI agent—her name is Randi Grimmel—will likely talk to you tomorrow in more detail about your mother's death," Clayton explained to Summerlin. "There might be a special agent from the Park Service with her too," Clayton added. "But if you don't mind, I'd like to ask a few questions relating to the missing paintings."

"Go on, Sheriff. I doubt I'll sleep much tonight and I still have to go to Alpine."

"I'll see Deputy Rangel gets you there and back."

"I appreciate that."

They gathered around the table again, Aurora offering to make more coffee, but both Gina and Clayton declining.

Gina seemed composed, so Clayton decided to be blunt. "Do you have any concern that Mr. Bottaio may have stolen the missing items? Or that their removal is in some way connected to what happened to your mother?"

Gina was silent for a moment, but then rose to her feet and walked up to a dark window, her faced mirrored in it.

"I don't want to believe that," she said calmly, "I cannot believe that. Mateo owes so much to us both, but especially my mother. He loved working with her and learning how to be an artist from her. He's a gifted photographer already—don't you agree, Aurora? He would never, never, do anything like you're suggesting."

"The paintings were valuable?"

"I explained that to your officer on the phone."

"Remind me."

"A quarter of a million at least," Gina said. Clayton caught the look on Aurora's face. She probably earned more from selling t-shirts at her gallery in Marathon than from her paintings.

Gina turned away from the window. "But who would Mateo sell them to? Especially now, with my mother dead. Sure, they'd be worth even more—much more. But no respectable buyer or gallery would touch them without authentication."

Clayton nodded politely. He guessed plenty of disreputable or overseas collectors would pay dearly for paintings with a notorious pedigree. *Last works of a murdered genius.* Regina read his thoughts.

"I'd stake my reputation on Mateo's good character," she said. She looked to Aurora Mendez for confirmation. "You've met him."

Aurora nodded. "Mateo would do nothing to harm Iris Cobb. Working with Iris and Gina was the golden ticket for him. I know that. He said it every time I saw him."

Aurora's warm endorsement surprised Clayton. "How long has Mateo been here exactly?"

"More than a year," Gina said, sitting down again. "I hired him while Iris was away at our gallery in Taos. She spends a few months there every year."

"And he came from . . . ?"

"Mateo had lots of jobs in lots of places," Gina said, sounding defensive now. "Mostly doing commercial photography or working in galleries. He sold Navajo rugs at Jacob Lake Inn when he was younger and spent time in Page. Very good recommendations from a place in Austin too. I think he was in the Navy, wasn't he Aurora? Or maybe the Coast Guard? Right out of high school."

"Junior college," Aurora said. "But he got a degree eventually at the University of New Mexico."

"We'll get his employment records," Clayton said. "And I guess I'll try to talk with Mr. Bottaio tonight."

Gina shook her head. "He doesn't have a cell phone. Doesn't believe in them."

"Where does he live? He must have a number."

"He lives here at Cobb. He has his own cabin. I checked it before I called you. But he's not there. And his car is gone too. An old blue Volvo station wagon. I don't know the year or plates."

"Easy enough to find out." But the guy was coming into focus, Clayton thought. The FBI would be on him quick.

"Got a photo?"

"On my phone. He's not forty yet, shorter than you, but not by much. Thick black hair, dark eyes."

Clayton sensed Regina was holding something back. "Ms. Summerlin?"

"Mateo has been living with Iris these past several months."

❖   ❖   ❖

NEITHER CLAIRE NOR Beatrice could tell Alex who'd been murdered since they didn't know themselves. But he understood now why the sheriff left Billy's party in such a hurry. And at least he knew the victim wasn't Piper Robinet.

Alex would have preferred to leave the celebration immediately to sort through what Piper had said to him. (He didn't mention her to Claire or Beatrice. Clayton had to know first.)

But to be civil, the three of them stayed until almost 10:30 at the Lamb's, sampling food on the patio and allowing more guests to mingle with the actor. Alex was sure he spoke to every woman in the main house before he departed, some of them twice. He signed their clothes, purses, paper plates, exposed body parts. Eventually, he asked Beatrice to stand behind him to keep his butt from being pinched. *Damn the tight jeans.*

But after appreciative hugs from Nikki Lamb, they eventually made a clutch-grinding departure from the McCann property, sitting three abreast on the front seat of Beatrice's ancient GMC pickup. There was no back seat. Beatrice wrestled with a floor shifter two feet tall, rowing it between Alex's legs. He'd gallantly taken the middle position to save Claire the discomfort.

At Claire's house near the university, Alex realized his sister assumed he'd be moving back in this Friday night—and he wasn't ready for that. For one thing, he needed to talk with the sheriff. Fortunately, Beatrice pointed out that his clothes and gear were in Clayton's cabin. Reading disappointment in Claire's eyes, Alex reminded her that they'd spend all day Sunday on the River Road.

"And you will come again for dinner tomorrow evening too, Claire," Beatrice insisted, sealing Alex's stay at the compound through Saturday too. "I have invited my sisters and brothers-in-laws for the usual Saturday night chicken fried steak and pumpkin pie."

Claire played the good sport, even as Alex pulled out the fob for his Range Rover, still in the driveway next to her Wrangler. He'd arranged with the Legesons earlier that day to extend the lease at his cost. "I'm gonna take it so Beatrice and Clayton don't have to chauffer me anymore."

Clayton returned to his cabin about an hour after Alex settled in. It was very early Saturday morning. Somber and withdrawn and still in party clothes, the sheriff nonetheless seemed relieved to find Alex awake, checking email on the sofa, both dogs asleep at his feet.

'Dude," he said, nodding to the boy like he belonged there, and then dropped into a chair to ease off his boots. The dogs were up instantly and eager to get in the way. "There's Shiner in the fridge," he said.

Alex figured Clayton counted for parental supervision so he opened two.

"Enjoy the party?" Clayton asked. It was a pro forma question. But an opening.

"Yeah. But something happened you should know about."

"Oh?"

"Piper was there. At the pool with Billy and his friends. She arranged to talk with me."

"Did she say much?"

Alex filled him in, slowly realizing how little she'd revealed.

"She didn't tell you how she got to the party? Where she's staying? What she's doing now?"

Alex felt like a dope. Just shook his head.

Clayton grunted. "Dudn't matter. She's an adult. And way past twenty-one." He lifted an eye to catch Alex's reaction.

"I never guessed."

"Claire did."

"Dang."

They drank in silence for several minutes, both studying the label on their beers. Clayton eventually set his on the coffee table and pointed with his chin to the pen and ink drawing on the wall.

"She's dead," he said. "The woman who did that. Murdered this afternoon in the national park."

"I'm sorry," Alex said.

"Me too," Clayton said. "Me too."

Chapter 21

Sheriff Clayton Shoot had met FBI special agents before. Tall, lean men with shiny shoes who'd barely shake hands whenever Artie Paulsen, the former sheriff, steered them to his office. Suits, white shirts, ties—no matter the weather. Somber Yukons and Suburbans in the lot. Conferences going mostly one way: *Here's what we expect from you.* No small talk, especially with underlings.

But this guy—Elliot (call me *Lee*) Perciak, a recent transfer out of Michigan—seemed wholly different. For good reason: he was the special agent from the National Park Services Investigative Services Branch. ISB, not FBI. He'd arrived at the sheriff's department at 9:00 AM Saturday morning in jeans and a denim shirt after a long ride from Midland–Odessa in a Fusion, taking a room at the Holiday Inn Express near the university.

He informed Clayton that Randi Grimmel, the FBI agent out of El Paso, had driven directly to Big Bend. She was the El Paso office's expert on drug operations along the border, relevant because Iris Cobb had been murdered just miles from Santa Elena Canyon on the Rio Grande.

Perciak, however, was intrigued by the disappearance of Iris Cobb's paintings and hoped to touch base with the artist's Alpine connections before maybe heading south to the national park himself. He'd learned about the missing works in a call with Velma Furcron, who'd passed along information that Clayton radioed to Gus Stumpf the previous night. Stumpf herself was back in Alpine now after working the Old Maverick Road crime scene with park officials—happy, Clayton guessed, to be home with her husband and boys. She'd earned her overtime. Probably up real late writing a report too.

Perciak wasn't an outwardly impressive man. He stood much closer to five than six feet and would be hard-pressed to tip a scale at one-forty. Early middle-aged,

Clayton guessed, and drifting toward baldness. Yet nervous energy made him move like a teenager. He seemed genuinely eager to work with Clayton, Gus Stumpf, Alonso Rangel, and other personnel from the sheriff's office on the Cobb murder. However, Alpine's Chief of Police Fiona Tusk passed on this early-morning meeting, likely figuring her boyfriend would fill her in. Clayton was uneasy because Fiona rarely missed a chance to hobnob with feds.

A staff member passed material around the small conference table, the folders including photographs of the crime scene. Perciak then rose to shake Clayton's hand. "The hero out there at the Window Trail," he said. Clayton was impressed. The guy had done homework to know about the episode that practically made Clayton sheriff. Others seemed pleased by the gesture too.

"We do what we have to out here," Clayton said. Then he introduced his people to the special agent who took a moment to explain what exactly the ISB was. Nobody in the room had met someone from the unit before.

"We investigate everything from homicides to drug cases to missing persons in national parks and historic sites. Lots of missing persons," Perciak said. "Understand you just had one of those?"

"Not missing long," Alonso chimed in.

Perciak then summarized what little they knew about the Cobb murder without seeming to take charge. He explained Chief Ranger Furcron's working theory that Iris was in the wrong place at the wrong time.

Clayton frowned. "Crime of opportunity?"

Perciak nodded. "Maybe drug runners crossing Santa Elena Canyon and heading out of the park over that Maverick Road. Or, less likely, migrants heading north."

"Not impossible," Gus Stumpf said. "The Maverick's a graded, four-wheel-drive two track. Patrolled, but not on the ticket for most tourists. Bad guys see an old lady out there with a Cadillac? Easy target."

"For robbery, sure," Alonso said. "But murder? And who'd cross the river at the canyon with all the tourists there?"

"Use them as cover, maybe?" Perciak countered.

Alonso shrugged, but the ISB agent's tone impressed him. He wasn't treating Alonso like the rookie he almost was.

Perciak asked what exactly was taken at the crime scene and learned what everyone already knew: Iris's satchel with her wallet, IDs, and credit cards. Summerlin had mentioned her mother was fond of carrying cash too.

"And where exactly was her vehicle and what was in it?" Clayton's question was to Gus, the only one in the room who'd been at Luna's Jacal. The sheriff hadn't found time to review the paperwork yet, already piling up on a case less than twenty-four hours old.

"She parked it right along the road where it widens up in front of the jacal. One of them long-wheelbase Escalades. Art stuff in back like you'd expect. Brushes, rags, paint tubes, water bottles, beach umbrella, folding chair. Big wooden container called a *wet carry box* took up a lot of room. That's where she'd put finished stuff to dry. One of the park people onsite explained it. No paintings inside it though, just blank canvases."

"And the easel?" Clayton and Perciak asked the question simultaneously.

"Just a few yards back from the jacal. Either knocked or blown over. And a canvas on the ground next to it. Just barely started. There's a picture in your folders."

They all paused to look. Cobb's quick sketch focused on the jacal's facade and entryway, with its long, sagging roof pulling up to the base of a towering cliff behind the dwelling. Iris had roughed in a few mesquite bushes in the background.

Gus continued, "She was maybe working when the perp showed up. Maybe he knocked it down during a scuffle or afterward when he left. You can see Iris's paint box on the ground too in the photo."

"Assuming just one perp?"

"No reason to," Gus admitted. "Ground is too graveled and hard to show footprints, at least last night. It was dark already when we got out there and the lights sometimes distort what we'd see better in daylight. But enough wind to scatter surface grit. I wouldn't expect footprints."

"Any thoughts why she was shot in the jacal, beyond the obvious one of getting the crime out of sight?" It was Perciak's query, but everyone was wondering the same thing.

"Might have muffled the shot," Alonso suggested to nods.

"But no one would likely hear anything out there anyway, it's so remote," Gus said. "Not even a pistol shot."

"Or maybe they went in to get out of the sun," Clayton said. "Maybe Iris didn't expect the person following her to kill her."

"And Iris maybe knew her killer?" Alonso added.

Clayton closed his eyes, imagining the scene. "Say a car pulls up. Tourist seems interested in what she was doing. Iris could've just kept on working, while talkin' to them. Then invited them into the jacal to cool off."

"Her YETI was in there. Better place to store it than a car. But it wasn't opened," Gus said.

"No time to," Clayton said. "I'm guessing our killer wasn't in a sociable mood."

"Might have seemed that way though," Perciak suggested.

The group thought that over.

Perciak finally raised an eyebrow and stared at Clayton. "So, what's the likelihood the guy already had four or five Cobb paintings in his station wagon?"

The sheriff nodded. "The missing man. Mateo Bottaio."

"Matthew Cooper," Perciak announced. "His birth name is Matthew Cooper."

Clayton was impressed. "Fake ID?"

"No, the guy changed his name legally, about the time he started selling photos at major galleries, including Iris's in Taos. Probably hoped *Mateo* would sell more prints than *Matt*."

"You figured this out over night?"

"Not hard, given FBI databases we can access." Perciak flipped through notes in front of him. "Too early to say if the guy is a murder suspect. But we need an interview asap. Trouble is he could be anywhere by now—halfway to California or Florida. There's an APB out on his Volvo. A 1998 V70. Pretty rare vehicle."

"Regina Summerlin said she hired Mateo," Clayton said, figuring Perciak had read his report from the previous evening. "Her mother was in a relationship with the guy."

Perciak winced. "Regina is Iris Cobb's daughter—she'd be about the age of the photographer?"

"Right. Cobb's husband Jock Summerlin died a good many years ago, leaving her the girl from his previous marriage. Seems Regina's birth mother died in a light plane crash. And Jock had an embolism in his brain."

"Wow."

"For what it's worth, Gina Summerlin's convinced this Mateo guy had nothing to do with the missing paintings or what happened to Iris Cobb."

"I gotta get these relationships straight," Perciak said, biting his lip. "And look into Iris Cobb's will too. Rich woman like her is sure to have one." No one disagreed. "But let's say this isn't a crime of opportunity or isn't connected to the disappearance of the paintings. What else is on the table?"

Clayton frowned. "If Fiona Tusk was here—Alpine's Chief of Police—she'd mention that Iris Cobb wasn't real popular in our community."

Gus nodded and the sheriff encouraged her to speak. Clayton's captain faced Perciak squarely. "You should talk with the Nixons. Ella and Barney. They run a news site down here everybody reads called *Big Bend Mercury*. All last year, they covered an oil pipeline story. Most people against building it in this county, but Iris sure wasn't and so the Nixons interviewed her and she got lots of pushback. Same with frackin'. Iris even published an op-ed in the weekly paper supporting it.

"Not a fan of immigrants neither, though she'd have more allies there. And she didn't get along with Police Chief Tusk for that matter." Gus turned to Clayton. "Iris was in your corner last spring when you ran against Fiona for sheriff. I heard she even talked to one or two commissioners on your behalf."

That was news to Clayton.

"Wouldn't guess any of these are killin' matters," Gus shrugged. "But you never know with people these days. Iris just had her nose stuck in everything."

It was evident Gus preferred people who kept opinions to themselves.

Perciak smiled but appreciated the insights. "There's business issues here too," he said. "Ms. Cobb's gallery in Taos for one. Prime real estate and highly profitable. And her net worth is huge because of how she's marketed her brand. Upscale stores around the country sell Iris Cobb custom greeting cards and pottery and such. Everything from jewelry to tableware with her name on it."

Clayton sat back in his chair. "I guess we knew she was even bigger than Alpine," he said, thinking about all her acreage in Brewster County.

"And she's got land investments in the Permian Basin too. Fracking *has* been good to her." Perciak glanced around the table, almost apologetic. "I got most of that info from Randi Grimmel—the FBI agent."

"So, *cui bono?*" Clayton said.

Perciak laughed. "Not words I expected down here. But, yeah, who benefits from her death?"

"Who doesn't?" Gus frowned.

⇜ ⇜ ⇜

"WOMEN'S TROUBLE," WAS Fiona Tusk's reply to Clayton Shoot's inquiry about her health. *Words that silence any man.* The blond young sheriff with the boyish cowlick settled uncomfortably into a chair in her office following the meeting he'd just had with Elliot Perciak of the park service. *Investigative Services Branch special agent.* Whatever that was, Fiona sniffed.

Without any good reason, she found herself resenting Clayton Shoot this Saturday morning too. Sure, he'd invited her to the meeting, but what would she do there? Probably throw up on the table. Her city police had little stake in Cobb's murder. It happened beyond city limits. Just like they had no hand in the recent fire in Jeff Davis County that nearly killed Ella and Barney Nixon. (Clayton didn't belong there either, but he showed up anyway and got glowing coverage in the *Mercury*.)

Or that recent business at Big Bend National Park with the lost actress? Fiona's department spent two nights chasing teenaged girls in Alpine's streets screaming for Claire Harp's little brother. And, naturally, Fiona hadn't been invited to Billy Lamb Jr.'s birthday blowout at the McCann Ranch last night either just because she'd falsely accused the lad of a murder last spring. *Petty of them.*

She had every right to feel sorry for herself this morning.

Except Fiona was beyond all that. Because, for months now, *a twenty-three-year-old man curled her toes almost every night.* That's what she felt like saying to Sheriff Shoot.

But instead she nodded patiently beneath her ever-lengthening row of Rotary Club plaques while Clayton summarized what he and ISB agent Perciak discussed. She mostly concurred. "It's ridiculous to think migrants or drug smugglers murdered Iris Cobb," she said. "They'd want to slip into the country unseen. Why attract *almost* every arm of the law just for a lousy wallet and paintings they won't be able to sell?"

Clayton didn't disagree. Couldn't, because she was right. "Iris had enemies in this town," she added, "enemies she earned because she was a mean woman who didn't suffer fools gladly." The remark made Fiona flinch because it suddenly reminded her of when the artist called her a *dope*. In public.

She consoled herself by offering the fledgling sheriff her best wisdom. "The photographer is the obvious suspect. *Mateo Bottaio.* Sounds like a gigolo. And the man absconds with a quarter million dollars in artwork on the day the woman he's living with is murdered? Coincidence? I think not. Find him, Clayton. He should be in jail already."

The sheriff nodded.

She sniffed. "And what in heaven was Iris Cobb doing with that youngster in her bed, at her age?"

Her words left Clayton speechless. *Good.*

DEPUTY ALONSO RANGEL liked Mr. Perciak, but wasn't sure the ISB agent was being upfront with the sheriff's office. Or maybe he was as confused as they were—with a murder on his turf, a robbery on theirs, a dead artist in a Lubbock morgue, and her boyfriend on the lam. Alonso didn't know what *on the lam* meant exactly, but guessed it fit this situation.

Clayton had ended the morning's meeting by giving assignments to his small Cobb murder task force. First, though, he made sure to ask Perciak to share any info he got from Border Patrol checkpoints, especially whether their cameras recorded Iris Cobb's Escalade or Mateo Bottaio's Volvo coming or going on Highway 118. And then he added one more vehicle to the list, Gina Summerlin's SUV—which turned out to be a very cool (in Alonso's opinion) Toyota 4Runner TRD. His view of the lady went way up when he learned that.

Gus's task was to interview owners of art galleries in Brewster County to see what their buzz was. Lots of socializing in that assignment and a certain amount of schmoozing, not something Alonso could have handled.

The assignment he got seemed less complicated: drive this Saturday afternoon to Fort Davis National Historic Site and interview anyone who might confirm that Gina Summerlin was there painting when her mother was shot—as she claimed. Clayton got Perciak's okay for this inquiry. It would save the ISB agent a trip on his own to Fort Davis.

Like Big Bend, the old fort from the Indian Wars was a federal park, but *way* smaller. Alonso thought a phone interview might get the info Clayton wanted, but the sheriff preferred one-on-ones. Said they made people more honest.

Alonso sure didn't mind a 30-minute cruise to the tourist spot in Jeff Davis County, familiar as it was. Easy miles and eye-popping horizons separated Alpine from the neighboring town. He particularly liked the spot along Highway 118 where you could look up and see the domes of McDonald Observatory gleaming on the mountaintops. They made Alonso feel important. Not sure why. But it was cool to think important scientists worked there.

The superintendent at Fort Davis had heard about the murder of Iris Cobb and quickly directed Alonso to a handsome middle-aged ranger who'd worked the visitor's desk the day before when Regina Summerlin said she was there. *Ms. Alicia Cortez.* Cortez checked him out and he returned the favor. There was a time when ladies her age were off the radar, but that had changed since Alonso hooked up with Fiona. Not that he was eyeing the ranger seriously because Fiona was all he needed. But his appreciation for women had matured. Even for this female ranger and *despite* her uniform.

Better yet, Ranger Cortez didn't have to examine a database of visitors (if there was one) or study a guest register to answer Alonso's questions. She absolutely remembered the painter arriving bright and early Friday with a portable easel and backpack, all ready to hike the Ridge Trail.

"Got here at 8:30 yesterday morning," Alicia smiled. "Hoped to paint at the first few lookouts, especially the one way above the barracks and parade grounds. Said she'd been here before, but not in the fall. I could tell she had because I didn't need to warn her about all the cactus or how steep the trail was in places."

"Could you describe her?"

"A little younger than me. Healthy looking. Wearing a big floppy hat with straps and sunglasses hanging around her neck. Said her name was, I think, maybe Virginia? Oh. And she worked at the Cobb Institute down south below Alpine."

"Yes, ma'am," he'd said. He showed a photograph of Gina Summerlin.

"That's her, for sure! Plein air painters, they're called. Pass through here pretty often now, though not all climb the trail. I thought they just painted skies. Hold on a minute."

The sociable ranger paused to check in a pair of visitors with senior passes, handing them maps and a brochure.

"I remember the woman so well because she came on back through here again just as I was getting off duty."

"What time was that?"

"Maybe 4:00 PM or later? Undid her backpack to show me what she'd done. Had three small paintings in a box—real nice. One of an unrestored ruin, just the foundation left. Two others from up on the trail. Very colorful. I remember saying I was surprised she found prickly pear in bloom this time of the year because one painting showed a couple big plants on the trail. Well, she told me it's easier to sell paintings with cactus in bloom rather than not. I thought that was *so* smart."

"So, she definitely left here after 4:00?"

"Yes," the park ranger smiled. "Like I say, I was just about to go off duty myself. Deputy Rangel, is it?" Glancing at his badge and ring finger.

No ring.

She smiled even more.

Chapter 22

Gus Stumpf had figured on spending maybe two days talking with artists at the dozen galleries in Alpine alone, and then doing the same in Marathon, Terlingua, Lajitas, maybe even Sanderson and Presidio. She didn't feel better when Clayton told her to skip Marfa because the art there didn't look like anything Iris Cobb painted. *Just boxes and rocks and crushed cars*, he said.

Gus would have enjoyed crushed cars.

But two tiring days of official interviews got compressed to less than two hours in a dress, mostly because Clayton showed some sense. Right after their morning meeting with the undersized ISB special agent, Clayton took a call from his girlfriend Claire Harp. Turns out, Claire had been invited by her friend Aurora Mendez to a hasty gathering of local artists at the Cobb Institute to memorialize its dead founder this Saturday afternoon. Claire thought Clayton should know. The gesture would get the artists inside the Cobb Institute where they could spend an afternoon drinking and gossiping about dead Iris, a woman they didn't much like. And they could console Gina Summerlin, with whom they had more in common.

Clayton considered the gathering a bad idea at first since the Cobb Institute was a potential crime scene—those missing paintings and all. But Gus persuaded him that alcohol among friends might free up tongues. (Clayton couldn't attend the memorial because he was the sheriff and a man, and Gus was neither.) So, the sheriff finagled an invitation to the event for Gus from Aurora—who the sheriff knew from high school.

Perfect. Gus could now meet people she needed to interview in one place instead of a dozen—with follow-ups as needed. Just as important, she already knew many of the folks who'd be attending. And talking is what Gus did best.

Clayton advised Gus to dress appropriately and, when she asked what that meant, he shrugged his big shoulders. *Like an artiste?* he said. *You'll fit in fine.* Gus thought maybe she wouldn't, but no one would care.

⊸·⊱　⊸·⊱　⊸·⊱

CLAIRE FELT OUT of place entering the Cobb Institute grounds mid-afternoon on Saturday, where she'd never been before. But Aurora Mendez insisted she belonged with this group of West Texas painters, sculptors, photographers, printmakers, even a few musicians.

"You'll get so much press when *Madrone* is republished we'll be too jealous to ask you back. You'll be like Iris Cobb, an artist big enough to ignore us."

"Iris is dead," Claire noted. "And I met her just that one time." Aurora had made the introduction.

Still, Claire agreed to attend the memorial because Clayton believed it would be useful. She even forgave the sheriff for not telling her about Iris's murder sooner the previous night. But why should he? She didn't know the woman except very secondhand. *Oh*—and from a certain pen and ink sketch in Clayton's cabin she'd seen.

Claire arrived at the Cobb promptly at 3:00 PM and found parking hard to find, a rare concern in West Texas. Inside an impressive adobe building, she made her way to an austere gallery very much in the minimalist style—white walls, plain furniture, cold floors. Claire knew that Iris Cobb herself was a down-to-earth Texan fond of the horses, cattle, and rugged men she painted so realistically. So it seemed odd that the Cobb Institute, at least this part of it, felt as detached from the region as the Judd Foundation in Marfa. Except that these plain walls were full of Iris's dazzling art. And several lesser pieces by her daughter.

The salon was already crowded with talkative women and a few quiet men from the local Arts Council. It didn't take Claire long to realize they identified far more with Gina Summerlin than Iris—even if she lacked her mother's genius. Like many of them, Gina doggedly pursued an artistic calling in a corner of the world where ranchers and oilmen mattered far more.

Claire felt better about her assignment when she learned Augusta Stumpf would be there too, mingling with guests. Because Gus was in civilian dress, Claire didn't notice her at first. But, with heavy red lipstick and a fifties-style do, Gus fit right in, looking positively counter-culture. Clayton's captain moved easily from group to group.

Claire wasn't as good at small talk, especially when surrounded by such remarkable art. But she was happy to sip wine, gaze at paintings, and keep her eyes and ears open.

The gallery was a collection of pieces Iris Cobb evidently loved too much to sell. Claire soon found herself staring at a striking unframed painting that still looked wet, admiring how Cobb had turned a run-down two-story shack into a study of desert colors and textures. You could almost smell dry wood and hot stone. Claire pulled out her phone and photographed the piece, suspecting she might be breaking protocol for both a gallery and memorial service.

"It's called *Terlingua Townhouse*," a voice from behind Claire whispered. "Iris wrote that in pencil on the back." It was Regina Summerlin, somber in a simple gray dress with a touch of red on the collar. *Designer piece?* Claire wondered.

"It's barely dry," Claire said and introduced herself.

"I know who you are," Gina replied. "Thank you for coming this afternoon, Claire." She touched the side of the painting, almost caressing it. "You're right to photograph this. It's likely the last piece Iris finished. Not even signed yet—and it represents a new direction to her work, focusing on ruins now, not just natural scenery. I think she painted it a week ago in Terlingua Ghost Town, then finished it in the studio here at the Cobb. Iris preferred slow-drying oils, so she could do that."

"It's exceptional," Claire said and meant it.

"Iris was never a pure plein air painter. Made fun of us who thought we could complete a work in one sitting."

"I didn't realize there were conventions . . ."

"Iris always took her own path. Always." Gina suddenly looked cheerless. "That's how she managed all this—I mean the art, the Cobb Institute, our gallery in Taos."

"You must be proud."

"That painting is worth $200,000 now. Perhaps more."

The remark struck Claire as off key, even if Gina seemed on the verge of tears.

"And yet it's all come to an end. Some illegals cross the river and snuff out a life for what little they might find in her purse. It doesn't make sense."

Claire felt uneasy. Was Gina using her to send a message to Clayton? Why else single her out in this crowded room? But that was unfair. Maybe the woman was just grateful Claire had paused to admire a milestone piece by an artist now passed. Claire understood the feeling, given her own project, which involved recovering the words of a dead writer.

"I wish I knew your mother better," Claire said. A safe sentiment.

Gina smiled and leaned in. "She certainly shared your admiration for Clayton Shoot."

Claire hesitated. "I know she sketched him when he was younger."

"And made a copy for herself . . . She had an eye for beautiful men."

Well, that was news, Claire thought. But maybe not something to share with the sheriff.

A change in subject seemed in order. "So plein air was a new style for Iris?"

"Oh, yes. She scorned it for so long and thought I should be more ambitious in my own art—since that's all I did. Plein air. But then she tried it and you see the results. Of course, some of the paintings in this salon are earlier studio pieces. That was her *métier*."

Claire nodded.

"That and those simple designs she drew for pottery and plates and figurines. There's even a line of Iris Cobb holiday cards. And she did design quite a few herself or at least approved what she was shown. Have you ever seen them?"

Claire was oddly grateful when, on the far side of the room, Aurora Mendez tapped a glass to get the group's attention. Gina nodded to Claire and walked slowly toward Aurora who needlessly introduced herself and then delivered a tribute to Iris Cobb, rattling off a list of achievements that began to sound like a corporate report. Her fellow artists admired Aurora's good intentions, if not her eloquence.

Gina thanked Aurora for the tribute and then made much briefer remarks, praising Iris Cobb's commitment to art that ordinary people could understand. As she wound down she was interrupted by a heavy-set woman in a dark polka dot crepe dress waving an empty wine glass.

"We like you Gina because you're one of us. But your mother wasn't. *No, she was not!* She looked down on all of us in this room as amateurs and poseurs. People who did not belong in the same studio she did. You know that yourself. You must have felt that!"

Women standing next to the outspoken artist persuaded her into silence by offering another drink.

But Gina wasn't offended and nodded. She gazed slowly around a room her taller and more stately mother would have dominated.

"I am so grateful to you for coming today. I turned my phone off because of the horrible calls I got yesterday evening—you can imagine what the press is like. So I didn't know what Aurora was up to until a short time ago, organizing this tribute. I didn't expect you'd all be here. Your support means everything to me, now and over all my years as a painter. You helped me develop my craft despite relentless criticism." The last remark was obviously aimed at her mother.

Gina continued. "Let me promise you that things will change. I'm going to open the doors of the Cobb Institute to more artists and craftspeople in this region, from the Rio Grande to the Davis Mountains." Her neighbors and colleagues applauded and they watched as her face suddenly colored and bloomed with delight. But she wasn't looking at them any longer. She was staring at a tall, curly-haired man standing in the open doorway. He looked tired and unkempt.

"Mateo!" she almost screamed.

⇥⇤ ⇥⇤ ⇥⇤

"I MUST TALK with you, Mr. Bottaio," Gus Stumpf barked from back in the salon even before Gina reached him. But she was inaudible above the crowd. And there was no stopping Gina Summerlin, shedding tears, pushing others aside, and then wrapping her arms around Mateo tightly enough to force him to do the same. Too short to land her kisses, she tugged the lapel of his jacket and caressed his unshaven cheeks.

Gus wasn't by any means a psychiatrist, but she sensed the guy wasn't feeling the love Ms. Summerlin was showing. Gus noticed Claire Harp already on the phone, likely to Clayton. That left her to push toward Gina at the entrance of the gallery. Unfortunately, others in the group had the same idea, eager to capture the moment on their phones. Certain to be online in seconds.

"They think you stole her paintings," Gina said in a voice that carried better than Gus's. "Five paintings from the vault."

"That's crazy," Mateo replied, just barely above a whisper. "She told me to deliver them to Taos."

"They think you did it. Killed Iris."

A gasp from the crowd overwhelmed Gus's demand that Mateo say nothing.

137

"Iris is dead and the police are after *me?*" Mateo looked stunned, his voice still lower than Gina's.

"Robbed her and killed her."

"Iris said she'd leave a note. In your office. Didn't you tell them?"

Gus was almost to the front of the room now, behind other guests transfixed by the drama.

"I didn't see it. I haven't checked my office."

"I spoke with the office manager last night . . . tried to call all morning from along the road wherever I could find a phone."

"I haven't spoken with Lydia today . . . I've been so busy with the FBI. Don't even know where my own phone is."

Then Regina grabbed Mateo's arm and pulled him out the gallery door he'd just entered and outside to the grounds, her friends funneling behind. Gus dumped the pumps she'd worn, swearing *never again,* and ran after the couple, barefoot over a graveled walk. It slowed her down.

"Mr. Bottaio, I order you to stop!" had no impact. Gina and Mateo were both younger than Gus. And it occurred to Gus that maybe she didn't look like an officer of the law to Bottaio—though Gina Summerlin surely knew she worked for the sheriff's department. *Or maybe she didn't.*

By the time Gus caught up, the couple had crossed a manicured field and another graveled road, to enter a handsome add-on to what was possibly Gina's residence (leaving a door open behind them—which Gus took as license to enter).

Gina flipped on lights and was at her desk with Mateo, rifling through parcels, mail, and catalogs scattered across its surface. "Here it is, here it is!" she shouted, looking not only at Mateo now, but at the group of witnesses pushing around Gus in the doorway. "Iris's note!"

"Put that down immediately," Gus said with as much authority as she could muster. "That's potential evidence in a felony."

It was as if Gina Summerlin had just noticed Gus. She slowly lowered the piece of personal stationery, covered in thick purple handwriting, and began reading it aloud. "Dear Regina . . . Matthew left late Thursday morning while you were out. He's on a trip to photograph Guadalupe Peak and then on to Taos. I asked him to take some recent oils to our gallery there. He may be gone several days. The staff will be expecting him. Iris." Gina teared up, looking at her friends and the captain. "Her last words to me."

"We'll need to authenticate that," Gus said. But she could see where this was going.

Chapter 23

"**A**nd have you met Sam Vogt yet?" Ella Nixon asked Alex Harp, now seated on the deck of her rental home on Saturday afternoon. The handsome adobe was perched high above other properties in sprawling Alpenglow Estates—a neighborhood carved from a working ranch a dozen miles south of Alpine. The web journalist behind the *Big Bend Mercury* noticed him studying a conspicuous peak in the distance.

"Cathedral Mountain," Ella said.

"Yep," Alex replied. "'Bout what I'd call it."

"Practicing Texan?"

"Yes, ma'am," he admitted, from under the cowboy hat he'd picked up at the Saddlery. She grinned. Ella was cute and cheery, short hair emphasizing every facial expression. Her blind husband at the picnic table stroked a ragged mustache and grunted.

"She dragged me up here for the view, knowing I can't see it. We could have got something way cheaper."

"Don't mind him. He's cranky in his dotage."

"I got just sixteen months on you, old woman." Oddly, Barney Nixon aimed the remark at a second guest, seated with them. Ella had already introduced the distinguished gray-haired man to Alex as Rawdon C. Muckelbauer, professor of theater at Sul Ross State.

"The collaborator on my project these past few months," she explained. The professor wore a yellow bow tie and tweed jacket that rubbed Alex the wrong way. A fussy goatee didn't help.

"People will talk when they hear where we're leasing," Barney Nixon muttered. "*Old hippies living high off the hog . . .*"

"We're journalists, we want them to talk," Ella snapped, then recovered and refocused on Alex. "It was lucky to find this place and on such good terms. Our house burned down Monday evening, you know."

"Yes, ma'am, so I heard," he said. Alex had dodged unpacked suitcases and musty boxes as Ella led him out to the deck. She was careful to keep her two Persian cats indoors.

"Coyotes," she explained.

"Some drive up here," Alex said. But truthfully the Range Rover scooted over the ruts on the climb to their rental.

"And *so* kind of you to come to see us," Ella said for maybe the third time. Clayton warned Alex that the editor of the *Big Bend Mercury* would be charming and he'd found her so throughout the wandering interview. Sweet smile, eyes sparkling. But always prying for news.

"You're staying out with Sheriff Shoot, I hear?" Ella suddenly asked. "Such a good-looking man." Her eyes fell on Muckelbauer when she spoke.

Alex laughed to throw her off. "You know where I'm staying, Mrs. Nixon. And I think you owe my sister an apology for chasing me there."

Ella looked rattled. "We just report the news. Claire flat out told me you were returning to Alpine. I couldn't guess what teenagers might do."

Alex knew that wasn't true. "Doesn't make her feel better."

"I'm sure you're enjoying the Shoot ranch."

"Yes, ma'am." He held his gaze.

"And I *will* apologize to Claire."

He expected she might. "And promise to say nothing about Sam and me until I say it's okay?"

Ella didn't see that coming. "Well . . . if you insist."

"Thank you, ma'am—I do. And to get back to your earlier question, I'll be meeting Sam Vogt tomorrow. We're going off-roading in Big Bend."

That tidbit soothed Ella. "Just the two of you? Such a good way to get to know him."

"My sister Claire is coming. Maybe somebody else."

"The sheriff?"

"Too busy with the Cobb murder. You know about the memorial this afternoon?"

"We have somebody there. She'll text if anything happens—beyond the expected tears."

"Regular crime spree in the county," Barney grunted, stretching his neck. "Three murders in three years. What's this place turning into, eh, Muckelhead?"

The professor ignored him.

"Closer to four," his wife sneered. "Years, not murders."

Alex could see Ella enjoyed correcting Barney. She'd been doing it since he arrived. Probably fought like hell.

"No problem that Sam is gay?"

"No, ma'am. Not sure how that's relevant to off-roading." But Alex wasn't surprised Ella took that angle. "Lots of gay men in Hollywood," he added.

"Ella tells me you're even more fetching than Clayton Shoot," Barney said, picking up his wife's theme and wiggling the lure. Somehow the blind guy was now staring him right in the eye. "She tells me too Clayton blushes whenever he's embarrassed. Are you blushing, Mr. Harp?"

Alex couldn't decide if the old guy was laughing or sneering. Probably both. Ella opened her mouth, but Alex interrupted. "Wouldn't be where I am if I weren't a looker," he said, grinning at Ella.

"Damn," Barney said. "An honest man!"

"And is it true you've been working with Beatrice Shoot on your forthcoming role in *Romeo and Juliet*? Out at their ranch?"

Ella's question was so canned Alex almost looked for a camera.

"She's one hell of a dialect coach," he explained. "Biggest surprise of the trip, except my girlfriend running off."

"Hah," Barney snorted. All the major networks credited the *Mercury* for their coverage of the Piper Robinet escapade.

Ella feigned sympathy, but leaned in for something juicy. "Does what that girl did bother you?"

Alex said nothing. He sure wasn't going to tell her about meeting Piper Robinet at the McCann Ranch party. The Nixons were *not* invited, but likely had plenty of informants there—moneyed ladies courting Ella's good will.

Muckelbauer broke the uncomfortable silence. "You know, Alex, you're not what I expected at all. I've have directed at Sul Ross for decades and encountered screen actors before—lots of them. But meeting someone like you, so young and yet so serious about your craft, is just thrilling."

Almost a come-on, but Alex doubted Muckelbauer was hitting on him—mainly because something was up between the natty professor and Ella Nixon.

He'd put money on it. "Acting's mostly instinct for me," he said. "I got my TV show for singing at a baseball game."

"Not a method actor then," Muckelbauer teased, maybe testing him.

"James Dean made a movie down here, didn't he?"

"And you will too, Alex," Ella added.

Barney rolled his eyes. "Just stay away from the South Rim, hey kid?"

Muckelbauer leaned back in his chair and crossed his arms. "I do know Beatrice Shoot, by the way. She's reviewed Sul Ross productions in the local paper for years. A stern critic but a brilliant woman. She'll be an asset to you."

More ass-kissin' from the Professor.

"Well, you are a delight, Mr. Harp," Ella said, worried what her husband might say next. "I'm so happy we've had this opportunity to meet you, given what Professor Muckelbauer and I have been up to and knowing what your support means to the project. We are *very* grateful. And I must say, were I thirty years younger . . ."

Thirty?" her husband roared, jowls wobbling. "Forty years, my dear. Forty years, I'd guess, before any boy his age would glance at you." Barney was slapping his knee. "Kid, believe me, there *are* advantages to being blind."

Ella glowered.

Chapter 24

By the time Clayton Shoot and ISB Agent Elliot Perciak sat across a desk late Saturday afternoon from Mateo Bottaio—or Matt Cooper as Perciak insisted on calling him—the Cobb murder case was looking more and more like a border incident. Gus was in the room too, embarrassed.

"It was like the Keystone Cops," she said, summarizing events earlier at the Cobb.

Mateo didn't take kindly to the remark. Understandably, Clayton thought. He looked exactly like what he was—a man who'd lost a loved one. Or maybe he was just worn out by a long drive from Taos?

Claire described Mateo as blue-collar handsome when she'd called Clayton from Iris's gallery—the guy did have good features, dark eyes, strong chin. Clayton could maybe see him as a plumber in a commercial?

More important, the tale Mr. Bottaio was telling held up.

They would verify the handwritten note Iris Cobb left on Gina's desk Friday morning. But it looked authentic, even if Clayton didn't understand how Gina could have missed it. She explained that Iris routinely dropped handwritten notes for her to find: Iris disliked texting and had a key to Gina's office.

New to the story, however, was Mateo's road trip to Guadalupe Mountain National Park on Thursday, where he photographed McKittrick Canyon. He claimed he then drove on to Roswell to spend the night with friends before heading to Taos next morning. Perciak looked over to Clayton who nodded. *A plausible itinerary. Easy to corroborate.*

"Receipts?" Clayton asked.

"I threw them aside till I got home." Mateo suddenly brightened. "You could check that easy. Everything from the trip is on the passenger seat or floor—gas receipts, park admission, hotel rooms, all my meals, signed vouchers from the Taos gallery for the artwork."

Gus's phone buzzed and she stepped out of the room to take the call.

"About that car," Perciak said, interrupting the straight-line trip chronology Clayton preferred. "Where is it exactly?"

They'd driven Mateo to the sheriff's office in Alpine in a cruiser, leaving Alonso and two other officers to finish forensics on Iris's gallery and storage room—pointless now, Clayton realized, if Mateo's story held up. But Alonso radioed that he'd not located the Volvo station wagon they knew Mateo owned anywhere on the Cobb property.

"It's at BAM Automotive on 118," Mateo explained. "I took it there Monday to have the engine mounts replaced."

"Wait," Perciak interrupted. "How'd you get to Taos?"

"In one of the Institute's Toyotas. A blue Sequoia. It's in front of the studio where the memorial was held."

Perciak collapsed a little into his chair. Clayton got up to radio Alonso. They'd need to secure that SUV and its receipts.

When the sheriff returned, Mateo resumed his account of the last two days. After Roswell, he said, he stopped briefly in Santa Fe and then headed north to Taos where Iris had her gallery on the plaza.

Gus returned to the room, coughing softly to interrupt. "This is kinda relevant I'm afraid."

The three men stared.

"We just heard from the manager at Cobb's gallery in Taos. She confirms that Mateo Bottaio—she called him Matt Cooper—delivered paintings with serial numbers matching those Iris told them he would deliver. This was yesterday—Friday, October 22." Gus let the information sink in and then continued.

"Matthew arrived just after noon and they even videotaped him unloading the canvases. She said he was popular with the staff and his own photographs sell very well at the gallery. They were enchanted by Iris's new work too." Gus paused. "*Enchanted* was her word."

Gus then fiddled with her phone and brought up a date-stamped video she'd downloaded. She played it. It showed Matthew Cooper and staff members sliding paintings from under the hatch of a big blue SUV and carrying them through the front doors of the gallery. Patrons looked on. It was a celebration.

145

Clayton realized Iris had been shot at almost the same moment. He'd have been happy to say *We're done here*. And offer condolences to this Mateo Bottaio or Matthew Cooper. But there was more to investigate. Perciak concurred.

"A few more questions, if you don't mind, Mr. Cooper?" the ISB agent said quietly to a man looking haggard despite the confirmation of his alibi.

"What more can I tell you about a killing that happened here? We didn't get the news until late last night while we were at dinner—the gallery staff and me. We heard from Lydia Champlain, the office manager at the Cobb. I was drinking then. Not fit to drive back till this morning. I told that to Lydia. She said she'd tell Gina. I guess she didn't."

"Bear with us," Clayton said softly.

Matthew's eyes shifted between the two officers. He folded his hands across his chest.

"You think Gina is involved, don't you? If I didn't kill Iris, maybe she did?"

Perciak spoke before the sheriff could. "I understand Ms. Summerlin hired you?"

"A year and a half ago, yeah. I'd dropped in to visit the Cobb after a day in Marfa and I met Gina Summerlin in the book store. It's a gift shop too. We got to talking about our own work. She's a plein air painter."

Both Perciak and Clayton nodded, now too familiar with the term.

"We got along and she invited me to see Iris's studio. I was honored. Iris was in Taos then for an extended stay, working with the people who do her commercial products—cards, pottery, plates."

The cops nodded again.

"Long story short, I told Gina my work history, showed her my photography online, and she offered me a job. She'd just fired an assistant and hired me on the spot. It was a dream opportunity."

"Where had you been working?"

"At a piss ant gallery in Austin. South Congress district. I figured I'd trade that cutthroat scene for a chance to work at a prestigious art institute. No brainer."

"Other perks?" Perciak asked the question with his head angled just right.

"Gina and I began a relationship, yeah. But it didn't last long. I think I got bored first, but stuck it out . . ."

"Until?"

"Iris Cobb returned. She liked my portfolio and saw I was doing a lot better job than the woman in the position before me. Then she insisted I have my own place. I thought that meant an apartment in Alpine, but she offered a lodge on the Cobb. Where artists-in-residence stay."

"How did Gina Summerlin feel about that?"

"I think she was relieved. I was a disruption. She wasn't used to having a guy around. Clothes on the floor, doors not shut, music too loud—small shit. We actually got along better after I moved out, at least for a couple months."

"Then what happened?"

"Iris."

Clayton sat up. "You and Iris Cobb became . . . ?"

"Not what you think. Mostly platonic."

Perciak didn't like evasions. "How mostly?"

"I'll leave that to you," Bottaio said quietly. "Iris Cobb became my mentor. Motivated me to be a better photographer. She was proud of the recent turn in her own painting. Said real artists never stopped growing and showed me how."

He smiled just a bit. "She thought I should have stuck with Matt Cooper too."

Perciak frowned. "Bottaio was Regina's idea?"

"How'd you know?"

"Just a guess." The special agent did not look sympathetic.

The photographer stared at the table. "Ours was a better relationship than I could have imagined—Iris and me."

"With Gina on the side?" Perciak said. Not exactly a question.

"Gina Summerlin and I still work together to this day. Easy to do with someone compartmentalized like she is. And how could she object if her mother was happy?"

Maybe Cooper believed that, but Clayton had doubts and Cooper noticed. He looked intently at the sheriff.

"Iris Cobb loved men, Sheriff," Matthew said. "The way we are, not the way lots of people these days want us to be."

Clayton thought about the ten-year-old sketch above his sofa. He nodded slowly. Once Iris showed up, Gina Summerlin didn't have a chance.

⇥⇤ ⇥⇤ ⇥⇤

IT WASN'T LIKE Gus Stumpf to be contrary. But after Clayton and the little fed dismissed Matthew Cooper, she realized she'd witnessed what they hadn't—Gina Summerlin's hot-blooded reaction to her former boyfriend's return to the Cobb.

"She's not over him," Gus said to the sheriff and special agent. "She jumped on him when he came through that door. A woman whose mother was killed *yesterday* and her hormones raging like that? She thought she had Mateo back."

Perciak frowned. "Maybe just relieved she'd been proved right? Said all along Cooper had nothing to do with the killing."

Gus wasn't buying it. "When he walked into the gallery, she didn't know where he'd been or what he'd done. Didn't care. She just wanted *him*."

Perciak looked over to Clayton who shrugged. "Gus has a point."

Perciak smiled. "Well, we'll see how happy Ms. Summerlin is when she finds out what's in her mother's will."

The agent was holding information neither Gus nor Clayton had. Gus gave him her *spill the beans* stare and he folded. Just like her boys.

"The FBI showed me a document Iris Cobb amended two months ago. Gina Summerlin still gets the Cobb Institute and *very* healthy cash assets. But the Taos Gallery and 50% of the income from Iris's commercial products go to one Matthew John Cooper."

Gus and Clayton both studied their fingernails.

"Well," Gus Stumpf finally said. "That gives both of 'em a reason to murder Iris. He gets big bucks. She gets big bucks *and* revenge for stealing Mateo."

The men realized she could be right.

"But let me tell you about them artists at that reception Mateo broke up. They sure did plenty of hating on Iris Cobb first. Claimed she was mean-spirited and cruel. Would say horrible things just to make news. Or to make rich folks happy. *Corporate headquarters stuffed with Cobb originals*, I heard one of 'em complain.

"And they sure didn't like what she thought about 'em as artists. They made her the judge for a competition of local painters once. And when it came to announcing the winner, Iris gave the prize to *nobody*. Said nothing she saw showed *any level of distinction*. Her very words. The husband of an artist said somebody should string her up *and* shoot her. That was a couple years ago.

"Still, artists ain't the sort to use fists when they get angry, let alone guns. So who in this county wanted Iris Cobb dead? Maybe everybody. . . and maybe nobody."

Chapter 25

At the Shoots later that Saturday evening, the extended family was well into the Blue Bell Homemade Vanilla before Clayton arrived late from the office, shuffled into the dining room, and assumed his place at the head of the table. Claire had the seat to his right, across from Clayton's mother Anna, who immediately assembled a plate of chicken fried steak for her boy. Green beans and biscuits with cream gravy on the side. Texas comfort food. Claire guessed she'd done it thousands of times before.

Farther down the table, the two married Shoot daughters and spouses were folding their napkins—their noisy children already on their own in the kitchen.

A place would have been reserved for Alex at the opposite end of the spread, but he'd called earlier to cancel. Explained that he'd spent the afternoon in Marfa, met some guys there, and would be dining at tiny Cochineal if they could get Saturday evening reservations. Otherwise, Dairy Queen!

"Teenagers these days," a disheartened Beatrice sighed, sitting in his spot. But Claire knew she'd forgive her brother.

As soon as it was polite, Clayton invited his well-fed family to move into the more comfortable great room, saying he needed to talk with Claire in private while he finished up. He placed a hand over hers to keep Claire at the table. She appreciated the gesture. Beatrice rose reluctantly, warning she'd soon return with coffee.

"Long day?" Claire said when she and Clayton were reasonably alone.

Clayton nodded, wiping gravy from his lips. "Thanks for attending the memorial this afternoon," he mumbled. "Gus Stumpf filled me in. Seems we're back to square one on Iris's killing. Those paintings weren't stolen and Mateo Bottaio is off the hook."

"So he *was* in Taos?" Claire had remained in the Cobb gallery when most of the crowd scurried to Gina's office. Didn't want to be part of that scene. She chatted with several other artists who felt the same way.

"Yep, in Taos when Iris was shot," Clayton nodded. "Seems a decent guy. Real name is Matthew Cooper. Dazed and confused though."

"By Regina Summerlin?"

"You caught that too? Gus Stumpf said the woman went way overboard welcoming him back. Hugs and kisses and all."

"Gina's got to be emotionally fragile. Her mother's dead barely a day."

"The FBI woman thinks Iris's killing was maybe a crime of opportunity after all—though they're not having luck with that angle either. Gossip along the river. Some chatter about drug mules. Nothing solid."

"You think she's right . . . the FBI agent?"

Clayton twisted his shoulders. "I'm probably sayin' too much. Gus did mention bad blood at the memorial. People were there mostly for Gina—not Iris."

Claire let him know what she'd learned on her own about Iris's sorry reputation among local painters.

"That's exactly what we heard," Clayton said.

"But Iris was just as tough on Marfa types. Probably tougher."

"Aluminum boxes and concrete blocks," Clayton sneered.

Claire bristled, not sure why. "I rather like *those* installations."

"I didn't mean nothing . . ."

"You know Iris had followers she didn't even know about on Twitter and Facebook who cheered her when she attacked contemporary art? Especially after appearances on Fox News and *The View*. Some people think Iris liked making enemies." Claire realized she was talking too much.

"Iris was real kind to me," was all he said.

She winced. "Gee. I wonder why?"

He laid down his fork and stared. "You pissed?"

Claire paused, surprised by the response, then nodded. "A little."

Long pause. "Cause of your brother?"

"Where'd that come from?" she said. But he'd nailed it. *And who were these guys Alex was eating with in Marfa tonight? And why'd he blow her off again?*

"I'll make him go back to your place tonight."

"Don't you dare! I'm spending the whole day with Alex tomorrow. And I get why he's happy here. I'm boring and parental." Claire managed a smile. "And I'm glad he likes you."

Clayton pushed his empty plate away and stared at her.

"I'm sorry I can't go off-roading."

"Not your fault."

"Don't do anything crazy."

"Do I have that reputation?"

Clayton stared at Claire, frowned. "We've had some rough months, huh?"

She tried not to tear up. "Too many changes in our lives. So much to do. You're sure Alex isn't in the way?"

"He makes Beatrice happy . . . and me too."

"The brother you never had?"

"Too damn smart for that. He'd have made me jealous."

"My sisters felt that way about me," Claire admitted. "So Alex hasn't crossed any lines . . ."

"I don't know what you mean," Clayton said. Claire thought maybe he did. But it was kind of him to reassure her. She needed to change the subject.

"Piper Robinet," she said. "What's going on with her?"

Clayton scrunched his eyes. "Off the radar. Bigger problems."

"But you know Alex talked with her at Billy's party?"

"He told me."

Probably more than he told her. "And?"

"And what?"

"Aren't you going to investigate? Find out why she did what she did?"

"She seemed happy in that video," he said, "safe and not under duress. Same thing at the party."

"But it would be easy to find out more."

"I don't poke around in private lives."

"Are you implying . . . ?"

Fortunately, Beatrice rolled a cart to the table at that moment with a carafe of coffee, three cups, and all the sides. Claire and Clayton welcomed the interruption. Beatrice served the couple and settled in herself, sitting across from Claire at the table with Clayton between them. *More Downton Abbey than Reata*, Claire thought.

"There is a matter I would like to address," Beatrice began, "given what I have myself heard about Iris Cobb and Regina Summerlin and given what I am certain you have been discussing."

"Beatrice, you have no idea," Clayton said, needling gently.

"You are perhaps unaware that Iris Cobb and I sometimes talked. We were never friends because she was an arrogant and intrusive woman and I do not like that type."

"Who does?" Clayton kept a straight face.

"Yet Iris was a brilliant person who could be honest with people she respected."

"Like you?"

"Indeed."

Claire smiled. *Who says* indeed *these days?*

"You have probably heard that Iris was at the Big Bend Park and other sites recently delving into a painting technique relatively new to her, *plein air?*"

Clayton nodded immediately, expecting the women to be impressed.

"What you may not know is Iris was concerned that adopting the style might upset her daughter Regina, who had long been doing such work. Rather crudely, in Iris's estimation, and I am certain she did not leave that judgment unstated. She could be *quite* tactless."

"I've heard that, Beatrice," Clayton conceded.

"Yet Iris admitted to me recently," Beatrice said, "that she was wrong to feel so and even regretted mocking Regina's choice of technique. Not that Regina's paintings weren't crude, but Iris found the method and style itself admirable. Painting *al fresco* stimulated her genius Iris found and, well, you perhaps have seen the results. Brilliant paintings that command a hundred times what her daughter's scratchings do."

"And you think *what?*" Clayton asked. "That Gina killed her mother because she was jealous?"

"Heavens no, Clayton," Beatrice said, grinning like a Cheshire cat. "But I just thought you should know."

Chapter 26

Prepping early the next morning for the long-anticipated River Road trip, Claire was nonetheless surprised when her doorbell rang at 7:30 AM. Sam said he'd drop by about 8:00 and she'd forwarded that starting time to Alex, who'd been punctual from pre-school.

More surprising is what she found at her door, a young man in his mid-to-late twenties geared up for the expedition and looking like he had stepped out of an outfitter's catalog. Longish brown hair, carefully groomed scruff, roguish eyes, he seemed like a cross between a first-year grad student and a surf park attendant. She expected *dude* to be the first word out of his mouth.

"Donnie Majewski, ma'am," he said instead. Claire thought *native Texan*. He stood on her porch with a ruck sack and emergency medical kit. "Alex told me we'd leave from here?"

Donnie noticed Claire checking the driveway to see where his vehicle might be.

"I got dropped off, ma'am, by a friend headin' to Fort Stockton this morning. I live in Terlingua so I figured to hitch a ride here. At the end of the day, y'all can just leave me off near my place not far from the park entrance or maybe we can have a bite to eat in Terlingua?" He was soften-spoken and polite with a dimpled chin. He politely removed a Tilley hat as he crossed the threshold. Claire was cautious, but cordial.

"Alex didn't mention anyone coming by. How do you know him?"

"We shared a tent at the South Rim the night his girlfriend ran off. I had a single tent and she commandeered that, so I moved in with your brother. I'm one of the guides the movie company hired for the night."

Claire realized she knew the story—just didn't have a name for the fellow. She apologized to Donnie for keeping him standing on the porch and watched him step into her house, distracted by muscular legs beneath khaki shorts. It had been almost a year since she'd been with a guy and she was okay with that, given her relationship with Clayton. But she had eyes and Donnie warranted full attention. Good thing Clayton wouldn't know about him.

"Can I get you coffee? Just brewed a pot."

"That'd be mighty nice," he nodded. She headed into the kitchen watching him settle into the sofa. "Alex told me you have a Rubicon?" he said.

"That's right. Will it be okay for today?"

"Way more than all right. I seen stupid people do the River Road in rental Mustangs. There's only a problem in washes after real heavy rain. I take tourists pretty regular in an old Xterra."

Claire knew what that was. "So, you live down here fulltime?"

"Yes, ma'am. I've been settled in Terlingua two years since college."

"Where'd you go?"

"Texas Tech in Lubbock. Natural resources major."

She nodded. "I went to graduate school at UT-Austin. Now I'm at Sul Ross."

"Alex said you were a writer . . . and quite the looker too." The guide smiled genially, teeth pearly white. Claire rattled the cups as she set them on the coffee table and offered cream and sugar. He took the sugar. She sat next to him.

"And you like it? The work?"

"Oh yes, ma'am. Right now, I'm with a local company, but hoping maybe to set up something of my own in Lajitas, guiding rich folks coming through. More and more of 'em now. I can take 'em on the river or cycling or campin' overnight in the parks. Anything under the sky suits me."

Claire realized she was smiling through his remarks like a schoolgirl.

"Can you have much of a social life out here?"

The question didn't unsettle Donnie. "I manage," he said, brown eyes twinkling.

I bet he does Claire thought, suddenly anticipating an entertaining Sunday. Nothing wrong with flirting. She knew from experience that Clayton did when he stopped women for speeding—at least back when he was a deputy.

Then she thought about Alex and this guy and Piper Robinet on the rim. *Shit.* Was it possible Alex had, well, paid attention to Donnie? And what if Piper, already upset at losing the part in *Romeo and Juliet*, finally had enough? Wanted out of a sham relationship? Hollywood, after all, had its closet. Maybe a clueless trail guide had been the catalyst for some nasty business on the rim?

But surely not . . . she had to snap out of this.

Claire had no time to consider the notion because a rumble outside announced the arrival of her brother in his Range Rover and Sam in a slightly worn two-door Jeep, its roof and doors removed. Claire's introduction of Sam Vogt to her brother pre-empted any immediate decision about what wheels to take.

Alex was aggressively friendly. "Privilege to meet you finally," he said with a wink to the slim towhead, suggesting he knew all about Sam. Her brother always did his homework, that's for sure. "And when Clayton couldn't make it," Alex continued, "I thought to invite a guy I met on the South Rim. Sam, this is Donnie. He's an outfitter in Terlingua."

It was obvious Claire and the outdoorsman had already met.

"Awesome, dude," Donnie said as if meeting a celebrity. "Donnie Majewski. Can't believe how you saved that guy on the Window Trail."

A local *would* know about Sam. But Claire could see how the accolade embarrassed her former student. Still, she caught Sam eyeballing both Donnie and her brother. Handshakes all around and then the guys got serious, silently appraising the off-roaders on the street around her house.

On their own, Claire guessed the boys would have preferred Sam's wide-open Jeep. But its back seat was tight and they'd be covered with grit by the end of the day. They gallantly settled on Claire's four-door Rubicon with its fancy sliding roof. Open air, but shade as needed. The Range Rover was off the table from the start.

They quickly calculated they had ample supplies, mostly because Beatrice sent Alex off with a basket of delights she'd prepared. Fastest way to any man's heart. Sam brought sandwiches, a cooler, and two cases of bottled water. Donnie was sharing Clif bars even before they settled in. And sunscreen. They antici-pated a full day.

Claire drove the opening leg of the trip, more than a hundred paved miles just from Alpine alone, first traveling east to Marathon and then south toward the border, across the less scenic side of the park, mostly low hills and desert scrub. Donnie sat in the passenger seat next to Claire with Sam and Alex in the back. With the roof fully open Claire could catch just snippets of what they said, Alex easing Sam into more conversation than she ever got from him. Before long, the two were passing Texas expressions and pronunciations back and forth, with Sam the instructor. Claire hoped Sam would like her brother and it was obvious the good vibes were mutual.

They had the vast park pretty much to themselves so early on a Sunday morning, only Claire's respect for speed limits slowing the drive. It would take two hours just to reach the turn-off to the River Road proper, including a stop near park headquarters to top off the tank.

Donnie played tour guide for Claire, because that's what he did, calling out features of the arid, sometimes drab, terrain, filling Claire in about the Hallie Stillwell Store when they'd passed a turnoff near the park entrance, and recommending that they save a fossil exhibit for another trip when they had more time. She learned there'd once been mining on this side of the park, with ore transported to Marathon by mule trains and a tramway. Donnie knew his stuff.

The turnoff for the River Road came just ahead of the hot springs, which Donnie described as another spot worth a visit someday. Claire drove until they reached a sign that said *Gravel Pit*, where a short detour led to a campground and then access to the Rio Grande, narrower and more placid than she expected. They spent just a few minutes, Sam passing around bottles of Ozarka in the bright sun. Temperatures were still cool but rising steadily and there was no chance of rain—perfect weather for off-roading.

Donnie pulled out a ballcap for Claire. The others had their own. Sam rotated into the driver's slot, slipping the Jeep into 4-high, and Claire became the front seat passenger, freer now to enjoy the ride. Claire found the route less rugged than she feared and maybe less interesting. On knobby tires that rolled over rocks and plowed through gravel, the Jeep shrugged off what the trail offered. Sam didn't mind stirring up dirt, driving faster than Claire would've, but he slowed wherever scrub or ocotillo threatened her doors with desert pinstripes. When the road flattened, their eyes were drawn to the Chisos Mountains, the entire range contained within the park's boundaries. The Rio Grande remained close just south of the road, but mostly out of sight.

In the back seat, Alex and Donnie celebrated their reunion—less than a week after their moonlight hunt for Piper on the South Rim. They punched and shoved and even grabbed an occasional knee. Just boys being boys, Claire hoped. Donnie ribbed Alex about the few hours they'd shared a tent, arguing that being naked in a sleeping bag—as Donnie had been—bested socks and skivvies, apparently her brother's preferred attire. Passionate disquisitions on sweating, layering, heat transfer, and butt cracks enlivened several miles of creosote and gravel. Claire assumed the point was to embarrass her.

"Real men sleep naked," Donnie concluded.

"Not if'n they still live at home," Sam said quietly, grinning so only Claire could see. The kid was always levelheaded.

"Okay, okay," Alex conceded. "Clayton Shoot sure does."

"The sheriff?" Donnie was surprised. Claire too.

"How the heck?"

"Staying at his cabin. I have to use a bathroom in his bedroom."

"Never seen a naked cop," Donnie said pensively. "No, I take that back."

Alex punched his shoulder.

Sam leaned in and pointed. "There's the Mariscal Mine."

Or what remained of it—a cluster of abandoned stone and metal structures sprawled across a slope excavated decades earlier. The nearest building, reddish in hue, was crumbling, but three towers aligned above and behind it were better preserved—they resembled a Tibetan temple. Workers had mined cinnabar here and then pulled mercury from the ore, a task Claire assumed was hideously dangerous in this remote desert.

Claire wondered whether the laborers—almost certainly Mexicans—ever imagined one day that tourists in shorts and air-conditioned vehicles would stop for lunch at their worksite. And then scramble over what remained of their pits, furnaces, ovens, and even outhouses—which is what her suddenly rowdy companions were doing late this Sunday morning. Claire eventually rounded up Donnie, Sam, and Alex and pointed them west again, with Donnie now at the helm.

Claire slid into the back for the first time, sitting behind the driver and next to Sam—who she realized was as attracted to their travel guide as she was and now had the better view. In the front passenger seat, Alex continued his colloquy with Donnie, this time both more serious about the geography and history of the region. Her brother's curiosity knew no limits.

"Different breed of people out here then," he concluded.

"We still are," Donnie insisted. "But now we gotta deal with professors—and actors." Donnie laughed. More punches thrown and they were at it again. *Buds*, Claire smiled weakly.

The thirty miles of road west of the Mariscal Mine were much rougher than the twenty miles Sam drove. The trail had them reaching for grab handles. Claire admired the outfitter's skill on the hills and dry washes. Lava flows crossed their path too, with gravel and rocks lining the bottom of almost every hill, pulled there by raging waters in gullies now bone dry. She understood how heavy rain might make the road impassable. Donnie was in 4-low now and he occasionally locked the differentials. Claire had never done that.

They encountered few travelers along the road and just one animal bigger than a road runner—a bulky sheep-like creature with magnificent horns.

"An aoudad," Donnie explained. Claire made him spell *aoudad* before she believed him. The creature just stared from a hillside at their odd machine and the weirder creatures inside.

By mid-afternoon, fifty miles of off-roading left Claire and company sore but satisfied. Claire decided the terrain was remarkable more for its isolation than beauty. Yet, as they returned to pavement on the western side of Big Bend, Donnie immediately suggested another off-road route along the western border of the park, one that would save them some miles but not much time on their way to Terlingua. The Old Maverick Road.

It was where Iris Cobb had died just three days ago.

Donnie's idea was irresistible to Alex because he'd also get to see the towering cliffs of Santa Elena Canyon very near the turnout to the road. But Claire wasn't sure. She was the only one in the group with any connection to Iris Cobb.

"It might be closed," she hoped.

Donnie shook his head. "I checked this morning with a ranger."

Exactly what you'd expect from a tour guide.

"Luna's Jacal and the area around it are off limits—where they found that woman's body," he said. "But the road is open."

Claire shrugged, uncomfortable, but not enough to spoil the guys' afternoon.

Chapter 27

Clayton Shoot drove away discouraged from a hastily scheduled Sunday afternoon meeting at Big Bend National Park with Special Agents Perciak and Grimmel and Chief Ranger Furcron. Gus Stumpf in the passenger seat of the Durango and Alonso Rangel in the back shared his sour mood. The Cobb investigation was generating little more than paperwork—though plenty of that.

Clayton, at least, had finally met Velma Furcron face-to-face, a handsome African-American woman in her early forties, with hair that curved delicately around her neck. And warm, soft eyes. He liked her. If he could work it out, he'd make sure her daughters met Alex Harp—*Charlie* to them, Furcron explained.

Agent Randi Grimmel? Just the opposite. Short blonde hair, eyes like daggers. All business all the time. She'd look forty her entire career. Probably end up running the FBI. He noticed that Gus Stumpf's homey truisms were like nails dragged across a chalkboard to Grimmel, though she smiled a time or two at Alonso. (Clayton almost wished Fiona Tusk had seen that.) Lots of eye contact between Perciak and Grimmel too. Opposites attracting?

Perciak ran the meeting, but Grimmel was the more assertive—a woman impatient with Texas drawls. She did good work though. She'd already verified a spike in prices for Cobb's paintings since the artist's death. As a result, the Taos gallery was currently closed more to reappraise its inventory than to honor Cobb. Cobb had been prolific and the new gallery owner—Matthew Cooper, if Iris's will held—was growing richer by the day. Clayton expected the feds to talk with him again soon, though the guy had no control over market values. Gina Summerlin might have claims on the fast-appreciating works too, depending on how the will was written. And there could be as many Cobb paintings, drawings, and sketches in the Cobb's vault in Alpine as in Taos.

Representatives of the Border Patrol and DEA at the table on Sunday remained skeptical about immigrant involvement in the killing. They restated what they'd argued before: the crime's intent was petty theft, its consequences catastrophic, takings trivial. Border criminals might hijack an Escalade and run the vehicle across the border into Ojinaga. Such things happened.

But to kill an old woman for her purse and wallet? Just stupid. In any case, there was no activity on her credit cards, no hijacking of her identity. And thieves didn't usually wait. Not much buzz up and down the border about the crime either. Just fears that surveillance would get even tighter if someone from the *other side of the river* killed Cobb.

Clayton raised the issue Gus Stumpf had been pursuing, the intense dislike for Iris Cobb among local artists and political activists. Perciak, Grimmel, and even Furcron seemed ready to take that angle more seriously now.

"We'll be talking to painters and gallery owners ourselves—including everyone at that memorial yesterday," Grimmel insisted, the *we* being feds. Clayton guessed Claire might be included in that group too and wondered how she'd feel about it. But she'd dealt with cops (and lawyers) last spring and could be tough as nails. He liked that. In any case, her connections with Iris Cobb and Gina Summerlin were minimal.

Perciak and Grimmel also intended to quiz local journalists and, Clayton guessed, a host of political activists and oil and gas lobbyists. His people would be pushed to the sidelines now, he assumed, and that was fine. They'd be available if serious suspects emerged. But that's also when the feds would likely clam up and solve the crime on their own. Or maybe not. Perciak at least seemed like an upfront guy.

"So we sit on our asses until needed?" Alonso said from the backseat. Gus seemed resigned to that role already.

"Not exactly," Clayton's eyes were fixed on Highway 118. "Let the feds do what they're good at. We can track what they miss."

Gus frowned. "Okay," she said. "So, what *are* we good at?"

"Looking for holes. *Cui bono?*"

Gus rolled her eyes, but Alonso got it. "Gina and Mateo. They're both getting rich."

Clayton nodded. "And right now, who do we think *couldn't* have killed Iris?"

Gus's turn. "Gina and Mateo."

"Yep. So who do we investigate?"

Clayton paused for a reply that didn't come. He sighed. "We reexamine what we *think* is settled. Study all those travel receipts Matthew Cooper came up with, check the people who claim they saw him on the road, analyze that video from the gallery in Taos. Could our curly-headed photographer have faked such stuff—maybe with Gina's help? They were lovers once. Might they still be in cahoots?"

"But Gus says Cooper didn't seem that into Gina at the memorial yesterday," Alonso objected.

"And how hard would that be to fake?"

The deputy saw what Clayton was driving at, even if he wasn't convinced. "But Gina's story is solid. She was in Fort Davis when Iris was shot. We know when she got there, when she left, even what she painted."

"Right," Clayton said, "Cactus blooming out of season."

"Huh?" Now Gus was confused.

Clayton nodded to Alonso to explain.

"The ranger at the desk wondered why one of Gina's paintings showed prickly pears in bloom this time of the year. Gina said buyers like them that way."

"Makes sense," Gus nodded. "What's wrong with that, Sheriff?"

"Nothin'. I'm not saying Gina's lying. But we can't take anything at face value."

"Still don't get it."

Alonso smacked his forehead. "What if she didn't paint it that day?"

"Well, there's a thought," Gus said. "How could we tell?"

"Let's not get ahead of ourselves either," Clayton said. "We just gotta worry every detail—like a kid with a loose tooth. Think of Gina and Matthew acting maybe separate or maybe together. And reassess their motives. For instance, why would a woman kill her mother for an inheritance she'd get eventually?"

Alonso coughed.

"What?"

"Stepmother," Alonso said. "Gina's biological mother died not long after she was born. Her father Jacob Summerlin married Iris Cobb about when Gina started kindergarten."

Clayton nodded. "Good reminder."

"And that explains why they didn't look alike," Gus added. "But if someone raised you all your life, she's your mother. You wouldn't remember any other, would you?"

Clayton didn't reply—with four kids, Gus would prefer to believe that.

Instead, he put another issue on the table. "Claire told me the two women had different ideas about art. Maybe they went head-to-head over intellectual stuff?"

"Maybe," Gus said without enthusiasm. "But Gina was still in Iris's will, whatever their differences."

"But her share got halved when Mateo came along," Alonso said.

"So, she waited too long. Should have killed Iris earlier."

"Maybe," Alonso frowned. "Or Iris might of split up with Mr. Cooper eventually and given everything back to her stepdaughter."

"Or married the guy and taken even more away from Gina," Gus countered, turning to Clayton. "You think the feds will follow up on all this?"

"I'm not sure I can follow it now," the sheriff laughed. "But my point is we don't have to wait. Better to go all-in upfront than stretching out the investigation. Chili Festival is just around the corner." The annual Terlingua celebration early in November routinely strained their resources. Participants these days were less rowdy and naked than in the past, but they'd grown in number. Just as much trouble as ever.

Clayton slowed at the border checkpoint. They were waved through. Nearly back in Alpine.

"And there's that too," Clayton added. "Checkpoint cameras support both their alibis. Mateo left for Taos Thursday morning in a car that belonged to Cobb and he returned Saturday afternoon. No other recent sightings except taking his Volvo to Bam Motors—I forget exactly when but earlier in the week.

"Same with Gina. They caught her truck heading to Fort Davis early Friday morning just like she claimed and she doesn't appear on camera again on Highway 118 until late Friday afternoon, well after Iris was killed. Border Patrol validated those times. She was in Fort Davis all day."

"We got our work cut out," Gus said to Alonso in the back seat.

"I'm up for it," he responded.

"Bet Fiona hears that a lot," Gus laughed and watched Clayton's ears turn red.

Chapter 28

Because Donnie made such good time off-roading, Claire and her crew could pause at Santa Elena Canyon and view it from atop a steep trail on the American side of the river. Thousand-foot cliffs funneled the Rio Grande toward a flat and sandy shore, populated by more tourists than they'd seen all day, many wading into the cold and muddy water. Donnie confirmed Claire's guess that he sometimes led rafting tours down the canyon, pushing off, he said, at Lajitas Crossing some miles west of the park. The river looked wider here than where they viewed it earlier at the Gravel Pit campgrounds. But it was far from an intimidating barrier.

Conveniently, the turnoff to the Old Maverick Road began just about where the pavement ended at the canyon turn-off. Alex took the wheel and Donnie assured him that the fourteen miles to the ranger station at the park exit would take far less than the hour tour books claimed—unless he drove like a grandma. Sam sensibly pointed out that law enforcement might be around, working the murder site about half-way up the road.

Still, the Maverick was flatter and more recently scraped than the River Road, its creosote flats, dry washes, and low hills familiar terrain to them by then. Stands of yucca added character. As for road hazards, the washboard surface was rough in places and recent rains had hollowed out ruts and moved boulders. But Claire's Jeep might as well have been on an interstate.

With Sam now in the passenger seat, Claire overheard Alex questioning him about his closest friend Mote McCrary, author of the book Claire was editing. Sam was more forthcoming than usual, describing trails they'd shared and nights under moonless skies. He spoke frankly too about the harrowing events at the end of the Window Trail that had made him famous. Donnie chimed in, as knowledgeable as any local about a murder that made national news only months earlier. Being guys, they pretty much now ignored the mildly freckled girl in the back seat who'd been in the thick of the case herself. Sam got all the questions and, for once, seemed eager to talk.

Claire couldn't decide whether to be amused or miffed. Sam and Donnie were almost the same age, and Alex—if a tad younger and much richer—was still one of the *boys*. Was Claire just an older lady to them and a school teacher to boot? Over the long day, even Donnie Majewski's courtesy from the morning (tour guides like him must deal with mature folks all the time) had become merely dutiful.

Or maybe he didn't find her as attractive as she did him?

Donnie and Alex of course had shared an adventure on the South Rim. And Sam had all of Donnie's passion for the Big Bend region. How could she compete? Couldn't begrudge Sam for finding Donnie appealing either. *And maybe more was going on?*

Their mood sobered when they spotted two white SUVs and plenty of bright yellow barricade tape just where they expected, roughly halfway up the Maverick Road. Without the police presence, they might have driven right past the stone-and-wood shelter off to the right at the base of a towering hill dotted with scrub—Luna's Jacal.

It was maybe a dozen feet wide and thirty feet long, with timbered beams supporting a sagging roof of rock, ocotillo branches, and protective black tarp. Its far end backed right up to a massive rock. Claire guessed the dwelling cleared barely five feet at its peak—no one in her Jeep could stand up inside. She wondered how Luna had raised his family with no more refuge than this. Just rocks, cactus, and dirt, as far as the eye could see. She assumed a spring or creek was nearby.

But now Iris Cobb had died here too. That would become part of its lore. In rugged country like this, death happened. People perished on backcountry trails from heart attacks and heat exhaustion or bad decisions to hike alone. Elderly hikers lost their bearings and walked right past springs that would have saved their lives. People fell off cliffs. But to die while bringing life to oil on canvas? At someone else's hand? Someone who wanted to steal what—a few dollars, credit cards? They hadn't even taken Iris's car. The crime seemed pitiful.

Alex slowed and Donnie and Sam instinctively doffed their hats. A park ranger saluted and waved them on. Chatter in the Jeep ended until Luna's Jacal disappeared behind the dust they stirred in passing.

"You knew her?" Sitting next to Claire in the back seat, Donnie whispered the question.

"I met Iris just once in company. A hello and handshake."

Donnie nodded. He was being polite.

"Easy place to rob someone," Alex said.

"But not a place you'd expect to find someone to rob," Donnie replied—sensibly it seemed to Claire. She shared Clayton's doubts about a crime of opportunity. But the alternatives seemed worse.

For the next few miles, they were subdued—contemplating the murder and maybe thinking about what remained of the afternoon. The washboard surfaces seemed rougher now and the Jeep skittered in spots. But there was plenty of daylight left, Claire knew, so they could share a proper meal in Terlingua before dropping Donnie off and then returning to Alpine. (Beatrice's basket of delights was gone after the Mariscal Mine.)

But then Claire remembered the photo she'd taken of Iris Cobb's last painting—a two-story adobe ruin with a timbered porch set against a blue sky and red hill. *Terlingua Townhouse*, Gina said when Claire spotted it only the day before in the artist's private gallery. Iris Cobb's last finished work.

"There's something I want to show you, Donnie," Claire said, fumbling in the back seat for her phone. The photo was easy to locate. She'd taken dozens today but it was the only shot from Saturday.

Donnie studied the image. "An abandoned building? Nice colors though."

"Iris Cobb painted it just recently—in Terlingua. The oil still looked wet when I saw the picture yesterday. Recognize the spot?"

"Can't say I do. But Terlingua's got lots of broken-down buildings, especially around the Ghost Town. That's a settlement that got abandoned when mercury mines went belly-up after the war. Shouldn't be hard to find, if it's there."

"Could we do that?"

"Sure. But I got my hot tub on a timer heatin' up right now. I thought maybe we could soak before we eat?"

"Somebody say *hot tub*?" It was Alex from the front seat, with even Sam chiming in.

Claire smiled. Maybe Donnie had something in mind after all. But she didn't intend to drive the hundred miles back to Alpine in damp underwear.

"How about you guys hit the tub and I'll explore Terlingua on my own? I'd be safe doing that on a Sunday afternoon?"

"Sure. It's a tourist place," Donnie said. "Just don't get pulled into too many conversations. Some of the locals like to jabber, especially those on the front porch by the Starlight Theatre."

"Maybe I should go with you?" Alex was being dutiful.

"There's a bookstore and an art gallery too," Donnie added.

"Perfect. I'll go shopping," Claire said, knowing the impact of those words on men. "And I'd rather do that on my own."

She was being honest. Alex would have more fun with his bros and she wanted an hour without them.

❊ ❊ ❊

CLAIRE WAS GRATEFUL her Jeep came with navigation because she needed its map of the oddly sprawling town, famous now for its chili cook-off in November. Much of the town surrounded Highway 170, the only route west to Presidio and the larger Mexican city of Ojinaga. The road ran parallel to the Rio Grande much of the way and so was also called the River Road by locals. But this one was paved and curvy and, Claire heard, far more beautiful than the one they'd explored today.

Beautiful was a word that didn't fit Terlingua itself. Bustling under a late afternoon sun, the place was full of small businesses catering to tourists seeking desert adventures. Claire noted casitas under construction along hillsides, RVs and trailers shaded by metal awnings, and numerous offbeat shops and galleries—even a famous underground restaurant. Enough growth to worry an elderly resident she spoke to. Claire found it too dry and rocky to feel homey, even if locals seemed content. She guessed they were comfortable with scorpions and rattlesnakes too.

Just off Highway 170, Claire located the Terlingua Ghost Town, remembering Gina Summerlin thought Iris had painted *Terlingua Townhouse* in this area. Its hardscrabble properties along a dirt road and just past a cemetery were few enough to check quickly. But the two-story adobe depicted on Iris's canvas was nowhere to be found. Was it possible she invented the dwelling, with its crumbling walls, rotten beams, and odd reddish dune in the background?

In the Ghost Town, Claire browsed a giftshop and bookstore and then chatted with the men Donnie warned her about—drinking beer on the porch of the Starlight Theatre and Restaurant. They called her *pretty lady* and studied the

166

photo of *Terlingua Townhouse* on her iPhone. No one thought the building was north of Highway 170 and not likely south of it either. Least not in Terlingua. Someone suggested Presidio or even Study Butte, a tiny settlement almost at the entrance to Big Bend National Park.

They wished her well on her search, especially after she mentioned that *Terlingua Townhouse* was maybe the last painting by Iris Cobb—a name they now recognized but wouldn't have a week ago. *The murdered lady*, they called her. They seemed of two minds about the crime. Drug runners had done her in or she was up to something herself. Not sure what, but it got her killed. Claire promised the garrulous drinkers that she'd return shortly for dinner with three strapping young men. That disappointed them.

But it *was* time to pick up the guys. Donnie's casita south of Highway 170 was a twenty-something's paradise—complete with a jacked-up Xterra under a carport up front and something like a patio behind, with its hot tub surrounded by a cedar deck decorated by hubcaps. Donnie had even rigged a canvas sunshade. The place seemed more serviceable than pretty when she'd dropped Donnie, Sam, and Alex off there an hour earlier and headed into town.

Returning now, she parked her Jeep in front of the garage. With its engine off, she could hear the roar of a pump pushing water and the flyting of young men. Turning the corner too quickly, she caught then sitting on the deck thirty or forty feet away, their feet in the tub, steam rising from bubbling water—Donnie's broad back and Sam's slimmer one in view. On the other side of the pool, she could just make out Alex's thick hair. Donnie leaned a tanned shoulder into Sam and pulled back and then Sam leaned into Donnie and held there briefly. Naked as jaybirds. Two gay guys—maybe three?

They didn't see her. She scooted behind the garage, returned to her Jeep, tooted the horn. In an instant the pump ceased and she heard Donnie.

"Give us a second," he said and that's about all she allowed, coming around the corner a second time. They were pulling up shorts, wet but decent.

Donnie laughed. Sam looked embarrassed. Alex was Alex.

"Nearly caught us bare-assed," he smiled. "Donnie says we should eat at the Starlight."

"Sounds fine," Claire said. "I stopped there to show my photo."

"Any luck?" It was Donnie, toweling moisture from the back of Sam's neck as Claire approached.

"None," she admitted, noting the gesture. "But I learned a lot."

Chapter 29

"Mother?"

Taking the call in the bedroom with her husband snoring quietly, Eugenia Harp noted two oddities. No, *three*. Her eldest and only unmarried daughter was phoning *her* for a change, they'd spoken just three days earlier, and it was almost midnight—either an hour earlier or later in Texas where Claire lived. (Eugenia despised time zones.)

"Claire?" she replied, joining the conversation where she usually opened it. "Are you all right?"

"Am I calling too late?"

"Of course, you are. It's Monday here already. But I assume you have a reason?"

"Not sure I do." Voice tentative and quivering. "I spent the whole day with Alex. Off-roading in a national park."

"I'm so sorry, dear. Did you get it fixed?"

"What?"

"Your Jeep. Did you get it back on the road?" She knew what Jeeps were for, but since Claire presumed her mother was clueless about popular culture, Eugenia happily obliged. Her daughter ignored the question.

"We drove more than two hundred and fifty miles."

From Cleveland to Cincinnati, Eugenia estimated, to put the trip into a perspective she understood. A tiresome day. "Did you have a good time with Alex? Did you finally talk?"

An ominous pause on Claire's end. *Maybe she'd had a drink . . . or several?* That would explain calling so late.

"That's just it. We hardly spoke at all. He paid more attention to the guys."

Eugenia said nothing. Claire would elaborate. *She was a teacher, after all.*

"I invited Sam Vogt. The trip was actually his idea."

"The gay boy with the blue eyes from the book you're editing?" Claire sighed on cue.

"Yes, mother, the gay boy. And Alex invited Donnie, a trail guide he met on the South Rim."

"Where that actress of his disappeared?"

"Yes."

"And you found this trail guide attractive?" *Motherly intuition.*

"What? How did . . . have you talked to Alex?"

"I have not. But it sounds exactly like something he'd do. Set up his sister with a handsome friend. He's a bit of a yenta."

"He wasn't matchmaking. I'm almost ten years older than Donnie."

"And he's not your type?"

From the pause that followed, Eugenia guessed *very much her type.* And Claire was upset about something.

"I'm sorry, dear. We play games too much when we talk. You called for a good reason."

"When we got back to my place at the end of a long day—Alex, Sam, and me—Sam went home in his car and Alex got into the Range Rover he'd rented and just drove back to Clayton Shoot's. Just like that. Didn't even consider staying with me."

"Did you say anything?"

"He said his stuff was at Clayton's."

Eugenia sighed. "We went over this last time. It's only natural that Alex enjoys staying on a ranch. Clayton Shoot is the novelty for him on this trip, not you."

Since taking the call, Eugenia had wandered from her bedroom to the bar downstairs and poured herself a bourbon, neat. From a bottle of Texas Blue Corn she bought her husband for his birthday. Clayton Shoot recommended it—yes, they talked sometimes. Claire didn't know.

So if Claire too was drinking on the other end of the line, it was a family trait. She heard Claire breathe deep, like before diving to the bottom of a pool.

"Okay, here it is, mother," she said. "Have you ever thought your son might be gay?"

The liquor was timely. Eugenia sipped before replying. "Not once," she said. "But go on."

"That girl Alex was with on the South Rim—."

"Piper Robinet," Eugenia remembered.

"She and I talked the night she stayed at my place. Alex was upstairs showering. I sensed something off in their relationship. The girl was hiding something."

"Was she as attractive as the news reports said? I've seen photos."

"Very beautiful. And oddly mature for a seventeen-year old—which she admitted she wasn't. And then you know what happened in the park. She up and left Alex. Decided to sleep on her own and then disappeared."

"Yes."

"And not just because she lost the movie role, I think."

"Juliet?"

"Then Alex spent that night in a tent with the same trail guide he brought on the road trip."

"Donnie again?"

"A very attractive man."

"You thought so?"

"I did, mother . . . And I thought maybe he was interested in me."

"And you liked that?"

A long pause. "He wasn't."

"And so for that reason you suspect that Alex and Donnie . . . ?"

"It surprised me how Alex fussed over Sam Vogt too. They'd never met before, but Alex knew all about my student, who he was and what he'd done. Like he'd studied him."

"That's the way your brother is. He knew what happened with you and this Sam fellow last spring because I sent him the news. All the stories and links. You'd be complaining even more if Alex ignored your life."

"They sat in the backseat of my Jeep like old pals—and Sam's not one to warm up to most people. I just haven't met many straight guys as comfortable right off the bat with gay men as Alex."

"He's an actor."

"I know. But Alex hung on Sam's every word."

"With Donnie too?"

"Oh yeah. Those two were like juvenile delinquents in the back seat when it was my turn to drive."

"Boys are like that." Eugenia remembered Alex with his football buddies. Claire was already in Austin then. But it occurred to Eugenia that, for the moment, Claire sounded like she was still in high school too. Jealous no one was paying attention to her.

"Near the end of the day, I drove to Terlingua for an hour on my own, shopping and looking for things." Claire explained what the Terlingua was like. "So I left the guys at Donnie's place. He lives just outside the town."

"That at least was thoughtful of you. Men do not like to shop—except at REI and AutoZone." Eugenia doubted Claire heard her.

"When I got back to go to dinner, the three of them were in Donnie's hot tub, pretty tight. Bumping shoulders. Drinking, I guess."

"Oh *my*."

Claire caught the sarcasm. "They were naked, mother."

"Three men in a hot tub who might not want to dine later in wet shorts."

Claire sighed. "I mean there's nothing wrong if Alex is gay. But that he doesn't feel close enough to share that part of his life. That's what gets me."

"So you're sure he's gay? You have the habit, you know. As I recall, you've raised a question about Clayton Shoot once or twice. A captain back then in the sheriff's office . . . with a gun and a horse."

"That was a joke. I brought it up when Clayton said he didn't want to have sex until we married."

They both paused, Eugenia sipping her drink in Ohio and certain Claire was doing the same in Texas. Claire's bourbon was surely not as good.

"You know, Claire," she said slowly, "of my four children, you'd be the only one I'd have questions about. A striking woman—movie star looks, just like your brother—but already in her early thirties and never a boyfriend serious enough to bring home. And the men you did date? Academics, theatre majors, even that writer fellow. Not exactly awash in testosterone. And when a real man finally asks for your hand, you turn him down flat. It broke your father's heart. He really likes the idea of a cowboy in the family."

"Surely you know, mother . . ."

"Do I? I'm quite certain my boy is straight, but would not care if he weren't. Because I love him, just the same way I do you . . . Why don't you simply talk to Alex, Claire? Ask him?"

The advice struck Eugenia as astonishingly wise. It took Claire many heartbeats to respond.

"Because Alex might hate me forever if I'm wrong," she finally said.

OR MAYBE I just don't want to know? But why? Claire ended the call with her mother quickly.

She'd never had issues with gay colleagues or students and positively cherished Sam Vogt. And how had her mother come out on top in the conversation—the righteous one despite her sketchy track record on social issues?

Claire sighed and drank deep. Perhaps loving someone involved selfishness and possession. She felt a need—maybe the right—to know what was inside the heart of a little boy she'd helped raise. Even now when he was old enough for secrets of his own. She wanted him in her life again, knew he hadn't been there in a long time. *If ever.*

And somehow these feelings now involved Sam Vogt and, damn it, Donnie Majewski and his brawny legs. Even her cowboy sheriff understood basic human relationships better than she did. Clayton and Alex were like jam on toast. And it wasn't supposed to be that way.

Despite another drink, Claire tossed too long in bed. She knew her book project would require concentration the next morning after a long and very odd weekend. But she needed a path forward in her personal life too and suddenly realized who might have an answer.

Piper Robinet.

If Clayton Shoot wasn't following up on the girl's South Rim disappearing act, Claire would investigate on her own. And do a better job than the tabloids too, currently reporting sightings of Piper in Las Vegas, SoHo, and Butte. (She'd scanned tabloid headlines in the checkout at Porter's Groceries.)

Her ticket to locating Piper was obvious now too: Billy Lamb Jr.

Billy had to know either Piper's whereabouts himself or somebody who did. Because that *somebody* likely drove her to the party at the McCann Ranch just two nights earlier and *might* even be shacking up with Piper somewhere nearby. Brewster County had lots of hidey holes. You could conceal an army regiment in this corner of Texas, let alone a single girl. Even a pretty one.

Of course, Alex might also know where Piper was. Might even be communicating with her. But Claire couldn't ask *him*—not unless he brought the subject up the next time he wandered into her life. Or maybe, just maybe, Alex was still at the Shoot Ranch *because* he was shielding both Piper and himself from Claire's curiosity. Keeping private matters private. Even from his sister.

Whatever. Claire had questions only Piper could answer.

To find her, she'd pressure her former student, Billy McCann Lamb. He'd once come to her for advice about his own dalliances. And she tried to help. So Billy owed her.

Despite the alcohol, her fingers moved faster than her brain. She'd dispatched an email message to Billy before she remembered it was well past midnight and he was still a student at Sul Ross and her conduct might be misconstrued. *What the hell was she thinking?*

Which is likely why Billy replied immediately. *Happy to talk about Piper tomorrow. Won't be on campus. Come out to the ranch early afternoon? Sending directions right now.*

And there they were.

Hope springs eternal for young men. Billy spent the semester in her spring course signaling interest from a backrow seat—sunglasses, leather jacket, tight jeans.

Yep. She was sure she could get Billy to tell her how to locate Piper.

Chapter 30

"So Perciak and Grimmel are maybe a thing?" Alonso asked Gus Stumpf, stifling a yawn.

The odd couple were working even earlier than usual on this Monday morning following Iris Cobb's murder. Alonso sat behind the wheel of Brewster County's most trail-rated 4x4—complete with brush guard—just outside the entrance to the Cobb Institute, the designated starting point for their experiment. Clayton had okayed it.

They'd spend the day retracing the route Gina Summerlin would have to follow from her residence at the Cobb to Fort Davis, and then to Luna's Jacal and back to Fort Davis—*if* she were the one who killed Iris at the national park. No presumptions or shortcuts. Tires on the ground, feet on the trail. Could Regina make the loop in the time available? And, crucially, could she evade the Border Patrol's checkpoint cameras on Highway 118?

To avoid suspicion, Alonso and Gus started their circuit out of view from the woman's residence. But they were less than a tenth of a mile away.

Their first benchmark was the Border Patrol station on Highway 118—which Summerlin's 4Runner clicked past on Friday, October 22, at 7:28 AM, no doubt just moments after she'd turned north out of the Cobb's handsome carriageway entrance. Alonso and Gus hit the checkpoint at 7:30.

"Can they do that—Perciak and Grimmel?" Gus wondered, "fraternize between the IBS and FBI?" Alonso was driving away from the Border Patrol turnout very slowly, searching the shoulder of the road. The landscape to the east was unusually lush because of a wet autumn—the rolling hills thick with tall grass and scrub.

"I couldn't with Fiona in the police department," Alonso mumbled. He figured everyone in town knew about their May/September affair about ten minutes after his boots slid off.

"But Fiona was your *boss*," Gus objected. "And you were low guy on the totem pole in her department. *No offense.*"

"None taken," he replied, still studying the roadside at 15 mph. A Subaru passed them. "But I had to leave my job. Chief Tusk and a skinny Mexican kid from Candelaria? I mean, we couldn't even take lunch without people thinking I was getting favors."

"You *were* getting favors."

"Not them kind. I mean like the best assignments and shit."

Gus looked at the dark-haired deputy maternally. "I don't think Agent Perciak is Grimmel's boss or vice versa. They're both special agents."

By this time, the checkpoint was already a mile or more behind them and out of sight. "You gonna drive like this all day?" Gus finally asked, figuring Alonso was up to something. "At his rate we won't be in Fort Davis . . ."

Alonso slapped the top of the steering wheel. "There. Break in the fence. Big one. But you need to look close to spot it, in all that brush."

"No cattle grazing here, I guess."

"Most everything on 118 is fenced. But not here—and this is all ICS Group property. Clayton said so."

"ICS Group?" Then Alonso saw Gus grin. She got it. *Iris Cobb Summerlin land.* He gave the big hemi under their hood more throttle, smiling himself now too.

⊰⊱ ⊰⊱ ⊰⊱

THERE WASN'T MUCH chatter for the next forty-five miles. The drive north on Highway 118 through Alpine and then to Fort Davis was routine for any local law enforcement officer. As anticipated, they arrived at the fort's information desk easily by 8:30 AM, when Gina Summerlin claimed to be there—and found the same attractive ranger Alonso interviewed on Saturday at her desk in the Visitor Center.

"Hello, Ms. Cortez," he said. She seemed tickled Alonso remembered her name. Paid no attention to Gus.

"Good to see you again too, Deputy."

"We're just verifying some details of Ms. Regina Summerlin's visit here on Friday, October 22, when you saw her check-in and then go off to paint."

175

"Right, I saw Ms. Summerlin on Friday and recall you asking questions about her the day after."

"Had she been to the fort before then—Gina Summerlin?" It was Gus's question.

"A few times," Cortez nodded and smiled. "She liked to sketch views from the palisades and seemed fond of our ruins." Not all structures at the fort were restored.

"And to confirm," Gus continued. "She talked with you here at about 8:30 AM —as we are now."

"Right."

"And then headed up to the trail. But you didn't, in fact, see Ms. Summerlin again until 4:00 PM?

Cortez's eyes narrowed. "That's right," she said. "I can't tell where visitors go once they leave this desk. Don't need to."

Gus nodded to Alonso significantly.

"But I did overhear a child some hours later mention a lady painting up on the trail. At a scenic overlook. The painter even put a brush in the little girl's hand and let her add some color to the sky. Is that important?"

"Could be," Alonso said quietly. "Can you be surer about the time?"

"Midmorning? Closer to ten than eleven, but I'm guessing."

After several more questions, Gus and Alonso left the visitors center and marched toward the trailhead where Gina began her day. Assuming the child was telling the truth, Summerlin did exactly as she claimed—spent at least part of her morning painting on a trail roughly three hundred feet above the fort. The child even mentioned buildings she could spy far below her, so Ranger Cortez assumed the youngster met the painter near the main overlook, with the parade ground beneath it and rows of barracks laid out like dominoes. And Gina claimed she also set her gear down near two benches up there—so the officers assumed she'd been to at least one other viewpoint. It gave Gus and Alonso a specific path to follow.

The weather was cool and the trail empty so early on a Monday. Neither officer minded the hike up and around scarred rockfaces and lots of cactus. They wore hefty backpacks to approximate Gina's climb with a full painter's box. On Sunday, Clayton thought to ask Gina to furnish snapshots of the works she did that day and the artist quickly returned the images, along with approximate locations. Gus and Alonso had those photos on their phones and they supported the artist's account. The officers even identified a massive prickly pear featured in one painting—clearly *without* the blooms Gina told Ranger Cortez she'd added to please potential buyers. So her story was consistent.

But this didn't surprise the officers. Gus and Alonso assumed Summerlin visited the fort, climbed the trail they were now on, and stopped where other park visitors might notice her—as the little girl conveniently had. But it was Clayton's hunch (and nothing more, at this point) that, on Friday, Gina might have just touched up canvases she'd painted previously. Because, to murder her mother, she'd have to depart Fort Davis by 11:00 AM, drive 150 miles south to reach Luna's Jacal by 1:00 PM—the estimated time of the murder—and then be back at the historic site around 4:00 PM to be sure someone in the visitor center noticed her departure. With supposedly new paintings in hand.

For this *what if* scenario to work, the officers made two critical assumptions. First, Gina Summerlin knew where Iris Cobb intended to paint on Friday. But that was *easy peasy*, Gus had argued. Her stepmother might simply have told her: *I'll be on the Old Maverick Trail today in Big Bend.* Better yet, *I'm gonna paint Luna's Jacal.* They had only Gina's word that she *hadn't* spoken with Iris Friday morning.

The second assumption was dicier. Somehow, Summerlin had figured out how to evade the automated license plate readers at the Border Patrol checkpoint twice. First, late in the morning when she would have raced south from Fort Davis to intercept her stepmother at Big Bend National Park and then again when she returned north to the fort after the alleged murder.

Right now, those cameras supported her alibi. They'd photographed her vehicle leaving the Cobb early in the morning and then again late in the afternoon returning there—but not at any times in between. Gina could argue convincingly that she was at Fort Davis and miles away from Iris Cobb at the time the crime occurred.

Alternative routes to the murder site in Big Bend, either through Pecos County or south from Marathon, were simply too lengthy to be plausible *and* even these were surveilled by Border Patrol cameras, none of which snapped Gina's license plates.

Gus and Alonso estimated that Summerlin would spend at least an hour up on the Fort Davis trail, long enough for visitors to notice her painting there. But they didn't stay quite so long themselves, assuming they'd need extra time on the road to figure out what Gina surely knew when she set out on Friday (if she committed the crime)—how to evade those plate readers.

"Game is afoot," Alonso said as they started the trek down from the scenic lookouts above the fort and back to where they'd left their pickup. He was not quite sure what the expression meant. But he guessed it applied here.

Chapter 31

Clayton envied Gus and Alonso in the field this Monday checking out a theory about the Cobb murder any clever lawyer might tear apart. Maybe even a dumb one. But he was also happy to sit down with Lee Perciak to discuss their other *unlikely* likely suspect, Mateo Bottaio, aka Matthew Cooper.

"Don't waste your time," the special agent said, over red enchiladas at Alicia's Burrito Place south of the railroad tracks in Alpine. The breakfast crowd had already filtered out so they could talk freely. The abrupt dismissal surprised Clayton, so Perciak leaned in. "I got no problem with going over suspects with a fine-tooth comb. I'm eager to hear what your officers come up with on Regina Summerlin. But we already gave due diligence to Mr. Mateo."

He spit out the name.

"Don't like the guy?"

"My mother's generation used to talk about *gigolos* and to my mind Mr. Bottaio-Cooper fits the bill. Using women to get ahead . . ."

"A no-talent photographer?"

"He's actually pretty good. An agent in New Mexico—photography buff—knew Bottaio's work even before we checked into him."

"So where's the problem?"

Perciak surveyed the empty dining room. "My own lack of objectivity," he admitted. "Cooper just rubs me the wrong way, especially given what he's stepped into."

Clayton looked confused.

"The guy's suddenly a millionaire. I wouldn't resent it if *you* or Gus Stumpf or Agent Grimmel stumbled into a fortune because you're working stiffs like me. But even Grimmel got squishy with Cooper when she finally met him—

an ex-army guy who spent his late twenties working at upmarket resorts and spas doing who knows what. Then he picks up a camera, starts communing with nature, and *bingo* he's got a career. Sleeps with an old lady, and he's in the money."

"That's Coke you're drinkin'?"

"Just an unprofessional way of saying we checked and double-checked Cooper. Followed up every damn receipt, even reviewed security videos at gas stations. And he was where he said he was, doing exactly what he said he did, from here to the Guadalupe Mountains to Santa Fe to Taos and back."

"Humph."

"No prior knowledge about what Cobb left him in her will either. Cobb's lawyer said his client kept Cooper out of the loop when she added him to it. In case she changed her mind. Iris genuinely admired the guy."

"Clean as a hound's tooth."

"Eisenhower expected that from Nixon. But, yep, apparently. I was suspicious about Cooper swapping his Volvo for a Cobb Institute truck, but that checks out too. Even if his station wagon hadn't broken down, he'd need the bigger vehicle because the paintings Iris sent to Taos wouldn't fit into his ride."

"So, no point wasting time on him?"

Perciak shrugged.

"My people could maybe help more with the interviews," Clayton offered.

"Grimmel wants to keep the interrogations in-house now and consistent. And she's right."

"*House* being FBI?"

"Yep. But be grateful. Interrogating academics and pseudo-intellectuals is the worst. They complain when we call them in for the interviews. Then they won't stop talking or stay on point. All except maybe Ms. Harp."

"You know she's my girlfriend?"

"Oh, yeah. Don't remember how that came up."

Clayton knew the feds were thorough.

"Still, we can't skip the interviews or something might slip through. And we don't want to be bit in the ass later."

"So?" Clayton wanted to get Perciak on record.

"You guys stick with the follow-up on Gina Summerlin's day. Most everyone we talked to spoke well of her, but no one seems to really know her. No intimate friends, except Cooper for a few months. I can guess why she's stuck on him though. She's not bad looking, but Cooper is out of her league."

"Iris Cobb could attract him."

Perciak rubbed his finger together. "Rich and famous. That's a powerful aphrodisiac. Must have been tough for Gina living in the shadow of a prominent mother."

"Especially one that ends up with your boyfriend," Clayton said.

"Yeah. But Regina and Mateo split up even before Iris got involved."

Chapter 32

It was roughly 145 miles from the parking lot at the Fort Davis National Historic Site to Luna's Jacal on the Old Maverick Road, where Iris Cobb was shot. But Gus and Alonso got back to their truck at 10:30 AM—plenty of time to cover that distance before 1:00 PM, the estimated time of Cobb's murder. Speed limits were generous and they had to cover only seven or eight miles of dirt road once they were in Big Bend.

"We got some leeway in that time of death estimate too," Gus observed as they turned out of the parking lot and into the town of Fort Davis, heading south on Highway 118.

Alonso agreed. "Could go either way."

"True."

"But Gina wouldn't be on a schedule like us. She just needed to get to Big Bend, find her stepmother . . ."

"You know, that little girl who remembers Summerlin worries me," Gus said. "Makes it all real. Gina *was* on that ridge, for sure."

"We expected that," Alonso insisted—he didn't want Gus goin' squirrelly on him now. "We figured she worked at the fort on Friday."

They were silent for several miles, the big all-terrain tires of their truck howling beneath them.

"Real problem is ahead," Gus sighed, more to herself than to Alonso.

"I checked those satellite photos close."

"I don't doubt it. But engineers who set up the checkpoint probably did too." Gus had the most recent satellite images in her door pocket. "They wouldn't put it where drivers could just scoot around."

Alonso shook his head. "The checkpoint's real old. Built before 9-11. Before real good satellite cameras and the kind of off-road trucks we got now. And Cobb sure owns lots of property along 118."

"Maybe the checkpoint uses radar or ground sensors too?" Gus did know Clayton vetted this trial with Border Patrol agents.

Alonso grinned like one of her boys up to no good. "They're being cagey. But they'll tell us if they detect us."

Forty miles later, now well south of Alpine, they were approaching ground zero for their experiment. The deputy slowed just out of sight of the Border Patrol checkpoint, with the turnout to Cathedral Mountain Trail coming up on their right. Alonso spotted the unfenced break he'd seen earlier in the scrub running along the eastern side of Highway 118. He slowed. Noticed some tall grass just barely crushed—a deer path or javelina crossing. Or maybe a vehicle had pulled in here recently just as he was about to do?

Time to head off road. Alonso signaled a left turn, crossed the empty highway, drove slowly over the shoulder, and then aimed down and across a series of humps, their truck kicking up dust.

"Mother of God." Gus clutched the grab handle.

Conveniently, the game trail (if that's what it was) angled away from the road, where healthy cedars and yucca and thick shrubs immediately screened their movements. But it was slow-going now as they pushed southeast, creating a path as much as following one that took them between and around hills high and far enough from the highway to make their 4x4 invisible. They needed their laptop GPS and in-vehicle navigation screen to be sure they were steadily moving southeast, both away from the highway and then eventually past the Border Patrol station, still to the south.

As they'd planned, Alonso headed slowly toward a large uplift in the distance, one easily visible on their satellite photos. There, they eventually came upon two cabins in the shadows of its cliffs, well east of Highway 118. The wooden structures showed up as smudges in the aerial shots, which Gus now held in her lap. A hunting camp, they realized—perhaps rarely used, but not quite abandoned. The windows in two small cabins were intact and somebody might have parked nearby recently.

"Need to remember this place," Alonso muttered.

"Do much hunting?"

"Nah, but sometimes it's good to get away."

"Don't let Fiona hear that . . . You ever live with a lady before?"

"Not like Fiona. Clean sheets. Washer and dryer. Breakfast every morning."

"Ain't love grand?"

"You have no idea." Alonso's grin tickled Gus. She *did* know the feeling.

Past the hunting camp, they tracked the base of the hill south until they found yet another rough path running north and south. Deer or javelina run? Nothing showing on their photos of course. Gus expected they might even be on someone else's property this far from the road, not on Cobb land at all. But the scrub was manageable and Alonso rolled on.

GPS showed them heading south now and parallel to the highway. Gus felt their tires crushing cactus and young mesquite. Then Alonso aimed the truck up and over a berm that looked like it might have been bulldozed into place years ago. He pointed to where one or two other vehicles had left marks on the same ridge.

On its other side was a narrow path maybe gouged by farm equipment working this distant corner of what they figured had to be the Cobb Institute proper. They followed where it took them, confident they were by now past the border checkpoint. And soon they spied a few metal barns—the first of the institute's outbuildings. Not long after, they swung east on a graveled road that circled the perimeter of the main property, providing access to the Cobb's fields, fenced corrals, barns, and, eventually, its main buildings and residences. From inside those structures now, anyone looking out a back window might spot their hefty vehicle. But Alonso doubted they could read the Brewster County seal on its front door.

Pleased with themselves, Alonso and Gus drove another mile through the southern half of the property, knowing exactly where the graveled road intersected Highway 118 just beyond the checkpoint.

Alonso beamed. "Cleared now to the park and Old Maverick Road. ETA at Luna's Jacal, maybe 12:45."

"Just in time for a murder," Gus replied. But no smile on her face.

She radioed the news to Clayton who made it clear they still had to complete the full circuit. "Make sure there are no surprises on the Maverick. Or on the ride back."

※ ※ ※

MATEO BOTTAIO—WHO MUCH preferred Matthew Cooper these days—glanced out of a second-floor administrative office at the Cobb just in time to spot a white truck, jacked up like an off-road special, on the perimeter road. It was too distant to make out its logo. Sheriff's department or FBI, maybe? They'd been all over the complex already, interviewing employees, demanding computer files, combing through offices and galleries, asking annoying questions.

All in their day's work.

He pointed the truck out to Regina who'd just stepped into the office on her way to God knows where, files and papers in hand.

She'd been feverish since his return to Alpine . . . could it be just two days ago? Gina was responding to her mother's death as she did to most things—with intensity and discipline. Their brief relationship had been like that too: she made love like a Prussian general.

She'd spent the whole morning on the phone with lawyers, business agents, Cobb administrators, and people in Taos. As if nonstop activity might erase tragedy.

She decided there'd be no public memorial in Alpine—contrary to promises made to community leaders not invited to the gathering on Saturday. There *would* be one in Taos once Iris's remains were released. She would be cremated and interred there too, even though her roots were in Texas. The Cobb in Alpine would resume some activities in January. Maybe.

But no time for tears.

More worrisome, Gina assumed their relationship was *on* again. Just like that. Regina Summerlin and Mateo Bottaio (she insisted on the name). Not only business partners, but lovers, as if Iris wanted it. Gina didn't ask if he did.

The FBI had set Iris's house off limits. So Matthew willingly returned to a small lodge on the Cobb property he'd never quite relinquished. He'd kept some clothes and photographic equipment there. Gina initially insisted he move in with her, then decided to wait until they set up housekeeping in Taos. Perhaps she didn't want to compete with her mother's ghost?

But Matthew wanted none of it. They drove each other over the edge during the few months they lived together earlier. He didn't intend to repeat the mistake. Besides, his eyes were already elsewhere.

Gina needed to come to terms with Iris's will too—and so did he. The news had just about floored him. Matthew could only imagine the complications Iris's surprise bequest would now cause. How exactly would a Cobb Institute in Gina's hands interact with the Taos Gallery, which fell to him? Gina assumed a continuation of present arrangements. He didn't see how it could work. Wasn't sure he wanted it to.

❖❖ ❖❖ ❖❖

"I'M SURE IT'S nothing," Gina said, glancing out the window just in time to see the tailgate of the truck.

"Big rig," Matthew said.

"Ram Power Wagon," she muttered, looking interested, despite the dismissal. But she hurried down the corridor before he could ask why.

Chapter 33

Monday afternoon—at about the same time Matthew Cooper spied the truck on the Cobb property—Billy Lamb Jr. was in a field with two other cowboys moving cattle. Claire spotted him easily when she drove up, following his directions to a working part of the ranch, not to the big house she'd visited twice for parties. He saw her immediately too. On a tall brown horse, he made his way through a gate and headed toward her Jeep. Rope still in hand and squinting in the afternoon sun, he dismounted.

Billy was covered in mud and dust and smelled like what he'd been riding. Claire felt like she'd stepped into a movie.

"Good to see you, Professor." More formality than she expected from her former student. "Let's head to the run-in."

The shelter was a sturdy tarp over a metal frame in a rocky field—a safe place for horses in storms, but shade for Billy's crew today. It had a small camp stove, rucksacks, and folding chairs. Two double cabs were parked nearby. An older cowboy lifted a coffee pot from the stove and assured Billy it was full, leaving Claire and his boss to themselves.

Claire took Billy's offer of a cup—black only because they didn't have cream. Ironic with all the cattle around. The stuff tasted like hard liquor. Billy laughed at her expression.

"It's a percolator," he said, tapping the battered pot and doffing his hat. "Leave it on the stove too long and coffee gets tart."

Sure does, Claire thought. "So this is all yours now," she said.

Billy hunched forward, hands on his knees. Calloused and scarred, she noticed. "Yes, ma'am. Pretty much."

In the bright sunlight, an October breeze ruffled Billy's hair. The squint made him look older.

"And how does it feel?"

"Diff'rent. I knew there'd be responsibilities. All my life I seen my daddy more in his office than on the land. So he's easing me into the business side now. Gotta keep up with the times, but I don't want to lose traditions, you know? There needs to be places like this that still respect the cowboy way."

Claire smiled at a guy she'd regarded as a jerk in the spring.

"My dad thinks we could market what I want to maintain and maybe even open up this place for environmental tourism. I ain't against that. I gotta learn the revenue side of the business. My dad and Nikki can cover only for so long."

"You're going to finish school?"

"Sure. Just need the six hours I'm taking this semester. Sul Ross will be happy to see me go."

"And ask for contributions for the rest of your life."

"All the more reason to graduate me. I was surprised by the *B* I got from you last spring."

"You shouldn't be. You wrote good stuff, even if you breezed through your papers."

"I wrote 'em myself."

Claire smiled. She never thought otherwise because they sounded exactly like Billy.

"I suspect you're a guy who doesn't want other people knowing how smart he is." According to Clayton, Billy once went head-to-head with Alpine's police chief and won.

The young cowboy shrugged. "The ranch has been mine less than a week. But I already spend time every morning readin' and signin' stacks of papers."

"As Billy McCann?" she asked, surprising herself with the question. "You sign as Billy McCann?"

Billy hesitated. "You know about that?"

"Clayton told me," she explained. "Said it was a tough decision for both you and your dad—changing back to your mother's last name."

Billy folded his hands. "Clayton just lost his father. I been thinkin' about that for some reason. I was at the funeral."

"You might talk to him. About father–son stuff."

"Clayton always makes sense," Billy admitted. "I coulda changed my name at eighteen according to the lawyer, 'cept my mother's will didn't give me the ranch until now. I saw no point to hurryin'."

"I get it," Claire said, thinking he also could make the change even later in life.

"*Billy Lamb*," he said.

"What?"

"Still using Billy Lamb for now. Billy McCann Lamb. I haven't filed those legal papers yet. I thought I'd wait until after all the birthday shit. Need to be stone sober when I get to 'em."

"You seem mighty clearheaded out here."

"Shoulda seen me Friday night. You know her—the woman who died?"

"A friend of a friend. But still a shock."

"Sorry I didn't say hello to you and Clayton. I know the sheriff left early 'cause of the murder, and I pretty much stayed downstairs after blowin' out the candles."

"We arrived too late for that."

"I met your kid bother."

"I saw you escorting him down to the pool. That's why I'm here—I know Piper Robinet was at your party too."

"Cool guy. Head screwed on straight," he said, deflecting her query. "Honestly, I knew nothin' about your brother or Piper before this last week, except my stepmom sure wanted Alex to show up. So did one of my friends."

"Who was that?"

Billy smiled and turned his head. "I promised not to say."

"But you knew Piper Robinet was the actress on the South Rim last Tuesday with my brother . . . ?"

"Dumped him there. I know now, but didn't until Friday night. My stepmother mentioned something about movies and Oscars, but I don't follow stuff like that."

Says a kid who dressed like James Dean all semester. Claire smiled.

Billy went on. "I did hear about some girl lost in the park, but it was like kids robbing a Stripes station to me. No connection to my life. But then this beautiful woman shows up at the pool with . . ."

Claire dipped her head to signal interest.

Billy closed one eye. "You wanna get in touch with her?"

"I'm guessing you know how to do that."

They stared at each other.

"Yeah well, somebody I know brought Piper as his date Friday night and when I pushed, he filled me in about what went down. So, what's *your* interest in Robinet? Your brother must know why she dumped him. Why not just talk to him?"

"You think Piper dumped Alex?"

Billy paused, like he was deciding what he could say without betraying his friend.

"Come on, Billy. I'm not the cops and they're not interested in this story anymore."

He nodded. "Too busy with Iris Cobb. You know we got one or two of her paintings. She sketched horses real good. Happy to show you next time you're at the big house."

"I just want to help my brother. Figure out what went wrong on the South Rim. I know Piper was upset about losing the movie part."

"To some Brit with a shitty name."

"Tabreetha Bree-Jones."

"Wouldn't name a sow that."

Claire burst out laughing. Billy did too. It changed the atmosphere.

"Look," he said. "That friend I mentioned also wanted me to invite Alex to the party. I thought it was strange cause it's not like Tyler's queer or anything . . ."

"Tyler?"

"Shit. Yeah . . .Tyler."

"Billy, I'm not interested in the guy, whatever his name is." *Though she was.* "I bet there's maybe a hundred Tylers in Brewster and Pecos Counties. I need to talk to Piper Robinet—about what happened between her and Alex. Simple as that."

"Your brother in trouble?"

"I don't think so. Maybe a little mixed up."

"Have you ever met Piper?"

"She stayed at my house the night before they hiked the South Rim."

"They sleep together?"

"Why do you want to know?"

Billy colored and laughed. "Fantasizing."

Well, that was honest. "He slept downstairs and Piper was in the guestroom upstairs."

Billy seemed relieved to hear that. "Here's the deal," he nodded. "Tyler filled me in about Piper while she was talking with your brother down by the pool. Their relationship's real complicated and I'll leave the details to her . . ."

"So you'll give me her number?"

"I'll put you in touch. Her and Tyler have stopped using cellphones and there's not a signal out where they're staying anyhow. Police and park rangers aren't after her, but tabloids sure are. And, well, Tyler's a good friend, so I let 'em hide out at a cabin on the ranch south of here where no outsider's gonna locate 'em. Tyler took her there Friday right after the party."

"They could find the cabin in the dark?"

"Tyler's been there lots of times with me. Good place for drinkin' and huntin'. And gettin' away from angry parents. By the way, Tyler works at the park."

That clicked. Billy flashed the charming smile Claire remembered. "Thank you, Billy," she said and meant it. *This was progress.*

"I'll call her on the hardline and she can arrange to meet you *if she wants*. She's less'n thirty minutes from Study Butte. Maybe you could meet there?"

"I can't go to the cabin?"

"You'd be welcome most anytime. But not in this situation."

"I owe you, Billy."

"Other way around. You treated me decent last spring and so did Clayton Shoot. And tell him I need to talk with him."

"I will."

"So what's *your* number?" Billy smiled when he said that.

Chapter 34

"Monday night football tonight, Sheriff?" Alonso asked. They were in Clayton's office at the end of a very long day—Gus, the sheriff, ISB agent Perciak, and the deputy. Fiona was invited but declined. Not feeling well again.

"That still on TV?" Perciak grunted, studying the sheriff's bare workplace. "Haven't watched in years."

Clayton felt embarrassed by his mostly empty walls. Former Sheriff Artie Paulsen carted off thirty years of plaques and accolades when he resigned in May—including photographs with two presidents and a college national championship football coach. His items left shadows. It would take decades to replicate Paulsen's collection, but Clayton had stuff of his own, including, it occurred to him now, that pen and ink drawing Iris Cobb had done of his horse. A way to honor her. Lots of people would see it.

With everyone settled in, Clayton nodded to Gus. Gus turned to Perciak. "We spent the day . . ."

He waved her off. "I know what you and Deputy Rangel were up to."

Gus frowned.

Perciak continued. "I called the Border Patrol myself to see if they detected your run-around their checkpoint." He paused.

"And?" Clayton pushed.

"They did not."

No one spoke as they pondered the implications.

Alonso broke the silence. "It was tight though. Ms. Summerlin didn't give herself much room for error. We just barely got back to the desk at Fort Davis by 4:30 when we know she talked with the ranger."

Clayton shook his head. "She had plenty of leeway."

Alonso didn't understand.

"Regina got there around 4:30 because that's when she got there," Clayton explained. "The fort is open until 6:00."

"And if something had gone wrong on her way down to Big Bend," Perciak said, bouncing a finger on his lip, "she could have tried again another day."

"But we did prove she *coulda* done it. That's something, no?" Alonso needed affirmation and looked for it in Clayton's body language.

"The key point was getting around those license plate readers at the checkpoints," the sheriff said. "I'm thinkin' she reconnoitered a path across Iris's properties weeks ago, real careful not to wear a trail doing it. They've got horses on the Cobb she might have used too."

"She likely tried it with a truck though," Gus said, "to see if Border Patrol reacted. And if they'd called her out, she'd just be on her own land. Nothin' suspicious."

"What does she drive?" Perciak asked.

"4Runner TRD." Alonso remembered because he wanted one himself.

"And the Cobb has other off-roaders," Clayton noted.

Perciak studied the grain of the table. "I can already hear her lawyers blaming you guys for any paths across her property."

Clayton disagreed. "We know where Rangel and Stumpf were."

"And there was other tracks out there already, 'specially around the hunting camp," Gus added.

"Just an observation, not a criticism," Perciak said. "You guys added to the investigation today. I give you that."

"So, where are we?" Clayton said, knowing how he felt. But he wanted Perciak on the record.

The agent winced. "Despite an alibi that suggests otherwise—I guess Regina Summerlin *could* have killed Iris Cobb. And given the Cobb Institute's location, she might have used those border cameras to enhance an alibi she already had in mind. Painting all day in Fort Davis."

"Okay . . ." Clayton began, but Gus interrupted.

"I got a boy who reminds me whenever I suspect him of somethin' that 'cause he *coulda* done it dudn't mean he did. Same here."

"Might say as much about migrants or drug runners on the Maverick Road," Perciak said. "But your kid's right. *Could have* doesn't mean *did*."

Feeling left out, Alonso chimed in. "What about Mateo?"

"Well, that gets complicated," the sheriff said slowly. "Matthew Cooper expected Iris to paint on Friday because she usually did. But remember he left for Taos on Thursday to deliver her paintings. He couldn't know what happened Friday morning.

"But I'm convinced Summerlin knew Cooper was on the road—if nothing else, from that note Iris left on her desk before leaving for the park. Or Gina could also have found out from Iris herself Friday morning. Whatever. But then she used the note on Saturday to clear Cooper when he turned up. Pretended, too, that she didn't know he was returning Saturday—said she had her phone off after Iris died. But that seems real suspect now."

"Lots of movin' parts," Gus muttered. "Gina waited until the right ones came together. And maybe they did last Friday."

Alonso looked puzzled. "Couldn't Cooper still be in cahoots with Ms. Summerlin on the murder?"

Perciak shook his head, which surprised Clayton, knowing the agent's dislike for the photographer. "It was Iris who told the Taos gallery to expect Cooper with the paintings," he explained. "Gina didn't control that, but she maybe took advantage of it. And what would Cooper gain by killing Iris anyway? He says he didn't know about the will and she was already his mentor and lover and—what's the female equivalent of *sugar daddy?*"

"Sugar momma," Alonso said too quickly. Then flushed.

Clayton felt bad for the kid. "I'm tryin' to keep an open mind," he said. "We're obligated to. But my gut tells me Gina planned the murder and did it on her own. Damn it, though, if I can see a way to prove it."

Chapter 35

It was just after 8:00 AM Tuesday morning when Claire's cell phone rang. She was up and finishing breakfast, light streaming through her kitchen windows. Claire didn't have a good view of the sky from her residential street. But sunrise on a cloudless morning was brilliant anyplace in West Texas.

"Am I speaking to Professor Harp?" She recognized the caller's voice.

"You are."

"Pardon if I don't identify myself."

"I understand." Billy warned Claire that Piper was paranoid about tabloid reporters listening in.

"Can you meet me in Study Butte this morning? Do you know where that is?"

"I drove through on Sunday." *Just a string of shops and gas stations along Highway 118.*

"We could have lunch and talk. There's an Alon station where 180 meets 170. It's where you'd turn for Terlingua."

"I've stopped there for gas."

"Behind it is the Big Bend Café. I'll get at a table under the photographs by the entrance. Let's say 11? Can you get there by then? I don't know distances around here."

"Everything's far apart," Claire said, guessing a trip of eighty miles. "But I'll make it easy. I appreciate the call."

"Billy was persuasive."

Claire wasn't sure what Piper meant. "Did Billy explain why I want to talk?"

"Kinda. To be honest, I wouldn't mind a chat—especially with a woman."

"Anything you need? Magazines or newspapers?"

"I'm fine. I don't want to read what's being said about me."

"Then I'll see you in a few hours."

"Big Bend Resort and Café," Piper repeated and hung up.

Good. Claire had time to finish breakfast and swing by her office to handle a swarm of emails from her publisher. She was in jeans, boots, and a long-sleeve blouse, but grabbed a floppy hat on her way out. Sunglasses too. Easy to look stylish in the desert.

Claire worked at her Sul Ross University desk until just after 9:30, then walked to the parking lot, hoping a sprint down Highway 118 would clear her mind. She set the cruise control for 75 just outside town, a stiff wind tossing her boxy Jeep.

Nearing the Border Patrol checkpoint, she slowed to study the Cobb Institute on the left where she'd been on Saturday, just three days earlier. Aside from the studio where Cobb's memorial was held, she now noticed a cluster of low-lying office buildings, handsome residences, and what might be barns or warehouses. These structures barely registered before.

She reset the cruise control and thought about her upcoming conversation. Certainly, she'd ask Piper why she deserted Alex on the South Rim, humiliating him. Was it because she lost the movie role or something else? She'd pursue *something else* as far as necessary. She wanted the truth.

After all, Piper had been an adult playing a high school kid on *Brainiacs* while Alex was the real thing. Hadn't she foreseen the complications—the legal issues in their relationship, whether in California or Texas? And who, if anyone, helped her off the South Rim? Someone from the film company or even the crew? Donnie Majewski wasn't the only trail guide working for Throng!Media that day.

Claire suddenly wondered how Clayton might interrogate Piper in this situation, how he'd get information from her. Because, well, Clayton was almost always on her mind—if she was being honest. Right now, she imagined him in his office, fretting over the Cobb case, maybe with that special agent from the park police. Or maybe he'd taken the morning off to check cattle or crops with Beatrice. Alex along too.

She'd been with desirable men before the sheriff—with more men than Clayton had women, she'd wager. But none had his easy charm and simple grace. How he leaned against a car, played with his dogs, settled calmly into a chair. She could picture herself growing old with this guy.

He was the first man to make her think about kids too. Beautiful sons and daughters growing up with mountains and wide horizons. Could she really do better? Did she want more—maybe some mystery or risk or edge?

Claire recalled a conversation months ago with her blunt-spoken elderly friend Miss Lucy. A woman made wealthy by a string of marriages who now lived alone on a luxurious property near Fort Davis, still pining for Clayton's father Finis forty years after she'd turned him down. Too distraught to attend the man's funeral last May.

Some mistakes are irrevocable.

Claire found herself braking near the Terlingua Ranch turnout still ten miles from her destination. Open spaces and a sky bright with desert sun. Empty road. Simple choices. She suddenly realized what she'd been denying.

Her restlessness this week had almost nothing to do with Piper and Alex. Or who Alex slept with or why he was at the Shoot Ranch rather than with her in Alpine. She wasn't angry because Alex chose Clayton over her. Her problem was she was not with Clayton herself. And that was her fault, not Alex's and not Clayton's.

What after all *did* she want? Claire had spent five years at the University of Texas earning a PhD in literature and then veered into the low-rent (if high revenue) sideline of writing composition textbooks. Hoping to escape family pressures, she'd applied on a whim for a teaching position at a school she'd never heard of in a town she could barely find on a map. She planned to stay at Sul Ross State two, maybe three, years at most. Then discovered she liked West Texas more than she expected—not just its astonishing landscapes but the people it attracted and sustained.

And Clayton Shoot.

Yet because of what happened in Alpine—solving a murder with Clayton and recovering an important manuscript—Claire now had job offers she'd only fantasized about in grad school. A senior editing position with the publisher of *Madrone*, in her choice of its Boston or New York offices. Prestigious schools across the country calling her repeatedly, urging Claire to visit, to apply. Once-in-a-lifetime opportunities.

Except it was unthinkable that Clayton would follow her. He was rooted in this arid place, and yet his talents weren't wasted. He was already the highest-profile official in Texas's biggest county. He might follow up with a career in the State House, which would give them, assuming they married, plenty of time in Austin. Washington could be in the cards too. A recent Congressional District 23 representative came from Alpine. Why not Clayton Shoot?

But she couldn't imagine Clayton thriving elsewhere. He was as native to Far West Texas as ocotillo. Did it come down to Clayton versus her own career?

She knew which choice would keep her warm at night and smile at her for no reason and make her feel protected and loved. And yet . . .

Without realizing it, Claire had cancelled the cruise control and drifted twenty miles below the speed limit (almost criminal in Texas). And Highway 118 was turning twisty again, the surrounding hills scraped raw by mining operations the previous century. Study Butte, she realized, was just over the hill and she now regretted even making this appointment with Piper Robinet.

Because Eugenia Harp had been right. Claire's problems with her brother were of her own making. If Alex found Clayton and Sam and Donnie attractive—more power to him. Claire liked the same men. And whatever happened at Big Bend between Alex and his Liz Taylor look-alike co-star mattered not at all.

Which embarrassed Claire since Piper Robinet was at this moment waiting for her in a greasy spoon. Claire had to finish what she'd started. And elements of Piper's story *did* still puzzle her. The girl said she wanted to talk. Okay. Claire could do that.

Chapter 36

About the same time Claire neared Study Butte Tuesday morning, Matthew Cooper (aka Mateo Bottaio) was finishing a long session in Iris Cobb's office, a spacious room just off her studio. Working with Lydia Champlain, the Institute's office manager, he'd reviewed Iris's papers and recent correspondence to identify items that required immediate attention. The FBI had already examined the materials and authorized their return.

Not a stickler for business details, Iris had for years left overall management of the Cobb to her stepdaughter Gina, who in turn relied on Lydia to handle mundane stuff—paying bills, corresponding with the public, dealing with contractors.

But in recent months, Iris made Matthew privy to business matters too, sharing passwords, silently copying almost all her professional correspondence, soliciting his advice about matters as routine as maintenance, and even occasionally asking him to review Gina's policies and initiatives. She clearly wanted him as involved in her professional life as he already was in her private one, possibly as a counterweight to Gina. Or maybe to be sure he gained the business savvy he'd need as a successful photographer.

As a result, Matthew quickly came to appreciate Lydia's role in running the Cobb. Wavy-haired, down-to-earth, and smart as a whip, Lydia didn't give a hoot about art. But she was loyal to Iris, who rewarded her dedication and common sense handsomely over the years. Matthew and Lydia sifted through message after message this morning—most of which made better sense to the office manager than to him. Matthew sensed Lydia was assessing his moves and weighing his emotions too.

"Do you think Gina should be doing this instead of me?" he'd finally asked midway through Iris's emails. They were having to explain, over and over again, that Iris Cobb was dead. *Not easy.*

"Just the opposite," Lydia said after a pause. She pushed away from the desk and drew the office door nearly closed. "I've been debating whether to tell you what I've noticed recently. With Regina. I know you've been close with her in the past."

"In the past, yes."

"And maybe you two are still on the same page. Hell, I'm probably going to get fired anyway."

"Fired? Why would we fire you?"

"I can't explain exactly. The past months have been so *peculiar.*" Lydia paused, folded her hands on the table and stared silently at Matthew, as if asking permission to continue. He nodded, realizing she was just about his age.

"Sometimes when talking business, Iris and Regina barely noticed me in the room. But I was privy to all their dealings, so there was nothing to hide from me I guess. When it came to money, Iris was the artist and Regina the manager. She was a huge asset to her mother, maybe unappreciated. Iris was delighted by the Cobb Institute programs Gina set up and profited from all her daughter's marketing schemes—the greeting cards, pottery designs, towels, candles. You know what I'm talking about."

Matthew certainly did and would soon benefit from these enterprises himself, given the terms of the will.

"But she rarely gave Regina any credit. Feature stories and interviewers always praised Iris's business flair. But that was all her stepdaughter's work. To Iris, business was beneath the dignity of an artist. At best, Gina was just a useful subordinate."

Not news to Matthew. "The problem went both ways," he objected, "Gina thought she could be as serious a painter as Iris. Even I could see her talents weren't on canvas. Maybe I should have been more honest with her."

Lydia shook her head vigorously, curls bouncing. "No, you've got no liability here. Regina's problems run deeper, I'm sure. But we're off track. Or maybe not.

"What I've watched for months is Regina making decisions about Iris's assets—both the Cobb and the Taos enterprises—mostly on her own. Taking Iris out of the loop or injecting herself into the business in odd ways."

"Such as?" Matthew asked, leaning back in his chair, impressed by Lydia's mettle.

"It was Regina who thought you should be in Iris's will. She pushed for that change a few months ago."

"Why in the world . . . ?"

Lydia's dark brown eyes went wide. "Mr. Cooper . . . she's still in love with you."

It took him thirty seconds to grasp Lydia's insinuation. The office manager was patient.

"So Gina set it up that, if something happened to Iris, we'd be joined at the hip?" he said.

"And elsewhere." Lydia should have resisted the taunt.

"And Iris went along with this?"

"Because Iris really *did* appreciate how happy you made her. She told me so herself. And that's all she told me about your relationship, Mr. Bottaio."

Hint of a smile on Lydia's face. Or maybe disapproval? Matthew reddened. Couldn't hide much from this clever woman, he realized. Maybe Gina should have been more careful.

"And so?"

"There's no grief in Regina now that I can see," Lydia frowned, "just a determination to move on. She's closed off her emotions and is making one major decision after another on the fly. She seems so cold and out of touch."

"That's maybe how she deals with grief?" Matthew said, having witnessed the same behavior. It worried him, but he didn't think Gina was acting out of character. She'd always been hardnosed and driven.

Lydia leaned in closer across the desk. "She's ordered us to prepare all the important works of art for immediate shipment to Taos. She's determined to transfer the whole operation to New Mexico. Even arranged with movers to pack her furniture and personal items, though she now intends to leave ahead of them—maybe early as today. Says she'll stay in Iris's condo in the mountains there and that you'll follow."

That *was* news to Matthew. "What happens to the Cobb in the meantime?"

"Closed down until spring and maybe for good."

"She said that?"

"Not in so many words. But she knows New Mexico generates the real income. The Institute represents Iris Cobb's ties to her Texas roots. Regina doesn't feel the same attachment."

Not quite shut, the office door now opened slowly, Regina Summerlin standing calmly in the hall.

"That will be all for now, Ms. Champlain," she said, signaling for Lydia to leave while stepping into the office herself. Lydia dipped her eyes and did as requested, but not before gazing back intensely at Matthew when she passed behind Gina. No regrets there, Matthew realized.

Gina waited until Lydia stepped down the corridor. "We'll have to let that one go," she said with a tight smile, as if she assumed Matthew agreed.

"Is she wrong?"

"About closing the Cobb? You and I have talked about that, haven't we? Just temporary until we get matters settled in New Mexico."

"And you're leaving now?"

"And you too soon after, I'm thinking. You can decide what maintenance staff to keep here through the winter and secure whatever art we leave behind. All the good stuff is going to Taos, the very best of it with me."

"Right now? And the FBI is okay with this?"

"I'm not sure what you mean. I don't need permission to go anywhere. Neither of us is a suspect."

"But leaving might raise questions."

"About what?" Gina took the open chair still warm from Lydia and reached across the desk to grasp Matthew's wrist. "Don't you see, Mateo, what's happening in this investigation? The FBI and ISB and even that Furcron woman at Big Bend already know who killed my mother. Oh, they've made a show of verifying every detail of your whereabouts and mine when Iris was robbed and shot. But they know beyond a shadow of a doubt you were in New Mexico and I was painting at Fort Davis.

"And they're going through the same motions in interviewing dozens of artists and activists not only in Brewster County but across the whole region, right into Midland and Odessa. They're drawing out the process until people forget about what actually happened just a few miles across the Mexican border at Luna's Jacal."

"And that would be?"

Regina used the little finger on her right hand to pare grit from under the nails of her left.

"The feds won't admit the obvious truth—that Iris was killed by illegal aliens expecting an easy score against a frail old white woman with a Cadillac. That's not the narrative they want told about the border. Such a crime gets in the way of larger political and social agendas their agencies support. Investigators will do as they're told until people forget Iris Cobb. And there's nothing you nor I or even Sheriff Shoot can do about it."

Matthew Cooper said nothing. He'd caught similar chatter on talk radio yesterday, both local and national, even the same phrases—Gina had no doubt heard it too. Or maybe she'd initiated it. *Did she believe it?*

Gina's eyes darted from the window to Matthew and back, all the while drumming the desktop with her fingers. She looked out of place in Iris's office, cluttered as it was with mementoes of a rich and complex life. Matthew could imagine Gina ordering these shelves cleared and made tidy for future visitors . . . or owners.

He wondered if the cruel event of last week had strained his former lover beyond her limits. Matthew was familiar with Gina's obsessions and manias. He quit her in part because of them. But he felt an obligation to her too.

"Maybe we should take time off tomorrow and head for Chinati Springs?" he said. "It's going to be warm, you can paint, I can bring my cameras. We'll enjoy the waters."

"And spend the night?"

He shrugged. Couldn't bring himself to say *yes.*

She laughed. "You don't get it. My truck is almost ready to go right now and I'm heading for Taos soon as I can. I may only get as far as Carlsbad or Roswell tonight, but I need to be on the road. To secure our future and protect our interests."

"A few days won't make a difference."

"But they will. This is a crucial moment for Iris's brand—the gallery, the Institute, and especially her merchandise. We need to secure her legacy while she's still in the public eye."

"For being murdered?"

"That's not something we can change. But, yes, she's a bigger figure now because of what happened. Think about Versace or the attempt to kill Andy Warhol. We can't bring Iris back but we can lock down her reputation and our own artistic positions by what we do in the next few weeks with our place in Taos."

Perhaps she sensed his skepticism. She sat back in the chair and smoothed her denim shirt—though it still looked bulky. She was in work jeans too, sensible attire for serious hauling and packing. Not a trace of makeup. Oddly attractive, he thought. But, right now, scary.

"We'll rebrand the Taos properties as the Cobb Museum and Gallery and establish a permanent collection of Iris's best works there, right up to her very last painting. I've already shipped more than two dozen pieces from her personal collection to Taos and I'll take four or five more myself.

"Then we'll use the prestige of these masterpieces to attract a higher caliber of artist to the gallery. People who will want their work associated with the Cobb name. Of course, we'll auction off or sell what remains of Iris's work, but very gradually and selectively, making sure buyers have no idea how many paintings we have—and there are many. We'll push prices as high as possible."

Gina rose from the chair to skim the dust off one of Iris's crammed bookcases, suddenly avoiding eye contact. "Naturally, your photographs will have a prominent place in our reconfigured gallery, as will my plein air works."

Matthew saw this coming. Iris had for months featured his top images in the Taos Gallery and they sold well. But she'd never allowed Gina to hang her canvases there—and with good reason.

"This is extraordinary," Matthew said slowly, "but there is the matter of the will. Iris gave the Taos gallery to me."

Rather than be offended, Gina turned around, smiled, and then stroked his arm. "Oh, Mateo. I'm doing all this more for you than me. I know what the will says. But it'll be in probate for months, maybe years, especially since we'll be working across state lines."

Gina's argument made sense, but was it sincere? He couldn't say. Given the size of Iris's estate, settling it had to be complicated. Gina could even challenge what her stepmother left him—though that would be more difficult if she'd suggested the legacy herself, as Lydia claimed.

Or maybe Iris had left him even more than Gina intended?

Gina, however, was insistent. "We can't ignore this opportunity, Mateo. It breaks my heart to lose Iris. But we need to act maturely, bracketing our grief for now while we secure my mother's legacy and our own."

Matthew was sure she'd rehearsed those lines. *Bracketing our grief?* Lydia was right. Gina wasn't struggling to control her sorrow. She didn't have any.

And she wasn't finished yet. "There's our commercial lines to tend to as well. It's too late to do anything for this Christmas season. The Iris Cobb cards are printed and shipped already. I checked. But we'll advertise the hell out of them and then redo all the products next year.

"I'm thinking we'll move the brand upscale, expand what we offer, and market the new lineup as the Iris Cobb Heritage Series. We can run with it for decades like what's been done for, say, Georgia O'Keeffe or R.C. Gorman. Just think of the opportunity for posters, jewelry, ceramics, maybe even western furniture. Iris was sometimes too fussy about what she'd put her name on."

Gina couldn't conceal her glee. It frightened Matthew—because she didn't have the sense now even to conceal it.

Chapter 37

Fluorescent lights, fake wood tables, stackable chairs framed in chrome. To Piper, the Big Bend Resort and Adventures Café seemed as down-to-earth as Arkansas. She and Tyler Tribble dined there on steak rancheros several nights ago. He'd worried then someone might recognize Piper. But today, a full week since her escapade on the South Rim, locals had mostly forgotten her. And nosey tabloids couldn't stake out every diner in West Texas.

Still, she took precautions for the meeting with Claire Harp. Eased up on the makeup and tucked her hair under a battered cowboy hat borrowed from Tyler. A little paper in the lining made it fit. Piper play a fatigued tourist, scruffy and bored, even if she felt darn near blissful inside.

A little less so when she saw the reaction Claire Harp got entering the diner. Tall and slim will do that. Almost as attractive as her brother, Piper thought—same profile, same confident stride. Pulling off sunglasses, the professor scanned the room. Didn't spot Piper. It was humbling. She wasn't used to being a wallflower.

She waved on Harp's second pass.

They hugged. Piper wasn't sure why—they had little in common, except Alex. But seeing the professor snapped the South Rim back into focus. Claire would expect the whole story now. And Piper wanted to talk. Needed to, in fact. She'd been mostly isolated, beginning at Tyler's Study Butte apartment for two days following her hike on the South Rim—she ventured outside just once on her own then.

She and Tyler *had* made a dash last Thursday into Fort Stockton, a hundred miles from Study Butte, to photograph her standing beside a giant roadrunner statue. *Paisano Pete, was it?* Miles of empty range, there and back. Tyler said reporters would think she was heading to Los Angeles if she appeared in a selfie taken near Interstate 10. At the time, Piper and Tyler figured on staying in Brewster County for a while because of his job at the national park.

Life became much more comfortable a day later when, at his party, Billy Lamb offered Tyler use of a cabin near the southern boundary of the McCann Ranch. The guy was proud of the place. Built by his mother Delia McCann in the early years of her marriage to William Lamb, the getaway ended up in Billy's hands after Delia died. Billy's father was too heartbroken to revisit it.

Tyler and Piper headed there right after her meeting with Alex Harp in the pool pavilion. Billy had even slipped trays of cold cuts, fruit, and desserts into Tyler's back seat before they drove off. (Bottles of champagne too.) Practically a honeymoon. The lodge looked out upon more stars than Piper had ever seen.

The next morning brought swirling fog and antelope right to their door. Tyler had the weekend off, so they could figure things out. No phone service, no cable, just the two of them after so many years apart. They'd made good use of a copper-paneled bed in the guest room.

Now, she watched Claire ease into a hard vinyl chair across from her at the café. The professor looked calm and reserved, not uptight like she sounded on the phone.

"I'm grateful you were willing to see me," Claire said.

A sturdy waitress stopped by the table to take their early lunch order. It was not yet eleven. Claire suggested chips and salsa to start and maybe beef enchiladas?

Piper agreed, not terribly hungry. "You didn't recognize me just now?"

"Not at first. You're invisible under that hat."

"I'd take it off, but my hair's a mess. Billy's cabin doesn't have a proper vanity in the guest room."

Claire scanned prints on sale on the restaurant walls. "I'd assume he's had more than a few girls there over the years."

Piper shook her head. "Doubt it. The big house is much closer to town. But the lodge is more romantic, even if it's all guns and antlers and cow paintings." Piper fingered the tabletop. "Did Alex fill you in about our meeting at Billy's?"

"He didn't say much."

"I didn't tell him much," Piper admitted. "When Tyler first mentioned the birthday party, I said we *had* to go and that Billy should invite your brother. That way Alex could see I was okay. More than okay. And I needed to admit to him finally how old I was."

Claire frowned.

"You figured it out soon as we met in Alpine. But you didn't tell him, I guess. It's possible Alex was onto me anyway. But the age difference didn't matter in Texas. We were legal here . . ."

Claire's eyes darkened. "Technically."

Piper nodded. "I'd have been happy to be Alex's first love, even in a tent—if he wanted that. But it wasn't my reason for coming to Texas."

"Oh?" Claire said.

"Not what you suspect. Even at Billy's party, I didn't quite explain to Alex what I was up to or why I left him on the rim. I just said everything fell apart after Tabreetha Bree-Jones got the role I wanted. But I assured Alex I was all right. I'd have said more, but he stopped me."

"He stopped *you?*"

"Alex told me point blank that he'd share anything I told him with the sheriff. Because, for some reason, he'd gotten all close to the guy and was rooming with him?" Piper couldn't stifle a smile.

"Alex wasn't at my house because . . ."

"Billy explained what happened. Must have been tough for you. But Billy thinks real highly of Clayton Shoot. That's the guy's name, right?"

Claire nodded.

Her reserve annoyed Piper. "Okay, here's the deal. Your brother barely knew me, not on the rim or all the months we worked on *Brainiacs*. He could find publicity stuff in my network bio—teenager from Arkansas, regional acting experience, committed to world peace and clean oceans. But I didn't see any point in sharing my life story. I doubted Alex would believe it."

Claire at least looked interested now. The waitress interrupted them with refills of ice tea.

When she left, Claire pushed back in her chair and stared at Piper. "You might be few years older than Alex," she said, "but I'm nearly twice his age. I've spent much less time with him than you recently. Honestly, I don't know how to talk to him anymore or to get him to be open with me. I was hoping you might."

"He's not a mystery man," Piper said.

Claire frowned. "Just tell me. Was anything between you and Alex real? Did you leave my brother on the rim for this Tyler guy you're with now? Or did Alex let you down in some way and then Tyler stepped in?"

Piper was genuinely puzzled. Claire was at least talking. But what could she mean by Alex *letting her down?*

Piper removed the cowboy hat, pulled out the paper lining, and shook her hair into better shape. She decided to start over. "How I got where I am is a long story," she said, "and a mostly sad one. Tyler knows it now and I'll share it with you. Then maybe you'll see why I didn't tell your brother much. You can decide what more he needs to know—if anything."

Chapter 38

Alex knew something was up when a text from his Los Angeles-based agent Bob Markus buzzed his phone midday on Tuesday. He was on a deck outdoors at the Shoots' main house with Beatrice, working off her prompt, *Art thou not Romeo and a Montague?* They'd been at it since breakfast. Instinctively, he checked the message.

"From my agent," he explained.

Beatrice sighed. They had discussed Bob Markus before. Beatrice thought he should hire a more aggressive representative. "A woman would work even harder for you."

Alex supposed she was right. Markus's terse text announced a conference call with Throng!Media executives the next day at 10:00 AM PST. In Texas time, twelve noon, Wednesday, October 27. He read it to Beatrice.

"And what do you think is the agenda for this sudden meeting?" she sniffed. "You certainly should know."

He didn't disagree. Alex called Markus but got an answering service. He left the message Beatrice suggested: *I cannot participate without more information.* On his own, he'd have used *can't*.

Markus called back before they reached *What satisfaction canst thou have tonight?* Bob specialized in handling actors on teen networks. Easy money and quick turnover. Most just morphed into undergrads or baristas when their series ended. Alex Harp was the stellar exception, and Markus was happy now to be dealing with top-tier producers and media executives.

"Not a contract issue—I don't want you to worry about it," Markus explained. But it sounded like he should. Alex switched to speakerphone, so Beatrice could listen in. "Bree-Jones's people want to explore artistic matters."

"Some people will be in England then?" Alex guessed, calculating the time difference—and wondering whether Tabreetha would join the mix. They'd never spoken.

"Right. I think it will be 6:00 PM there. End of the work day. But I don't know exactly who'll be in the conference. Expect Throng!Media executives, the producer, screenwriter maybe, Bree-Jones's top people."

"No shit?" Alex said.

Beatrice intervened. "And those artistic issues concern *what* exactly?"

There was a pause. "Who's there with you, Alex?"

"My acting coach—Beatrice Shoot."

"Didn't know you needed one."

"So good to speak with you too, Mr. Markus," Beatrice said. "Now, again, what issues will Alex and I be discussing tomorrow and with whom?"

"I don't know everything I'd like to about the meeting, Ms. Shoot. I do know executives are considering how best to make use of Ms. Bree-Jones's talents, now that she's aboard the project."

"Surely they thought about that before they signed her to a contract."

"Alex?" Rob Markus seemed uneasy with Beatrice's condescension.

"She's my senior artistic advisor too," Alex explained, making up the title. Beatrice smiled. "When I signed more than a month ago, the studio had a strong concept for the film. What's changed?"

Markus did not respond immediately. All he knew for sure, he admitted after some hedging, was that the call concerned *Romeo and Juliet* itself, not salary or contract matters.

"But trust me on this, Alex."

"A conference call out of the blue? Good news rarely arrives in so peremptory a fashion," Beatrice scoffed. "Perhaps your employers do not take you seriously?"

I'm just a kid, Alex conceded with a shrug to Beatrice, but then spoke directly to Bob. "I should know what's on the table at a meeting like this."

"It will be fine, Alex," Markus said. "I guarantee Throng!Media wants to keep you happy. You're crucial to their plans right now and they know you have other offers." Markus's voice dipped into a more personal register as he signed off. "You know I'm on your side, always."

"I do."

"Here's my advice then. Be Alex Harp and say what's on your mind."

In the quiet that followed the call, Beatrice looked about as uneasy as Alex felt.

"So there are *sides*," she observed. "That is important, even if we do not know precisely what the divide is or who stands where. Perhaps all our work on *Romeo and Juliet* will be for naught."

"I'll talk to my dad tonight and he can notify my lawyer. They're personal friends and she vetted my contract."

Alex and Beatrice remained outside on the deck, but they set *Romeo and Juliet* aside. Beatrice broke a lengthy silence.

"When he was a junior in high school, Clayton played Macbeth."

Alex couldn't imagine Clayton as the Scottish king. "Was he any good?"

Beatrice stared at a cloud in the western sky. "Legend says King James I—for whom Shakespeare wrote *Macbeth*—preferred short plays."

Alex didn't interrupt.

"That evening, everyone in the audience was grateful."

Chapter 39

"So, love at first sight between teenagers—you and Tyler Tribble?" Claire said, skeptical of the story Piper was spinning. The couple had met almost a decade earlier as sophomores at Hope High School in Arkansas.

"I'd been around rough men all my life, most of them jerks and blowhards—my father included," Piper explained. "Tyler was different. Quiet, always with a smile, respectful to a fault. He treated me as more than a face and body. There'd been interracial dating for decades in Hope, but we still became an item at school. It wasn't easy, especially with our families—mine barely white trash and his social climbers pushing Tyler to go away to college."

Piper sounded rehearsed, like she'd dreamed up the tale for tabloids. But Claire let the girl go on.

"We dated almost two years. Our friends saw no future for us. He was a science geek and I just wanted to escape to California and do my thing. I acted in every local play I could. Got good notices. Tyler at least believed in me, said I was real talented.

"But after graduation he headed to a forestry program at Colorado State and I was stuck in Arkansas. We grew apart. It's what happens to high school sweethearts. Then everything at home just broke. I never had much family life to begin with, but daddy abandoned my younger sister and me after our mother got sick. Went off with another woman. Haven't heard from him since.

"After our mother passed, we lived with a grandma, supporting ourselves on the old lady's social security and my job at K-Mart. Eventually, my sister and I started out to California. My idea mostly. We left as soon as Piper was old enough to be emancipated. Nobody noticed."

Confused, Claire interrupted. "Piper?"

The girl gazed at the acoustic ceiling. "Yeah—sorry. I'm running ahead of myself. Piper was my younger sister's name. I'm actually Pippa Robinson."

The young woman saw Claire's skepticism.

"I know—a soap opera," she sighed, "and it gets worse. We headed to California in a car so old that it had an airbag only on the driver's side. We crashed in Nevada. I survived but my sister in the passenger seat didn't. I awoke in the hospital alone. People couldn't have been nicer, but I felt like an alien. No relatives or friends to call. No place to return to. If I thought about Tyler, it only hurt more. We hadn't spoken then in maybe two years?"

Claire was puzzled by the name thing. But she'd let Piper or Pippa tell her tale. The only concrete facts seemed to be Tyler, who Billy Lamb actually knew, and the girl's undeniable TV career in California. Tabloids didn't waste time on nobodies.

"There's a happy ending—sort of," Piper said. "We'd been hit by a drunk driver in a Mercedes. Son of a prominent Nevada politician. By the time I got out of the hospital, I had a check in hand and a new Chevy. Nothing grand, but enough, I thought, for a start in Hollywood. I'd get an apartment, wait tables, or maybe work at Target until I found something at a studio.

"I sure got a lot of attention from men at the hospital—orderlies and even a doctor or two. Nurses made a big deal about how lucky I'd been to be unscarred because what a shame that would have been. By then I knew what my assets were and what I could do with them.

"The settlement check was made out to Piper Robinson. I think our purses got switched because the funeral home that cremated my sister's remains recorded the deceased as Pippa. So when I headed to California, I became Piper and was suddenly four years younger. And that's how I sold myself to the WetBTE network, then casting a show about high school nerds. Just a kid—with boobs like Liz Taylor."

Claire smiled at that. Maybe some of this *was* true.

"I lied about my age initially but was careful to use my real social security number and IDs when I got one of the leads in the show. I do think Piper was a better stage name than Pippa and I went with Robinet since it sounded classier."

"You wouldn't be the first actress to lie about her age," Claire said.

"The network never raised questions. I wasn't difficult or a troublemaker. They were happy with me."

"And that's how you ended up in *Brainiacs* with Alex."

"Yep, a tough twenty-three-year old who could look, maybe, fifteen? And just like with your brother, cameras loved me, I knew my lines and was good with dialects—and I was ambitious."

Seductive smile too, Claire conceded.

"I got hired just before Alex and so I remember when he first walked on the set. All eyes checking out the new guy, who somehow managed to seem humble. Acting, even then. I wanted to dislike him because he had what I didn't—family, friends, a home. He was even staying with an aunt in Los Angeles. What I wouldn't give for someone like that to look out for me.

"Alex asked me about my parents, my high school, Arkansas, the shows I did there. I was so hungry for attention, I made stuff up. Turns out he treated the whole cast and crew the same way. But I didn't care."

Claire nodded. She'd seen Alex's charm when he interacted with Clayton's relatives and friends. He got along with everyone from prickly Beatrice to that little niece at the BBQ who'd called him *Charlie*.

"Right off, two of our episodes won awards. Network executives couldn't be happier, especially since the parent company—Throng!Media—wanted to grow beyond kiddie TV. They needed a star and they found one in your brother. I could see where he was headed and decided to hang on. He got a bit part in a movie and then another, and then—well I don't have to tell you. Oscar buzz after barely a year in the business."

Claire read more admiration than envy in Piper's dark eyes. And she couldn't blame the girl for ambition. Even academics glommed onto rising stars in the profession.

"To make a *very* long story short," Piper said, "your brother and I, after some rocky weeks, hit it off. He might have been a high school jock, but he was the sharpest guy I'd ever met. Except when it came to women."

Finally, Claire thought. Unfortunately, lunch arrived.

⋇ ⋇ ⋇

"WHO'D GUESS WE'D find enchiladas this good two hundred miles from the nearest city?" Piper said, mouth full. "Of course, Mexico's just across the river."

Claire nodded, but wanted to stay on point. "That's exactly what I came to talk about this morning," Claire said, wiping her lip.

"Enchiladas?" Piper laughed.

"No. My brother's relationships with women."

Piper lowered her fork slowly. "Is that really your business?"

"I wasn't home much during his adolescence. We've grown apart."

"You know he'll be eighteen in a few weeks?"

Claire sat back in her seat. "I'm not sure how to put this . . . I think now maybe you've been good for Alex, and I expect you've been protecting him, and for that I'm grateful."

"From what?" Piper seemed genuinely bewildered. "I don't know what you're talking about." It was her turn to look skeptical.

Claire was embarrassed she couldn't just say it. But then she did. "I think Alex might be gay and you've been helping him seem . . ."

Awkward pause.

"Not gay?" Piper finally said.

Claire nodded and Piper laughed so loud they attracted attention. She lowered her head.

"The boy couldn't be more straight. I've never slept with your brother, Claire. But I've had close-up scenes with him in the show and sometimes he just can't keep it down. It's a joke on the set how horny he is."

"Really?"

"Oh, yeah. I know sex wasn't Alex's initial reason for coming to Texas because he'd planned a trip here before I got involved. But once I did . . . well, he expected a memorable night on the South Rim. And I broke his—I'd say *heart* but that wasn't the body part involved. Cruelest thing is, I set him up that night to share a tent . . ."

"With Donnie Majewski," Claire said slowly.

"He told you?"

"I've met Mr. Majewski."

"And that made you more worried . . ."

"A very fit young man." Claire was not about to admit her own attraction to the trail guide.

"You know for what it's worth, I think your brother is still a virgin. He allowed me to pretend I was too, but knew I wasn't."

"He does seem comfortable around gay men." Claire had to put that on the table. "Very comfortable."

"And that's why you think . . . ?" Piper laughed again and Claire was starting to resent it. "When it came to starlets, your aunt in California policed Alex like the Gestapo. What the poor woman never figured out was that maybe half the men on our set—actors, crew, studio executives—were head over heels for her nephew. But Alex was totally okay with it. Not above a little flirtation for the sake of community spirit either."

"So, not gay?"

"Gay friendly. Hell, people friendly."

Piper reached across the table and grabbed Claire's hand. "I adore your kid brother. Everything might have been different on the rim that night if I hadn't got the bad news about the movie. And if Tyler Tribble hadn't turned up."

A long silence. "That can't have been a coincidence," Claire said.

Piper pulled away. "No, it wasn't. And that's the other half of the story. God, this is getting longer than *Ben-Hur*."

Claire laughed, relieved now and interested. "Go on. I'm all ears."

Piper crossed her arms atop the table. "Out of the blue maybe a month ago, I got an email from Tyler, forwarded up the network's PR chain. They screen the thousands of messages we get from *Brainiacs* fans—most from kids. But Tyler's email stood out because it seemed professional and legit, so it was sent forward. He identified himself as federal employee working in resource management at a place I never heard of."

"Big Bend National Park," Claire said, seeing now where this was going.

"Said he was *pretty* sure I was the Pippa Robinson he knew from high school in Arkansas, apologizing profusely if I wasn't. He'd searched for me on the Web in the past only to discover that Pippa Robinson died in a car crash in Nevada. But seeing is believing, he said."

"And you responded to the email?"

"Took me a day or two. So much had happened—more in my life than his, at least emotionally. But I couldn't ignore Tyler. I knew it the minute I read his message. And after I googled him."

"You hadn't done that before?"

"No. I was ashamed." Piper shrugged and stared out at the graveled parking lot. "Not long after I heard from Tyler, Alex tells me he might visit his sister in Texas when *Brainiacs* wraps and then hike in a national park near where you live. I put two and two together and invited myself along.

"Alex was up for it, of course. And my agent was ecstatic. He saw a chance to use the trip to promote me as Juliet in Alex's new movie. *Two actors already in love soon to play history's most famous lovers?* He thought the studio would eat it up and they almost did."

"How did Tyler feel about that?"

"He just wanted to see me. He'd already offered to come to California for his next vacation. And Tyler and I weren't committing to anything. I didn't know how college and work changed him, any more than he knew who I'd become. But I was curious and attracted, given how Tyler looked in photos we shared. He had the advantage on me there, since I was on a show every week. But he doesn't care enough about TV even to own one."

Claire liked the guy better. "How'd he find out about you then? You said he emailed the network, so he must have seen your series."

"He spotted me on a really old TV set—the kind with a *tube?*— in an employee lounge one evening. Just about floored him. But he went back a few times to be sure, then followed up online since WetBTE has a huge website. It was almost romantic how he stalked me."

Chapter 40

Claire picked up the check at Big Bend Café so fast Piper didn't have time to object and wouldn't have anyway. She was enjoying her time now with a woman who seemed open-minded and almost vulnerable. So, with Tyler at work, Piper was in no rush to return to Billy's cabin. She suggested a stroll through Study Butte.

"Let me show you were Tyler and I hid out for two nights after I left the Rim," she said. "You won't believe how guys live." Claire was game, relieved that her suspicions about Alex were off base.

They left their cars at the restaurant, sure nobody would mind. Piper explained that she drove Tyler to work this Tuesday because of the meeting with Claire. She'd pick him up later in the afternoon—probably putting more than a hundred miles on his Camry before the day was out.

They meandered down Highway 118 where it passed the turnoff to Terlingua and then veered east toward the Big Bend park entrance, still some miles off. No sidewalks of course, just tarmac and gravel and a bright sun warming their big hats. Two fetching women out for a stroll. Drivers in pickups and SUVs honked.

"So you arranged to meet Tyler on the South Rim?" Claire asked. Piper figured she would get around to that question.

"Not exactly," she said, looking up at the taller woman. "I thought we'd get together the next day—after Alex and I got down from the South Rim. I'd have told your brother about Tyler by then. The three of us could have had lunch in the Basin."

"Tyler and Alex together? That would have been odd." And suddenly Claire again didn't look happy.

Piper paused beneath a fake stoplight next to a sign for the Study Butte

Mall—a tiny store promising liquor, beer, ice, and diesel. "Take my picture," she said, handing Claire her phone. Piper hammed it up for a series of shots. But Claire waited.

"How could I know how I'd feel when I saw Tyler?" Piper said. "We'd been close in high school, but five years later? I figured with Alex along the meeting might be less awkward."

Claire passed the phone back to Piper, the last photo still on its screen. "Seriously? The day after you slept with him?"

"I wasn't thinking straight, was I?"

They were headed east now, following the road toward a converted gas station some yards off with a sign that read *Many Stones*. Piper liked the name. It fit the surroundings.

"So what *did* happen on the rim?" Claire wanted an answer.

"No mystery at all. Tyler heard from co-workers about the event Throng!Media was arranging for Alex and me on the South Rim. Female staff were buzzing about it—you can guess why. So Tyler volunteered to be one of the park people managing it.

"Alex and I were surprised by the turn-out Tuesday and so was Tyler. People everywhere having a good time. And suddenly I spotted him in the crowd. I realize now I would have been disappointed if Tyler hadn't shown up. We were able to talk because your brother was busy with fans of his own."

"And?"

"High school all over again. Tyler looked fantastic. I think he felt the same about me. Thirty seconds erased five years.

"But Tyler was smart enough to be careful. He told me he'd hang around and we could talk later. It was still miles to the rim and he was spending the whole day. If your brother noticed anything that afternoon, it might have been a cute ranger named Sebastián I fussed over in case he'd noticed the attention I'd paid Tyler."

Claire was about to speak, but Piper stopped her.

"Alex wasn't looking at Sebastián *that* way—though I couldn't blame him. The guy was a hunk."

"You seem to attract them."

"Oh, and you don't? I've seen Clayton Shoot." Piper wished immediately she'd held her tongue.

But Claire smiled. "You and Tyler *didn't* plan to dump Alex on the rim?"

"No. But things happened to keep us separate most of the hike. Guys crowding me and girls all around Alex." Piper was shading the truth. She didn't want to mention the bad vibes she was getting from Throng!Media.

Claire paused to study the asphalt beneath her boots.

"I know what you're wondering, Claire. After seeing Tyler, no, I couldn't imagine spending that night with your brother."

"Good," Claire said. "Right answer."

But Piper felt hurt. "It wasn't easy. Everyone on the rim assumed Alex and me were together. Even locals—like Donnie Majewski. He arranged the tents in the campground to give us privacy."

"Was your agent there?"

"No. But I told you what his strategy was and I went along. I thought, okay, Alex will be happy and so will I if Throng!Media thinks we make the perfect screen couple."

Claire said nothing.

"Then it all crashed. Nobody on the rim expected executives in Hollywood to cast Juliet that afternoon. Or choose Tabreetha Bree-Jones. We might not have heard the news till the next day if the one Throng!Media bigshot in our party didn't have a satellite phone."

"Was he in on it—the executive?"

The question surprised Piper. "I didn't think so. Maybe? It was so abrupt and cruel. One minute, I'm seeing this awesome view off the edge of the rim. And the next minute everyone's buzzing about Bree-Jones and treating me like a leper.

"I got the word from a nobody who worked for Throng, not the executive. Then I just ran down the trail back toward the campsite, hoping no one would follow. I wanted to be alone.

"The last I saw your brother there, he was talking with that Throng!Media guy right on the rim. I don't even remember the guy's name. I just kept running until, maybe a quarter mile down the trail, Tyler was right beside me. He'd followed me. You can figure out the rest."

They'd reached the rock shop—the only customers there. They quietly examined items on makeshift tables all around them, mostly stones, geodes, and some cactus. Piper watched a pickup throttle by.

"But I heard others went looking for you," Claire said. "Why didn't they see you and Tyler?"

"I wanted Tyler to get me away from the South Rim and he did. We moved fast enough not to be spotted through Boot Canyon and eventually hid in a park service cabin maybe a hundred yards off the trail and not all that far from the campground."

Claire hadn't been on the South Rim so Piper explained how trees and rock formations and different elevations in the canyon blocked longer views.

"I sure didn't notice the place on my way out to the rim and I guess no one else did either. Just a shack, dark and dirty inside. Maybe rangers use it in bad weather? But it was exactly what Tyler and I needed.

"Looking back, I think we should have just hiked down to the Basin then and there. No one would have blamed me. But I insisted on spending that evening with the crew like a good sport. I also didn't want Tyler drawn into the mess. And I sure didn't want to humiliate Alex—though I managed that pretty good, didn't I?"

"You scared him more than anything."

"And hurt and confused him. I guess Donnie was the only one to come out ahead after I persuaded him to share a tent with Alex."

"How'd you know Donnie was gay?"

"By the way he *didn't* look at me?" Piper said. Claire was amused, then embarrassed.

"I assured Tyler I'd return to the campsite like nothing happened and that he could find me later that night in the only single tent. I'd be packed and ready to go."

"And if Donnie or Alex had screwed things up? Not wanted to share a tent?"

"I'd have gathered my stuff, picked up Tyler at the cabin, and left. But I didn't have to. And Tyler waited as promised until things settled down before midnight and we hiked down that trail in the moonlight."

"You must have been exhausted."

"Never felt more alive. I lost the best movie role I'd ever get, but found the only man I'll ever love. Fair swap."

"Wow."

"Yeah."

"I almost envy you," Claire said, like she meant it.

"We knew it would be a mess in the media, but didn't care. Tyler said we'd hole up in his place in Study Butte until we figured things out. I was mainly worried he'd lose his job. And he still might when this all comes out. But I have savings and Tyler's up for a move. The publicity might even get me talk show gigs in California until better things come along. And there are lots of state and national parks where Tyler can work there."

Claire seemed placated and suggested it was time to head back to their cars. But Piper nodded toward a dirt road just across the highway lined by stucco and adobe buildings in various states of disrepair.

"Let me show you Tyler's place. I have a key." They crossed Highway 118 and walked a hundred yards down a rutted, unmaintained drive.

"Glad I wore boots," Claire said.

At least Tyler's two-story unit had a solid door and awnings—which was more than could be said for the other dwellings. An air conditioner hung from a window on his second floor.

"Cheap rent—and Tyler doesn't need much," Piper smiled. "There's employee housing at Big Bend, but he prefers privacy."

"He's sure got it," Claire said.

"Electricity and a well," Piper noted. "But no cell service. It's a dump. Tyler's saving for a rock house in Terlingua. But that's not gonna happen now."

Claire studied the neighboring properties while Piper fiddled with a key, yanking the door handle up and down.

"Shit," she said the very instant Claire did too.

"See something?" Piper asked.

"That place there. I need to get closer." Claire headed toward a two-story ruin maybe fifty yards down the path. Slow at first, then almost running.

By the time Piper caught up—having failed to open Tyler's apartment—Claire was standing in front of the structure, awe-struck. Just another crumbling adobe, Piper thought, with bare windows and broken timbers across what remained of a second story porch. Behind it was a hill of red dirt.

"This *is* the building I saw in Iris Cooper's studio at the Cobb on Saturday. From a painting Gina Summerlin said was her mother's last work. Except here it is in Study Butte."

"What?" Piper didn't follow anything Claire had just said.

"I've seen a painting of this place," Claire explained. "By Iris Cobb. The woman murdered last Friday."

"Murdered? On Friday?" Piper was confused. "I didn't hear anything about that."

"You've been at Billy's cabin."

Piper nodded. "No internet there. Not even a radio."

"The woman who painted this house was robbed and shot in Big Bend National Park Friday afternoon."

"That can't be possible," Piper said, hand over her mouth now.

"What?" Claire asked, surprised by the girl's distress.

"I was here Friday by myself after Tyler went to work. He took the car and I got bored in the apartment. So I wandered out late in the morning and spotted a woman with an easel, an umbrella over it, and a big SUV. She was finishing up in front of this building."

"You're sure. On Friday?"

"It wasn't lunchtime yet, but I was going to head down the road to eat—where we just did. Instead, I walked up here and we chatted for maybe fifteen minutes. She dabbed at the painting a few times and then said it was finished. I congratulated her and told her it was beautiful.

"She was very nice. Said I was beautiful too . . . I'm almost certain she guessed who I was. But then she talked about how important old buildings can be. How she thought about the people who lived in them once. How she wanted to bring this one back to life."

Claire was pacing, trying to sort things out. "You might be the last person to see her alive—except for her killers."

"She said she was going to Big Bend to start a new painting. I helped her load the one she'd just finished into her Cadillac. Slid it into a box."

"She called it *Terlingua Townhouse*," Claire said.

"I know! She told me. Said no one would buy a painting called *Study Butte Studio*."

"So you really did see her."

"Sure."

"And you could describe the woman?"

"Tall, elegant, older lady dressed for working in the sun."

"You'll have to talk with them—the police." Claire was breathless. "They need to know this. You're certain about the day and time?"

Claire seemed annoyed when Piper pulled out her phone and spent half a minute flicking through items on its screen. But it dawned on the professor what Piper might be searching for.

Piper's fingers slowed and then she stared at an image. She held it up for Claire. A selfie.

Of Piper. And *Terlingua Townhouse*.

And Iris Cobb, smiling.

Chapter 41

At the sheriff's department, a dispatcher routed a call from one Matthew Cooper to Captain Gus Stumpf because Clayton Shoot was at Alpine High School on Tuesday, taking lunch with high school kids interested in law enforcement careers. Gus heard Matthew Cooper out and assured the photographer that the sheriff would call him back right quick.

He did, canceling the tail end of the student event and hurrying to his office. Figuring that Elliot Perciak and maybe Special Agent Grimmel needed to hear the news firsthand, Clayton directed his dispatcher to arrange an immediate conference call if everyone was available. They were.

Just twenty minutes later, Matthew Cooper was on the line with Clayton Shoot, ISB agent Elliot Perciak, FBI agent Randi Grimmel, and Gus Stumpf. All were in Alpine except Grimmel, who was with the Border Patrol at Big Bend.

"Tell us what's happening," Clayton asked the man who'd soon be sharing a big chunk of Iris Cobb's empire with Gina Summerlin.

Cooper was agitated. "I've been worried about Gina since I got back from Taos. Her behavior. I thought it was grief and stress. That would be normal."

"Go on," Clayton said. The sheriff was glad he'd had time to eat because he sensed something was up.

"But she's beyond that now. Manic. Delusional, even, about what to do with the Cobb Institute. And what she expects from me."

"But that's not why you called," Perciak guessed.

"No, sir. Right now, Regina has people here shutting down her house and Iris's studio. She's packed up to leave, maybe within an hour or two. Cargo box on her SUV's roof. Says there's work she needs to handle personally in Taos involving restructuring Iris's whole business and revamping the gallery there."

Randi Grimmel chimed in. "The property Iris left you?"

"Yeah, but that's not the issue right now. With the murder investigation still up in the air, I told her she should stay here in Alpine."

Clayton asked straight out, "Do you suspect she had anything to do with Iris's death?" His colleagues weren't surprised by the question, but Cooper was.

"Hell, no! I mean . . . strange stuff *has* been going on. I just learned today it was Gina who talked Iris into putting me in her will. That was a few months ago. And now Gina has this idea that she and I are partners again—and not just in business. Like I say, delusional, and now this fixation on getting to Taos . . ."

Clayton wished he could see how Grimmel and Perciak were reacting.

Cooper continued. "She thinks your investigation is a fraud too. That you already know illegals killed Iris, but won't follow up for political reasons."

"So we're part of a cover-up?" Gus said.

"She didn't use the word—but, yeah, cover-up fits."

Clayton reacted before others could. "You do what you can to keep Iris in place for now. Stall her until I get there with Special Agent Perciak—you remember him?"

"I do—though I don't know exactly how to keep Regina here. Disable her truck maybe?"

"Men!" Gus hooted. "Always complicating things. Just play along with her. I bet the woman's hungry after all the packin'. Suggest lunch before she goes off on that long trip. Open a bottle of wine. Smile at her." Clayton heard Randi Grimmel groan.

"I can try that," Cooper said. "But she's a single-minded woman."

"We all are, kid," Gus said.

"We'll be there asap . . . maybe half an hour," Clayton promised. "Now, if you'll hang up, the rest of us need to consider our options."

The instant Cooper left the call, Randi Grimmel cut to the heart of the matter. "Suspect—or person of interest? We can hold her for sure if the first, *maybe* if the second?"

"Y'all know where I stand," Clayton said. Perciak quickly brought Grimmel up to speed on Gus and Alonso's experiment the day before.

"So Summerlin might have been in the national park at the time of Iris's murder," Grimmel said.

"But we don't have physical evidence she was," Clayton admitted. "No weapon.

No witnesses. Checkpoint cameras still support her alibi. Far as we know, she was in Fort Davis when Iris died. Still . . ."

There was a moment of silence.

"Say what you're thinking, Sheriff." It was Grimmel putting Clayton on the spot.

But he dodged. "I think we should discourage her from leaving Texas. Things get complicated once she crosses state lines."

"Grimmel and I would still have jurisdiction," Perciak said. "Since the crime occurred in a national park."

"I get that and don't intend to violate her rights. But I don't want Gina Summerlin leaving Brewster County. I hear what Matthew Cooper's getting at. Something's off in her behavior."

The callers took another moment to think, then Perciak made up his mind. "Where exactly are you, Sheriff?"

"In my building."

"I just finished an interview at a gallery on Holland Avenue," the special agent said. "I'll be at your place in five or ten minutes and then we'll head to Cobb together. Can we get there in half an hour?"

"Sounds like a plan," Clayton said.

When the call ended, Gus looked oddly excited. "Should I come along?" she asked the sheriff.

"You keep the fort here," he said. "Send Alonso to the Cobb if something comes up."

"Maybe Summerlin's behavior today makes her a person of interest?" Gus suggested. "Fleeing the scene of a crime?"

"Except there's no crime at the scene. Least not yet."

Chapter 42

By the time Clayton Shoot and Elliot Perciak headed south on Highway 118 for the Cobb Institute, Claire Harp and Piper Robinet, driving north on the same road, were more than halfway to Alpine. Claire realized immediately that investigators needed to see the selfie Piper had taken with Iris Cobb. It placed the woman in Study Butte just moments before she'd head into the national park and down the Old Maverick Road. You could even see her Cadillac in the background, tailgate open.

"Send me that photo and I'll forward it to Clayton," she'd said to Piper while still standing in front of the crumbling structure. Piper had Claire's number, and immediately texted the image. Nothing happened. *No service.*

Claire slapped her head and then hurried up the road and back to her car, Piper struggling to keep up and swinging her phone to find a signal. "We could maybe get service in the Chisos Basin," she sighed. "But that's dozens of miles in the other direction."

Terlingua was much closer, but Claire couldn't recall having phone service there two days ago when she'd searched for the very building they'd just found. She didn't think so, but hadn't tried to make a call. GPS worked, but that was a satellite thing.

"Maybe I could take your phone with me to Alpine and then bring it back?" she suggested.

"The picture's that important?"

"Yes!" Claire said, sounding more certain than she was. She recalled Gina Summerlin approaching her at the memorial on Saturday to talk about the work. *The last piece Iris finished,* she'd said. At least Gina would have the satisfaction of knowing where *Terlingua Townhouse* had been painted. Not in Terlingua at all.

Piper interrupted Claire's thinking. "I could just go with you—to Alpine."

"What? . . . No, that would put you out and you still have to pick up Tyler at work."

"It's not even noon and I am bored," Piper smiled. "Maybe a cop could get me back to Study Butte? And you need me to check cell service while you're driving."

Claire quickly relented. She wouldn't mind company on the ride up Highway118 yet again.

So Claire had pointed her Jeep toward the county seat, eighty miles north, ignoring an already generous speed limit and grateful the wind had died down. They let Big Bend Café know that Tyler's Camry would be in their lot for a while. The waitress shrugged. Parking wasn't an issue on a weekday in October.

Claire pointed Piper to a cable in her glovebox and a USB port in the center stack to keep the phone alive while they searched for a signal. As the miles passed, Claire explained all she knew about the Cobb case—who the murdered woman was, what kind of work she did, even where she was shot. Piper really knew nothing about it. She was impressed though that Iris Cobb had sketched Clayton Shoot when the sheriff was the same age as Alex.

"There's a screenplay here whenever they find out who killed her," Piper said. "And I bet that sketch of Clayton is worth something now." Claire nodded, recalling Gina's estimate for *Terlingua Townhouse*. Two hundred thousand dollars.

"That's odd, though," Piper said, checking again for service while studying the scenery.

"What is?"

"That the painting would already be in Cobb's gallery on Saturday, the day after her murder. How'd it get there?"

Claire was lucky the road pointed straight ahead for several miles. Because suddenly she wasn't thinking about driving. She pounded the steering wheel as she worked through the implications. Piper had nailed it.

⋅⋅⋅ ⋅⋅⋅ ⋅⋅⋅

FORTY-FIVE MINUTES LATER and just minutes after Clayton Shoot and Elliot Perciak headed for the Cobb Institute in Clayton's Durango, the dispatcher in the sheriff's office transferred a call from Claire Harp to Alonso Rangel. Claire had asked to speak with Clayton Shoot. Alonso Rangel picked up instead.

The deputy was itching to be at the Cobb with the sheriff, especially after Gus Stumpf explained that Gina Summerlin was packed up and ready to leave Texas, heading to digs in New Mexico. Alonso imagined hot pursuit to the border. The woman wouldn't get far.

But he was happy to talk with Claire too, who he knew was Clayton's girlfriend. They'd been introduced a few times. Not the sort of woman you forgot. And today she seemed *real* wound up.

"I've been trying to reach Clayton, but didn't have a signal for a long time."

"Oh, yeah? Why's that?" he said. Most of Alpine had good cell service.

"Because I've been driving up Highway 118 from Study Butte."

"That's mostly a dead zone."

"I've noticed. But he's not been answering even after I got a signal. I'm about twenty miles south of town now. Clayton still won't pick up."

High maintenance girlfriend, Alonso thought. He explained to Ms. Harp that the sheriff was tied up at the moment with important matters and wasn't taking personal calls.

"I understand. But I have critical information about the Cobb murder . . ."

⚜ ⚜ ⚜

AFTER A QUICK fifteen-mile drive down Highway 118, Special Agent Perciak and Sheriff Shoot turned left into the Cobb compound and pulled up in front of what they assumed was Gina Summerlin's residence. Nearby, a carport big enough for a motorhome shaded a white 4Runner. A blondish woman with wavy hair and a clipboard was checking items already loaded into its cargo area.

Clayton parked his Durango right behind the vehicle, realizing Gina could still pull out easily by driving across a dry lawn and over a small curb. Her high-clearance SUV would have no problem at all.

"Can I help you, Sheriff?" Lydia Champlain asked, introducing herself as office manager to Iris Cobb. No mention of Gina. Clayton wasn't surprised that Lydia recognized him, and she nodded too at the rumpled guy with him. The special agent in civilian clothes looked tired after a morning of fruitless interviews.

"We're looking for your boss?"

"Right there in the house having lunch."

"With Mr. Cooper?"

230

"How'd you know that?" But given the look she gave Clayton, Lydia seemed glad he did. Maybe Cooper positioned her out here?

Clayton rang the doorbell and the photographer answered quickly. He looked drawn and nervous.

"We'd like to speak with Regina Summerlin," Clayton said loudly enough to carry.

"Who is it, Mateo?" Gina asked from inside, maybe in the dining room or kitchen—if Cooper persuaded her to have lunch.

"It's the sheriff and . . ." Cooper stumbled.

"Elliot Perciak," the ISB special agent said loud enough to carry. "We need to talk with you, Ms. Summerlin."

Gina appeared at the entryway in field pants, shooting shirt, and formidable Schnee boots. She was groomed for travel, hair pulled back tight and virtually no makeup. Her dark eyes expressed curiosity more than concern.

"We have questions," Clayton said. "But it looks like you're all packed to go somewhere." He saw the relief on Matthew's face. The guy was off the hook for blowing the whistle on Gina's departure plans.

"Come in gentleman. No point standing out there. Mateo just grilled up ham and cheese sandwiches. Can we make some for you?"

The woman seemed more at ease than Clayton expected. Had Cooper jumped the gun? Maybe Gina thought they just wanted to update her about her step-mother's murder?

"Might I ask where you're going?"

"Remind me who you are?"

Elliot Perciak reintroduced himself, then added, "I was with Special Agent Grimmel. We talked to you yesterday, Ms. Summerlin."

"The FBI lady. She did all the talking," Gina smiled. "As I think I told you then, I'm leaving for Taos to handle Cobb business there. We have a gallery and financial interests that need attention right now."

Clayton knew she hadn't mentioned travel plans to Perciak or Grimmel in any previous meeting. They would have told him immediately. *Probably*.

Perciak was about to respond when Gina invited them into the kitchen. "Let's sit around the table. It's more comfortable there and I'll make another pot of coffee."

Cooper shrugged, perhaps baffled by her composure too.

"You're looking tired, Sheriff," Gina said as she ground fresh beans. Wood and chrome in her kitchen sparkled. She was either a meticulous housekeeper,

Clayton thought, or had good people working for her. "This murder has been hard on us all," she sighed as the mill went silent.

"Yes, ma'am, that's so," Clayton said. "None more than you. But with our investigation incomplete, it would be best you stay in Brewster County. Issues could arise only you could explain. And we'll likely have more questions."

Perciak interrupted. "We're interviewing new people every day and might need you to assess what we learn."

"And what have you found out from all the painters and political activists you've talked to so far? She raised a hand to stay Perciak's response. "I'll tell you myself. Absolutely nothing. I know many people did not like or agree with my stepmother. They talked to me all the time about it. But they're no more capable of murder than you or me. Have you had questions about them for me so far?"

"No, ma'am," Perciak admitted.

"I didn't think so . . .You know there's been lots of illegal border crossing in this county lately—isn't that true, Sheriff?"

Clayton nodded. His office had posted notices of increased immigrant activity around Marathon recently and just apprehended two Guatemalan citizens in the country illegally. She didn't need to know the details.

"Yet you deny the obvious," she continued.

"That's not true. Border Patrol and the Park Service have been working the river hard—both sides—following up every lead. FBI Agent Grimmel is there right now . . ."

Gina dismissed Perciak with a wave. "Well, you guys keep looking." She glanced at an unsmiling Matthew Cooper. "In the meantime, we have business with impatient people in Santa Fe and Taos. They want to honor my mother there too, just as we've done here in Alpine. So, unless you have other questions or seriously believe I am a suspect . . . or a person of interest?"

The latter phrase was a challenge, Clayton guessed. Had Gina lawyered up?

Clayton felt his phone vibrate. He checked the screen while the others glanced around the table in silence. Text message from Alonso: *Claire headed to Cobb. Delay Gina!*

What the fuck? Clayton thought and blushed. Couldn't help it.

"Are you all right, Sheriff?"

"Yes, ma'am."

"Well, am I a suspect or not?" She looked back and forth between the two lawmen.

"Not a suspect, ma'am," Perciak admitted. "And we can't hold you as a person of interest because you've cooperated and answered all our questions to this point."

She got up to pour the fresh coffee.

"Good to know, I'll try not to be insulted," she said, filling their cups. "Now, if you don't mind, I need to get back to my office and give final instructions to the staff. And to dismiss one of them." She looked pointedly at Cooper. "Then I'll be leaving. You have my cellphone number. I expect to be on the road for two days, arriving in Taos late tomorrow night. And you'll be following me in a week or so, Mateo?"

"Yes, ma'am," he just about whispered.

Cool as a cucumber, Clayton thought and Matthew Cooper a wet rag. "We can't stop you then," Clayton said, "though Special Agent Perciak and I have some matters to settle with Mateo right now. If you don't mind, Ms. Summerlin?"

"*Gina*, please, Clayton. And, of course I don't mind. Finish your coffee. But I do want Mateo to see me off in a few minutes."

"We'll join him, ma'am, to wish you a safe trip. Fine vehicle you got there. Packed to the gills."

A triumphant Gina rinsed the coffee pot and left the men in the kitchen.

"What the fuck?" Perciak said to Clayton.

Clayton looked out the window as Gina marched a hundred yards down the graveled road, a spring in her step, and turned into her two-story office. Moments later, from the opposite direction, he saw Claire's Jeep approaching. Behind her some distance was a Durango like his. He guessed Alonso was at the wheel.

"Somethin' is up and we're about to find out what," he said to Perciak.

Chapter 43

Alonso had quickly transferred Claire's call to Gus. The captain was swift on the uptake—once Claire explained the photo she now had on her cell-phone. Gus determined where Claire was exactly and where Clayton was, and how soon Alonso could arrive at the Cobb as their backup. Then she set them all in motion.

"Wait for Alonso when you get to the Institute," Gus said to Claire, "and then find Clayton, wherever he is. But don't show that picture if Regina Summerlin is with him. Drive safe, but get there pronto."

Claire hoped Gus would give Alonso more explicit instructions because she wasn't sure what was happening at the Cobb.

Piper squirmed in the passenger seat, even more confused.

"You're gonna stay in the car," Claire said.

"Like hell I am. That's me in the photo."

"I don't want you getting hurt."

"I've been taking care of myself a long time."

"You're a witness now."

By then Claire was making a sharp right turn into the Cobb's main entrance, just south of the Border Patrol checkpoint. There was no time for more argument with Piper. She spotted Clayton's Durango and then Clayton himself—as well as two other men—waving them down. Alonso's cruiser arrived from the opposite direction and was quickly right behind her. No siren or lights. The institute's grounds looked remarkably peaceful.

And that made sense. No one knew what was up.

Clayton opened her door before she shut off the engine.

And Piper reached over Claire to hand the sheriff her own cellphone with the selfie of Iris Cobb up on the screen.

"Holy shit," Clayton said.

"It was taken in Study Butte," Claire explained before Piper could. "Look at the date and time." Clayton handed the phone to a federal agent she barely recognized—*FBI maybe?*—and then to Matthew Cooper, who she clearly did. He *was* almost as tall as Clayton.

"We need to check the gallery where the reception was held Friday," Claire said. "That's where *I* saw the painting."

"Can we do that?" the guy in the suit asked.

"I have a master key," Matthew said. "I guess that means I can let you in." He led the way to an adobe structure already familiar to Claire.

"Where's Gina?" she asked.

Matthew shrugged. "Firing people . . . She'll be awhile."

But the gallery was a disappointment. Most of Iris's works had been removed, replaced by hastily hung plein air works of lesser quality, even to amateur eyes. Alonso pointed out two items that Gina said she'd painted at Fort Davis on the day of the murder.

Claire moved from wall to wall.

"It's not here," she said.

"What's not here?" They all turned. Regina Summerlin had walked in unseen through a back entrance.

Claire regretted she'd not yet fully explained to Clayton what she and Piper pieced together on the ride up from Study Butte. But she'd leave this confrontation to him and the guy in the rumpled suit. *Or try to.*

"We're looking for a painting by your mother called *Terlingua Terrace*," Clayton said.

"*Townhouse*," Claire corrected him. "*Terlingua Townhouse.*"

Claire saw the woman stiffen, but it might have been an effect of the gallery lighting.

"*Terlingua Townhouse?*" Gina seemed puzzled. "I'm not sure I remember it. And why would you be interested in the painting?"

"I saw it here Saturday—at Iris's memorial," Claire insisted. "You talked to me about it then. Said it was her last work. I took a photo . . ."

"I don't remember that, my dear. Who are you exactly? You look familiar."

Claire figured Gina might be evasive, but didn't expect total denial. The federal agent looked uneasy, maybe worried by Claire's intrusion into his case.

"Iris was so prolific," Gina smiled. "We have so much work of hers now in storage. Are you *sure* you saw that painting here?"

Clayton intervened. "This is the one we're looking for," he said, showing Regina Summerlin the selfie of Piper and Iris and *Terlingua Townhouse* on the actress's phone. Gina stared at it for an uncomfortable interval and then seemed to notice Piper for the first time.

"You're the girl in the picture with my stepmother?" The words came slowly. *Gina buying time*, Claire assumed. Thinking through the implications—which hadn't hit Claire immediately either when she first saw the image.

"That's *Terlingua Townhouse* right beside them," Claire said. "Look at the time stamp, Ms. Summerlin."

"I do see it," Gina said. "Oh, yes. The day Iris died. And what a beautiful painting. Do you think it was stolen by the people who killed Iris? Clayton, is that what you've come to tell me? Is that why you're really here?" Gina covered her mouth in horror.

Feigned, Claire was sure.

Then Gina slowly pointed to Piper. "Unless *you're* the one who killed her. Who is this girl? What is she doing here?"

Claire was startled. *Could that be possible?* Was Piper so skilled an actress that . . . but why would she photograph someone she intended to murder? And then share the photo?

Regina turned on Clayton. "That's what happened," she said slowly. "That's what happened. This young thing killed my mother for the painting and then drove her to Luna's Jacal in the Cadillac and left her there." Gina was suddenly breathing fast, hugging herself, staring down at the floor, as if horrified.

Clayton looked at the carpet for a moment too. "And how did she get back to Study Butte?" he said, as much to himself as to Gina. When he looked up, Claire could see the cogs turning behind his blue eyes.

"Yes, exactly!" Gina seized the sheriff's question. "Whoever you are, how did you get back to . . . where? Terlingua, was it?"

"Study Butte," Piper said softly, as Iris Cobb's stepdaughter came apart right in front of them. Flushing white, then red. Trembling. Perspiring.

Perciak intervened. "I think you need a lawyer, Ms. Summerlin."

"Don't talk of lawyers. They cost too much," she said softly. Then, pointing to

Piper, Gina almost shouted. "She's going to need them more than me . . . Tell them, Mateo. Did you ever see this *Terlingua Townhouse* painting here? In this studio?"

Gina's former lover—and Iris's too, Claire recalled. The handsome man was struggling to keep track of what was unfolding. Clayton shared Piper's photo with him.

"No," he said after a careful look. "I never saw it. But that *is* Iris in the photo and that's her Escalade too."

"No one else—except Claire Harp—saw the painting here then?" Gina sounded more confident. "Isn't that the crux, Sheriff? Isn't that the crux of this theory?"

"I have a photo of my own from Saturday that . . ." Claire began.

"What theory is that, Ms. Summerlin?" Clayton interrupted. "Why are *you* upset?"

"Always with her nose in other people's business. And Claire Harp's your girlfriend, isn't she?"

Just moments ago, she didn't recognize me, Claire recalled, convinced now that Gina Summerlin was delusional, lying, or both.

"You need a scapegoat for my mother's murder—all of you—and now you'll hang it on me."

Alonso, standing protectively near the front door, let someone Claire didn't recognize into the gallery. Not noticing, Gina turned on Piper again. "Who *is* this girl? Will somebody please tell me! What did *she* do with my mother's painting? That's what you should be asking, Sheriff."

"We can look into that, ma'am." Clayton was trying to calm Gina.

"Maybe she had an accomplice? A boyfriend, I bet. That's how she got back to Study Butte. They've probably sold *Terlingua Townhouse* by now. And how'd she get here today?" Gina turned on Claire again. "Did she come with you? Did she blackmail you because you're sleeping with Sheriff Shoot?"

Gina turned helplessly to Matthew Cooper, her eyes wide. "It all fits, Mateo. *Terlingua Townhouse* is worth a fortune and all of them want a cut."

He looked almost heartbroken. "Maybe you shipped it to Taos already? You've been so busy and confused. Or maybe one of your people removed it?" Matthew said.

Claire shook her head slowly. That still would not explain how the work made its way to the Cobb gallery within a day of Iris's death.

"Call the gallery there right now. Ask if they've got it. Ask them to check tomorrow or every day next week. It doesn't matter. It never will be there."

"It's in your truck, Ms. Summerlin. I packed it myself. You told me to."

Gina and everyone else turned toward a handsome woman standing next to Alonso. The one he'd let in moments earlier.

"I fired her, I just fired her," Gina hissed. "And for good reason, Lydia Champlain. You schemer. You gold digger. Don't believe her, Mateo."

"The painting *is* in the truck. It saw it in the gallery for the first time Saturday. Others did too, I'm sure."

"You couldn't know it was by Iris. It wasn't signed yet. You couldn't know that." Perhaps realizing what she'd just admitted, Gina wobbled backward and dropped onto a circular sofa in the middle of the gallery, hands caressing her face, breathing hard.

No one moved. They let her settle.

"I couldn't just leave it in the Cadillac . . . Stupid now, but it was so beautiful. I was going to claim I painted *Terlingua Townhouse*. But no one would believe . . ."

Elliot Perciak stood above Gina. "Ms. Summerlin, I need to read you your rights."

She focused puffy eyes on him and then turned toward Clayton. Laughed. Laughed a second time. In control again. Like a switch had been thrown. "Don't bother. I know my rights, Mr. FBI. Don't care about them. You see, I did shoot Iris Cobb Summerlin."

"I'm Elliot Perciak with the Investigative Services Branch of the National Park Service . . ."

From out of a pocket of her sporting shirt, Gina pulled a handgun. Claire was close enough to read *Kahr* on the barrel.

"Oh, it's not for you," Regina said as everyone froze. "An insurance policy. In case something like this happened. And, no, it's not the one I used on Iris. I was smart enough to lose that one in the park. You'll never find it. But you don't need it now, do you?"

"Ms. Summerlin, please put that pistol down," Clayton said, steering Claire and Piper behind him.

Still seated, Gina played with the gun. "Iris Cobb only went through the motions of being my mother. I was baggage to her after my father died. She called me the little queen but treated me like a charwoman. Sent me to second-rate schools. Bullied me into doing what she wanted—she was a *mean* soul. But I was too entangled in her web to leave, especially as I grew older. *Major in business* she said, so you can at least do my books. But I was so good at it—wasn't I,

Matthew Cooper? I had all the ideas. Made Iris millions selling designer plates and Christmas cards and then buying oil land people thought was depleted. And I even made you a photographer, didn't I? Encouraged you. Changed your name. Introduced you to Iris."

Alonso shifted slightly against a back wall.

"Don't try anything, kid," she warned, caressing her cheek with the pistol. "I'd hate this gun to go off and hurt Ms. Champlain there. By the way, Lydia, have you enjoyed Mateo yet? Has he seduced you too? I expect he will. He was good in bed the first few weeks. After that . . ."

They heard vehicles crushing gravel on the drive outside the gallery.

Regina stood up and stepped away from the sofa. "Don't know how you did that, Sheriff. But use your phone to keep them outside. Let me hear what you say."

Clayton did.

"Now, where was I? I want you to get this right. The murder was easy to work out. I just needed to wait for the right opportunity. Iris eventually took to doing her plein air works in Big Bend and always told me exactly where she was going. When she mentioned Luna's Jacal, I realized that would be perfect. I'd painted there myself. Adequately remote. And I had the perfect alibi ready, once I figured my way around those Border Patrol cameras."

"Knew it," Alonso snapped. Summerlin gave him a strange look.

"Oh, for the record, Mateo had nothing to do with Iris's murder. I'd hate to think of him in prison as somebody's bitch. I used his trip to Taos just to throw suspicion on him so I could also be the one to exonerate him. Worked as I hoped, except he wasn't grateful enough. I killed her because she took you from me, Mateo. Feel guilty about that?"

"We'd already broken up," Cooper mumbled. "I liked you, Gina. Just never loved you."

"You preferred a rich old bag." She waved her hand to prevent a response. "Don't bother. I killed her because she stole my art too. The one style of painting I was good at. The *one* thing I had to myself. She mastered it the first time out and flaunted it. Plein Air Painters Salon winner, right out of the box." She caught Piper rolling her eyes.

"And what are you good at, Ms. Robinet? Seducing boy actors? Of course, I know who you are. If I knew about that selfie with Iris, I'd have framed you. You look dumb enough. And what a movie *that* would make."

Gina finally turned to face Claire. Stared at her for a moment. "You know, Ms. Harp, this feels really good. Speaking my mind. I should have done it years ago." She raised the gun to her temple and pulled the trigger.

It didn't go off.

Clayton had Gina disarmed and on the ground in seconds. She smiled up at him. "You know, sweetie, I think I'm thoroughly deranged."

"Not enough to convince a Texas jury."

Chapter 44

Alex was asleep before Clayton got in late Tuesday night. On Wednesday morning, he was up and around the main house by 8:00 AM, again without seeing the sheriff. Alex found Beatrice preparing breakfast in business attire—clothes she might wear when she handled financial matters in Midland–Odessa. He was in a western shirt, jeans, and boots. He hadn't showered though because he didn't want to wake her brother.

"We have much to cover before the conference call," Beatrice said. "But I cannot get my mind off the murder of Iris Cobb." She slid a perfectly segmented half of grapefruit in front of Alex.

Like the boy, she'd spent time before breakfast reading the *Big Bend Mercury*, catching up on the previous day's events. "To murder your own stepmother because you envy her talent *and* the man she is sleeping with . . ."

"The guy slept with her too," Alex reminded Beatrice. "Matthew Cooper."

Beatrice sneered. "*Mateo Bottaio* on the photographs he sold. It is like a second-rate Jacobean play." Alex didn't understand the comment.

"To plot so deliberately where and how to kill someone," she went on, "to wait for your opportunity, to contrive an elaborate alibi. This Summerlin woman had more criminal talent than she knew, though I had my suspicions. And your sister once again solved the crime. She found the one piece of evidence Summerlin could not explain away."

Beatrice was furiously squeezing oranges for fresh juice. "If she had just left that painting in her mother's car, her alibi might have stood. And she would have owned the work anyway. What was she thinking?"

"Clayton's gonna be busy."

"Most of the work will fall to the FBI and Park Service, he told me. Making a federal case of it, as they say." She frowned. "But everyone in that gallery yesterday will be questioned thoroughly—especially your actress friend, Ms. Robinet."

Alex figured as much.

Beatrice stacked pancakes in front of the boy, offered maple syrup and the juice. "I apologize it is not chilled. There will be coffee shortly."

"You're spoiling me, Beatrice."

"Maybe you have heard already that Ms. Robinet has a boyfriend—who works at the park?" she almost whispered. "That has been confirmed. They were staying in Study Butte."

Alex nodded. He'd read the same story in the *Mercury*. "And then they moved to Billy Lamb's cabin—the same night I saw her at Billy's party."

"And how do you feel about that?"

"Explains a lot. But I'm totally okay, Beatrice. Really."

"Then I am totally *okay* as well."

Beatrice truly was his friend, as if he didn't know that already. "I'll probably go back to Claire's tonight. Spend time with her, after all that's happened."

Beatrice nodded. "Clayton will miss you. He may want you to stay."

From her sad look across the table, Alex guessed Beatrice was speaking for herself.

"But we face challenges of our own today," Beatrice said moments later. "Tell me more about these movie people."

Alex was happy to. He explained that Throng!Media—a new player in films and streaming services—wanted to raise its profile with serious critics. That's one reason they'd hired him to do *Romeo and Juliet*.

Beatrice nodded.

"But the company can't neglect its fanbase either—people who watch *Brainiacs* or dating shows or talent competitions."

"Like the *Idle Americans*."

"Which is probably why the company hired a popstar to play Juliet."

They chatted for more than an hour, Beatrice schooling Alex about the great studios of the past and Alex explaining how a TV sitcom earns as much revenue from product tie-ins as from the program itself.

Alex was impressed when Beatrice suggested that the sides likely to be taken in their forthcoming conference call might mirror career differences between Alex Harp and Tabreetha Bree-Jones. "I wonder who at Throng is on my side?" he said. "Maybe I *should* look over my contract? I can access a copy online."

"That would not be a bad idea."

⇥⇤ ⇥⇤ ⇥⇤

THE TERMS WERE as generous as he remembered. Alex talked briefly to his lawyer in Ohio before the call. She had a court session coming up and strongly advised that the discussion be delayed. But Alex wanted to go forward, remembering his agent's straightforward advice. He promised to keep her in the loop.

At noon in Beatrice's office, Alex dialed the call-in number and code sent him by text and stated his name when prompted by a computer-generated voice. Almost immediately he was greeted by his agent Bob Markus, Throng!Media executive Sherman Farr (who he'd last seen on the South Rim Trail), the film's producer, several writers, and—big surprise—studio head Ayala Topfer. He recognized Topfer's name, but had never spoken with the CEO before. She was a big deal in Hollywood.

Alex assumed he'd entered a conversation already in progress. But clicks on the line announced new arrivals too—among them Tabreetha Bree-Jones's manager Alistair Connell, her senior advisor Sienna Wragg, and maybe another assistant whose name Alex didn't catch. But no Tabreetha.

Alex dutifully introduced Beatrice Shoot as his language coach and artistic advisor. The participants chatted briefly about Texas food and London weather. Then Ayala Topfer got down to business.

"We're calling, Alex, to discuss suggestions your co-star has made about our film *Romeo and Juliet*. I'm going to leave it to Mr. Connell, her business manager, to outline those proposals. Briefly, I hope."

"Hey, there, Alex. Good to talk with you this afternoon." His accent—Oxford smeared with Cockney—made it difficult to guess his background or age. "Tabby has been reading a preliminary script for the movie and, frankly, she doesn't much like it."

Alex looked at Beatrice and shrugged. "I haven't seen any script," he said. "We've been running through scenes from the play here we assume will be in the movie."

"Aye, there's the rub," Connell said, sounding amused by his cleverness. "Tabreetha is unsure about the whole Shakespeare thing. She doubts her fans

243

will put up with old-fashioned dialogue and medieval words. So she wants to update the story and characters and make it more *today*."

Alex recalled Sherman Farr on the South Rim talking to him about *Mercury* and *Tebow* and now understood maybe where those character names came from.

"How modern?" Alex asked.

"Well, twenty-first century language and tunes."

"Tunes?"

Sherman Farr jumped in. "Hello Alex. Good to hear your voice again. Hope all is well with you—and Piper?"

"We been busy since the rim," Alex said.

"Yes, we all heard about that," Connell interrupted and moved forward. "As you know, Alex, Tabreetha brings immense experience as a stage performer to this project. She envisions this film opening at a halftime show for a sports spectacle where she sings and then meets Rocco for the first time."

"Rocco?"

"Tabreetha thinks we don't want our audience thinking *Romeo and Juliet* when we'll be doing something so different. She also believes the old title is sexist since *her* character will be the obvious hero of the story."

"Heroine, perhaps?" Beatrice chimed it, unable to remain silent.

"A heroin addict!" Sienna Wragg said. "That would be so cool. I like it."

"I did not mean . . ."

"Back to Rocco," Connell said, possibly annoyed by Bree-Jones's senior advisor. "It's Tabreetha's hope that we might rebrand the project as *Juli and Rocco: A Love Story*." He spelled out the names for them, and then took Alex's and Beatrice's silence for assent.

It wasn't.

"Juli is a once-struggling performer now at the top of her game and Rocco is a street thug and drug pusher she takes a fancy to."

"Imagine the trailers!" Wragg said. "*West Side Story* for the Twenty-First Century. Only the setting is, maybe, Bali or Mexico City or a town in Italy."

"It *is* set in Italy," Beatrice noted.

"No, I think it was Los Angeles." Wragg again. "The one with Leonardo DiCaprio?"

Beatrice sighed audibly.

"Who is that woman?" someone with a British accent whispered too loudly.

Alex knew it was time to speak. "I'm pretty sure this isn't the project I signed up for." London and LA muttered and coughed. After a pause, he added, "Shake-speare's *Romeo and Juliet* set in Italy? The way he wrote it?"

More silence.

Then Wragg spoke again, as if Alex had said nothing. "You see nobody's into tragedy anymore, so Tabby's got this different idea for the end. Naturally, Rocco overdoses and dies, but Juli cleans up her life and closes with a rap trib-ute to her dead boyfriend a year later at another halftime show. That way, she could do sequels."

"Perhaps even *Juli and Caesar*," Beatrice deadpanned.

Others on the line were unsure who'd offered the suggestion. But the assis-tant whose name Alex missed loved it.

"Marvelous! We could do three or four films that way, maybe even a prequel? Sort of a classy *Fast and Furious*."

Connell coughed to silence his eager team in London. "We didn't mean to ambush you, Alex, with all these changes. Tabreetha Bree-Jones simply hopes to give fans worldwide something fresh and exciting—quite unlike anything produced before."

Beatrice didn't doubt that.

Connell continued. "Tabreetha needs to play to her fanbase and her strengths as an arena performer and doesn't want to be confined by words in a world that expects images and music. Of course, there can still be Shakespearean echoes in her performance . . . and yours. We'd be sure to keep it classy."

And for the next ten minutes, London and Los Angeles buzzed with more ideas. Texas stayed mostly on the sidelines.

Someone noticed.

"Alex, this is Ayala Topfer. I need to hear what you're thinking." She hadn't said anything to this point.

"Honestly?"

"Of course." A click on the line. Someone coughed.

"Okay—I appreciate Tabreetha's *concepts* and know where they're coming from," Alex said, ". . . but I'm not sure I can be part of this project anymore."

"Oh, Alex. That's so uncool." Tabreetha had entered the building. "And you have *such* a marvelous voice. We'd write a song or two just for you."

Alex looked over to Beatrice who was so red he feared she'd faint.

"Look," he said, remembering his agent's advice. "I've got my contract on a screen in front of me. It commits me to playing the part of Romeo in

Throng!Media's production of—and this is the exact language—'William Shake-speare's *The Tragedy of Romeo and Juliet.*' Not *Rocco and Juli . . .*"

"*Juli and Rocco,*" Bree-Jones interrupted.

Alex ignored her. "The contract says what it says. *The Tragedy of Romeo and Juliet.* If Throng!Media now has somethin' else in mind, I guess I'm not your boy."

"Oh Alex," Bree-Jones said, "you will so regret not being part of this." But her voice hinted his withdrawal might have been the goal of the call to begin with.

"Doubt that," he said, looking to Beatrice, now white as a sheet.

"We'll give you time to think about the project," Tabreetha said, as if in charge. "I have a late recording session and apologize for just popping in like this. So good talking with you, Alex! I love your little show. Cheers."

They heard clicks on the line and a mechanical voice announced that three participants had left the conference, then three more.

"I'm still here," said Markus, Alex's silent agent.

"And I am here, Mr. Harp," said Ayala Topfer. "And, though I have to leave now as well, I *will* get back to you."

❧ ❧ ❧

"DID YOU INTEND to go so far, Alex?" Beatrice asked when the boy exited the call, leaving his agent hanging. "Should you have talked with your father and lawyer first?"

"Why? I still have a contract. The ball's in Topfer's court. She didn't tip her hand. Neither did the producer or Sherman Farr for that matter. I said what I said."

This tough Alex was new to Beatrice. Had she pushed him into a corner with her own remarks—*all* of them true?

"Your agent didn't say anything either."

"He told me to be honest."

"You were. But can you afford to lose the film?"

"I can't afford to make it," he said. "Career killer."

"Let us go outside," Beatrice suggested. "Perhaps a walk around the farm will put things in perspective."

Alex didn't disagree and they left the ranch house and headed toward a corral.

"The head of the studio called you *Mr. Harp,*" Beatrice said, as her two new cattle dog pups ran up. "What do you make of that?"

"Nothing. I didn't notice."

"If she felt bad for you, Ayala Topfer probably would have said *Alex*. But she called you Mr. Harp. The woman is either very angry with you or very impressed."

Alex looked toward an ancient cottonwood near a tiny stream.

"Is she an intelligent woman?" Beatrice asked.

"I know her just from signatures on my contracts."

"What will you do now?"

"Wait and see. And spend a few days with my sister, if she'll have me."

Chapter 45

Wednesday found Claire proofreading the latest draft of her edition of Mote McCrary's *Madrone*. She'd been at it all day. Immersion in work—that was her safe mode after trauma. She'd done it in graduate school when she blew a mock interview prior to a Modern Language Association meeting. Did it for several weeks the previous spring following her first encounter with murder. And now, she was glued to a computer screen in the wake of the previous day's drama. *Second* murder case in one year. According to the *Big Bend Mercury*, Clayton Shoot and Claire Harp were a crime-fighting duo. Midland–Odessa media picked up the meme.

And maybe they were? Escorting her to her truck yesterday following interminable and repetitive interviews, Clayton kissed her memorably, with Piper looking on. But all she'd done was spot an important photograph and deliver it to Clayton right when he needed it. No one could foresee what followed at the Cobb. Second time in her life Claire faced a gun.

Officials grilled Piper much longer than Claire. Understandably. For hours, the FBI agent strained to connect the actress's escapade on the South Rim to Iris's murder—largely because Piper hadn't reported her Study Butte encounter with Cobb immediately. Being off the grid for so long with her boyfriend seemed particularly implausible to Special Agent Grimmel.

The agent needed to spend more time in Far West Texas. Piper now loathed the woman.

Poor Tyler Tribble got pulled in too. Though he had nothing to do with the murder and hadn't seen the selfie, he was scheduled for interrogations today. Piper worried Tyler would lose his job immediately for not reporting that he'd helped Piper off the South Rim. But neither of them really cared. Too much in love.

Even getting Piper and Tyler back together had been a struggle. Without reliable cell service, Piper's boyfriend had no idea why she failed to pick him up after work yesterday. A coworker at the park drove Tyler to Study Butte. Thanking the guy with a burger at Big Bend Café, Tyler spotted his own car through the restaurant's window. Long story short: Tyler spent Tuesday night alone in Billy's cabin while Piper occupied Claire's guest room in Alpine a second time, Tyler agreeing to pick her up Wednesday after his interview with the FBI.

But what an odd night it had been for the two women. They ordered pizza and Claire opened a bottle of cabernet. Two, in fact. The traumatized actress wanted to talk about her dead sister and what it felt like to have no immediate family. Claire described her relationship with her own sisters. Complained about her mother Eugenia. And then Claire admitted she'd never been close with Alex.

The gay one? Piper said, deep into the wine. Claire deserved it.

They talked about their men too. Piper was head over heels for Tyler. Could it last? Claire wouldn't offer an opinion, but admired how sensible the pair seemed about their future. They assumed Tyler would become the breadwinner once Piper's savings from *Brainiacs* ran out.

I don't see a place for me now in Hollywood, Piper said.

For her part, Claire confessed to feelings she'd barely admitted to herself. Blame the cabernet.

I don't know what I'm holding out for, she told Piper.

You do know you could propose to Clayton? Piper replied.

Claire shuddered, remembering it.

⁂ ⁂ ⁂

BY LATE AFTERNOON, Claire was flagging. Reading her manuscript backwards word by word to catch spelling errors in *Madrone* was tricky since its author Mote McCrary used lots of Texas lingo. *Cain't, dudn't, fixin' tuh.* But at least her office at Sul Ross felt safe. She was reluctant to leave.

Then there was a knock on the door. Claire had asked the staff in the Languages and Literature Department not to give out her location or phone number to anyone today. She'd even switched door cards with a colleague on leave to deceive reporters persistent enough to search Morelock Hall. *Thinking about you, Ella Nixon.*

The intruder knocked again. Then she heard, *Claire?* A note of Eugenia Harp in the voice, but lower. It was Alex. She hurried to the door and unlatched it.

He looked lean and tall and not like a high school kid at all. Even the cowboy hat and denim seemed right.

"Hey, sis," he said. "The ladies in the office told me where to find you."

Of course, they would. Probably offered to make him dinner too. Claire burst into tears. Alex steered her to her desk and dropped in the chair beside it. He let her cry—what any smart guy does under the circumstances.

"You've been through a lot," he said when her sobs abated. "Not sure I could take all the stress of living in Alpine."

Claire laughed and dried the tears. Then grabbed and hugged him.

"What's this all about? You're the one what coulda got shot."

"Stop the Texan. Talk like an Ohioan."

"Yes, ma'am."

"Stop it. Are *you* okay?"

"Why wouldn't I be?" But she sensed something off.

"Mind if I move in for a coupla nights before flying back to La La Land? I got my stuff in the Range Rover outside. Figured you'd be here when you weren't at your place."

"Clayton didn't throw you out, did he? How is he?"

"Didn't even see him this morning. I got up before he did, and then Clayton headed into town while Beatrice and I were in a meeting."

"But you two are square?"

"Me and Beatrice?"

"No, you and Clayton. But you and Beatrice too. Just tell me you're okay."

"I'm okay, 'cept I feel all guilty leaving you alone this week."

Claire looked him in the eye. "Piper spent last night here in Alpine. With me." That got his attention. "Tyler probably picked her up by now. He had to talk with the feds first. I think they'll head to his place in Study Butte instead of Billy's cabin."

"I guess the police grilled you yesterday too?"

"Second time this week. Last night Piper and I were both at the sheriff's office until late explaining what happened at the Cobb. And Piper's fine. *You* should talk with her. Let her tell you about Tyler Tribble."

"The boyfriend."

"Yes. He really is."

"Billy Lamb filled me in some last week. Hope they're happy."

"Really?" *Wait till he learned the full story.*

"Sure." He took a deep breath. And then he unloaded about his confrontation with Throng!Media and Tabreetha Bree-Jones earlier that day. Claire was shocked and worried.

"You're walking away from the movie?"

"They're the ones doing that."

"You tell daddy?"

"Yep, and my lawyer too. But the decision's mine."

"Alex, you are just a kid. Growing up way too fast."

He stared at her, maybe disappointed.

"Can you afford it? Are you going home to Ohio?"

"Hey, I have other work," he smiled vaguely. "And this *Romeo and Juliet* thing's not settled."

It sounded like bluster to Claire. Her heart broke for her little brother.

"What a terrible time you've had in Texas," she said. "I feel so sorry . . . and I know Clayton's going to feel the same way. And Beatrice. And Sam. And . . . everybody else. You'll probably never come back."

Claire realized it sounded as if she planned on staying in Alpine a long time herself.

Alex removed his hat, ran fingers through his thick hair, and then stared at his boots, now scuffed and a little broken in. A gesture he might have stolen from Sam Vogt.

"Just the opposite," he said, shaking his head like he was waking up. Staring through her like he'd missed something until now. "Wow. I've had a *helluva* good time here. The people I met. Things that happened. Stuff I've seen. Mystery, murder, broken hearts . . . All what's lacking is a happy ending."

Being an English teacher, Claire thought Alex was speaking metaphorically. He wasn't.

Chapter 46

"Alex Harp still at your place?" Billy Lamb Jr. asked, sitting across from Clayton Shoot at Reata on Thursday. Lunch at the Alpine landmark was always crowded, but Lambs or McCanns never had problems getting served. Neither did the sheriff. The staff gave the two young men a corner table for privacy.

"He left yesterday after the Gina Summerlin stuff. I guess he figured I'd want time to myself and that his sister needed a man in the house. The boy's life got real complicated of a sudden. Be headin' back to California soon, I expect."

"Not that quick," Billy said, ordering up carne asada and enchiladas without checking the menu. And a glass of wine because he finally could. The sheriff went with tenderloin tacos and iced tea.

"Thanks for meeting," Billy continued. "Claire said we should talk."

Clayton nodded. "But whaddya you mean *not that quick*? Alex stayin' on?"

"Into the weekend, yeah. He called early today about a gig at my place Saturday night for his new Texas friends. Wants my help settin' it up. You're likely invited."

"Your folks had a party a week ago."

"This one's gonna be at my cabin. And it's Alex's thing. Mostly."

"So you're going along?"

"Hell, yeah. Never know when I might need a Hollywood bud."

"Heard that place was just a hunting camp."

"Never been there?"

"No."

Billy winked. "Heard wrong. Momma built the lodge as a getaway. Basic, but sweet. Firepit. Pool table. Garage and barn. Alex's picking up costs, but I'll kick in. Won't be much. Food and drinks for maybe two or three dozen people. Keg. Somebody pickin' a guitar."

"Wonder why he didn't use my place? Closer to Alpine."

"Not everyone invited is from town. Besides, the Shoot Ranch is parental."

"*Parental?*"

"You're the sheriff, Clayton, and Beatrice is Beatrice." Clayton winced. "Did I make you feel old?"

"Kinda."

"Weird kid, your future brother-in-law. But in a good way. Friggin' genius, I think."

Clayton shrugged. "Might be. But I'm a worried about him. Claire mentioned his movie deal blew up yesterday."

"Alex didn't say nothin' about that. He seemed real upbeat, you know?" Billy was still processing the sheriff's non-reaction to *future brother-in-law.*

"The boy takes things in stride," Clayton mumbled, thinking aloud. "Lotsa energy."

"Couldn't disagree."

Clayton refocused. "But speaking of *parental* . . ."

Billy studied his plate a moment, then looked up. "I haven't filed them papers yet. To change my name."

Clayton folded his arms atop the table. "So, what's that tell ya?"

"Huh?"

"I woulda thought you'd file 'em soon as you got 'em."

"I'm learnin' to be a thoughtful and deliberate person?"

"Bullshit."

"It's like this, Clayton . . . I want any son of mine to be a McCann, just like what it says above our ranch gate. Been there a hundred years or more."

"Then sign the papers."

Billy gazed at his plate again and grinned. "I see what you're doing—making me feel all guilty."

"About what?"

"You know."

"Then say it. Put it in words." Clayton was serious. "What's botherin' you?"

Long pause while Billy sipped his wine.

"Say it," Clayton pushed.

"Maybe I'm makin' my dad feel like he's losin' his son . . . but that ain't true. And how's come you're not Finis Shoot, named after *your* father?"

Clayton looked uneasy and Billy felt bad. Finis was dead only a few months. "Didn't mean to be hurtful."

"Didn't take it so, Billy. And I'm not Finis Shoot 'cause I was named for my granddaddy, who died before I came along."

"So you *were* a namesake. From a generation earlier."

"Yep. And if I'm ever blessed with a boy, I'll likely name him Finis. Second one will be Clayton."

"If Claire lets you."

"Runnin' ahead of yourself, dude." Clayton closed one eye. "I think her dad's name is Beverly, and no son of mine will ever . . . If you tell her I told you, I will kick your ass."

"I'd deserve it. But that means Alex Harp isn't a junior either—though he's an only son like both of us."

"But he *is* a Harp and I'm a Shoot. Last name matters too. Maybe more."

"I get it."

"Look. I'm not gonna pull the dead dad card on you. But think about it. You're the most important thing your father's got."

"Nikki . . . ?"

"She might not like to hear it. But it's true. For your dad, McCann's a brand. He's part of its history only 'cause he married your mother. And then they made you. So you're his real legacy, not the ranch."

"I'm just thinkin' of my own kids—sons or daughters. McCann is already my middle name. Right there on the birth certificate. I just want it to be their last name, that's all."

"And that's your choice, Billy. All I'll say is I saw that briefcase with the McCann name on it at the Saddlery when your dad picked it up. He wanted to give you his blessing without saying a word. That's how men are. But it still broke his heart."

"I didn't mean to do that."

"Course you didn't. And he'll get over it. Probably already has."

"But?"

"No buts. That's all I got. And I'll see you Saturday if Alex invites me to his shindig."

"If he don't, I just did. My house, my rules."

Clayton slapped the rich young man gently on the side of head and picked up the check.

Chapter 47

A text arrived late on Thursday morning from an executive assistant at Throng!Media asking Alex Harp to be available for a call from Ayala Topfer at 1:00 PM PST. That would be 3:00 PM in Alpine. No more details than that. The assistant assumed he knew who Topfer was. Assumed, too, he'd know the reason for the call.

Right on both counts.

Alex sent his confirmation. He briefly considered calling Beatrice and his father. Thought, too, of consulting Robert Markus, his agent. But decided to handle this next round with Throng!Media on his own.

Ms. Topfer chose to approach him one-on-one. That must mean something, given that he was technically a kid. She'd have to be careful. Maybe Topfer was just softening up a gullible minor for bad news. But, still, he was flattered.

It had already been a busy day for Alex. He'd spent its early hours working through his plans for Saturday night. Claire had left him on his own after making waffles and apologizing profusely. She faced a deadline on her book manuscript. Said she felt terrible, but couldn't delay the final proofreading.

He'd smiled. Told her he'd be on the phone much of the day anyway. And he had been, even before the heads-up from California.

He called Billy Lamb first. He had both cell and hardline numbers because the young rancher gave him his card at the birthday party not quite a week ago. Handsome embossed item with a bronco rider.

Billy heard him out and liked what Alex was proposing for Saturday. He signed on immediately. Except Alex figured his gathering would take place at the Lamb ranch house and Billy countered by offering his cozier lodge—where

Piper and Tyler stayed. "More down-to-earth than the big place. You're talking maybe two dozen people?" Billy asked.

Alex hadn't counted, but it sounded right. "Maybe more, cause parties always grow."

"Unless you want to have it down in our pool pavilion?"

Alex thought about Piper—and maybe somebody else—in a bikini. But deferred to Billy.

"I'm guessing your cabin's out in the boondocks somewhere?" Alex said. "Hard to find?"

"Good graded road to the place. I'll have hands put out signs and park a pickup at the one tricky turnoff."

Billy had done this before.

"Okay."

"Now about food and entertainment . . ." the young landowner continued. "This is short notice if we're talking *this* Saturday. But I know a guy with a chuckwagon and he owes me. I'm pretty sure I can get decent music too—coupla fellows on guitar who pair up with a washtub bass?"

"I don't know what that is."

"Trust me," Billy said. Alex felt he could.

"Money's not an object," Alex added.

"Between us, we can swing it."

"Nah, this is my show, Billy."

"McCann Ranch always goes first class."

They settled on a time and Billy promised to confirm on the food and entertainment. Which he did very quickly, long before Alex received the text from Throng!Media. Billy also emailed a helpful map to his remote lodge. "Made it for a few girls I couldn't bring to the main house," he explained—in some detail.

After speaking with Billy, the first person Alex formally invited was Claire, except her phone defaulted to *leave a message*. And he did. Pretty much, just *save this date* because he'd see her tonight and fill her in, but just a little. They had dinner planned at the 12 Gage Restaurant in Marathon, which he knew was special to her.

Then he called the sheriff's office and tried to talk his way past the dispatcher. Didn't work. Clayton, he learned, had a lunch appointment in town— with Billy! He expected Clayton would call soon as Billy spilled the beans about the party.

He had more success with Beatrice, who quickly accepted his invitation and mentioned several other members of the Shoot clan she'd bring along. "How could we not attend?" she said. Then Beatrice asked Alex about the status of *Romeo and Juliet*. But he kept the upcoming call with Ayala Topfer under his hat. No point in worrying her. And he had a good feeling . . .

Alex's next priority was San Vogt, who he thought might be tough to reach. (The kid didn't have a cell phone until recently.) But his hot tub buddy picked up immediately when Alex dialed a number Sam had shared after their dinner in Terlingua. Alex explained what he had in mind, yet Sam hung back.

"I don't know, Alex."

"We gotta tell people sometime and this seems like it."

Sam was silent for a ten or fifteen long seconds. "I got somethin' else planned."

"I'm leavin' Texas in a few days."

Another lengthy pause. "Donnie and I was fixin' to go out Saturday night. First time."

"Oh," Alex said, grinning at his end. "Well, hell, I was gonna invite him too."

"You sure?"

"Absolutely, I tell ya—here's what we'll do . . ."

And he explained. Sam, a trifle reluctant, still said *okay*. Even giggled. That was new for Sam.

"I'll send you guys a map. Just be sure Donnie comes. Tell him we're gonna have a chuckwagon and a guy playin' a washtub bass."

"Cool."

Alex checked the time.

And then, taking a deep breath, he called the excellent Navajo girl he'd met on the South Rim—Gracie Allen Yazzie. He still had her card stuffed in his wallet. She sounded as giddy accepting the invitation as he did offering it.

"You could bring a friend," he added.

"Now why would I wanna do *that*?" she said. The young actor construed her words in the best possible way.

They might have talked longer, but Clayton, back from lunch with Billy, finally returned Alex's call.

"When were you gonna tell me about this little *thang* you're having with Billy Lamb?" he drawled. "And how's come it's at his place?"

"He's got more money than you do, Clayton."

"But I'm taller and carry a gun."

"Yes, sir."

"Hey, do me a favor. You gotta invite Captain Gus Stumpf and her husband and Deputy Alonso Rangel. They work for me and had a helluva week and both would enjoy meetin' you. Same with Velma Furcron. She's Chief Ranger out at Big Bend National Park. And there are a coupla feds who helped out too."

"Gimme their numbers."

"How's 'bout I talk to 'em? You won't have to explain so much. And, oh—are kids okay?"

"What?"

"Is it okay to bring kids?"

"Hadn't thought about it. There's gonna be alcohol."

"This *is* Texas," Clayton reminded him. And so Alex's party list grew.

Half an hour later, Deputy Rangel called. He had to remind Alex who he was and Alex confirmed that he'd be getting an invitation from Sheriff Shoot.

"I already got that," Rangel said, "but you see I need to check on something else. I'm calling from Midland." Alex remembered the Midland–Odessa Airport. Seemed ages since he and Piper wandered through the terminal with the Legesons. "We'll be back by tomorrow."

"Okay?" Alex had no idea who *we* was.

"It would be so cool if I could bring the Alpine Chief of Police to the party. As my date."

Alex paused. He actually knew who the chief was, but decided to have fun with the guy. "I'm cool with that if Clayton is. Really. Bring him."

"No, no, no! The police chief's a woman. Fiona Tusk."

"That's even better," Alex said.

"But you oughta check with Billy first 'cause—"

"What?"

"Chief Tusk accused Billy Lamb of murder last spring. But she's *really* sorry. And it would be so cool if we could both come to this party. Because . . . well, you'll see."

"I'll check with Billy."

And he did.

Billy hooted and hollered and, if Alex heard correctly over the phone, either slapped his knee or something harder. Then he laughed. "Tell Alonso the bitch can come."

Which Alex did later, in not so many words.

Shortly thereafter, Billy called Alex again to check whether it was okay to invite his own dad William and his stepmother Nikki. Billy sounded oddly serious and deferential. Alex sure remembered Nikki. "Can't leave 'em out," Billy explained.

Easy answer. It *was* their damn ranch—or had been.

Not much later, Alex heard from one *Gus Stumpf*. But it sounded like a woman. He recalled Gus was on Clayton's invitation wish list. Alex was getting confused.

"Yes, Gus?" he said.

She/he was *real* direct and very Texan. "Clayton said Piper Robinet might be at that thar party you're throwin' Saturday. I'm grateful for my invite, but wonder if I could bring two of my boys? You see, they have a thing for Ms. Robinet? They ain't teenagers yet, so they won't be no trouble."

"I told the sheriff kids would be okay."

"Well, I didn't think of 'em when he mentioned the gatherin'."

"Sure, bring the boys. But I can't say for sure yet Piper will be there. And there's definitely gonna be alcohol."

"They're used to it. We won't stay long. T'ain't often kids get to meet TV stars. And she *is* a beautiful woman."

"Yes, she is," Alex confirmed.

"Then the four of us will see you Saturday night. And thank you, young man."

Might need to order more food, Alex thought.

"Oh, one other thang." By now, Alex was certain Gus was a woman. "I passed this by Clayton and he said to check with you 'cause you really don't know these people. But a Matthew Cooper and Lydia Champlain here have had a *real* rough week, what with the murder and all, and they could use a little boost from the community."

They were just names to Alex, but in for a penny . . . "Tell you what," he said, "Ask Clayton to invite them and we'll leave it there."

"Thank you, Mr. Harp," the captain replied. "You know, I gotta confess I'm kinda eager to get a look at you myself. I seen your show."

"I appreciate that," he said, sounding way too mature.

"Now, if I told Clayton *that*," Gus laughed, "he'd blush right down to his toes."

Alex laughed, but got out of the conversation quick. Gus sounded like she wanted to talk. And his next call might take time.

It did. For good reasons, he *had* to invite Ella Nixon from the *Big Bend Mercury*.

"Now, some of this event has to be off the record, Ella," Alex explained.

"It will be," the woman promised.

"And not for use."

"Damn," Mrs. Nixon said. "You know the difference?"

"I need your promise. You'll know what's news and what's personal."

Ella hesitated, considering her options. "Okay. We have common interests. And I wouldn't miss this for the world. Our coming out."

"You'll tell your husband?"

"Maybe."

"And Professor Muckelbauer?"

"Definitely."

They schmoozed some because you had to do that with Ella. And she liked him, so he didn't mind. But Alex checked his watch and signed off soon as it was polite. He just had time to plug his nearly dead phone into a charger when the summons came from Ayala Topfer. He took a deep breath.

"Hello, Alex. I have news for you and I'll get right to the point. Then we can discuss details."

No nonsense woman. She sounded like the bigshot she was.

"Should I get my lawyer on the line?" Alex said.

"That's an option. But I don't have any people here myself. It's just me and you. And you're a smart boy."

"Okay . . . ?"

"So, Tabreetha Bree-Jones will create *Juli and Rocco* for Throng!Media's streaming service, with her production people in charge. There's an audience for what she wants to do."

"I see." His stomach fell. Not what he hoped.

"And you and an actress yet to be named will make *Romeo and Juliet* for regular theatrical release. A prestige film for us, but intended for general audiences too. Including mature adults who've read Shakespeare. Top director and production values. The full deal, just as we promised you originally. It's what *I* wanted from the start."

"Thank you."

"Rob Markus said you had guts."

"Yes, ma'am."

"I wanted to be sure you did."

"Yes, ma'am."

"I hope you're smiling."

"Wide as Texas. But can I offer a suggestion or two?"

"I figured you might."

Chapter 48

Claire hoped to catch a ride with Alex to his Saturday evening shindig, but he left for Billy's ranch hours early to help with set up. Clayton was a desirable second choice, but he had police business in Terlingua that afternoon and would head to the party from there. And she'd been unable to persuade Aurora Mendez to join her. The painter and gallery owner was, understandably, broken up by what happened with her friend Gina Summerlin.

So as evening approached, Claire Harp drove across miles of cattle range herself. Fortunately, the weather was perfect and the map Alex supplied clear. She spotted the pickup marking a key turnoff from a mile away. A fine-looking cowboy there waved her on.

What her brother had arranged in mere days amazed her. Truck after truck (and just a few cars) lined both sides of a graveled driveway crossing a pasture up to Billy's place. The terrain seemed ordinary until you got near the lodge itself, poised on a ridge with jaw-dropping views south and west. Hills and mesas in a fresh coat of autumn ginger. And just the right clouds gathering to guarantee a showy sunset in maybe an hour or so.

Claire counted three dozen people gathered around a fire pit and honest-to-goodness chuck wagon—both separated from Billy's log-and-stone lodge by a tile patio. Guests were already dancing. Enough boots and cowboy hats to stock a Sheplers. Claire knew about half of the crowd, which included a handful of kids being herded by a pair of single-minded border collies.

How had Alex connected with all these folks in just the few days he'd been in Texas? Not a mystery to her any more, she admitted. His gift was knowing how to talk with people. He was a good ol' boy with Clayton, a student with Beatrice, a sweetheart with Sam, and God only knows what with Ella Nixon and her Sul

Ross State colleague Rawdon Muckelbauer, the only guy in tweed standing around the firepit. The journalist and professor were gabbing with her brother like old pals. They were a short throw from the musicians—two mustachioed men with a guitar and fiddle and a third guy clinging to a pole while standing atop what looked like a washtub. Right then, they were crooning a song about *long johns?*

Suddenly Clayton was at her ear, whispering, "If your jeans were any tighter . . ." He carried a paper plate piled high with ribs, nodding her toward the chuckwagon. Some moments earlier, Claire had seen him chatting up a handsome blonde woman—the office assistant who'd blown the whistle on Gina Summerlin. *Lydia something.*

"Finish your sentence, Sheriff," Claire said, pique in her voice.

"I could read the credit cards in your wallet?" He was staring at her backside.

"Eyes up, big fella. Do you always attend parties in uniform?"

"It does attract ladies. But I been workin' all afternoon and no time to get home. Hope I ain't gamey?"

"All I'm smelling is . . ." Claire sampled the air. "Mesquite cooked brisket, grilled chicken breast, cowboy beans, potato salad, maybe peach cobbler?"

"I'm impressed."

"Alex told me the menu. And I think I want something a bit stronger than sweet tea right now."

✂ ✂ ✂

ALEX WAS SMART enough not to compete with the setting sun or the country tunes accompanying it. Happy group, all around. He thought Billy sure hit the mark with the music and food. Though the McCann Ranch had a chuckwagon of its own, he'd hired a guy who catered for dude ranches throughout West Texas. Gourmet eats, with everything made on site in Dutch ovens and iron skillets. The rolls were good enough for dessert.

Friendly folks strolled up to talk with him, many of them people he hadn't met before, even a surprisingly grabby FBI agent. He explained he'd be saying a few words to thank everybody for his good times in Texas. (And he had even more to say now than he expected.) Then they could dance and drink as deep into the night as they pleased.

He'd worried through the awesome sunset that some guests especially important tonight hadn't appeared yet. But then Piper and Tyler Tribble slipped into

263

the crowd. He realized now Tyler had been one of the park staff on the South Rim so many days ago. Handsome guy. You couldn't miss him.

Not long after, Gracie Allen Yazzie tapped him playfully on the shoulder and he kissed her cheek. Just what she wanted! She looked great in jeans and a simple pearl-button cowboy shirt, hair braided in pigtails of the kind he loved to yank as a kid.

William Lamb Sr. and his wife Nikki made a late appearance too. Billy pointed them out. "Checking out my first rodeo," he whispered. "And your sister Beatrice just rolled in."

So with the crowd moving without much herding toward benches and soft chairs surrounding a now-blazing firepit, Alex rang the triangle dinner bell on the chuckwagon and stood on a stone ledge. He opened with profuse thanks to Billy Lamb Jr., giving his friend credit for everything from the food to the weather. Billy blushed at the hearty round of applause—he wasn't used to it. His dad standing in the back looked proud.

Then Alex introduced himself. Proper protocol, he knew, unless you're the pope. The crowd mostly recognized him, none more than two little girls with Velma Furcron, Chief Ranger at Big Bend. He remembered her from an interview after his South Rim debacle. Her daughters giggled and waved at him and he waved and giggled back. The crowd ate it up—though Claire rolled her eyes.

"I don't know if Texas is always like it's been these last two weeks," he began. "But I sure enjoyed seeing this part of the state and meeting so many good folks—even if under somewhat *peculiar circumstances*. A party to thank everybody seemed called for since it's what Texans do at the drop of a hat. Get together and eat."

Cheers and a few yee-haws.

"Y'all know I'm an actor, and I gotta say, these past few days I been feelin' like I'm in a mystery movie. The kind where all the folks hidin' somethin' git together at the end and then the truth comes out. Well, here we are. But I'll keep this short and promise not to arrest nobody."

Murmurs, and laughter too, especially from the law enforcement types finishing their cobbler.

"I do have some surprises," he explained. "I'm gonna start with a local hero who I just met on Sunday but who's been part of my life for several months now. Sam Vogt, where are ya?" He scanned the crowd, though he knew exactly where the blue-eyed towhead sat, close beside Donnie Majewski, maybe the only guy in the crowd in shorts instead of jeans.

Alex waved Sam up to stand next to him, the fire now bright enough to add drama to a darkening scene. Sam was shy as ever, hands in his pockets and head down. Spotting Claire in the crowd, Alex grinned at her, pulled Sam up close, gave the local hero a hug, then a quick peck on the cheek.

"Sam and I have a special relationship," Alex said and paused. Claire caught her breath and she even grabbed Clayton's hand. "The last few days, I've been practicing my Texan with him and getting to know how he thinks. Because you see—"

Alex nodded to Donnie Majewski.

"I'm gonna play Sam Vogt in a movie based on what happened here last spring—when Sam and my sister and Clayton Shoot not only figured out two murders but that the murderer . . . well, y'all know that story." Alex ruffled the hero's straw-white hair. "I guess I'll need a dye job if I'm gonna look like him."

Sam looked embarrassed but Majewski pumped a fist. Alex knew Sam and Donnie had decided to go into business together in Lajitas as trail outfitters.

Claire, however, couldn't quite close her mouth. Clayton Shoot sitting next to her applauded while Piper Robinet laughed, amazed by what Alex Harp could pull off. Maybe a little envious too?

"Now, I came down here to Texas not only to meet Sam," Alex continued, "but also Ella Nixon from the *Big Bend Mercury* and Professor Rawdon Muckel-bauer at Sul Ross State. You see, these guys wrote the screenplay for the movie, and it's a *fine* script. Someone at a big studio figured out my family connection to the story and the next thing you know, I got the part."

Ella and Muckelbauer stood up and took lengthy bows. Alex noticed Ella's husband wasn't with her. Strange, since Barney Nixon seemed not the sort to miss a free meal.

"Now, don't ask me whose gonna play Clayton Shoot or Claire Harp or Billy Lamb or a bunch of other folks in this audience. 'Cause I don't know. But the movie's gonna be filmed right here in Brewster County."

The crowd cheered. But both Claire and a very red Clayton Shoot sat quietly, the implications settling in. Alex noticed and shrugged. "Hey, blame Ella and the professor, not me." But Alex expected he'd get grief all night for not saying anything until now.

He went on. "I need to introduce two more people." He said it twice to settle a crowd buzzing about film crews in the region. "The first is a guy by the name of Tyler Tribble who I've never spoken with. But I'm told he's that presentable dude sitting there next to my co-star from *Brainiacs*, Piper Robinet. You may have heard of *her*?" The crowd laughed, recalling tabloid stories from a just few days back, overshadowed now by news of the local murder and arrest of Gina Summerlin.

"I think this is Piper's first public appearance since she dumped me on the South Rim," Alex explained, "—for Tyler Tribble. Can't say I blame her."

It was a delicate line, except Alex delivered it just right. Piper and Tyler bumped heads, smiled, and gave Alex a thumbs up. The crowd cooed.

"And Piper, as you know . . ." Alex paused to look toward the FBI woman and a park police agent with his arm around her shoulder. "Piper actually helped my sister and Clayton Shoot and others solve a murder just a few days ago. We gotta be happy about that."

The crowd hushed, maybe uneasy about all the crime in their community. Alex did notice two youngsters waving and winking at Piper. Gus Stumpf's sons, he guessed. He'd seen them eyeing Chief Ranger Furcron's cute daughters too.

Waiting for the crowd to settle, Alex felt like Bob Hope addressing soldiers in grainy videos he'd seen.

"Now this is for you, Piper. I bet everybody here already knows about the movie part you *didn't* get, playing Juliet opposite of, well, *me* as Romeo." Alex figured this would be dicey and both Tyler and Piper looked uncomfortable. It was quiet enough suddenly to hear the fire crackling and wind blowing across the pastures.

"You can expect a phone call Monday, Piper. From Throng!Media. They've changed their minds and want you for that part—assuming y'all can come to terms on salary and put up with a shitty co-star."

Piper went from slack-jawed to barely able to breathe to heaving sobs. Tyler rocked her in his arms. The crowd figured this must be good news and cheered—whatever those tabloids said about the woman. Piper mouthed *thank you* as soon as she was able.

"Details to follow," Alex promised. "I've gone on too long. But just one more thing. Where's Beatrice Shoot?" Again, he knew exactly where she was, but pretended to study the crowd. Beatrice rose slowly, giving Alex a wary frown.

"Beatrice, you've helped me so much this past week and more that I asked Throng!Media to bring you aboard officially as my dialect coach for *Romeo and*

Juliet. Yes, the one Shakespeare wrote. So if you can manage it this coming summer, it means a few weeks in Hollywood and Italy?"

Beatrice waited for friends and neighbors to stop hooting and cheering.

"Thank you, Alex Harp," she said without a trace of emotion. "I will check my schedule and get back to you."

Alex doubled over.

"Finish the food and enjoy the music," he said when he was able and signed off with a hook 'em Horns. But Billy grabbed Alex around the shoulders and said he had something to say too. Guests already rising from split logs or canvas chairs settled down again.

"Sorry," Billy said. "Sorry. This ain't gonna make sense to no more'n four or five people. But I wanted to do it publicly so there's no going back." Alex remained standing with him because his friend looked like he needed support.

Billy reached into his denim jacket and pulled out a thick white business envelope.

"Daddy," Billy said. "You kin probably guess what's in here." The crowd turned to where Billy was pointing. The tall man who used to run the McCann Ranch was standing against a rock column supporting the cabin's veranda. Nikki Lamb was next to him, turquoise sparkling in the moonlight.

"Them papers changing my name to just Billy McCann are all signed and ready to file."

The crowd went silent. Alex didn't know what this meant, but he read tension, maybe sadness, in Clayton Shoot's face. Same expression on Billy's father.

Billy held the envelope out in front of him for a tense moment, almost as if he expected his father to come up and take it. Then he threw it into the fire pit where it flared and crumbled in seconds.

"I'm Billy Lamb for the duration." Silence. Most guests didn't know how to respond. But Clayton Shoot stood and applauded, Claire joined him, and then everyone else did too. The tall guy in the back saluted Billy and wiped maybe dust from his eyes.

"Thanks, man," Billy whispered to a confused Alex. "And thank your future brother-in-law for me too."

But it wasn't over even then. Alex found a very large, middle-aged woman in jeans and a lambskin jacket standing right behind him, arm-in-arm with a lean and much younger Hispanic guy. Billy didn't look especially happy when he noticed the pair, though his eyes were fixed on the woman.

"Please can I have your attention for just a moment?" the young man asked, waving his hands. "Won't take but a minute." He paused while the crowd settled down yet again.

Gossip enough to last a year, Alex thought.

"For those of you who don't know, I'm Deputy Alonso Rangel and I work for Clayton Shoot."

Murmurs of approval and a few friendly hoots.

"And y'all know Alpine's Chief of Police Fiona Tusk." Louder hoots and a smattering of applause.

Alonso turned to Alex. "We've been a couple for a while," he explained, "Me and Fiona. She used to be my boss and then Clayton hired me."

"Not news, Alonso," a woman shouted. Maybe Gus Stumpf, Alex figured—the lady with the two squirming boys. But she was smiling, as if encouraging the guy.

"But we do got news we want to share and this is a good place for it. You see, Fiona and I was in Midland the last two days—where we got married!" He flashed his ring finger.

Clayton nearly fell out of his seat and even Billy and his father way in the back laughed and then applauded.

"Now y'all been 'specially nice the last few weeks when Fiona hasn't been feeling real good and that's why we was in the city. To have tests too."

Alex noticed Fiona staring at her fancy boots, hint of a smile.

"Turns out Fiona ain't sick," Alonso said. "She's pregnant."

Stone silence for five seconds, then boots stomping. And the musicians playing "The Eyes of Texas."

⊰⊱ ⊰⊱ ⊰⊱

CLAIRE GUESSED SHE wasn't the only one whose head was spinning after the evening's *entertainment*, as Clayton described it—especially after Billy and Alonso's remarks. The story of Billy thinking about changing his name circulated like wildfire so even outsiders like Velma Furcron and Elliot Perciak could appreciate what the kid had done, burning that envelope.

Alonso's announcements didn't need much amplification, given the visual impact of the skinny twenty-something groom standing beside his forty-plus bride (age and dress size). FBI agent Randi Grimmel asked Claire if they were actors making a political statement. But no one could doubt that Alonso and Fiona were blissful.

So the guests danced and ate and drank deep into the evening, Claire all the while trying to wrap her head around her little brother's performance. She guessed her mother Eugenia tipped Alex off after the phone call Sunday night. *Claire thinks you're gay.* And he'd run with it.

But Alex sure held the news about his next movie and the screenplay close. Ella Nixon did too—and why had she just now apologized to Claire for outing Alex's location in Alpine more than a week ago? And why was Professor Muckelbauer working with Ella on that screenplay instead of her husband Barney? Claire suspected a story there.

And the complete turnaround on *Romeo and Juliet*? Again, Alex hadn't said a word even at dinner on Thursday. Great news, of course, though Tyler Tribble didn't exactly seem thrilled. But Piper assured Claire he was, making a point of introducing him to her over more cobbler and Blue Bell. She and Tyler would be in California within days.

And then, once again and as always, Clayton had to leave early—this time because of a major accident on the road between Alpine and Marfa, under a railroad bridge. Just when she needed to talk. Let him know how her feelings were evolving.

It was Piper's words from Tuesday night that unsettled Claire this evening: *You do know you could propose to Clayton?*

She wouldn't go that far.

Because she was sure she could get Clayton to propose again and hoped to set the mood this evening. It might have worked. Out here around the fire, under the stars and waning moon, and in the wake of all that happened with Regina Summerlin and Iris Cobb. She and the sheriff had faced peril once again. Pulled together. Been first in each other's thoughts, she was certain.

And she knew she needed someone. Felt it in those silly moments with Donnie Majewski. And now even Sam Vogt was part of a couple. He'd driven off early with his handsome partner, talking a mile a minute. Sam never ever did that.

And Fiona Tusk and Alonso Rangel united too! An implausible pair, but happy enough to make her jealous. And with a child on the way.

Then there was Piper Robinet and Tyler Tribble. How likely was it that their relationship would survive beyond high school, with both families opposed?

Or after years of separation and Piper's loss of a sister? And yet, here they were this evening with life streaming their way, passion undiminished.

Even her brother wasn't spending the night alone. After the speeches and dancing, Alex had sidled up to Claire to introduce a girl. Gracie Allen Yazzie. Just a slip of a thing compared to Piper Robinet, with all *her* curves. Alex said he'd met this young woman on the South Rim, probably exactly as Gracie intended, and, well, it just felt right. The girl seemed as clever and determined as her brother. "And we're both virgins," she declared, pointing with her chin at Alex who then told Claire they'd be spending the night in Billy's cabin.

And Claire *was* happy for them. Delighted. Wouldn't say a word to Eugenia. Knew Alex wouldn't care if she did.

"You're okay?" he'd asked Claire, maybe sensing something wasn't right. But she waved him off, saying she had an hour's drive ahead. Congratulated Alex on his film deals. Wished them both the best.

And wished she felt as happy as Gracie.

The crowd was dwindling. What else was there for Claire to do then but walk back to her Jeep? The sky seemed as magical as it always did in this corner of the world. Both moonlight and stars tonight. Maybe she'd glimpse a meteor?

With her vehicle almost in sight, Claire heard boots crackling on the gravel. Someone walking behind her, maybe even picking up the pace. Somebody she knew? Likely, given the crowd. She felt curious, not nervous, but didn't turn immediately. Maybe for fifteen seconds.

"Claire Harp?"

The voice was male—cool and resonant and cordial. No threat, for sure.

"Claire?" he said again.

She had to stop. Turned. Tall, strapping, familiar.

"Sorry. I didn't mean to scare you."

"You didn't," she said. Moonlight revealed large eyes, high cheekbones, curly hair. Just the hint of a beard. Or maybe he hadn't shaved close today?

"We've met," he said. "But, like your brother put it tonight, under *peculiar circumstances.*"

Claire cocked her head and nodded. She hadn't paid close attention to him then.

"At Iris Cobb's memorial."

"I was there," she said. Remembered Gina Summerlin embracing him.

Understood why. Claire turned slowly toward her Wrangler. Glad no one else was around.

"And then on Tuesday when Gina pulled that gun . . ."

"Seems a blur to me now," Claire said, stretching the truth.

"We weren't introduced."

"No. Not the best time for it."

"I'm Matthew Cooper," he said, offering his hand.

"I know," Claire Harp said, taking it.

Afterword

I hope you've enjoyed *The South Rim Trail*. If so, please consider posting a review on Amazon or Goodreads. Even brief comments make a difference. Thank you!

For more about the Big Bend Country Mysteries, check out the series website at www.jjrbigbend.com. There you'll find information on forthcoming books and events, as well as photos and links—including to Amazon, Facebook, and Instagram pages. I update my blog regularly and welcome your comments and suggestions for entries. You can leave them on the Contacts page or sign up for the Big Bend Country Mysteries mailing list.

MANY PEOPLE DESERVE thanks for their contributions to *The South Rim Trail* and to the first Big Bend Country mystery *The Window Trail* (2018).

I'll begin with the real Clayton Shoot. I met him when he built a garage for me several summers ago in Alpine, Texas. I warned him then that, if I ever wrote a mystery novel, one of its characters would borrow his inimitable West Texas name. I kept my word. And he said *okay*. Thanks, Clayton.

My meticulous proofreader (and sister-in-law) Janet Ruszkiewicz deserves a shout-out. I brought her into the project after she spotted three errors in a recent C. J. Box novel—and how many copyeditors must that guy have? Any slips you encounter in *The South Rim Trail* are the result of my own last-minute tinkering. Don't blame Janet.

Mark D'Antoni of eBook Design Works formatted the text and designed the cover of *The South Rim Trail*. He did such a splendid job with *The Window Trail*, the first novel in my mystery series, that I knew where to go for this latest book. I am grateful not only for Mark's skill and artistry, but also his patience. I must have told him a dozen times I need to make one final change. He never flinched.

I owe a significant debt to good neighbors in West Texas who've supported and encouraged the series—most especially Peggy Hughes, Frank Cargo, Jayson Woodward, and my almost-agent Kay Pogue. When these fine people said I'd captured the spirit of the region in *The Window Trail*, I felt like a success.

My good friend (and former student) Douglas Taylor literally saved *The South Rim Trail* after two puppies with nothing better to do ripped apart the sole copy of its detailed outline. Doug helped me reassemble it, piece-by-piece. It took many hours. Doug was also the first reader of *The Window Trail*. Without his enthusiasm for an early draft, I might never have finished a book that Texas Authors went on to name its Best Mystery/Thriller for 2019.

Thanks, too, to another former student Rob Markus for introducing me to Balcones Texas Blue Corn Bourbon. For good reason, Eugenia Harp enjoys it in *The South Rim Trail*. And a certain Robert Markus appears as Alex Harp's Hollywood agent.

LIKE MANY WRITERS, I do take occasional license with geography, topography, and plausibility in *The South Rim Trail*. This is, after all, fiction—which can move mountains and mesas and campsites. Or even put a rack of tabloids in a supermarket that doesn't carry them.

Regional writing is always at the mercy of circumstance too: restaurants and businesses for example open and close with abandon. Still, I prefer to use real names whenever I can to recognize interesting places to eat, shop, and relax throughout Far West Texas. Visit them when you're here.

The problems my characters in *The South Rim Trail* experience with cell phones will be familiar to residents of Far West Texas. But I must admit that cellular service is improving. There are far fewer dead zones in the region now than in the past—when, for example, I had to wander down my street to make calls. During a recent drive through Big Bend National Park, I was rarely without a signal.

Finally, for those of you who might wonder, *Terlingua Townhouse* is an actual plein air painting by award-winning artist Jill Carver. Thank you, Jill, for letting me slip it into this novel. However, don't look for the building it depicts using my directions in *The South Rim Trail*. I had to move it so my characters didn't have to walk too far in the midday sun.

JJR

Made in the USA
Coppell, TX
20 March 2021